Children. Elderly. Mothers. Fathers. The strong. Weak.

And the marauders. About two dozen.

Goddamn them.

The sleep of reason . . . words from somewhere *. . . produces monsters.*

Memory feeding on madness.

The horror of familiar faces, distorted and bloodied. And when she couldn't see their features, she recognized fabric, boots, a belt, or a bag slung over a shoulder. In this grievous moment she shocked herself by giving thanks that Ananda and the others had been taken, for surely they would have been murdered in the frenzy. Thanks even knowing their plans for the girls because the abduction bought time.

Tire tracks began a few feet away, leading into the vast emptiness of the reservoir. In this world, tracks could last for months. She would follow them forever.

JAMES JAROS

BURN DOWN THE SKY

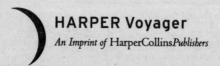

HARPER Voyager
An Imprint of HarperCollinsPublishers

This is a work of fiction. Names, characters, places, and incidents are products of the author's imagination or are used fictitiously and are not to be construed as real. Any resemblance to actual events, locales, organizations, or persons, living or dead, is entirely coincidental.

HARPER Voyager

An Imprint of HarperCollins*Publishers*
10 East 53rd Street
New York, New York 10022-5299

Copyright © 2011 by Mark Nykanen
Cover art by Getty Images (dry lake bed)/Stewart Cairns (sky)
ISBN 978-0-06-201630-0
www.harpervoyagerbooks.com

First Harper Voyager mass market printing: May 2011

Harper Voyager and ❯ is a trademark of HCP LLC.

Printed in the U.S.A.

10 9 8 7 6 5 4 3 2 1

For the future leaders of the rebel forces,
no matter their age or state of grace

Acknowledgments

My deep gratitude for the insights and suggestions of a great group of friends and family who read various drafts of *Burn Down the Sky*. Many thanks to Dale Dauten, Darryl Santano, Monte Ferraro, Tammie Andison, Kim Nykanen, Tina Castanares, and Anika Taylor Nykanen. Special thanks to Mark Feldstein, who pored over these pages with his keen author's eye and empathic editor's instincts. Special thanks, too, to Ed Stackler, who has lent me his enthusiasm, expertise, and wise counsel for more than a decade.

My editor at Voyager, Will Hinton, championed this novel and made numerous wonderful suggestions. And thanks to my agent, Howard Morhaim, who made publication possible by picking up *Burn Down the Sky* late on a Friday, only to find that he couldn't put it down.

I'm also deeply indebted to the many scientists, authors, and journalists who have written about climate change. As a member of the Society of Environmental Journalists, I'm privileged to receive a digest of the most significant environmental news of the day. These reports, from a wide variety of scientific and news sources, have provided me with critical stores of information. Likewise, important works of nonfiction, including *Climate Wars* by Gwynne Dyer, *Dark Age Ahead* by Jane Jacobs, *Collapse* by Jared Diamond, and the books of the independent scientist James Lovelock, proved both enlightening and frightening. But *Burn Down the Sky* is fiction, and while I think it presents a plausible outcome for our present myopia, I do not wish to suggest that it reflects the opinions of the aforementioned.

BURN DOWN THE SKY

Chapter One

Texas School Board Demands Equal Time for Climate
   Change Challenge
"Warming is only theory," board says
   Associated Press

"Nonessential" Plane Travel Banned
Desperate measure to cut greenhouse gases
Critics call it "too little, too late"
   Washington Post

Sweat dripped from the tip of Ananda's nose, darkening the dust. The girl raised a shovelful of dirt from the cracked bed of an empty reservoir and topped off a sandbag. Her mom tied a quick knot, heaved it aside, and snapped open another hand-sewn sack. Two men raised the wall behind them.

"Don't stop, hon. We're almost there."

Her mother had caught her staring at the steep sides of the basin—rising like cliffs, crumbling like chalk—before nudging the shovel with her foot. Ananda sank it back into the hard ground, the sun brutal on her back. Every story she'd ever heard about disasters called for gray skies, stormy skies, but there had never been a disaster like this one—

that's what her dad said—and the sun rarely strayed. The evidence surrounded them in ring upon ring of shimmery, deadly heat. There was the reservoir on which she stood, a moat of parched earth and insects extending miles from the camp in every direction. Then high above her at the top of those clumpy cliffs lay the shoreline where huge summer homes had once peered down at unthinkably cool blue water before the flames claimed them, too. And beyond the circle of charred houses rested the silent forests, burned to oblivion by the same relentless force that had gutted those lavish homes—the savage orb that would not waver.

Ananda had never known the world beyond the fallen forests, but she imagined the fiery rings radiating all the way to the sun itself, sparking those death rays in the sky.

The wall now rose to her mother's eyes; only a few feet remained before the camp was enclosed. They'd been building it for seven days, but what could it keep out. *What?*

Her mother had been vague, her father less so. Before leaving to scout the perimeter this morning, he'd said it would keep out coyotes, wolves, panthers, bears, marauders.

He'd mentioned the marauders almost as an afterthought, but Ananda knew better: Another scout had spotted them moving south from Knoxville ten days ago. They'd always thought the camp was isolated, far from the plundering. Plans for the wall had begun immediately.

As she shoveled, she glanced through the narrow opening to the camp garden, shaded by a patchwork of old clothes, torn blankets, tattered tarps—anything that could defy the sun, even weakly. Sunlight in only the smallest doses, and each plant watered by hand, by drips. The greens—chard and kale and spinach—hung withered as the faces of the old men and women who looked after every leaf, picking off the constant bugs and crushing them with fingers turned the dun color of earth.

Ananda and her mother formed half of a work crew that included the men who raised the actual wall and plastered it with a mud mix more precious than the jewels of old. Her father's brother, Uncle Rye, tall and lean like him, thrust the final sandbag into place as the sun slipped behind the distant cliffs, briefly backlighting the ruins.

Always the tang of wood smoke in the air, sulfurous and sweet, even when the fires couldn't be seen, as if the flames had stalked the last breath of the land deep underground, burning the roots and rocks and worms until the world above collapsed into the world below. Making a hidden hell to match the one they'd left to the eye.

Even the cracks in the lake bed appeared to smolder, though they'd built the camp as far as possible from the combustibles that formed the reservoir's towering, blackened border. Nothing lived down here but what they tended—the garden, themselves. Grains of hope.

"Is Dad going to make it back tonight?" Ananda always worried when he was gone, saying good-bye to him at dawn with pleading in her eyes.

"Yes, he'll be back." Her mother's hand fell to her back, rubbing it briefly as they walked past the picked-over berry patch by the camp's lone spigot, its lip dry as crust at the end of the day. It was drawing the last of the groundwater, and even the littlest children knew this. It might last another year. It might dry up tomorrow. No one wanted to contemplate the next step because it *would* be a step, maybe a million of them, each more dangerous than the last as a new search began.

Ananda looked around. At least here, she thought, we have the wall, *now.* Water, *now.* Food, *now.* Out there—beyond the cliffs and rubble and burned trees, beyond the empty cities—were only rumors of the worst the world can offer.

"Reduced to rumors." Her father had once said that while staring at the sky, as if bewildered by the breathless weight of his own words, no more believing them than the absence of clouds or rain. He'd put his hand on her shoulder and said, "I'm sorry."

She and her mom sat outside their tent on a sheet of pink plastic salvaged from the long journey here, a story she first heard as a toddler. Everything they owned held a story, for nothing had come easily, so a piece of plastic, bleached by the blazing sky to the palest hint of color, had a history and an imagined past in a better time.

A centipede crawled toward her foot. Her mother crushed it so quickly that Ananda only glimpsed it moving.

"Poisonous."

Her mom didn't need to tell her about centipedes or snakes, or the prickly toxic plants that could sprout in the cracks of the lake bed. Her parents had been graduate students in wildlife biology before the final fall forced them south. They taught survival classes in the camp, though only days ago Ananda had heard the other adults argue for a gentler name. But her mother had said the children needed to know "the stakes."

Her mother's eyes were never easy, always searching, like they'd seen too much, and having seen too much were forced to look for even more.

Looking now for Bliss. On the same day Ananda had been assigned to wall building, her older sister was given cistern duty. Critical work. Her mother's eyes looked through the long dusk for Bliss to return.

The camp had four large cisterns buried in the lake bed, and a network of gutters to harvest the rare rain. Not a drop could be wasted. Everyone grabbed cups and bowls and sheets of plastic and ran around catching it, mad with relief and laughter, and drinking their fill while they could. Festive, like a holiday. *Rain!* Without its sparse offerings, they would have dried up the groundwater long ago and been driven to the Gulf, dead and heating still, dark with velvety oil slicks and derricks long abandoned.

They'd come to Alabama ten years ago, though the names of states meant nothing now. Droughts knew no borders. Neither did the gritty wind or the thunderheads that devoured the sky before battering the land with vicious bursts, *flooding* it, washing away the rich soil until every remaining ounce became a treasure greater than gold. Hating the waste of so much water, and hating the passing of those clouds, too, the remote promise of their angry anvil shapes vanishing like a moment's rage.

Bliss and her work crew had been hiding the openings to the cisterns, drawn down to a nine-day supply. Rationing had begun with the building of the wall, a struggle for Ananda, who perspired heavily. Her mother had shared her rations.

"If marauders come, we'll claim the drought like a friend," her father had said last night, "because having nothing might drive them on without a battle."

"They want more than water," her mother had replied. "They want—"

Before her father could speak, her mother silenced herself. But Ananda knew what she would have said: "They want girls." And she knew why her mother had stopped speaking: the fear of Wicca.

Her parents had told her about the virus a little more than a year ago. They'd sat her down in their tent after the evening communal meal and closed the flaps. Bliss had stood outside to make sure the littlest children didn't overhear what was about to be said. Her mother had told her to listen carefully, that they didn't want to dwell on what they had to tell her, "but you're older now, and you need to know." Her mom began by saying that Wicca had a scientific name: Immune Disintegration Disorder, or IDD, but that "Wicca" had come into far greater usage after enraged fundamentalists of all faiths started calling it the "devil's disease."

Ananda had sat still as the air in the tent as her mother said that the Wicca virus confined safe sex between men and women to the twelve months after menarche. "After that, sex will almost always kill you. So sex can't happen, Ananda," her mother had said in her gentlest voice. *"Ever."*

"But you have sex. You had me and Bliss."

"No, not anymore. Sex is too deadly now. And it's a horrible death, Ananda. It's so bad it makes people kill themselves. It's madness." Then her mom stared at her so intensely that it frightened her.

"Meaning?" Ananda whispered.

Her parents had glanced at each other. Ananda watched her father shake his head.

"Can you just accept that for now?" he asked her. "That it's the most horrible disease ever?"

Her parents never talked to her about Wicca again, but every day since then the disease had felt as real as the ravaged earth. Even Bliss wouldn't talk about it. "The more you know," her sister told her, "the less you'll wish you knew."

Now, Ananda watched everyone in the camp return to their tents, sitting as she and her mother were, by the front flaps. Fatigue quelling boredom, as it did every day. They numbered almost 140 people, about half of them children, and were joined not by a common religion, other than a shared understanding that religion had failed them as surely as other earthly institutions; or by a common hope beyond survival, because hope in its most magisterial realms—home and land alive with the abundant fruits of labor—had failed them, too.

But survival itself was a powerful unguent, soothing their everyday differences and holding them together like the mud they made from sand and clay and compost, which turned fifty-pound sandbags into a wall. Joined also by the weaponry they shared. Ananda, along with the other children ten or older, knew how to use their eclectic collection of revolvers, knives, swords, chains, semiautomatic pistols, shotguns, and three fully automatic rifles. Firepower looted from an armory, back when armories still stood brazen against the world.

Well-armed for a camp, but not like the marauders who had the richest redoubts showering them with food, fuel, weapons, and armor-plated vehicles—all they needed to hunt girls. That was the scariest rumor Ananda had ever heard: that gangs roamed the land "harvesting" girls like her for sex.

Her parents wouldn't say, and neither had Bliss. But Ananda sensed that everything the girls whispered about sex harvesting was true. She'd glimpsed it in the eyes of her sister, turning cold when one of the older boys in their own camp let his gaze linger on her chest, which had grown in the past year. Ananda had also noticed Bliss's small breasts, and above them, always alert, her icy blue eyes.

Her mother was still looking for her.

"What if Dad doesn't get back tonight?" The sky was darkening.

"I told you, he'll be back."

Empty words. One way or another they said empty words every day, until they could have filled the reservoir with their meaninglessness.

Ananda stood, jumping up to look over the wall to try to catch sight of her father first. Nothing but the vast plain of lake bed. Her father had stayed away at night only twice before, both times after he'd spied marauders and couldn't risk capture. The marauders had little interest in men, she'd overheard her mother telling Bliss, but rendered their bodies for their dogs.

Dusk, thankfully, was slow this time of year, one of the few clues to the season. "You study the angle of the sun to know winter from summer," her dad had told her. But it seemed a crime to have to measure angles to know the season.

"It is a crime," her father agreed.

"Then someone's got to pay," she said.

"In the best of worlds, someone would."

Still, she welcomed the angle because when she jumped again, the late light revealed dust rising above a distant hummock in the lake bed. A wisp, that's all, and it might be no more than a dust devil dancing teasingly. But it was her father.

Running.

"Dad!" she screamed. "He's running!" She raced to the wall, hurling herself up to the top. He was running with Hansel, their mastiff mix, by his side. Hansel looked behind them.

Ananda heard her mother yelling, "Open the gate. Open it," before ripping off the chains herself.

Her father was a half mile away. At least. She'd never seen him run so hard. His rifle was strapped across his back and his bandolier flapped against his bare chest. His hair, long and banded, bounced behind him.

He screamed at Hansel. Ananda couldn't hear him, saw only the hand gesture that came with the command "Home." The huge dog slowed, as if torn between his master and the order, then raced ahead.

Ananda sickened when she saw her father's command, even more when her mother screamed "No" as an armor-clad truck roared around the hummock, churning up a hurricane of dust.

Her mom pulled her down from the wall. "You are not to watch."

Ananda broke free and hoisted herself back up. She saw Hansel nearing the gate, her father still so far away.

Her mother pulled her back down again, shouting, "Go to the hiding place now."

"But Mom," she pleaded, "Dad's—"

Her mother pushed her into the arms of a woman who rushed her to the root cellar on the other side of the camp.

Ananda hurried down the steps and slipped into the darkness carved out of the earth behind a false wall, hiding with other girls—nine-, ten-, eleven-, and twelve-year-olds. Even a fifteen-year-old. But not Bliss. One year after menarche, Bliss had been freed from having to hide. She would be at the wall with a pistol. Everyone had trained for this.

Ananda heard the root cellar door close. Not locked. Too obvious. But the entrance to the false wall would yield only to force.

"Nanda," whispered Imagi.

Ananda drew the girl close. A nine-year-old, but younger than the three years that separated them. "Down syndrome," Ananda's father had told her. Imagi had a big round face, wide-open eyes.

"We have to be quiet," Ananda said.

Imagi giggled and shouted, "Quiet."

The other girls hushed her at once. Bella, another twelve-year-old, said "You've got to keep her under control, Ananda."

They waited. So few sounds reached the root cellar, then the crack of bullets.

Imagi stiffened. So did Ananda, but she put her hand over the girl's mouth.

"Remember the game?" she said to her.

Imagi nodded in the blackness.

"It's starting now."

Chapter Two

Jessie saw in an instant that Eden would never win his race against the monstrous looking vehicles. Five of them now. From under their slabs of steel—a roughly riveted aspect so intimidating that it had to have been intended—there appeared to be a van flanking each side of the boxy truck. A burst of gunfire from Rye and her didn't slow them down, and targeting the drivers was hopeless: the windshield squinted like predators, with only a narrow horizontal slit across the middle of their metal shields—aperture enough for them to fan out in a precise chevron as they ground up the earth and bore down on Eden, nightmarishly short of the camp.

Hansel joined her at the open gate, heeling at the flick of her finger. She watched Eden's progress, counting the seconds. Maybe ten till the marauders caught him, another fifteen till they roared into the camp.

Each vehicle was crowned with a steel-sided metal carrier. She saw men crouching below the pipes that formed the upper railing, their helmeted heads bobbing briefly into view, their bayoneted gun barrels dark spikes in the dusk. Dogs crowded beside them, forcing their frothing muzzles into the wind, howling.

Night falling, heavens whirling, and down below, blood and bone and seething hate.

"Close it!" Jessie cried.

She couldn't risk the camp. Eden would have to come over the wall, a belief broken immediately by the brutal vectors of distance and speed.

Two dark-haired sisters in their forties, escaped slaves with branded backs, slammed the huge iron gate. Eden had found it mostly buried in the barren reservoir, looped chains around its hinges, and hauled it inch by inch across the fissured lake bed to the camp, believing that someday it would prove useful.

The sisters now hooked the chains around the door and anchored them to scavenged steel posts, locking him out.

Eden was still running well ahead of them, which made no sense to Jessie. Then she sensed the lupine cunning: the drivers had held back, trying to lure them into keeping the gate open. With it closed, they sped up.

She'd told Ananda not to watch but she herself could not look away as the truck at the center of the V shadowed Eden, an animal come to feed.

Twenty-two years to learn his every mood and expression, to read the fine lines of love on his face. An instant to know the bold print of his terror.

She counted again, as if numbers could add measure to life. The final seconds, *six, seven, eight*. Then she raised her rifle to the sandbags and eyed her husband's panic through the scope. They'd made a pact years ago: never to be taken alive. And when the girls arrived, they'd christened them with the same vow. Cruelty born of kindness.

She glanced at Bliss, twenty feet down the wall with a revolver. The girl's eyes bored into hers. Jessie turned back to her husband, forcing the crosshairs on his bare chest, her aim muddied by his wildly flapping bandolier. Two quick rounds. If the first found casing, the second would find flesh. She had no doubt she'd hit him. She'd hunted since childhood. Meat had already been scarce then, and she grew up with shortages of all kinds—food, fuel, compassion.

Her finger froze.

"Rye, I can't do it."

Her brother-in-law grabbed the rifle, faltering as he looked in horror at the truck. A huge man in the carrier was whipping Eden with a heavy chain, raking his back, pitching him forward. Eden's legs buckled and he lurched left and right, making him harder to shoot. The man ducked down, rising a second later to whip him again, catching his head. Eden still didn't fall.

Jessie grabbed back her rifle, cursing her weakness. Bliss looked away. Both of them watched the truck race in front of Eden and skid to a stop, brakes screeching. The vans on both sides of the truck sped past them before executing the same maneuver, plowing up twin plumes of dust. Then the vans pulled nose-to-nose, blocking all targets save metal and mystery.

Jessie heard the dogs, feared the worst, imagination a pale friend. She heard the engines rumbling, too, their threats drifting over the camp on the angry arms of shouts and fumes.

Minutes passed like the miles of a graveyard. The two vans gunned their motors, belching black smoke, more earth to stain the sky. Their tires spun, thumping the ground and churning up fresh dust as they reared away from each other. The truck rolled like royalty through the cloud, with Eden chained to the front, strapped sideways like a trophy deer left to drain.

Back in formation, they moved slowly toward the camp, Eden in the middle of the spreading V, war whoops and howling behind him.

Jessie forced herself back to the scope. Her husband's eyes blinked in terror.

"He's alive," she said to Rye and Solana, who'd come up beside him. "I've got to hear what they want."

"We know what they want."

"Then what they'll settle for."

"And we know what *he* wants." Rye.

She shook her head. "Not yet."

Eye back to the scope, she watched those bayonets dancing up and down, the rifle butts pounding out a dark promise worse than the dogs'. She'd been a sniper before they slipped away from the hills up north to come here. Pregnant with Ananda, she'd renounced her means of killing. But fury and reflex had her searching for a head, or a limb to sever. The scope proved stingy. Only dogs and the hard skull of armor.

Headlights awakened the night. In the long ago, they called them "high beams" or "brights." Blinding but for the bulbs that haloed Eden's head and legs.

The distance closed like a fist. Close enough that she could hear her husband. "The promise. Jessie, the promise." No strength for screaming, but his plea was plain enough.

"You hear what he's saying?" Rye asked.

Not in her heart.

Behind her, elderly gardeners rushed to pick every edible vegetable, sorting them into bins, hauling them to the root cellar. A key part of the plan.

Girls, stay quiet. Imagi on her mind.

"Open the gate." An amplified voice stunning in its clarity. She hadn't heard anything like it since childhood. "Or he'll open it for you." The shock of her husband's plight on her now like a beast. "We'll respect your camp. *You* must respect our demands. We're taking half your water, and all the females between the ages of nine and fifteen must line up by your gate for a physical examination. You will open the gate . . ."

Driving closer all the time.

". . . or we'll crush him and bomb your camp."

A thick arm rose from the carrier on the truck, thrusting an RPG high above the railing, the grenade launcher's deadly silhouette etched by the dying light.

Fifty feet away.

"We will not stop. Open the gate."

Above the pounding of the rifle butts and the rising bayonets came a thunderous chant: "Open. Open. Open . . ."

"Jesus fucking God." She turned to Rye, who shared his brother's look of terror.

"We're here for the harvest," the voice louder, nearer. "Don't deny us."

"Open. Open. Open . . ." All the arms in the carriers in the air now, thrusting bayonets like they could launch them, too.

Thirty feet.

"We'll take the females anyway and kill all of you."

Twenty-five.

"We're skilled veterans of many campaigns . . ."

Twenty.

". . . We never hesitate to do what we must."

"Open. Open. Open . . ." Pounding, pounding.

Jessie saw light stealing through rusted holes in the door, heard tires crushing dirt in the looming darkness. She thought of bombs and the demolition of the wall. *Of the camp.*

Fifteen.

She rushed the gate. The two sisters grabbed the heavy chain and tried to unhook it from one of the steel posts. Couldn't.

"We're opening it!" Jessie screamed as she yanked on the stubborn link.

"We *never* hesitate," the voice repeated.

She smelled exhaust a few feet away, yanked furiously on the chain, wept in frustration and rage when it wouldn't move. Solana reached through the tangle of her anguished arms, shifted a reluctant link, and the chain broke free.

The four of them slammed their shoulders to the steel, opening the gate to the blinding light a few feet away. *Still* moving.

They jumped to the side. Eden stared at her, blood specks in his eyes, and shook his head.

Chapter Three

Abandoned dogs, cats hunted
California animal shelters stormed, looted for "food"
New York Times

Midwest Dust Storm Blankets Three States:
Kansas, Nebraska, Oklahoma
Nation's biggest aquifer empty, cities deserted
Secretary of Agriculture Emergency Report to President

he steel plating on the boxy truck shuddered as the vehicle ground to a halt halfway through the open gate, brakes shrieking like a jungle.

Jessie forced herself to turn from Eden, terrified that open concern would leave her family in even greater danger. Eden must have sensed this, too, because he stared straight ahead with no more expression than the high beams burning behind his body. They'd feared it would come to this. *Sooner or later.* But always hoping for never.

"Throw your weapons down *now.*"

Her eardrums crackled painfully from the abrasive, amplified voice.

Bayonets and gun barrels stared down from the truck's

carrier outside. Men jumped from the armored vans and SUVs, drawing her attention to the wall where weapons now aimed *into* the camp. A quick count indicated upward of two dozen marauders.

She rested her hunting rifle in the silt, every move alive in the headlights, and saw Bliss lay down the pistol. To make their surrender look real, they'd planned to give up a handful of their better weapons. But their most critical arms—the three automatic rifles, semiautomatic pistols, and shotguns, including Bliss's—had been stashed throughout the camp. A lethal collection of hooked and doubled-edged blades had also been left within easy reach. She felt a blood binge creeping through the shadows, near enough to make the frightened face of every child claw holes in her heart.

Men climbed down from the top of the truck. One of them grabbed her rifle while the others fanned out and searched everybody, even children. Practiced. Efficient. They tore down the tents and hurried the weapons out of the camp.

"I want all those young females lined up by the gate." The lone man left in the carrier pointed his sawed-off shotgun to the narrow opening between the truck and the wall. Only the dogs crowded him now, snarling, their eyes like the gun barrels that had been looking down. "Everyone else sit there," he said, thrusting his weapon at the open space between the gate and the garden.

Hansel growled from several feet away, and Jessie signaled the dog to be quiet. Lights suddenly flashed into the camp from the other side of the wall. Half a dozen narrow beams raked the darkness, passing quickly over stone cook stoves, crude benches, and the flattened remains of the tents, then stopping to study stricken faces that didn't dare move.

Bliss stood second in line behind Kayla.

A child cried in the crowd, which set off another.

"Shut them up." The man waved his shotgun at the children, huddling like refugees.

Mothers and fathers tried to quiet the young ones. Failed.

Jessie's groin tightened, seized by the memory of Imagi always running to the rescue of crying kids.

"You," thundered the gunman in the carrier, "go when he takes you." He was pointing to Kayla, who was still startled when a man grabbed her and forced her through the narrow opening by the gate, pushing her to a stained cot with a shredded length of canvas hanging from one end.

Jessie edged to the left to try to see what they'd do to Kayla. To Bliss.

But she hadn't shifted far enough, and as she stirred again the man in the carrier shouted, "Don't move."

She froze as he took off his helmet. Gray hair raked back. Beardless face turbulent with odd angles. Maybe from shadows. Maybe from beatings.

He climbed down from the carrier, appearing shorter than he'd looked up there, but even more frightening with his shotgun at the ready and a bone-handled knife sheathed on his hip. Then he strode into the headlights and she saw his burned hand, index and middle fingers fused by the flames that had left his skin mottled and scarred, frozen in an arc that mirrored the hard crescent shape of the trigger they cradled.

Kayla yelped from beyond the wall, shattering the momentary silence. Three minutes later she fled back through the gate crying softly.

Kayla was nine years old.

A hand clamped down on the back of Bliss's neck, fingers reaching all the way around to her windpipe, skin hard and hot as sunburnt leather. And strong, like he could snap her spine easily as a bird bone.

He shoved her past a phalanx of armed men, most in helmets. All of them holding guns like they'd shoot if she sneezed.

A lantern hung over the cot, giving off an oily black smoke that stunk. The camp had no fuel, but scavenged wood; no lights, but stars and the moon that came with her cycle. Now there was a lantern, and it smelled rancid enough to make her sick. What were they burning?

"Take off your clothes." An old woman stepped from the penumbra. Dirty gray braids fell past her shoulders, and her skirt and top hung in tatters. A rag of flesh and fabric compared to the men.

Bliss knew better than to pause. She had to bare herself to all these men as if she'd done it many times before, even though modesty in the camp was an "absolute must." Her mother's insistent words: "*Don't* cry or let yourself shake. You've got to make them believe that you've had a year of cycles. Act bolder, look older." Her mother thought that was such a catchy phrase. She'd hated it and every ill meaning those words suggested, but repeated them to herself now like a mantra. To fail was to fall into their grip and die.

"Take that off." The old woman gestured at her shirt with a speculum that had been hiding in her hand.

"Why?"

Four men lunged at her and lifted her off the ground, tore off her shirt and forced her to lie back on the cot. Then they stared, faces masked by shadows. They said nothing, but their furious breaths and her panicky heartbeats formed a strange rhythmic madness.

"Open your legs." The old woman stood at the end of the cot, staring, too.

Don't hesitate, she told herself.

As soon as she moved, the men stepped back. Their retreat stirred the black smoke, suffusing her, once again, with the stench of burning fat. If that's what it was.

The old woman glared at Bliss, making her wish for nothing so much as the sanctuary of privacy.

"Are you a virgin?

"No."

The woman continued to look intently at her. Strange eyes. Large. "Do your parents know?"

"Yes."

"They must want to kill you."

Bliss said nothing.

"You're lying, aren't you?"

"No." The most important lie she'd ever tell.

She heard a metallic click over by the wall. *A gun?* They wouldn't shoot yet, would they? Not without their harvest.

"Menarche?"

"Yes."

"When?"

"Thirteen months ago."

"How convenient."

"It's true," Bliss blurted, aghast at what she'd done. You *never* say more than you have to. It's the first rule of lying. And she'd just violated it, insisting on the truth when it was true but not when she'd lied.

For all their cruelty, the woman's touch was not rough. But when the speculum entered her, Bliss still stiffened. *That's a good thing,* she told herself between gasps. "If you fight the feeling," her mother had warned, "they'll know you're faking it. Don't let them ever think that."

The men, she noticed, had all turned away after she said she wasn't a virgin. Their survival was at stake, too.

The woman withdrew the speculum, startling her again. "Sit up."

Bliss sensed trouble, the air snaky with lies and the fear of disease. She pulled on her pants and shirt.

"I can't tell," the woman said to a man in a battered porkpie hat who had stepped from a vehicle. "She could have started a month ago. She could have broken her hymen the way they do now. She could be prime harvest. Girls lean as her usually start late."

"How old are you?"

The woman winced at his question. She'd forgot to ask, Bliss realized.

"Fourteen. Fifteen next month."

"You keep a calendar?"

"In my head. We all do."

He looked her up and down. Bliss felt her future, her *life*, in the balance.

"Look at this." She pulled her pants back down and watched *him* flinch. *Good, he's afraid.* "And here." She threw off her shirt and pointed to her underarms. "I can't fake hair."

He stared at her, but again she sensed fear, not prurience, frightened awareness that she could be carrying the virus that had devastated the world as much as the warming.

Bliss never wavered as he called for headlights. *Look all you want,* she almost screamed. *All of you. And then let me go.* She had her mother's rich hair. Maybe her boldness, too, but when Porkpie moved closer for a better look, her boldness felt fleeting.

"Have you had intercourse yet?" His voice shook, astonishing her. But he was still staring at her sex as if *that* could give him the answer.

When the woman moved to respond, he slapped her chest. "Shut up."

"Yes," Bliss said.

He raised his face to hers.

"It sounds like you rehearsed." He leaned forward till she saw the deep caverns of his eyes, like they'd been pounded halfway through his head. A carved key hung from his neck with the inscription DULUTH. She'd heard that they wore them like charms, like they might actually get back to their homes someday, their lives. *Idiots.* Look around you.

"I did." Holding the boldness. Pushing it further: "Wouldn't you?"

He smacked her so hard her head snapped to the side. She looked back at him, all wariness gone. *You're dead.* She'd never said those words to anyone. Never thought them. But in the silence she knew their force and promise: *Dead.*

"I thought so. You're watching every word you say." He

turned to the woman: "Keep her out here. Something's not right."

Enraged, Bliss yanked her pants back up and threw on her shirt, furious with him, and with herself for insisting on the truth. But every other answer was as it should have been, and they still weren't done with her. Even admitting the rehearsal had been the right move. "If they think it, confirm it," her mother had said. "They know everyone rehearses girls. The worst is if they sense a lie. Then they'll think the truth is a lie and the lie's the truth."

Two men forced her to sit in the dust about ten feet from the cot. Headlights threw her shadow into the camp, where her sister was hiding. If they found Ananda, they'd do more than strip her naked. They'd take her away forever.

Bliss met Tangiers's gaze as she came out. Empty and cold. Like she herself felt. She heard the dogs stirring and tasted the blood on her lip for the first time.

Dead.

Jessie kneaded the dust, her palms damp and streaked. They'd brought back all the girls but Bliss. *What the hell were they doing to her?* She was a tough girl, much tougher than Ananda, but to be out there by herself. With *them*?

Rye tapped Jessie's back and whispered from behind her. "We're not going to let them take her."

She nodded almost imperceptivity, whispering back, "I'll murder every one of them."

But with what? She looked around. There wasn't a gun hidden anywhere near her.

The gray, beardless man with the sawed-off shotgun folded his thick arms across his chest and stared at them, the muzzle pointing carelessly toward a group of small children. He called for "Gemi," and a man retrieved a big black mixed breed from the carrier. The dog raced to the gunman, circling him with his eyes on the prisoners, growling fiercely, his tail brushing the children closest to him. Wild-eyed, they scrambled onto their parents' laps.

Hansel rose, snarling and bristling.

"Down," Jessie snapped, commanding the dog's obedience and the attention of the man.

"Yours?"

She shook her head.

"His?" The man with the burned fingers nodded at Eden. She hesitated, then nodded back.

"Yours?" He nodded at Eden again.

"No," Jessie said.

"Yeah, he is. That dog's trained for you, too. I know dogs."

Hansel had lowered his chest to the ground, still ready to pounce, his throaty growl adding powder to the unexploded moment.

The gunman's eyes roved over the crowd. "Now we're going to search your camp for the harvest. If you're hiding them, there'll be no pity. There can't be. But if anyone wants to speak up now, save yourself and your other kids, I'm listening."

No sound but a child's cry. He stared as the beams moved over their tormented features, the deepening night bearing down like a beast, all teeth and terror.

Men patrolled the inside wall, pointing their bayoneted rifles. Several wielded only machetes that glinted in the glancing light, long blades that opened the memory of the blood mysteries, more timely now than in the long ago when Jessie had sat in a classroom for a lecture on matriarchal cults. Wars exploding in the cities, mushrooming outward, and they'd been innocent enough to believe they still had afternoons for the sweetness of study.

"There are three blood mysteries," Professor Janet Jacobs had said, a vibrant young woman who was among the first of the faculty beheaded on the campus commons. "Menarche, birth, and menopause." They'd been studying the evolution of consciousness, the way ancients were mystified by blood and its transformations in women.

But Professor Jacobs had been so wrong, Jessie realized as she surveilled the armed men and her nose filled with the acrid odor of the unseen lantern. Jacobs had missed the most important blood mystery of all. Maybe because it belonged more to the world they were about to become than to the world they'd known then. Maybe because the fourth blood mystery was—and always would be—murder.

"We have nothing to hide," she forced herself to say to the man with the sawed-off shotgun. The fear had bred a viral silence.

He looked at her. "Nothing to hide. Where's your kids? And don't lie because I'll find out from someone else." He pointed the shotgun at her.

Why had she spoken? Starkey and his wife and their twin sons were sitting near her, shaking. *Nobody's going to sacrifice their children for yours.*

"The girl who's still out there."

"Her? She told my men she's had sex."

"She has." Then quickly, "There's not much for them to do here."

He rubbed his chin with his gun-bearing hand, and she wondered if he was wiping away a skeptical smirk. "Get her in here," he yelled toward the gate. "You," he pointed the shotgun at Jessie again, "you got the mouth, so show me where you keep your water."

She approached him, noticing veins like cables in his ropy forearms. He shoved her ahead, and jammed the barrels into her back so hard that she thought he'd shoot her right then.

Jessie hurried to the garden cistern, showing him the spout they'd left exposed. Like her hunting rifle, it was another sacrifice of their surrender. They'd hidden the spigot for the ground water under a raised bed of carrots. If the marauders found it, there would be no hope of keeping the camp. Groundwater? In this world?

Worth more than all our lives.

A beam of light fell on her hands, and she heard boots behind her. She didn't dare turn around. The dog had his nose in the air, on the ground.

"You telling me one fucking tank's all you've got for all these people?"

"It holds two hundred gallons." Lying even as she asked herself if dying violently for water was worth it. *But they're not going to dig up the tank to check. Right?*

"How much is in there?"

"About thirty gallons. We haven't had any rain for a long time."

"We'll take it."

"But you said you'd leave us half."

He stared at her, and she quieted.

No, argue, she urged herself. If that's all the water you really had, you'd say something. "You can't. We only have a seven-day supply."

"We 'can't'?" He grabbed her throat and twisted it so hard that she thought he'd crushed her larynx. "Don't *ever* say we 'can't' to me. Next time I'll rip you open and leave you to him."

The dog, agitated by his master, growled and bared his teeth at her. Hansel flew toward them. Despite her pain, she put up her hand to stop him.

"Let them go at it," he said, but turned to one of the men backing him up. "I want all the bedding checked, and underneath. Get some help. Make sure they're not hiding down in some holes under where the tents were. You," he said to the man still by his side, "stick with me. We're going over there." He pushed Jessie toward the root cellar.

Staggering, holding her throbbing throat, she watched him walk inside with his dog. The bins were piled high all the way to the back.

"How come it's all stuffed in here?"

She choked out, "We wanted to put it away." The dog

sniffed the bins, floor, walls, as he slunk into the deeper shadows.

"Hiding it? From us?"

A noise. *What the hell was that?* She coughed louder.

"Yes," she gagged. Let him think it was absurd to try to hide anything in there. *Imagi, shut up.*

"We're taking all this," smacking the top bin with the butt of his weapon. "But this shit's not the harvest we came for."

She kept coughing, all the time wishing the goddamn dog would go away.

He grabbed her arm, shoving her toward the truck. "Your husband's looking kind of beat."

When she didn't respond, he cracked the side of her head with the shotgun. "I said, 'Your husband's looking kind of beat.'"

She nodded, pain still erupting from the blow.

"You've got a nice little family. Just the three of you, right?"

"Right."

"Sit down," he ordered when they reached the assembled group. Bliss was off to the side, knees drawn up to her chest. Jessie saw fresh rips in her shirt.

He signaled the men by the wall, and she heard rifles readied. The rest were still ransacking the bedding and what was left of the tents.

"How many of them?" he snapped to a man near Eden.

"A hundred thirty-two."

The gunman turned back to them. "A hundred thirty-two, and not one single girl for the harvest. You must think we're stupid."

He began to pace, twirling his sawed-off shotgun around his fused fingers like a gunslinger of old before pivoting to face Eden. He yanked on the chains by his head, releasing the top half of his body. Eden's face smashed to the ground with a thud. Then the gunman released his feet, and Eden's legs crashed down. Still bound by the chains, he lay on the ground with dust rising into the headlights above him.

The gunman smiled at Jessie. "You lied. You got a harvest. They're over in that root cellar having a fucking party. Gemi sniffed them right out, and he's making sure they don't move." He waved over several men, who abandoned their positions by the wall. "Go drag them out. I've got something to show them." He lowered himself to one knee and pressed the barrels of his shotgun into Eden's face, mashing his lips and nose. "Something that'll set them straight right from the start." He looked at the horrified faces staring at him. "You lie, you die."

Imagi yelled, "The game! The game!" as the girls were rousted from the root cellar.

Jessie stared at the sky, pleading silently for someone to start it. Someone near a gun.

Someone did, but not the someone she would have chosen.

Bliss pumped her shotgun and rose from the shadows.

Chapter Four

World Seed Bank Looted, Destroyed
10,000 seed samples seized, eaten; guards killed;
  children trampled
BBC News

New Virus Alarms Doctors
Violent hallucinations, vicious fever
Murder, suicide rates skyrocket
CDC alert

The gunman jumped up with his sawed-off shotgun as Bliss, so thin and spectral in the dying light, raced toward him. A helmeted marauder raised his rifle and drew the girl's eyes. His face exploded with lead shot, and a shank of flesh spattered the gunman's chest and arms. The explosion tore off the marauder's helmet and pitched him forward, blocking the gunman's blast with his belly. Bliss pumped and fired again, an errant shot that rent only the night.

The silence had ended. The reckoning began.

With a single soft groan, the marauder collapsed on Eden's chained body, legs twitching beneath the headlights, Eden lying still and quiet as stone.

The camp erupted. Gunshots cracking like thunder on rock, children screaming and crying. Men and women weeping. And beneath the shrieks and desperate clamor, the eerie gasps of sudden death in shadows.

Jessie rolled furiously across the ground, no regard or feeling for the booted and bare feet trampling her. Scrabbling for a wooden barrel. Plowing into it, pushing it over into the garden, seizing the automatic rifle hidden inside.

Rolling farther, the M-16 hugged to her chest like a child, she saw flames flare from a distant muzzle and heard the deafening roar of gunfire so close to her head that she thought she'd been hit. Startled that she wasn't.

In a column of darkness she fixed the rifle to her shoulder, elbows to the earth. Marauders hard to see in the mayhem, but three of them rushed forward and she issued her first burst. They spun into one another, spilled apart, crumpled.

The lights went crazy. Beams crossed, rose, fell, daggers slashing at the dark, flashing on kids, dogs, on marauders shooting like men unleashed. Bodies collapsed and squirmed in a madness of motion.

Two marauders raced past, Jessie's automatic a scythe cutting them down. But now she drew fire in return. Dirt sprang up around her. Stone chips sprayed her face, cutting her lip and nose. Bullets sounded like bees in the queer turmoil of attack.

She forced her retreat on her elbows, bloodying them to back into shadows. A flashlight beam followed her, darted left and right, creeping closer, a beast nosing the night, and flicked away when a second M-16 opened fire on the far side of the camp, leaving only the AK-47 unclaimed.

Grab it. Someone.

A girl stumbled over her, then a boy. Starkey scooped them up.

"Get a gun!" she yelled. "Don't run!"

But the screams of the dying drove the Starkeys on. Others, too.

"The harvest." A screeching amplified reminder from the gunman, intent on the girls as his men savaged their parents, siblings.

She studied the truck, looking for him. No movement, save the smoke in the headlights, sinuous and slow.

Another burst from the other M-16. No one fell, but she spotted two more shotgun blasts a hundred feet away, red and yellow flames demonic in the darkness. Ours, she hoped. Bliss and Ananda alive, *please dear God*.

Yards away three echoing shots as a marauder gunned down a bent man at close range. Jessie aimed, and the shooter grabbed his shoulder, dropped his gun, dropped to his knees. She fired again, dropping him facedown in the dust.

A girl's wail—pierced with grief and horror—rose above the gunshots and shrieks, then stilled, emptiness deeper than death.

Jessie lunged behind a garden bed, breath fracturing like bone. *Breathe. Breathe.* Eyes beaded with sweat, tears. She watched marauders raise a portable steel shield and advance from the gate. She shot two more racing toward it, then raked her weapon to the right, sending three of them diving for the ground; one of them caught by a shotgun blast, tumbled like a weed.

They're taking cover. Not all, she saw with revulsion. A huge marauder hacked at fallen bodies by the wall. Jessie shot him as he raised his axe over a small, twisting form.

A girl ran into her, jerked away in fright. Jessie pulled her close and dragged her behind the root cellar.

"Stay here." She rested the girl's head on the ground, then looked around the corner of the cellar to see a woman backing a marauder up before emptying her pistol into his belly. His body snapped like a snake till Jessie heard only a *click, click, click*.

She shouted for her to get down, but the woman reached up, arms pleading with the night, voice a mournful squeal.

Then she raced toward the truck, thrusting her weapon at the marauders hiding behind the armor. *Click, click, click, click.* Two of them jumped out with machetes.

As Jessie raised her rifle to cut them down, a bullet cracked the root cellar inches from her head. She whipped back around the corner, striking the girl's head with the rifle stock. "Sorry, sorry," she said as the child whimpered. Jessie shot back blindly. Rounds split sandbags before a vicious oath sounded from the darkness. A light swept over the fierce face of a bearded marauder crawling toward her with a handgun. She killed him with a short burst, watched the light flit away, and rushed out to retrieve his weapon.

In the same instant the light returned. She grabbed the gun and dived back around the corner, dragging the girl to the other side of the root cellar, the earth at her heels chewed up by a fusillade. When the shooting stopped, she gave the girl the revolver. "They come for you, you use it." Then she heard the sharp report of a clip jammed into a rifle. Froze.

"It's me."

Rye. He jabbed bullets into her hand and drifted back into darkness.

Jessie reloaded, fingers moist, slippery. Slammed the magazine in and looked up to see a friend plunging a sword into the neck of a marauder, who slumped a moment before his skull was cleaved with a frenzied blow.

In the glancing light, she saw far more of the camp murdered, wounded, or lank with the hope that life was best served by the pretense of death.

Half a dozen dogs raced through the gate as the lead gunman's amplified voice returned. "Kill, kill!" he shouted. Jessie and another immediately sprayed the snarling hounds with gunfire, setting off howls of pain.

And then an unaccountable silence fell. The lull didn't last but it signaled a calculation to the killing now that the first rush of madness had passed. She detected stealth, too, in a marauder crawling through the distant shadows. A glint of light showed blood on his scalp, but most of the invaders had taken cover.

She climbed to a crouch for a better view of him, and told the girl to play dead.

As soon as Jessie straightened, she was grabbed from behind.

"Drop the rifle." His voice was husky, breath unbearable. The M-16 his prize.

She nodded, her free hand trying to slip into her pants for a crude shiv when a bullet stunned him and his arms fell away. She turned shooting, tearing open his chest before she noticed the girl standing with the revolver. Willa, she saw now. The only child of a single mom. Ten years old. Staring at the man lying at her feet. Crying.

Jessie took the gun, warm from the child's hands, and rocked her like she was her own. Willa spoke into her ear.

"Are you sure?" Jessie asked.

The girl nodded.

She'd seen her mom murdered in the first seconds of the attack.

Jessie sat her down, had her curl up on the ground. Gave her back the gun.

"If they come for you, do it again, Willa."

The slightest nod. Eyes squeezed shut. Tears leaking in the dimmest light.

"You saved my life, you can save yours. You're a very strong girl."

Jessie swallowed her grief. Felt her rage. Scanned the grounds for the marauder with the bloody scalp. Couldn't find him crawling through the slaughter, but the shooting had slowed.

She looked for Bliss and Ananda. Couldn't find them, either. The only family she could see was Eden still buried under that dead body. They'd always feared the worst, and it had come at dusk to bleed the night, a dreamscape of death. A massacre in the moon's stony glow.

How long had it been? Ninety seconds? Five minutes? Longer? She knew even less of their dead, who, how many. Couldn't begin to count the men she'd killed, and knew she'd never want to. But the marauders were hiding. She no sooner thought this than three of them dashed out the gate.

"Burtlan?"

"Here."

"Grinder?"

"Here."

A bizarre roll call. Some of them answering from outside the wall, others from behind the boxy truck. Many not answering at all.

What's going on?

The portable shield shifted, retreating to the gate. More of them slipped out and pointed their guns into the camp. Then she spotted the grenade launcher and sickened.

The nearest wall was about twenty paces behind the root cellar, which could give her a few seconds of cover. She loaded the last of her bullets before sprinting through the shadows, going over the wall without drawing fire.

But she had drawn attention. *Christ.* Someone came right over after her. Her first fear was the crawler with the bloody scalp. She had her rifle up, trembling with relief when she saw Solana. Rye climbed over a moment later and hurried up to her.

"They've got the RPG out. They're going to bomb us, burn everything." He checked the action on his rifle. "We've got to take it to them."

"I know. I'm going this way." She gestured right. "You guys go left. We'll pin them down."

"Always the optimist." Rye forcing a smile. "You two should stick together." He headed off.

"How many you figure they've got left?" Solana asked hoarsely.

"No idea. A wild guess, I'd say half. Maybe a dozen in all."

Within a minute they rounded the wall, saw the vehicles

squatting like boulders in the moonlight. The boxy truck that had been blocking the gate backed up, its retreat stark confirmation of a final onslaught.

She held up three fingers to Solana, then two, and on one they rolled out into the open, firing on six men aiming their weapons over the wall, cutting them down in seconds.

Scrambling to their feet, shooting at the fallen shadows, they fled to the nearest vehicle.

"Cover me," she said to Solana, and peered through the slits in the van's armor. Empty.

As Solana raised her weapon beside her, Rye opened up from the far side of the gate, a burst stilled almost immediately by a heavy barrage of return fire.

"He's down! *Down!*" screamed a man. "Grab him!"

The truck stopped backing up, shielding the marauders.

"You see him?" a marauder shouted at Jessie and Solana. He was big, holding Rye's lifeless body in front of him, shaking him so hard the head snapped feverishly. "He's fucking lucky. We get you, we'll eat you *alive.*"

Trying to contain her grief and fear, Jessie turned to Solana, found her eyes blank as pits as the marauder threw Rye's body down and ducked behind the truck. She and Rye had been romantic partners in the long ago, before Wicca wiped out sex. Solana closed her eyes and screamed in desolation.

Jessie pulled her close, felt her wilting. "The girls. You've got to think about them. They'd never kill them. We can't let them leave. Let's get the tires while we can."

Solana stepped back, nodded weakly, then placed the muzzle of her rifle under the steel plating and shot the front tire as if it were an execution. Did the same to the rear one. The van slumped toward them. Then she shocked Jessie by bolting for the next vehicle, drawing a flurry of gunfire as she dived behind the front wheel.

"Don't. That's crazy," Jessie hissed. Grief and suicide partners, too.

More shots from Solana and that van listed. Then she raced to the next one. Jessie held her breath. *Someone's going to get her.* But no shots. Jessie did hear footfalls and turned. She saw the crawler, now standing, less than twenty feet away. She squeezed the trigger of her M-16, spitting up dirt and blood so fast that she never heard the shot that claimed her.

Writhing, she tried not to scream, to play dead even in its leaden grip. But her hands clawed the dirt and tore at her face, the agony beyond bearing, thick as the churning earth itself.

She opened her eyes to the night sky blazing with burning death, and knew that she had finally fallen.

The sun rose high, flooding the dried-up reservoir with its sickly rays, sparing only the dead in the stingiest shadows. Bodies lay strewn like refuse, blood spattered on walls, stuccoed on skin—countless streaks and puddles crusting in the heat.

No movement but the dust motes dancing on bones. No sound but the clack of insects, their belly membranes pulsing madly.

A bottleneck fly landed on Jessie's leg, feeding on her wound. She stirred, awakened and alarmed in the same breath. Brought back to the gruesome unknown of her family.

She hoisted herself onto her elbows and saw the wash of blood on her thigh, thick as paste from her groin to her knee. Dizzy with pain, she sat and lifted the leg, and saw blood cakes in the dirt. A bullet had passed all the way through her quadriceps, sparing the femur, but it must have nicked the artery. She was a biologist. She knew anatomy. Muscles didn't bleed like this. But if the artery had been fully severed, she never would have survived.

The vehicles were gone. The gate still stood open. Twenty feet from her the bodies of marauders lay piled by the wall where she and Solana killed them last night, limbs swelling, skin already alive with parasites. To her right lay the M-16, barrel crimped in a tire track. Ruined.

Turning, she saw the man who shot her lying on his belly, like he'd even tried to crawl away from death. The butt of his gun protruded from under his chest.

She hesitated only briefly before pulling the weapon from under him. Cracking the chamber, she found two bullets left. *One for them and one for me*

Still on her seat, she dragged herself toward the gate, wary of what hid behind the wall. But she had to find her girls, her husband, and gather them in her arms, no matter their life or death.

Holding the weapon ready, she pulled herself closer, the silence violated only by her anguish, which set off a sharp metallic retort. And hard footsteps that stopped short of the gate, raising dust that rolled out like a thunderhead.

Jessie aimed at the opening. The sun flashed on steel barrels as the bearer wheeled around the corner to kill.

Mother and daughter stared at each other, both bloodied, torn, shaking, squinting, fingers aching from shooting. Bliss dropped her shotgun and staggered toward her.

Jessie hugged her fiercely. Almost fifteen years gone by and she felt the boundless wonder of her birth anew, weeping now as she'd wept then: for joy, for sorrow, for the astounding appearance of life in a world strangled by hate.

And then she heard Bliss talking through her tears: "She's gone, Mom. They took her and the others."

Chapter Five

U.S. Southern Wall Sealed
Motion detecting machine guns slay Mexican refugees
General says "catch and release ends"
Report of the United Nations High Commissioner for Refugees

Gangs Seize Abandoned Oklahoma Prison
Inmates found dead in savage reprisals
Cannibalism common in final weeks, days
From survivor accounts

A nanda heard gunfire from the camp and caught glimpses of headlights bleeding through the cracks in the back of the boxy, armored truck; but she couldn't take her eyes off the marauder who guarded them. Neither could the other girls who'd been dragged from the root cellar. All of them watched him thumb his blade like he was getting ready to gut game.

The lock on the rear door slammed shut, loud as the gunshots that continued outside. The engine raced, like they'd take off any second. Ananda heard the shooting slow, and then another noise, like a crank. The marauder had flicked on a wind-up flashlight from the long ago. He pointed it up at his face. It made him look like a monster picture that Bliss had once drawn in the dust, lighting up the dark brim of his strange looking hat.

"Don't any of you fucking move," he said, lips as narrow as lines of blood, teeth as black as char.

M-girl, terrified that she was next to him, started to scramble away. Miriam was her name but she'd always gone by M-girl. Fifteen and tall, but stuck with the younger ones because she'd never had her period.

The marauder grabbed her, dropping his flashlight. She screamed and tried to break loose. Ananda's eyes were still on his knife.

"I tell you don't fucking move," he jerked M-girl's shirt so hard he tore it off her back, "you don't fucking move."

He pushed her down and whipped her again and again with the crusty shirt. Then, towering over her with the shirt in one hand and knife in the other, he pulled his foot back to kick her. But he didn't, picking up the flashlight instead. He wound the crank fiercely, charging it up before moving the beam slowly over the naked hunch of her long back, the spine so stark and straight, thinner than the welts already rising from the whipping.

He dropped to his knees and ran his fingers over her skin. The tips like a spider. He did it two more times, both sides of her spine. Ananda so scared she thought she'd shatter. M-girl's horrified breath a mad bellows.

He stood and stared at her in the sullen light. Then he threw the shirt at her bare back and yelled, "Sit up so I can see you, and put the goddamn thing on."

She snuck it over her chest, tucking the lengths between her arms and sides to stay decent. She crossed her arms when she finally faced him, holding herself as if she were freezing in the swelter.

The whole time, he stood over her winding the flashlight crank like crazy. Staring at her until the truck backed up, smiling as he crouched and flicked off the light.

Bastard. Ananda squeezed her eyes shut, too terrified to watch what he'd do next, preferring her own darkness to theirs. She fixed on the memory of her mom's face so she'd never forget her. Her dad's too. *Bliss.* She loved her sister. *Adored* her. Everybody did. The king girl of the camp.

She cried quietly, oblivious to the bumpy ride over the cracked lake bed. She'd seen her mom weep only once. When she was seven her mother had held her close at the end of the day, gazed at the sky, and said, "That's how it always was when I was growing up." Ananda heard her voice catch and saw her tears, then looked up like her mom, shocked by the pink streaks in the sky. It was usually the palest blue, and here was a burst of unimaginable color.

Her mom had wiped her eyes and said it looked like cotton candy, talked about county fairs, wondrous blue ribbon pies and red wattle roosters and watermelons so fat and juicy they could treat a whole class full of kids.

Ananda now understood her mother's sadness for the first time. Grief was tinder. Tears the flame.

When the gunfire faded completely in the distance, the marauders stopped the truck. A man unlocked the door, shined a light.

"Hey, Grinder, we got to change those tires or the wheels'll crack."

"You need me?"

"No, Ell says stay with them." Moving the light over the girls. "Party with the Pure Bloods."

"He say that?"

The door closed, and the lock twisted like the fear in Ananda's stomach.

"Pure Bloods." He chuckled and let his flashlight play over the girls. "And I've got five of you, one for each finger."

He held out his hand, moving his fingers like the legs of a beetle trapped on its back, brittle limbs harrowing the air. A sickening flooded Ananda, like he was already reaching for her.

Imagi had her head buried in her tented arms, and M-girl was crunched up in the corner. Bella and Gilly were holding each other like always.

The engine started and he put away his flashlight. Ananda lay down, drawing her knees to her chest and trying to keep her head from bouncing every time they hit a crack. She finally drew her shirt up under her head to soften the ride, hoping he wouldn't switch on the light to stare at her bare back. Darkness was a comfort when sight was a fiend.

She slept. Not much and not well, fear as haunting as the heat. *Kidnapped by marauders . . . Mom and Dad and Bliss dead.* With nightmares like that and a life like this, she could hardly tell one from the other.

Daylight seeped through the cracks, slicing the shadows on the wall. Light enough to see they were smoke darkened, the ceiling so black it might have been burned.

Ananda sat up quiet as she could, saw Grinder's head hanging down, greasy hair jiggling from the bumps. Asleep. She saw his knife, too. What would Bliss do? she asked herself. She'd grab it and kill him. Just like she'd started all that shooting.

Which might have got her killed.

He caught her looking, like he'd had an open eye behind his dirty hair, and clamped his hand over the blade. He laughed sharply, like a bottle breaking, and whispered, "Pure Blood looking for trouble?" He glanced at the others sleeping. "You all smell real good. Make a man's mouth get all sorts of dry." Then he nodded at her, like she knew what he meant.

He looked away as the truck stopped. Outside, a man yelled, "Pee break."

Grinder nodded at her again, like they shared a secret. It made her want to shoot him and never stop.

The door creaked open, waking the other girls. A marauder peered in, the one Bliss had run toward with her shotgun. A squat weapon rested on his hip. It had a worn wooden butt pocked with burn marks. Be a lot better than grabbing a knife, she thought at once.

He pointed to each of them with two fingers that had been melted by fire, holding them out like he wanted the girls to see his scars.

"You girls pee or whatever you have to do. We'll feed and water you. But *don't* try to run off because there's nowhere to run and no one's coming after you except us. And you don't want that."

Ananda took Imagi's hand and coaxed her toward the door. Bella and Gilly pushed past them. M-girl stayed huddled in the corner.

"What's wrong with her?" Burned Fingers leaned his head in the truck.

Grinder crawled over, shook M-girl's shoulder.

"Don't touch me! Don't touch me!" M-girl screamed, scuttling along the smoke-stained wall to get past him, one hand pressing the shredded shirt to her chest and the other out to fend him off. The welts on her back looked meaner in the morning light.

Burned Fingers eyed them as Grinder jumped out. "What happened to her?"

"That bitch was beating on me, screaming. I grabbed her and that piece of shit shirt ripped." He glared at M-girl, quaking horribly with her head down, hair jumping insanely like the lengths of her shredded shirt. Grinder's furious gaze took in the other girls. They said nothing.

"That's a lie," Ananda blurted, wishing she hadn't. Mouth as fast as her feet, her mom always said.

Grinder's eyes went cold and empty as caves. Burned Fingers stared at her and bent closer.

"What's a lie?"

"Nothing." She backed away, feeling the leader's anger.

"Nothing? You just said one of my men lied. And I think

I know exactly who's doing the lying. Stand still." His voice had grown louder, and he gripped her shoulder with those fingers. "So what is it?"

"He put a light on, and she was next to him and got scared and tried to move away. He grabbed her and ripped her shirt till it came off. And then he beat her with it really hard, and—" She seized up, sensing that if she said another word the two of them would tear off her clothes, too. Maybe kill her.

Burned Fingers tightened his grip on her shoulder and leaned his face inches from hers. "And then what?"

Her eyes darted away. Grinder had his hand on his knife again. The end was coming.

"Nothing," she mumbled.

"That's right. *Nothing!*" Grinder shook his head. "She's a goddamn fucking little liar."

She hated being called a liar. She did *not* lie. *Ever.*

"I'm going to give you about two seconds to finish your story . . ." Those fingers were still digging into Ananda's shoulder. ". . . and then I'm going—"

"He started to kick her, but then he didn't." Speaking fast, eyes on the cracked earth. "But he kept touching her skin, putting his fingers all over her back. And he made her put on her shirt, which she couldn't 'cause it was all ripped up, and he was keeping the light on her the whole time."

"You little fucking—"

"Shut up." Burned Fingers pointed those scars at Grinder. "You," he turned to M-girl, "is that true?"

M-girl shook worse than ever. Worse than in the truck.

Tell him. She was so afraid. *Please.*

M-girl didn't say a word, but she answered with a nod clear as the tracks in the dust.

Burned Fingers pulled out his sawed-off shotgun so fast the barrels blurred. He pointed it right at Grinder's gut. "Give her your shirt."

"I ain't gettin' no goddamn burn 'cause of these lyin'

bitches." Grinder snorted, like none of it meant anything at all. But Ananda could tell he was scared now.

A menacing metallic noise drew Ananda's eyes to those burned fingers closing around the curve of the trigger, like the flesh and steel had been forged for each other.

The rest of the marauders stared. They were scared, too. She saw them looking this way and that, but their eyes always came back to Grinder, now taking off his shirt. He threw it at M-girl. "Don't stink it up, bitch." It hit her legs and fell to the ground.

"Pick it up."

M-girl bent over.

"No," said Burned Fingers. "Him."

Grinder grabbed it, held it out. She snatched it, refusing to look at him.

"Now get over there." Burned Fingers waved him away from the truck with his stubby shotgun.

"They're fuckin' lyin'. Can't you see that, man?"

"That's what you said last time. You can park yourself right there."

A mile or more behind Grinder the reservoir walls rose to the skeletal ruins of the lakeshore homes.

Burned Fingers let his weapon slouch by his side. "See, what bothers me is that they're *not* lying. Those red marks on the girl's back? They're not lies. The way she's shaking? That's not a lie. Did you see her pants?" He glanced at M-girl. "She urinated on herself. That's not a lie, either. And this one . . ." He shook his head at Ananda like he couldn't believe the sight of her. ". . . she doesn't even have the good sense to lie."

"I've had it with you." His voice suddenly boomed at Grinder. "With *all* of you. If any man touches any one of these girls in a way that isn't right," he lifted his weapon, "he'll pay."

A shattering noise. Flames screamed from the barrel. The

blast opened a hole wide as a bowl in Grinder's bare belly. Ananda backed up as he gripped himself, trying to hold it in. Then he sank to his knees, thighs running red, eyes still like caves but on the man who'd shot him.

He pitched to the side, raising dust, the morning sun making it all brighter than it might have been. His hat rolled on its brim, circled once and settled.

Ananda was so shaken she could scarcely stand. She'd heard gunfire at the camp, and now saw the damage blunt and deep. But she was glad he was dead. No sorrow for him. He would have killed her after she'd told on him. She was sure of it. And he'd scared M-girl so bad.

But what she couldn't get straight as she smelled the gun smoke, and felt the sun on her head and sweat trickling down her sides, was that if his death were just and fair, then Burned Fingers had made it so. And this scared her worst of all: that setting wrong to right had fallen to the likes of him.

"Sweet fuckin' Jesus, Ell, we're short already. Now we don't even have a man to ride shotgun with Wheez, and we got nothin' but skells from here on out."

Burned Fingers turned at the sound of his name. "We're not as short as we would have been with him." He looked at each of his men, eyes moving slow as a snake in the sun. They stood with battered hats and weathered hands shading their faces. "These girls," he swept his weapon over them, "are your life. They're more valuable than gold. If we get them up to Knox, we'll get all we need to live for a year. One more week of work and we're set. One more week of keeping your mind on the job and your eyes off of them. If you don't, if they get hurt in any way, we're dead. Not just me, all of us. And you know it. There's no room for mistakes. None. Wrench." He pointed to a pudgy man in a filthy blue bandanna. "You ride with them. And I don't want to hear one more word from any of you about being short-handed. We have what we have and we're going to make do."

Burned Fingers holstered his sawed-off shotgun and

walked over to the body. It was still on its side, innards all spilled out. He pushed it over with his boot so the empty wound eyed the sky, blind and red as a socket. Then he pulled Grinder's knife from its sheath and cut off the wooden key with DULUTH carved in its side. He reached back and threw it as far as he could.

Everyone watched, Ananda with her eyes on Burned Fingers's weapon. The holster didn't have a catch. That's why he could pull it out so fast. *I'm quick, too,* she told herself.

He caught her looking, just like Grinder had caught her staring at his blade. But Burned Fingers didn't clamp his hand on his gun. He just laughed and shook his head like he still couldn't believe the sight of her.

"She doesn't even have the good sense to lie."

Or to hide your eyes from your prize.

Ananda led Imagi behind a big rock with a nasty red streak, iron oxide when there was rain for rust. It bulged from the lake like a tumor. As they walked back from peeing, a murder of crows hopped up to Grinder's body and pecked at the crimson sprawl, their black feathers satiny in the sun. A seventh kept a distance. The watcher. Every murder has one. She tested him, feinting toward the body. The watcher squawked and the others looked at Ananda, beady eyes blacker than soot. High above, vultures wheeled, and storm clouds crept from behind the cliffs.

In seconds they felt the first few drops.

"Can we drink the rain?" Gilly asked, looking at Burned Fingers, then to Ananda.

"Let them," Burned Fingers told the men. "It'll be easier on the rations."

The girls gathered in a circle as they always had in camp, mouths open to the elements, holding out their cupped hands and gobbling water that always tasted cleaner and better than anything they'd ever known. Like rain came from another world.

The marauders raced to put out five-gallon canisters and

pale jugs made of clay or porcelain, topping each one with a funnel fashioned from an old tin can. More of the long ago for the here and now.

Ananda glimpsed an AK-47 in the back of the van where they stored the canisters. Stolen from the camp, she figured. She wanted to take it back *right now*.

A ginger-haired driver named Anvil saw her looking and slammed the door.

Rain chattered on the armor, and she wondered if it was falling on her mom, dad, Bliss. Everyone in the camp. The way they'd dance and sing when it poured like this.

Her hands fell to her sides. She'd had her fill, and watched Burned Fingers studying the water rising in the cracks in the lake bed. The cracks were deep, a foot in places, and three to four inches wide. Big enough to snap an ankle. Two men in the camp still limped because of the cracks.

If they're still alive.

"Load everything up," Burned Fingers yelled. "We've got to move out before we get bogged down."

He looked behind them. Ananda followed his gaze but saw only rain pounding the reservoir.

"Go-go-go," he yelled, herding them into the truck. All the girls were soaked, but "filled to the gills." That's what her mom would say after a great storm. Then she and Bliss would shout right back, "To the gills!"

No one shouted now. Quiet, but for the rain.

Wrench crawled in last, water dripping from a face almost as round as Imagi's, with lips fat and red as bloodworms. He slid aside a small, inconspicuous panel that opened to the cab, and sat leaning against the wall. Gray light swam into the cargo space.

The truck accelerated, swerving left and right.

"Get her in four-wheel!" Wrench yelled.

The driver braked, ground a gear, and the truck moved straight ahead.

Wrench smiled at them and clapped his hands like a kid

at a party. He didn't scare her like Grinder had, even though he also had a big knife on his hip. They all did. At least he wasn't thumbing the blade. He looked like the kind of guy who'd forget it was even there. She knew she wouldn't.

"I bet you're wondering why they call me Wrench . . ." He was a talker, she could tell, starting right up like he'd been starved for conversation. "See, I can fix anything: cars, guns, cards." Laughing a *hee-hee-hee* that was immediately annoying. "You never know. You can win a lot in a card game these days. One of you!" *Hee-hee-hee.*

He did look funny, with black bristles encircling those wormy lips, and more black bristles on top of his head, sprouting so randomly it was like a blind man had sprayed him with tiny darts.

"'Course, I can't fix this." He cupped his crotch. "So don't you worry none about that. Ain't got near to nothin' left down there. Long story."

She hoped never to hear it. Her mom would say he was "completely inappropriate."

"Do you know where we're going?" she dared ask. As long as he was so talkative.

His eyes got big and she noticed the swollen rims of his lids. Fat and red like his lips. "Now that's a good question. I can't tell you 'cause you're not supposed to know yet, but I can tell you it's a really nice place. You're gonna love it." He clapped again. She couldn't believe it. "They got nice toilets and warm showers and really great food." He shook his finger at them. "It's a lot better than that place you were in. It's gonna be great. You're gonna love it. All the girls do."

"What about my parents?" As long as he was *still* so talkative.

"Now that's another good question, and I rightly don't know the answer, but," shaking that finger again with a big wormy smile, "there's gonna be people there waiting to take good care of you."

I'll bet. Ananda knew why they wanted girls, and it wasn't to make sure they got a hot shower.

She didn't look up again until the brakes screeched. She must have fallen asleep.

Wrench crawled past her. She pulled in her legs. The door opened and he squeezed out. Burned Fingers looked in.

"Hey, all of you, come on."

They'd stopped at the edge of a huge pile of concrete rubble that had once been the reservoir's dam. It spilled down like a massive tongue lapping at the puddled lake bed.

The storm had passed and the sun burned ferociously, glinting harshly off the light-colored chunks. Mangled rebar rose like rusty ramparts across the jagged slope, as if to defend the defeated in their lapsed hour. But as her eyes opened fully, she saw that a path had been forged all the way up the rubble by pounding aside the twisted lengths, and that the large gaps in the base of this rugged trail had been filled with smaller pieces of debris.

"Sit over there." Burned Fingers pointed to a sliver of shade from an overhanging embankment. The sunlight felt rotten, like a dead creature left to hang and roast, drying her shirt and pants fast as her mouth and throat.

Wrench joined them, pulling off his bandanna to wipe the back of his neck. Then he rolled up his shirt to swab his sweaty face, wet belly, too. He had breasts like Bliss's. Small, but you could see them. Ananda wished she hadn't.

Where are you guys?

She stared at the flat land they were leaving, the walls of the reservoir the only boundaries she'd ever known. The scorching sunlight warped the view, baking the lake bed. The cracked earth looked bleak and fiery as brimstone. She squinted, hoping to see her mom or dad or Bliss. Anyone from the camp. It scared her when she turned back and saw the top of the broken dam. A bewildering and horrifying step.

Two of the marauders lugged a heavy piece of equipment from the back of a van to the front of the truck.

"That there's a winch," Wrench said. "And I sure hope it gets the job done fast 'cause this ain't no place to be sitting around like ducks in a shooting gallery." He was palming a small pistol.

"Is that for animals?" she asked, not without hope.

"Yeah, you could say that. You surely could."

He popped the magazine out. Fully loaded. He jammed it back in. Popped it out again. Nervous habit, she realized.

"The two-legged kind." In. Out.

"What?" she said.

He jammed it back in and walked his index and middle fingers down the short barrel.

She looked up and quickly saw that Wrench wasn't the only nervous one. Two of the other marauders had stationed themselves at the top of the dam, one with the AK-47, the other with a rocket launcher on his shoulder. Two more stood with shotguns halfway up the slope.

What are they *scared of?*

The gunman at the top slung the rifle across his back and looked behind him. When he turned, she saw his binoculars and knew he was glassing front, back, and center, like her dad used to do. *When he was really worried.*

"Yeah, you might not think we're the nicest guys in the world," Wrench said, "but let me tell you something you best remember: We're the good guys."

God help us. Her mother's words almost burst from her lips.

"What do you mean?" Ananda tried to keep her voice calm. She was the only one asking questions, but the other girls were leaning forward.

"We got some real Injuns out there. Take your scalp just to play ball with your head. They'd like nothin' better than to run off with the lot of you and leave us strung up like stuck pigs. And they would not be takin' you nowhere nice." He shook his head, rolled his eyes, whipped off his bandanna and squeezed out the sweat. It formed a stream that darkened his crotch. He didn't appear to notice. "No, they would not be doin' that. Them skells would be doin' things to you you don't even want to know about. Heinous things, like Ell says." *Ell.* The one she called Burned Fingers. "We ain't gonna let that happen, but just don't be kiddin' yourselves about where you should be puttin' your loyalties if the shit starts hittin' the fan."

Those skells sounded horrible. *What are they?* She couldn't bring herself to ask, and none of the other girls spoke up, either. They all stared at the top of the dam.

A man had lugged a steel cable up the slope, and now wedged an anchor between large chunks of concrete. He pulled on it and waved his arms. The truck's engine started, and the winch began rolling in the cable, dragging the vehicle up over the rubble. It listed side to side like the girls when they'd made themselves dizzy playing twirling games, but it didn't topple. An hour later the truck edged over the top. The men moved each of the vans and SUVs over in a third the time.

Wrench led the girls up the same path, clambering past the crumbling remains of a shattered spillway. When they climbed over the crest, they saw that the river bottom was built up on the other side of the dam to form a silty mound as smooth as the rubble had been rough.

"You seein' anything?" Wrench asked Burned Fingers, who had just walked up.

"Yup. We're moving fast as we can. There are signs."

"Oh, sweet baby Jesus," Wrench said softly.

"Get them back in and ready to go," Burned Fingers said to him.

The vehicles lined up behind the truck in single file. No one rode shotgun. The four men who'd stood guard at the dam now defended the convoy from the carrier above the cargo space. Ananda could hear them shifting constantly, like they were trying to watch all sides at once.

"You know what we call this place?" Wrench said as the

truck lurched forward, gaining speed so roughly that he had to sit with his back braced against the front wall and his hands firmly on the floor. The barrel of his gun peeked at Ananda from under his flattened palm.

No one answered him. Her stomach felt so sick she didn't want to hear. *Worse than them?* That's all she kept thinking.

"The 'gauntlet.' Right up ahead the river bed gets real narrow, and you don't want to be caught in no cross fire there. But don't you worry, we got our boys up top to take care of any mean business."

He lifted his eyes to the ceiling, as if to reassure them further, and in the next instant an explosion sheared off the entire front of the truck, ripping away the wall he'd been leaning against. In a *whoosh* he disappeared into a brilliant red fireball that sent a crackling wave of heat over Ananda and the others, incinerating the fine hairs on their arms and faces. The blast of heat lasted but a second before momentum hurtled the back of the truck past the tumbling, twisted, burning wreckage of the cab. Ananda clung to M-girl as they rolled to a stop. She stared at the smoke drifting past the sudden opening, only gradually becoming aware of the dozens of men with axes, clubs, chains, and knives who were running toward them, howling.

Their war cries grew louder, as terrifying as their tattooed faces and the bones piercing their lips, ears, noses.

And then she looked down and saw Wrench's gun a few feet in front of her, balanced on the charred edge of the open compartment. She lunged for it, and knocked it into the barren river bottom.

"No," she screamed, an outcry overwhelmed by the howling men pounding toward them and the shrieking panic of M-girl, Imagi, Bella, and Gilly.

Chapter Six

Australian Drought "Endless"
Total crop loss
"Interior Is wasteland": Ag minister
Oxfam Australia Report

200,000 Bangladeshis Drown in Massive Storm
   Surge
"Shark feeding frenzy"
Doctors Without Borders Special Report

Bliss raced to her mother with an old crutch made from a branch. Jessie, still on the ground, struggled to hold herself up. Gulping air, her daughter cried, "It's horrible in there, Mom. People. Children. *Everybody.* It's—"

The girl slid down the crutch to her knees, weeping too hard to finish. Her mother held her again.

Bliss had been awakened by Jessie dragging herself toward the gate. She grabbed her shotgun with little time to notice the devastation in the daylight. But to find the crutch she had to wade through the grisly remains, filling her eyes with carnage, and caking her feet with crimson mud.

Jessie let the girl grieve, knowing her own mourning could come only after she'd seen to the child in her arms and the one who'd been ripped from her world. Seen to Eden and the others, too.

Bliss wiped her eyes with grimy hands and helped her mother to her feet. Then she handed her the crude crutch, the top wrapped in rag. Jessie slipped it under her arm, gripping the bark-stripped length with her bloodstained hands. Primitive as it appeared, the crutch could have been a beaten relic of the Civil War, or the bitter price of a foundling future.

Standing left Jessie light-headed with pain. She clenched her teeth so hard that she feared they'd crack. Head down, she saw her pants leg stretched by the inflamed wound, daunting in a land where an abscessed tooth could kill, where little swelled but the dead and dying. And it *throbbed*.

That goddamned son of a bitch. Eyes raking the crawler who'd stalked and shot her. In her agony, she would have killed him a thousand times.

Where's Solana? Her oldest friend had been so reckless after Rye's death, risking her life to shoot *tires,* as if her sorrow were too deep for survival. But Solana had known so much pain for so long. A mother loses her only baby and she walks a barren plain, the promise of seeds turned to powder.

With Bliss at her elbow, Jessie took half hops, finding Rye's body near the gate. Face to the sun. But there was no sun, Jessie setting eyes on gray sky for the first time in months.

Maybe rain. She looked again.

Even amid death and ruin, rain meant life.

Bliss settled beside her uncle, stroking his face, then covering it with his shirt.

She stood, tears streaming.

Jessie spotted Solana facedown by the wall, hair a black fan on her back, clothes sheeny with blood.

"Bliss, help me."

Her leg was so stiff she had to hold it straight as she crouched, dropping clumsily to her haunch. "Solana?" Lifting the thick hair off her neck, staring at the hacked skin highlighted in blood and the slow drool of dirt. She smudged lines of both as she checked for a pulse.

"She's alive," Jessie whispered to the darkening sky.

Bliss patted her mother's arm and carefully pulled apart a cut in Solana's shirt. The wound was long and deep. They'd chopped her back, side, and legs. But her face, chest, and belly had been spared, protected by the hard shield of earth.

"Find Aretha," Jessie said. Not allowing for the murder of their healer. Not with Solana like this.

Bliss ran back into the camp, stepping around dozens of dead slumped over one another or lying alone with vacant eyes.

Jessie lowered hers to Solana. "The cuts need to be cleaned. We've got to close them." Charting the tasks aloud, defying cruelty as she could. "She needs blood, too." But they had no means.

She chanced another look at the butchery in the camp. Bliss still searching, calling, "Aretha, Aretha." A dog's cry the only answer.

"Gather your forces," Jessie said to herself, as if to gain strength from refrain. But she'd had to say those words so many times that she could scarcely speak them now.

Solana moaned.

"I'm here, baby. We're going to help you."

Solana's eyes opened. Bliss ran up shaking her head, confirming Aretha's death. She started to speak when Jessie raised a hand to hush her. Solana didn't need to know.

"She's waking up, Bliss. Can you get water for her?"

Keeping the girl busy. If her father were dead, Jessie wanted to find him first. Close his eyes. Cover his wounds. Compose his death.

And do what? she screamed at herself in silence. *Make it all better. Do Mommy magic?*

Bliss returned with a cup. The battle had saved the camp's water, if not most of their lives. Jessie strangled her anguish.

"Wet her lips. If she can drink, let her. We need to get as much water into her as we can. And help me up."

She hobbled to the gate, clutching her crutch, her strong leg folding at the full view of the slaughter. Death crowded the camp. Children. Elderly. Mothers. Fathers. The strong. Weak.

And the marauders. More than a dozen.

Goddamn them.

The sleep of reason . . . words from somewhere . . . *produces monsters.*

Memory feeding on madness.

The horror of familiar faces, distorted and bloodied. And when she couldn't see their features, she recognized fabric, boots, a belt, or a bag slung over a shoulder. In this grievous moment she shocked herself by giving thanks that Ananda and the others had been taken, for surely they would have been murdered in the frenzy. Thanks even knowing their plans for the girls because the abduction bought time.

Tire tracks began a few feet away, leading into the vast emptiness of the reservoir. In this world, tracks could last for months. She would follow them forever. On her crutch, if she had to.

Eden's body, she found, was under the marauder shot first in the face by Bliss and then in the belly by the gunman, blocking the blast aimed at the girl.

Her husband's cheek was pressed into the dust and his eyes were closed, unlike so many of the dead with their open unblinking stillness, their eerie look of life.

She lowered herself as far as she could, missing Bliss's help but unwilling to draw her near. Dropping again to her haunch, stroking his cheek, thinking it cool. Not surprised. Wishing only for the strength to push the dead marauder away, and to unleash the chains.

"Eden, Eden, Eden. I'm sorry I made you wait." *To die.* She could have fulfilled their vow never to be taken alive. She'd had a clear shot but was gulled by hope.

She'd kept every other vow they ever made until Wicca forced the sexes apart, leaving them with only longing, memory, and touch that could never escape the soft prisons of their own skin. The Wicca virus had proved much more virulent than AIDS in the long ago, and far more perverse, confining safe sex to those twelve months after menarche. Then there was no protection from the devastating effects, surely not with condoms, whose production had ceased with the annihilation of factories and herd animals.

Wicca raped the minds of men and women alike, bludgeoning them with psychosis, shattering hallucinations too wrenching to endure. No one counted the victims, no one could, but billions were said to have slain themselves. Off bridges, towers, with acid cocktails and tire irons, mass incinerations and poison chambers. A holocaust of willing horrors, of mad oaths for ending life. Waves of suicide so thick they'd left cities roasting with moldering flesh, the reeky heat of rot and waste rising from streets choking with corpses and the creatures that scavenged them—raptors, ravens, and vultures that darkened skylines and shadowed the dead, and rats and cats and carrion dogs grown huge as hogs.

"Mom, is Dad alive?"

Bliss stood above her, cup trembling in hand. Jessie couldn't bear the answer. A weight that would never ease. She reached for the water and sipped, then wet her palm and placed it by her husband's nose, delaying the news she must share.

Breath so faint it defied faith. Bending closer, she searched for his pulse.

"He's alive," she murmured, stunned by the thrum at her fingers.

Bliss nodded frantically. Dragged wildly on the dead marauder. She'll never move him, Jessie thought. But her wiry daughter hauled that son of a bitch off her father, and together they unhooked the chains. Eden's eyes never opened.

"I could help."

They spun toward an old woman with dirty gray braids,

filthy clothes. Bliss backed away, fear or fury on her face. Jessie tried to climb to her feet and fell back down.

"Who are—" But Jessie's question was lost to Bliss's rage. She'd snatched up her shotgun and advanced on the woman.

"Please," the woman said, backing away from Bliss. "I'm a nurse. I can help your wounded."

"We don't need *your* help." Bliss pumped the shotgun. Jessie flinched.

"Don't do it, Bliss. *Don't*."

"She stuck that thing in me and Kayla and all the rest. She's with *them*."

"You can't kill her for that."

"Get away from my mom." Herding the woman with the muzzle. Eyeing her down the barrel.

"I mean it, Bliss. Last night we were fighting back. This is murder. Don't do it."

Bliss started to cry, so softly that Jessie wasn't sure. And then she crumpled to the ground, hugging her shotgun.

"What's your name?" Jessie asked

"Hannah. Hannah Colmes."

"Help me up."

Jessie worked her way over to Bliss, crouching to comfort her. Easing away the shotgun. She asked Hannah if she'd seen any wounded.

"I found four."

"Children?"

"One of them."

"Have you checked everybody?"

"No."

Bliss stood, glaring at the woman. "I'll go check her friends. Make sure they're dead."

"I don't think you should do that alone," Jessie said.

"It's safer that way. I'll use the protocol." She reached for the weapon. Her mother held it back. "Mom, I'm not going to kill her, okay?"

Jessie handed it to her. "Be careful. Remember what Uncle Rye—"

"I'll *use* the protocol."

But first Bliss moved a cot to shade her father, expecting sun as she now expected pain or grief or the broken bonds of memory.

Hannah led Jessie to a young girl behind the root cellar, curled up where Jessie had left her.

"Do you still have the gun?" Jessie asked.

Willa brightened when she saw her and hurried to hand it over. The revolver went off, a deafening roar that fractured time and made their ears ring. The three of them looked at one another, stunned before realizing that no one had been shot.

Bliss came running from the other side of the camp.

"It's okay," Jessie said. "A mistake. No one's hurt."

"I'm sorry, I'm sorry," Willa cried.

Jessie stroked her flame red hair. "Come on, let's take a look at you."

She had a flesh wound in her calf. Hannah helped her toward the trampled garden.

At the far end of the camp, Jessie hobbled to a family of five awash in blood so thick that much of it remained moist. Her stomach lurched and she looked away. The Gibbses. Mother, father, sisters, brother. They'd died clutching one another. Or so it seemed.

"Maureen?" Jessie prodded her with the crutch.

The woman's eyelashes stirred.

"It's me. Jessie."

Maureen sat up, unsteady, then turned and shook her children, husband. "Get up, get up, they're gone."

At first her family didn't respond, which made Jessie question Maureen's sanity. But when Maureen shook her husband a second time, Keffer sat up, too. The children's eyes opened warily.

"Thank God. I thought you were dead." Jessie slumped on her crutch.

"I couldn't get a weapon," Keffer said. "They had us pinned down. Us and them." He looked at the dead surrounding them. "We did what we could to save the kids." His young were covered in blood. Faces, hands, chests.

"We rolled in it." Maureen shook her head as if she couldn't believe what she'd said. What they'd *done*.

Jessie hoped they'd find other families like the Gibbses. They didn't. But she saw the stock of the camp's second M-16 poking out from under the body of a dead teenage boy, and found three wounded adults; two of them had taken shots to the torso and looked likely to die. They also heard a boy calling for help, and found him stuck in a latrine.

Bliss checked the body of each marauder as if defusing a bomb. That was the protocol. Never approach them unarmed. Always have your finger on the trigger, shells in the chamber. Any sudden moves, shoot to kill. "And look for weapons *first*." Uncle Rye shouting that one.

She'd cleared nine bodies so far, most dead by automatic weapons fire. Four left to go.

This one lay on his back by the wall, eyes closed, a blood-smeared axe drawing flies by his belly, the brutalized bodies of his victims a few feet away. His shoulder had been shot open, bone expressed through skin and shirt. A sharp shattered extension showed marrow. Pointy enough to impale a foot.

She inventoried his hands. Empty. Eyed his pockets. Flat. Looked at his sides and between his legs. Nothing. But she was still uneasy because she found no wound but the shoulder.

So he bled to death. Good. He's a beast.

With her bare foot she jabbed his leg. It hadn't stiffened, but neither did it shake.

"If you're alive, give me a sign. But do it real slow or I'll kill you." Talking to the dead, one after another. But an eyelid fluttered.

"Jesus." She jumped back. Looked for her mother. Saw her on the other side of the camp with that witch.

Bliss turned back quickly to the marauder, aiming squarely at his face. How many had he hacked to death? Glancing at the savaged bodies. *Children.*

His eyes opened. "Go ahead, you're goin' to anyways. Do it, goddamn it. You can't figure the pain. *Do it.*"

"Don't push me!" she screamed, trying not to see those dead kids.

Hannah rushed over, her mother following as she could. Bliss swung the gun to freeze the witch, eyeing the marauder as she talked to her. "Don't worry, I'm not going to kill your friend. He's got plenty to tell us."

"Hannah," he grunted, "help me."

Bliss watched her shake her head. Her mother staggered up, eyeing the axe, children.

"I know who you are," Jessie said to him.

Her mom's voice sounded strange, reedy. And then she jammed the end of the crutch into his open shoulder.

The marauder screamed. Didn't stop.

Hannah moved toward her. Not soon enough.

"You bastard," Jessie cried, now raising the crutch like a club.

Bliss grabbed it, shouting, "No, Mom. We need him alive."

Keffer and Maureen Gibbs carried bodies from the camp, using precious pencil lead to record names on even more precious paper. Dates of birth, family affiliations, summarizing lives in the genealogical shorthand that had developed over the decades of scarcity predating the most virulent strains of Wicca.

Removing the dead would take at least two more days, and then they'd build pyres with the wood that they had children gathering from the edge of the lake bed, where every year hundreds of charred trees crashed from the eroding forest high above. They'd need branches and broken boles to feed the funeral fire for days. The work of the dead always hard on the living.

Jessie and Hannah helped the wounded to the tattered canopy, which they'd raised back over the flattened garden. They'd left the marauder with his ankles bound to a stake nearby. Jessie had just handed water to an elderly woman when Bliss screamed that she'd found Hansel.

The dog lay glassy-eyed on his side, panting feverishly, still bleeding from a rear leg chopped off an inch below the joint.

Jessie tore the rag padding from her crutch. "He needs a tourniquet fast. I'll get him water."

Bliss kneeled by his side and stroked his muzzle. "Easy boy, I've got to do this."

She tied a powerful knot around his stump. He raised his head but his howl weakened quickly.

Jessie returned with a cup. She handed it to Bliss, who dipped her finger and rubbed the water over his flews. He licked them, then lapped more from her hand.

"When he's had enough, find some rope," Jessie said. "We're going to have to cauterize him."

Bliss didn't understand.

"You don't want him to bite you. You're going to have to tie his mouth shut so we can put his leg in the coals."

Bliss closed her eyes and nodded.

"It's the only way he'll survive, and even then there's no telling."

Hannah waved Jessie over. "Your turn," she said, patting a rough-hewn table.

Jessie almost fainted when the old woman scrubbed her wound with the camp's acidic soap. But the bigger fear was always gangrene. Herbs and ointments were all they'd had since the collapse, weak weapons against deep infection.

As Hannah worked on her leg, she let on that she'd been

forced to travel with the marauders and do what they demanded. Bliss, passing by, snorted and shook her head; but girls her age were often rank with rectitude, and Jessie knew her daughter, wonderful in so many ways, was no exception in this regard.

Did it mean she trusted Hannah? Only as far as she could see her, and what she saw was a woman with the skills they needed most. She now used the camp's last needle to stitch Solana, who shuddered with each puncture of her back and kept her eyes fixed on Willa. The freshly bandaged girl cooked vegetables over the same fire that had boiled rags and sterilized the few medical instruments they salvaged from the long ago. Cannibalizing the past for its meager offerings, as the past had cannibalized the future for its air and water.

"They said they were going to take all the food from the root cellar." Jessie gripped Solana's hand as Hannah cinched the thread.

"I heard them . . ." Solana sucked air through clenched teeth as Hannah sewed another stitch. ". . . say there were only ten of them left. And someone," she gasped, "was still in the camp shooting at them."

"Me." Bliss was drawing water from the spigot for a young boy.

Solana gave up and cried when the needle pierced her again. "Go away," she said to Jessie. "You don't need to see this."

When Jessie didn't budge, Solana tried to push her. "I mean it."

She crutch-walked to Eden, who lay under the canopy on the broken cot.

"It might be a coma," Hannah had told her. Eden hadn't been shot, but the marauders smashed the back of his head when they ran him down. "Just talk to him. He can hear you."

Jessie knew he'd die soon if he didn't wake. No way to feed him or make him drink. All she *could* do was talk to him. And to God, whatever kind of God allowed this. She was always doubtful, now more than ever, but willing to pray if it worked, and knowing her suspicions would damn her in the eyes of believers. But they were a sorry lot, had worked most of the ruin on the world. Brought them to this, praying to some god-awful God, which probably had been their plan all along.

"I don't have a lot of time to talk to you, Eden. I've got to take this goddamn crutch and follow those tracks and find her. You hear me? I need you to come around, Eden. *Please*."

Hannah walked up beside her. "Solana needs a break. That needle's dull. She's going through a lot of pain."

"Where'd they find you?"

"What?"

"You *said* they made you go with them."

"Oh, I was living in a camp south of Knox when they grabbed me. They said I could go back when they were done. I had no idea they'd do something like this. I didn't even try to leave with them."

"Why should I believe you? You could have been left for dead like the rest of us."

Fat drops of rain drilled holes in the dust and struck Jessie's face. Then it poured. Bliss and the Keffers collected what they could with buckets, bowls, and tarps. Hannah started for the canopy, as if to help, but turned back to Jessie, who was staring at the sky. Blessed with rain after all this blood.

Wash it all away.

"I don't know if you should believe me," Hannah said, "but you're going to have to."

Jessie looked toward the gate and saw the tire tracks already turning into mud.

Chapter Seven

Pearl Harbor Falls, Hawaiians Declare Independence
Ancient monarchy restored, thousands celebrate
New nation slammed by typhoon, "massive life loss"
UN Report on Sovereignty Status

Aussies Invade New Zealand, 12,000 Land at Auckland
Country falls in day, starving troops plunder farms, widespread rape
From survivor accounts

The skells sprinted closer, their war cries deafening as Ananda dragged herself head first over the burned edge of the cargo compartment, eyes on the pistol lying in the sand, belly and thighs scraped and singed by the smoldering floorboards.

She tumbled to the river bottom and grabbed the gun. A bare-chested, thickly muscled man was running straight toward her. Inky snakes had been branded into his cheeks, the dark outlines of fangs burned into the skin above each eye, giving his brow the savage look of a canine's ravening mouth.

The gun wouldn't fire. Ananda looked up and saw him

charging into the truck's thin shadow, whipping a rusty chain above his head. She tried once more to squeeze the trigger before she remembered to rack back the semiautomatic's slide, firing twice at close range into a bloodred puma tattoo that stretched across his sternum.

He pitched forward, smashing his face against the smoking ruin of the truck. His open eyes never registered the impact.

Ananda heard footfalls and pivoted: marauders scrambling for cover. She turned back to shoot at three skells who veered apart the instant she aimed. Wasted bullets.

The guards? Why aren't they—

Before finishing her thought, she looked up. Two of them hung lifelessly over the front railing of the carrier. A third, bleeding from the waist, tried to raise the AK-47. The fourth, shaking, shouldered the RPG.

"Shoot it," she pleaded.

The long barrel shuddered, and a grenade with a fiery red tail exploded in a wave of skells, hurtling several into the air. One of them rag-dolled at least twenty feet before slamming into a flat rock with such a startling *crunch* that she heard it across the sandy divide. A sudden clatter drew her eyes back up to the carrier where the marauder with the RPG had collapsed.

M-girl leaped from the burned opening of the cargo compartment as three whooping, painted men unbolted the back door and dragged off Bella and Gilly.

Burned Fingers ran up and pounded the side of the truck, yelling "Kalashnikov" to the wounded guard, who dropped the rifle into his hands. Despite a gash in his upper arm, Burned Fingers neatly picked off two of the skells who'd grabbed the girls. The third lost his grip on Gilly, who lurched back in shock; but he held Bella as a shield, still whooping mindlessly as he retreated toward a forest of burned trees above the distant bank.

Burned Fingers sprinted after them without a word to

Ananda, or any notice that she was armed and could shoot him in the back. The thought never occurred to her.

A sharp choice did arise seconds later when a skell in a loincloth ran up behind Burned Fingers with a double-headed axe. Ananda aimed the pistol in the precise, two-handed stance her parents had taught her and killed the attacker.

Burned Fingers wheeled with his rifle raised, saw the dead man—and Ananda still poised to kill—and nodded his thanks.

The skells had scattered after the grenade exploded, and now darted everywhere at once with the crazed mechanical movements of brain-damaged men only dimly aware of their aims.

Anvil scaled the carrier quick as a primate, his frizzy hair disappearing as he picked up the RPG. Ananda watched him fire a rocket that ripped apart two skells whose paths were crisscrossing, adding blood and fury to the accelerating chaos.

She glanced in the cargo compartment for Imagi. Gone. *Where?*

Nowhere in sight. Ananda looked behind her and saw the riverbank, wondering if the girl had already fled the violence. She glanced at M-girl and pointed to the marauders fighting off the swarming skells. *This way,* she mouthed.

They struggled through the loose sand and stumbled over small boulders. The screams and crackle of automatic weapons kept their eyes over their shoulders, adding to their difficulties; but none of the guns had been turned on them. The only faces they glimpsed were distant, bizarre, and unmistakably fearsome.

Looming over the high, ragged riverbank were the skeletons of drought-stricken trees, many fallen, some still standing on the frail foundations of long dead roots. To haul herself up, Ananda grabbed a thick length protruding from the sandy soil. The crooked root crumbled. M-girl made a sling of her hands and gave her a boost, then Ananda laid aside the gun and reached down to help the tall girl claw her way out of the river bottom.

They looked up to see about twenty skells scurrying through the dead trees and upended trunks on the far shore. Ananda knew that if she could see them, they could see her. A dozen or more continued their helter-skelter assault on the marauders by darting from one fallen body to another; but the dead provided little protection, and the marauders, now sheltered by armored vans and SUVs, picked them off with impunity. None of the skells still running around looked like they cared if they lived, and none of them had guns.

But how'd they blow up the truck? She couldn't figure that. "Keep your eyes open for Imagi," she told M-girl.

"I just want to get out of here before they know we're gone," whispered the taller girl, whose eyes had returned to the killers who'd taken them captive.

Ananda grabbed the gun and the two of them crawled backward, always staring at the men who were slaughtering one another for the right to abduct them.

Filthy with dust old as the collapse, they finally stood after taking cover deep in the dark woods. They pressed their way past trees, forging a path through tortured limbs that snapped with the slightest touch. The twisted lengths were like the cracks in the lake bed, victims of a fiery heat that had sucked moisture from sap and soil till they'd turned brittle and broken.

But after living on the hard flat pan of earth, she felt a restless wonder at a world once lush and tall that had spilled seeds and twigs into a river swift and strong enough for spillways and turbines.

Their flight brought them over the crest of a hill, and the screams and gunshots hollowed. Poor Moony, she thought, feeling instant remorse over using Imagi's nickname. Bella's idea, "Moony Magi." Horrible the way it stuck. Maybe she'd balled herself up somewhere and hadn't moved, as she was apt to do in a panic, though with her Down syndrome, she was just as likely to run off wailing hopelessly.

When Ananda and M-girl reached a clearing, they both startled, stunned by the specter below them. The drought that had killed the forest must have turned the town to tinder. A fire had burned all the way to an eroded shore that overlooked the vast reservoir. Roads ran through carefully plotted subdivisions, past parks and strip malls and a two-story multiplex; but where homes and businesses once stood, only blackened foundations and brick walls remained, squares and rectangles, and a single charred arch that praised the persistence of stone. The community had become a crematory.

Ananda's eyes roamed the streets as a child might once have explored its many possibilities, rolling along on a bicycle or skateboard on summer softened macadam. Or in a car with her family for a week at the beach. But when the fire came, few cars had been left behind; and from a greater distance, these flame-darkened bodies would have blended into the background as blankly as shells on sand.

Nearby they spotted the remains of a church, a scorched cross bent over the belfry, like a suicide—arms spread wide—in the first second of flight.

Towns like this one had been part of her grandparents' youth. Though she'd never known them, the gutted buildings brought alive the sharp texture of their time. She saw a massive concrete square, and wondered with a peculiar excitement if it had been one of the "box stores" her parents had heard about, with aisles and shelves stuffed with countless products. "But it killed us in the end," her mother had said.

Death stared back at Ananda, as it had all her life. But here it looked so black and unrepentant, unburdened of hope. In the reservoir, they'd grown sweet berries and the reddest tomatoes. They'd saved seeds. They'd *lived*. Nothing appeared to live here but received memory, handed down by generations that would forget the collapse, if only they could.

They edged around the town slowly, wary of the walls that had not fallen, that could hide enclaves built of debris, brute shelters for the brute men of the river bottom.

She spied an intersection with what looked like a gas station on each corner, the pumps stripped to stubs. From the rise they still held, she also saw the foundations next to the cliff where the largest, most lavish homes had vanished into massive pits of gray powder. Beyond them an emptiness extended to a distant, hazy shore, a void so deep and complete that it was impossible to believe water had ever lapped at sand, or boats had moored on what was now only a bounty of blistering air.

"The towns were islands," her father once said, "in a sea of dying trees." And still people stayed and shopped till the fire came and the water burned away year by year, leaving cracks in the earth and a sky scorched of sparrows, starlings, and all birds of song.

Ananda and M-girl stopped only after skirting the last of the town, taking the shade of a large boulder. Both of them breathed hard. Ananda wiped sweat from her face, leaving dirt on her forehead and cheeks.

"You look funny," M-girl said. "You've got—"

"I'm-so-thirsty." Blurting it out. Ananda had no patience for this pain. Above all else, thirst was the knife in her life.

"We could go in there, look around." M-girl glanced toward the town.

"We need food, too."

"Let me see the gun."

Ananda handed it to her. M-girl popped the magazine. "It's half empty. Is that all?"

"I shot the guy who was coming at us, remember? And then I shot at some others and missed. And I used one on a guy who was going to chop Burned Fingers's head off."

"You should have let him."

"He was going after Bella."

"Like I said . . ." M-girl smiled.

Ananda shook her head. No mood for jokes. Not even about Bella.

"She owes you."

"Yeah, *if* she's alive."

M-girl handed back the gun. It was a given that Ananda was the shooter. Like Bliss and their mother and father, she had the eye, though she didn't think she had her older sister's courage. *But you escaped marauders and skells,* she reminded herself. *Escaped them all.*

For this?

M-girl leaned toward her. "Once it gets dark, we could work our way back to the dam and head back to camp."

Ananda groaned. "We were in the truck all day. They were driving super fast. The reservoir's huge. It's going to take us days to walk back. Without water? Or food?"

She wondered if they should have stayed with the marauders. But even with a swollen tongue and throat, she knew they'd had to leave. This might be their only chance to escape. To survive. The marauders weren't taking them on a holiday. They'd attacked the camp. They were murderers. The only reason they seemed halfway human was that the skells were utterly insane.

"A lot of these towns, I heard, had wells," M-girl said. "If there's water around, there'll be signs of people using it."

"And people. If you can call them that."

"I think they're kind of busy right now, and nobody's better at hiding water than we are. We'll find it."

So they stepped onto the first pavement either of them had ever seen. Hot, even with their thickly callused feet, and flat as the lake bed. Cracked and peeled open, too, exposing the parched crumbling underbelly of blacktop.

They scurried past the fire-stained foundations of homes, always alert for skells. Each black concrete square squatted in the middle of a lot that looked huge to Ananda, big enough for the camp garden, and there were tons of lots.

One after another. Her parents said that in the long ago most people grew only grass. Not even berries. And they'd cut the grass and cart it off to landfills, where it turned into methane gas that tore apart the sky. Grass that used up reservoirs of water to stay green. And now everything was black anyway, the lawns, land, foundations. Nothing grew in these ruins but bugs and snakes and skells.

They crossed a narrow strip of broken concrete that puzzled M-girl.

"Sidewalk," Ananda said, keeping her explanation brief to spare her throat. "People walked on them sometimes."

After searching three foundations for water pipes, and finding none that had survived the frenzy of scavengers, Ananda had to sit down, leaning against a wall that threw a shadow less than a foot wide.

"I'm sorry, but I think I'm going to be sick." The sun burned directly overhead, nausea itself. Long summer days were the worst. "I can't keep going."

M-girl glanced around, as if hoping to find more shade or water. "If I keep looking, you going to be okay?"

Ananda nodded, though she feared she'd pass out.

M-girl stirred the dust with her foot. "If they lived around here, wouldn't it make sense that they'd have a cistern set up somewhere?"

"Yeah, but do they *look* like they make sense?"

"I better get moving." M-girl hurried to leave.

"Take the gun."

She hesitated.

"Take it."

Ananda listened to M-girl's footsteps fade, then closed her eyes until a current of air fell over her damp skin. She looked up in alarm, but saw only the pale blue sky, and a tree that had once shaded the house in the full dress of summer. Though dead, it still stood. Nothing rotted anymore. Everything was like the orange peel her father had found when she was a little girl, decades after they stopped growing. It was mean-looking and hard as bark, like it would last forever.

She drifted on memory and speculation for almost an hour before she heard the war cries, bolting upright as M-girl jumped into the foundation, face rigid with fear.

"They're here."

"Did they see you?"

"I don't think so. I heard them coming and hid. Drink this. Hurry. We've got to get out of here."

She handed her a moist leather pouch. Ananda took several deep gulps. It tasted as bad as the marauders' water. But she was grateful for the way it eased her thirst, and offered it back to M-girl.

"I drank all I could back there. Drink it up because there's no way to seal that thing."

"Where'd you find it?"

"They've got a hand pump by one of those old gas stations. That's where they're living. And they're getting gas out of the ground, too. I think they're making bombs with it. They had cans all set up, and it looked like they were in the middle of packing them with some stuff that smelled awful."

"Fertilizer," Ananda gasped between mouthfuls. "Fertilizer bombs. My dad told me about them. Real powerful."

"I saw some of them sniffing the gas as soon as they got back. They'd put it on rags and hold it up to their face. Why would they do that?"

Ananda drained the last of the water. She felt much better, even with the chemical taste in her mouth. "I don't know. That sounds stupid. Did you see Bella?"

M-girl shook her head. "But I got away as fast as I could. Most of them were still coming down the hill."

Ananda held up the pouch. "Maybe we can fill it again."

"Not here. We've got to go. They were acting really crazy. But we better do this first." She scooped up ash and chunks of charred wood and smeared them on Ananda's clothes, skin, hair. Then Ananda did the same to her till they looked like minstrels in the long, long ago, the ones her mother had told them about in the camp school.

They crawled through burned backyards, inching forward to try to keep dust from rising in their wake. Movement, even of air, was always suspect in a land of the dead.

The shouting, screams, whoops, and war cries never ceased, joined now by a club or a pipe smashing metal. Then more. Drumbeats no more rhythmic than the madness of their voices.

Ananda and M-girl came to the only street separating them from the woods. They tested the blacktop with their hands. It felt so hot that Ananda couldn't imagine bellying across it.

"We've got to," whispered M-girl.

They both crawled onto the pavement, and they both sprang to their feet, palms scalded by the broiling black surface. They sprinted to the other side, huddling by a tree. M-girl looked toward the town. "I don't see anyone. Let's go."

"Run?"

M-girl shook her head. "And be careful not to break any branches."

They moved deep into the forest on their hands and knees. When they could no longer see the town, Ananda stood and shook out a few more drops from the pouch.

"What are we going to do now?" she asked.

"I think that as soon as it gets dark we should go to the dam and head back." Before Ananda could object again, M-girl said, "What choice do we have?"

The drumbeats and screams died at once. They looked toward the town as a slow-building uproar greeted the wrenching shrieks of a girl.

"Bella," M-girl said.

"No. That's Imagi." Ananda looked at her gun, at M-girl. "We have to get her."

"What? Almost half the bullets are gone. There must be fifty of them. They're insane. You saw them. They don't care if they live or die."

"You know what you just said about not having a choice? We can't leave her, not with them."

M-girl squeezed her eyes shut and gripped a branch. When it snapped, it sounded loud as a shout. But it couldn't be heard above Imagi's screams, thick and heavy as a blood-drenched blanket, or the chanting terror of the skells. Their thundering voices rose louder and louder, crazy and crazier still, as if to rip the sun from the sky and bludgeon the day with a final, senseless darkness.

Chapter Eight

L.A. Under Gang Control
Water riots end, 3,000,000 flee
From refugee accounts

French Muslims Announce Partition
Lyon to Marseille under Sharia law
1,300 die, women protest, stoned
Red Crescent report

One hundred twenty-one dead.

Funeral fires began two days after the massacre. Smoke rose denser than the blackest storm clouds, burdening the living with their final obligations to the dead.

Keffer Gibbs tended the pyres with a damp rag over his nose and mouth, after he and his family exchanged their gore-stiffened clothes for the pants and shirts of those who'd perished beyond the means of axe and machete. Keffer wore the frayed shirt of a man who'd fallen to small arms fire, two red-rimmed holes resting right above his heart. Eerie to see on a living man, but not so haunting as the sparks that had flared beneath a prized round of magnifying glass, setting off tinder hungry for the lick of flame and the taste of flesh.

The bodies of the two men who'd suffered torso wounds

had been added to the fires last night, and this morning a virulent infection from a minor cut finally felled a grandmother. Hannah covered her face with a dead child's skirt, then told Jessie that she should count her blessings.

Blessings? Jessie sat under the shabby canopy with her thigh throbbing ruthlessly, yet the pain felt tolerable compared to the blinding agony of having it scrubbed and dressed by Hannah every few hours, an excruciating ordeal that had left her briefly balancing a desire for death against the strict demands of life. The same gritty regimen prevailed for Solana, who was sleeping only feet from the marauder with his shot-up shoulder. Hannah had just swabbed and rinsed his exposed joint. The broken bones were pointy as spikes, and the open wound looked raw as a butchered beast.

"Don't cover it," Jessie ordered when Hannah lifted a steaming rag from the cook pot. "I want him like he is."

He lay in the spotty shade tied to ground stakes, forcing the memory of game hanging in a smoke shack. When Bliss started to strap him down, Hannah pleaded that Kruikshank, or KK, was "too weak to escape." Bliss had rounded on the nurse, responding bitterly that he wasn't too weak to kill us, and Jessie nodded at her daughter's use of thick leather bands to bind his hands and feet.

They'd fed him, given him water, and carried away his waste. Now she would question him. To find the girls, she needed to know details that only one of the killers could provide, and she figured she'd learn them faster with his shoulder bared.

Hannah put aside the boiled rag and stepped in front of KK, now claiming he was too weak for an interrogation. "Look, I can tell you what you want to know."

"How could you do that?" Jessie fired back. "You said they took you from a camp. So how could you know where they came from? Or where they're taking the girls? Or *do* you know?"

Bliss stormed up wielding her shotgun stock first, like

she'd bash Hannah in the head. Hansel growled at the woman, standing beside Bliss with his stumpy haunch protruding to the side at a grotesque angle.

"I don't know. I don't," Hannah cried, hands out to fend them off. "I'm just trying to help people."

"Yeah, like when you raped me with that plastic thing," Bliss shouted. "Move."

She marched her at gunpoint to the far side of the camp, where Maureen Gibbs pushed Hannah against the wall, cocked a revolver, and aimed at her face from less than five feet away.

A wave of vengeance had overtaken them. Jessie saw it in Bliss's and Maureen's fury, unleashed as lightning, but she felt its venomous sting most sharply as she lowered herself to a bench and stared down at KK.

"Remember me? I'm the one who jammed this," she held up the crutch, "into that." She poked the open wound with the sharply carved tip, hard enough to make him moan. "I would have beat you to death if my daughter hadn't stopped me. And I'm the one who shot you when you were chopping up kids."

"Not just kids," he muttered.

Jessie kicked his damaged arm, made him scream. "Killing their parents was okay?"

He shook his head as Bliss settled across from her, shotgun at the ready.

"You *answer* me. Don't just shake that fat head of yours. Is that clear?" Jessie held the crutch right above his wound. Dearly tempted.

He nodded, caught himself before she could strike, and said, "Yeah."

"Good. Now I've got a husband over there," she never shifted her gaze from his dull eyes, "who's dying because of you animals, and a daughter who's been taken by your friends. So I want quick answers. And I'm going to get them. We're also going to be asking Hannah a lot of the same ques-

tions. If you two don't agree"—she tapped his exposed clav-
icle, and he cried out—"I'm going to rip those bones out of
you piece by piece." She leaned close to him, feeling insane
with anger. Not caring. "I'd be lying if I didn't tell you that
part of me wants any excuse to tear into you right now. You
hear me?"

"Yeah."

"You better hear something else. There's no room for
anything but honesty here. I'm being honest with you. I'm
saying that if you don't spill your guts—and fast—I'm going
to make *sure* you drop dead from pain. Now how many of
you were there?"

"Twenty-two."

They'd killed twelve, so that left nine men for five vehicles.
Nobody to ride shotgun in one of them. Quick calculations.

"Where are you based?"

"Knox."

"Knoxville?"

"Yeah, but nobody calls it that anymore."

"In a camp?"

"Sort of."

"What's that mean? Get to the point."

"It's a setup near the people we work for."

The longer replies left him gasping. Good.

"Who are they?"

He looked away. She didn't pause, driving the pointy end
of the crutch into his wound, striking bone, wrenching it.
He shrieked. His body shook. Blood ran down his arm, pud-
dling like mercury in the dust.

She leaned close again. "I swear to you, I'll tear it apart
and then I'll rip out your eyes. That's my *daughter* you slobs
took."

"The Army of God!" he cried.

"Who the fuck are they?" Get a grip, she warned herself.
She felt monstrous rage and nothing to chain it.

Bliss put out a hand, whispered, "Easy, Mom. Not yet."

We need him alive. That's what her girl had said when she tried to kill him with her crutch, when he lay with the blood of children on his axe.

"They're a group that's having babies," he said.

"That's a lie," she said automatically. The implications were obscene. Lethal to those girls.

"No, no, it's not. They say they're blessed, they've inherited the earth. They have us harvest them, bring—"

"Don't!" she screamed, still whirling from his news about babies. "Don't ever use that word again." She raised the crutch with a grinding impulse to pin him to the lake bed. Tears ran past her mouth, under her chin. "They're *girls,* not some goddamned harvest."

"Okay, okay."

She was breathing so hard it sounded like she'd run through hail.

Maybe he feared her for the first time. His words came faster. "They have us find girls, bring them back. The Army of God's all men. They pay for them. Soon as they have a period, they try to make them pregnant. The first couple of months. After that the pregnancy would go on too long. The babies would get Wicca."

"What happens to the girls? After twelve months?"

"If they had a baby, they disappear. If they don't, they're sold."

Her stomach felt scorched. "Who buys them?"

"It's an auction, twice a year. Anybody can buy them."

"But they keep the babies?"

"The females."

"Why just the females?" But even as she asked, she knew the answer: The number of girls had dropped, so they were growing their own.

"That way they can—"

She held up her hand for silence. She couldn't bear to hear

it from him. One smarmy note and she'd kill him. But neither could she leave the worst unsaid: "Sex with kids. That's what it is."

"Not us," KK said. "We treat them right. Anybody touches them, they're dead."

"What about the boy babies?"

"They sell them. Rich people want babies."

"Rich people? There's money?"

"Just gold."

"Coins? Is there currency?"

"No. Nuggets, dust. Bags of it for the girls. They're more valuable than anything."

"Where do they get gold?"

"Some are traders."

"In what?"

"Anything."

"People?"

"Yeah. But a lot of it's family money. It goes way back." He still struggled to talk, but less so.

"Do they really believe they've inherited the earth?"

"Yeah."

"How long is the trip back to the Army of God?"

"Two weeks, if there's no problems."

"What kinds of problems?"

"All kinds. Cars break down. The roads are a mess. We get attacked."

"*You* get attacked? Who's doing that?"

"Shitheads called skells. They know what we do. They're always coming at us, but when they see us headed back, they know we might have a load."

Jessie glanced at Bliss, who was staring at him with the same disbelief that she felt.

"You mean there are men trying to steal them *after* you kidnap them?"

"Yeah. They ambush us."

"What do they do with girls?"

"Everything." He opened his mouth to go on, but stopped.

This time she didn't force him to say more. She feared for Bliss and almost asked her to leave.

"They don't sell them," he did add. "If they get them, they're gone for good."

She dropped her head against the crutch, stunned by the spiraling hell of the past forty-eight hours. She tried to get back on track. "So you work for the Army of God, and you're paid in gold?"

"Yeah, and other things."

"What other things?"

He hesitated, and now she did raise the crutch.

"Moonshine, some drugs . . ."

"You were about to say something else." A man who hacks children to death wouldn't hesitate over that. "Say it."

He looked at the tip of the crutch, already crusted with his blood. "A girl."

"Say that again."

"A girl."

"I thought you said you guys didn't touch them."

"On the way. But if we come back with at least five, we get to keep one. They pick her. Usually an ugly one. Or she's missing something, like a hand or a leg."

"What happens to her?"

"She goes with us."

"Then what?"

"We're careful. We make her last."

Jessie turned and vomited. Sickened, enraged, and angry at her own selfish fear over whom they'd get to keep. A flurry from Bliss forced her to look back.

Her daughter had pumped her shotgun and jammed it into his mouth. She was weeping, shaking. Tears splashed on the metal and drained to his teeth.

"Bliss, don't."

The girl yanked the barrel out and stomped away. She looked at the parched sky, poisoned with the smoke of the dead, and screamed so loud that she tore tears from her mother.

Jessie hobbled over and put her arm around Bliss's slight shoulders.

"I get to kill him, Mom. I get to do it."

"No, sweetheart. I can't let you murder anyone."

Bliss broke away and glared at her. "You heard him. 'We . . . make . . . her . . . last.' He's a *monster*." She beat her thigh with her fist. "They're all monsters, Mom. He made you sick." She raised the shotgun and used her shirt to wipe his mouth from the muzzle.

"I know what they are. We're going to find them, and we're going to make them pay."

"He can pay *now*."

"Not while he talks. When we're finished, he'll die."

"Promise?"

"I promise."

"I can't take any more, Mom."

Jessie watched her walk out the gate. She turned to KK, twenty feet away. His eyes had been boring into her back. She resumed the interrogation as if she'd never been sick, as if Bliss hadn't come close to killing him. As if she, herself, hadn't already vowed his death.

"Where in Knoxville? It's a big city."

"Not anymore. Hardly anyone's there. It's near the old Fort Knox."

"Where they keep the gold?"

"Not anymore," enjoying the repetition. "Gold's long gone."

"So there were twenty-two of you?"

"No, twenty-two in our group. The army's got other groups looking for harv—*girls*."

"Are they all there at the same time?"

"Hardly ever. We rotate in and out. Take breaks."

He might be telling the truth, she thought. He'd volunteered information. Maybe he heard her tell Bliss that he'd die. Maybe he was truly scared. "Where does the Army of God live?"

"About forty miles from us. They took over a bunch of places that belonged to some artists."

"You mean an artists' colony?"

"Yeah, that's what they called it. They've got water, grow food. They deal with a lot of traders."

"What kind of security do they have?"

"Not that good."

Could she believe him? "Describe it."

"About twenty-five guys. An RPG, two M-16s. They do perimeter patrols. They've got walls. Big ones. And all the men in the army are armed."

"Guns."

"Yeah."

"How many men?"

"Fifty. Maybe sixty. I'm not sure."

"That's all?"

"They have compounds all over. But each one keeps the numbers down."

Like the Mormon cults of old, she thought. Always driving out the boys to keep it flush for the men.

"How many acres?"

"About ten. It's hilly."

"If you were attacking, how would you do it?" Playing to his killing pride.

He brightened at that. "Depends on what you've got."

"You know what we've got. An M-16, like the one that got you. Some shotguns, handguns."

"How many people you got?"

"Not many."

"Take me."

"Never."

"Get more from somewhere then."

"And if we can't?"

"Forget it. They're not great but you're way outgunned."

"We're not going to forget it. Who does their security?"

He described former marauders, mercenaries, fanatical Christians. Then she grilled him on Hannah. When she finished, he asked if she was going to kill him now.

Jessie stood without replying and made her way over to the nurse, still sweating in the sun. Maureen kept aiming at Hannah's face as Jessie questioned her.

"Give me every detail on how they found you."

"He could be lying." Hannah's fear was palpable.

But their stories matched. She looked at Hannah trembling in the heat and decided to take her along when they went after the girls. It was not an easy decision. Hannah had been too willing to help her track the marauders, to point out how important she'd become to finding them as the rain washed away the tire tracks. And there were still wounded who needed care. But finding the girls was critical. Beyond the reservoir, in the world they left when Bliss was a baby, they'd face treacherous terrain that Hannah knew. Jessie hoped that self-preservation, if nothing else, would force her to guide them safely.

She told Hannah only that she'd have more questions for KK later, after she had time to consider their answers. But later never came. KK died as Maureen helped her husband lay the body of the grandmother on the flames, and while Jessie and Bliss washed blood from the cart. Everyone had been busy, even Hannah, but she was busy with the wounded. Right near KK. And though Jessie and Bliss listened, as they had all along, to make sure they weren't confiding, they couldn't be sure that Hannah hadn't killed him quietly—any more than they could say that in the middle of the night the marauder and the nurse hadn't agreed upon the story they'd tell Jessie later.

Jessie ordered Hannah to strip off KK's shirt so she could look for a fresh wound in his chest or back, eyes keen for a needle's narrow hole over his heart. Nothing. But Hannah could have suffocated him.

"No, I couldn't," Hannah said. "That's not me. I told you

he was too weak for all those questions, and what you did to him."

Maybe, Jessie thought, but her only regret over the murderer's demise was her inability to extract more information from him. Hannah covered KK's face with a familiar looking shirt. It took Jessie another moment to remember that it had belonged to the son of one of her oldest friends, killed along with her boy. Then she noticed that Hannah had changed into the dead woman's pants and shirt. Keffer and Maureen and their kids had claimed the clothes of their compatriots, but Hannah had come with the killers.

"What are you doing in those—"

"My stuff was crawling. They were rags," she said immediately.

"Those were Bethany's." Gunned down, and then left *naked*? "Did you put anything on her at all? Or did you just loot their belongings? When did this happen?"

"Last night. I covered them with my skirt and shirt. I've got to be clean to take care of people."

She couldn't argue that, but Hannah's presumption felt icy and left her furious.

"You get your buddy's body out of here. Get rid of him. *Don't* put him with ours. Drag him a long way away. Let the animals have him. They'll eat their own."

"He's not my buddy. He never was."

"So you say. Take him anyway."

Jessie refused to let her use the cart. They'd just cleaned it, and she wouldn't have his corpse soil anything of theirs.

It took Hannah more than two hours in the high heat to drag KK's body past the fires—but less than five minutes for the crows to find him.

Afterward, Hannah staggered into the camp soaked in sweat. She filled a mug and drank the water quickly.

"Sit down," Jessie told her.

The old nurse took the wooden bench by the ground stakes that had held KK.

"You're coming with Bliss and me."

Hannah shook her head. "Look, I'd like to get back to my people, maybe as much as you'd like to find your girls, but going back is going to get us all killed. The whole time I was out there I was thinking about this, and there's no way we're going to survive going back there. Once you're out of the reservoir, it gets really bad."

"What do you mean?"

"There are men that'll attack anything going by. They're insane."

Another detail that matched KK's claims.

"*They're* insane?" Just to see what she'd say.

"I know it's hard to believe, but they're worse than anybody who came here. We had cars and that truck, and they still tried to kill us. It was unbelievably scary. They had a bomb that just missed the truck."

"Do they live there?"

"I don't know. They came after us in a dry river right above the dam."

"What dam?" Still feeling her out.

"There's a dam. It's all destroyed. It's a long way from here. But you can get a car up or down it."

Jessie looked at Eden in his coma. Just what they'd found so many years ago: a broken dam.

"We'll never get past there," Hannah said.

"We'll get past."

The old woman looked dubiously at Jessie's crutch, then shrugged as if resigned. "There's a freshwater spring and a brine pool near there."

That was news. "In the reservoir?"

She nodded. "The brine would be good for your leg."

Jessie found her impossible to figure. Was her reluctance to leave sincere? Or was her self-promotion the real key to her self-preservation? Would she help them one moment by guiding them to water, and betray them the next by leading them into a trap?

By mid-afternoon they'd loaded the wooden wagon, so dark after years of use that the bloodstains from ferrying the dead blended right in. About three feet wide and four feet long. Hand-carved wheels. But it held several gallons of water in ancient jerry cans; dried fruit; dehydrated lizard loins and legs; and parsnips, beets, and turnips they could eat raw.

Weapons, too. The M-16, one semiautomatic handgun, a revolver, and three machetes they'd taken from the marauders. Jessie carried the ammo in a shoulder pack to prevent Hannah from grabbing a loaded gun. Bliss had strapped on her shotgun and bandolier.

Solana rose to her seat for their gentle embrace.

"I could go with you in another day or two."

"You need to heal," Jessie said.

With Hannah's departure, Maureen would care for the wounded.

Eden was the last to receive their good-byes. Jessie watched Bliss linger by her father. She finger-combed his hair, as she'd done as a little girl, and cried softly.

"I love you, Daddy. I love you. I want you to live. We're going to get Ananda and the others, and we're coming back. And I want to see you standing by the gate when we get here. Daddy, can you hear me? I want you standing by the gate. Daddy, don't die. I love you." And then she kissed his cheek so simply that Jessie's heart broke again, even after the massacre and its aftermath had pounded it to dust.

Her own words were no less urgent. She couldn't see how he'd survive another day. She was leaving him to die without family, but staying for his death might condemn the living. Already she grieved the loss.

"Eden, we had two babies together, and I've got to take one with me to find the other. Eden," whispering his name into his ear, the only kind of intimacy they'd chanced for years, "I'm going to leave you. I'm going to leave you to save what is ours. And if we don't make it back, and you live, forgive me for taking Bliss. Please know it was our only chance to be whole again. I could never do it alone, and we raised a fighter, Eden. She's all girl and she's a fighter. I couldn't leave her behind if I wanted to.

"Whatever happens, Eden, know that you'll live in me and our girls forever . . ." Her voice cracked, and she coughed. "You taught them so much. You taught them to be fierce for life, and oh, Eden, they are. They are. You're the finest man I've ever known. I loved you way back then. I love you now. I'll love you always."

Then her sorrow, too, moistened his skin, and she kissed his cheek, as Bliss had. And she felt the warmth of his living blood.

Mother and daughter nodded solemnly to each other. Bliss, tears streaming still, tied a rope harness around her hips and pulled the cart out of the camp. Jessie hobbled on her crutch with Hansel limping beside her. Hannah trailed steps behind.

Smoke funneled to the unrelieved sky, casting a shadow over them. Through the glinting waves of heat they saw vultures settle to the cracked earth, scattering the crows. Jessie gazed past the ungainly birds, and the cruel body they'd claimed, to the vast smoldering lake bed.

No tracks, but the defeated dreams of rain and the burning loss of children.

Chapter Nine

Spain, Italy, Turkey Aim Nukes at Northern Union, Demand Food
London Times online

Pacific Northwest Wildfires Scorch Portland, Seattle, Tacoma
One million flee, vandals terrorize refugee families
Federal Emergency Management Services

Imagi's screams kept erupting from the center of the burned town, echoing off the rubble of abandoned bricks and husks of blackened cars. When Ananda turned to go back and help Imagi, M-girl held her fast, too scared to speak. They stood beneath a twilight sky so strikingly red and gold that it could have been spattered with blood and flame.

Ananda stared into M-girl's eyes, and the older girl nodded at last. Together, they ran toward the town. Somewhere ahead, a stick or club resumed its brute drumming, a thunderous metallic pounding that girded Imagi's anguish.

Her volcanic screams stopped them blocks from the four-way intersection. So close that Ananda felt certain they must be holding her in one of the gutted gas stations. She pulled

M-girl behind a fire-smeared wall, popped the magazine on the semiautomatic, and counted the bullets.

"That's four for them and three for us. If we need to. Okay?"

M-girl cried. Nodded.

"Are you sure you're okay with that?"

"Just don't miss."

And leave me wounded. With them. Ananda knew her fear. "Stay close. And do what I say."

The younger girl had become the older.

The streets had cooled to sufferable heat, and they crawled toward the horror. The savage drumming ceased, and in its stark absence they heard an unnerving *whoosh,* like a candle loudly snuffed by a single breath, before Imagi screamed again. When she paused—for air?—they heard another *whoosh,* followed by a tortured cry sharp enough to cleave steel.

The babble of the skells rose and fell with Imagi's pain. They sounded incoherent, with jabber-fast outbursts followed by abrupt silences.

Ananda and M-girl slipped behind a pitted block wall that stood catercorner to the station where they thought the girl was held. The intersection reeked of gas. Peering through a small hole, Ananda saw Imagi naked and chained to a tall iron post that once might have braced an awning, or held an electric light above the stubby, stripped-down pumps. Skells in rags and scraps of animal skin crowded her, heads bobbing excitedly.

A man with a filthy halo of wiry hair dipped a cup into a tall tin container and took a drink. Ananda thought it was water until he spat it back. He lurched up to Imagi, breathed in her face, and struck a flint. The strange *whoosh* sounded as the fumes from his mouth flared into a foot-long flame that seared her twisting features.

A shorter man repeated the torture. Then a third, a fourth, and whatever order existed broke down as they jostled for the cup. They staggered up to Imagi, reeling from fumes and banging into one another, striking flints drunkenly. They burned her, burned themselves, and burned other skells who tried to burn them back.

The air blazed orange, thickening with soot and the sickly smell of burned flesh. Imagi cried hoarsely, wrenching her head to the side when a naked man with an erection tried to blow a thick stream into her eyes. The fire torched her neck and the back of her head, and her hair glowed brightly, briefly. Her face was red, puffy, blistered. Bleeding.

"They're cooking her to death," M-girl sobbed.

"Not to death," Ananda said softly. Sick with fear, with her own powerful reluctance, she raised her weapon. It shook in her hand. Stunned by what she was seeing, and by what she had to do.

We're going to die.

The words had the grave simplicity of stone, so direct and uncompromising that she never hesitated after stepping from behind the wall.

Halo Hair saw her running toward them and shouted. As they turned she shot into the thick of the mob, hoping to take down two or three with a single bullet; but it buried itself neatly in a man's back, and he fell without touching the others.

Ananda expected them to rush her, as heedless of her gun as they'd been of the marauders' more powerful weapons; but these were the survivors who had fled to the woods.

Only two of them ran away now. When she didn't fire immediately, the rest merely eyed her with a feral wariness, as if unwilling to cede the gas station after a lone casualty.

With her gun, she waved them away from Imagi, and watched as they crowded the tin container, protecting their prize. She spotted a cable snaking into the opening that had once been used to fill the underground tank, and still contained the dredgings they were trying to guard.

"Go get her."

M-girl edged over to Imagi and unclipped a carabiner that held the chain. The links clanked on the broken concrete.

Imagi looked too shocked to move, and M-girl had to pull her away from the pole. Then the girl groaned and tried to hug Ananda, bumping her gun hand. Ananda shook her off. The skells, still crowding the gas can, raped them with their eyes. One of them, reeling from fumes, sparked his flint randomly. Ananda flinched each time he did, afraid that he'd set off the whole corner. And then she saw what she could do.

"Run," she said to M-girl. "Just grab her and go."

M-girl looked petrified, but dragged Imagi away.

Ananda gave them two full seconds before she fired at the tin container, setting off a deafening explosion and a red and black fireball that engulfed the clustering skells. Death screams erupted from the billowing flames, and she heard the harrowing crackle of burning skin and hair and hide.

Shrieking skells hurled themselves on the ground or ran off trailing fire. The uninjured on the periphery stood and stared, as if struck numb by the explosion.

Ananda raced after M-girl as fumes rising from the underground tank burst into a fiery geyser six inches wide and forty feet high. White hot, it quickly melted the pole that had held Imagi, cheap metal slumping to the ground like a beggar.

The ground rumbled, shaking Ananda's balance. She staggered up to Imagi, who'd stopped to stare at the tower of flame, and shoved her. The girl sprawled into the intersection, and Ananda and M-girl had to haul her scalded body across the street as the tank blew up.

Concrete chunks as big as handcarts blasted into the air with the raging force of mortar rounds. Fire consumed the entire corner, heat so intense that Ananda feared she'd burst into flames before she could push Imagi behind the block wall that minutes ago had hidden them.

They looked up to see the darkening sky brighten like

morn with boiling clouds of fire. Fierce heat bled through the blocks. She worried that even the concrete would crumble.

Imagi pointed—her first sign of sentience—to a flaming arm spinning through the air, bent at the elbow like a boomerang. It landed less than twenty feet away, sizzling.

Seconds passed before Ananda braved another look at the inferno. "Jesus."

"What?"

"There must be fifteen of them coming up the street."

"Are they the ones who didn't get burned?"

"No, I think they're new."

"What are they doing?"

"They're just staring at the bodies and the ones screaming. We've got to get out of here."

She tapped Imagi's knee and put her finger to her own lips; but the girl's eyes were so fixed on the burning arm that Ananda doubted she could do or say anything that would register.

They crawled toward the hill that rose between the town and the river bottom. Imagi, perhaps sensing escape, moved without urging; and when they dared to run, she didn't stop till she faced the bony trees. Crying softly, she touched her burns. Ananda took her hand and led her into the barren forest.

M-girl trailed them to the clearing where they'd first viewed the devastation. The screams of the skells reached them loudly here, updrafts of agony riding the rise of the land. Ananda also noticed a peculiar orange glow above the intersection. Nothing left to burn but draining molecules of air.

"You see them?" M-girl's eyes streamed as she turned to Ananda and pointed. "Right over there." Before Ananda could pick out the skells, M-girl cried, "Oh God," and looked away.

Ananda caught the swinging of clubs, or pipes, or whatever they were using to bash the writhing, screaming bodies on the ground, silencing each one before trudging to the next tortured form.

Too late, she put her hand over Imagi's eyes. "Let's keep moving," she said to them.

"They're looking this way."

"They can't see us," Ananda replied, though she couldn't be sure.

"Why not? We can see them."

"They're kind of lit up." The orange glow still hung over them.

The clubbing stopped with seven stilled bodies. At least half a dozen others had died in the fireball.

A skell with a flap of skin hanging from his chest ran up to the killers. He held out a can and shouted. Ananda couldn't make out his words, if words they were, but she understood at least part of what he'd said when the others dipped their rags and breathed the fumes.

The chemicals worked quickly, and the men stumbled over the burned and mutilated dead. They never looked back as they clambered over the cratered ground till they came to the street, where they stood and swayed, looking drunk and crazed.

"Go away," M-girl begged.

Imagi forced down Ananda's hand. She couldn't have held it up much longer anyway. She checked the girl's shoulders for burns before cupping them gently.

"Not a word, Magi. *Quiet.* Now let's go."

As they retreated into the trees, the skells were still loitering on the street. Then a sharp branch raked Imagi's burned chest and the girl yelped piteously. When Ananda tried to hush her, she cried out, "Sorry!"

No-no-no. Ananda shook her head fiercely and whipped around. The skells were pointing, stomping their feet. Yelling. *Running.*

"Go, just *go.*" She pushed Imagi.

They climbed the hill smothered by night, trying not to break branches, each failure announcing their escape. Below them they heard the gibber of brain-damaged men and a thicket snapping under their stuporous assault.

The girls began to descend the other side of the hill, falling in the darkness. They had another mile, maybe two, before they reached the river bottom. *And then what?* Ananda asked herself. *Marauders?*

"It's too dark. We've got to hide."

M-girl found a narrow gulley long enough for them to lie head-to-toe.

They collected fallen branches before clearing out debris to make a soft bed for Imagi. Ananda gave up her shirt to cover the girl's chest and stomach burns before they piled on their gatherings. She dug herself in last.

The night sounds were no friend. Ananda heard insect scrapings, so close that she felt preyed upon by mandibles and prickly legs. She scratched her crawly skin, rarely finding life.

Worse, she heard the skells. They'd veer within earshot, then fade. Only to return.

Imagi slept, exhaustion overriding terror and pain. When she did awaken it was with a shriek so brief that Ananda feared it had escaped her own hellish dream, until M-girl shushed the girl.

Ananda lay still as silence, listening to heavy footfalls and breaking branches, the skells' breathless babble and Imagi's sudden whisper—"The game, the game"—delivered with a chilly reverence so unlike her fevered repetition of those words in the root cellar.

"Yes, Imagi, the game, the game," M-girl murmured as the sounds of the skells grew louder.

Ananda thought she could glean the first hint of daybreak. Had they passed the night? Or was this the false dawn of distant flames?

She eased aside branches and spied the dark outlines of

men careering toward the gulley. If they kept coming, they'd fall right on top of them.

The smell of gas reached them first, and though only her toe touched the back of Imagi's neck, she could feel the girl's overpowering fear.

Not a breath, Magi. Please.

But Imagi's panic deepened, and Ananda sensed her scream a full second before it revealed their crude refuge.

The skells stared at the gulley. Two of them howled to the darkness. Distant, muted shouts answered.

A torch flared and the smell of gas sharpened. A squat man waved the flames over the girls. They looked like animals trapped in a tindery burrow.

To the left, Ananda heard other skells thrashing through the forest. More noises rose behind the gulley.

She gripped the pistol tightly, knowing she didn't have nearly the killing power for the skells. But enough for Imagi, M-girl. Then herself.

A tall skinny man raised his arm and poured gas on the branches.

Imagi screamed again and Ananda sprang up, dripping with the cool velvety cloak of fuel. She aimed at him, counting "One" as she pulled the trigger.

The skells screeched but didn't retreat, as if they had no memory of the gun at the gas station. Or hadn't known the source of the explosion that burned the others.

But the gun wouldn't fire.

She snapped back the action. The trigger was jammed.

The skells whooped and surged forward. More smashed through the trees.

With a flick of his hand the torchbearer lit a vapor trail. Fire rushed toward Ananda.

She rolled over the back of the gulley, hauling Imagi out. M-girl threw herself aside as flames roared through the branches, chasing her like a serpent.

A man broke through a knot of trees behind them. Ananda

knew they were cornered. She pounded the pistol butt against her hip to try to unjam it and raised the gun to Imagi's head. But she faltered even before she saw who he was.

Burned Fingers emptied both barrels of his sawed-off shotgun, tumbling the torchbearer and a shadowy figure next to him into a large boulder.

He jumped through the flames to the other side of the gulley, cutting down two skells with a machete and beheading a third so quickly that Ananda didn't comprehend the damage until disembodied eyes stared at her from the fiery glow.

The marauder broke the barrels, reloading in seconds. Another blast slammed a skell into a tree, and Burned Fingers yelled, "Run."

Ananda pulled Imagi down the hill, racing after M-girl as the forest came alive with ululating skells and a fourth shotgun explosion. Then she heard Burned Fingers behind them, reloading on the run.

"Fucking *move!*" he bellowed, smacking Ananda's back with his weapon.

Dawn's gray light seeped through the woods, and she glimpsed the river bottom. She broke through trees heedless of scrapes and jabs, heard Imagi wail and didn't care. Just dragged the girl. Unstoppable in her fear.

She looked back and saw hordes of skells, as if the gunfire had hailed them from the gloom.

Burned Fingers turned and fired twice, still shouting, "Move!"

M-girl hurled herself from the riverbank to the sand, scrambling toward the armor-clad vans and SUVs. Imagi balked at the eight-foot drop. Burned Fingers seized the back of her burned neck and took her with him. Ananda landed beside them. Imagi was screaming.

As they struggled across the deep sand, the four vehicles fired their engines. The side door of the van last in line flew open.

Ananda heard branches breaking behind them and the duller *thump-thump-thump* of skells jumping to the river bottom. Her heart felt furious, her chest fractured. She tried frantically to keep up with Burned Fingers and Imagi but couldn't. She tripped and stumbled across the wide stretch of sand, deranged by the fear of falling.

M-girl heaved herself through the open door. Burned Fingers shoved in Imagi, lunged for Ananda, and pushed her in, too.

The van bucked forward, and he leaped aboard, reloading as skells sprinted closer. The heavy, four-wheel-drive vehicle gained speed slowly. Burned Fingers swore viciously, blasting a skell reaching for him and kicking another who snagged his leg and tried to drag him out. He raised his shotgun. Two skells, hidden by the side of the van, ran up and jerked him violently. Burned Fingers made a desperate bid to hook his bent, scarred fingers around an iron railing next to Ananda, but his grip failed and he dropped his weapon. The next instant he disappeared out the door.

The van braked. Ananda saw the three skells dragging him away by his legs. At least twenty more were flooding across the sand.

"Shoot those fuckers!" the driver yelled, turning, his face red and ugly as a wound.

"Go!" she screamed back.

"Fucking do it!"

She shoved aside her pistol for the stumpy shotgun and fired the remaining round with a shaky aim, surprised when two of the skells fell from the spray of lead shot. Burned Fingers rose to knife the third one in the neck.

The van accelerated as he dived back in and slammed the door. He reached for his weapon. Ananda handed it over, the barrel hot as a cook pot.

She searched the floor for her pistol, and found Imagi crouched over it naked, with the muzzle in her mouth.

"No!" she shouted.

M-girl looked up and tried to grab it. Imagi twisted away and squeezed the trigger, but the gun didn't fire. Before she could try again, Ananda had wrestled it from her. "No, god-damn it! *No!*"

"Give me that goddamn thing." Burned Fingers snatched it before Ananda could react.

He cracked the door and looked out, already slipping shells from his ammo pouch.

"Those fuckers gave up," the driver said.

Burned Fingers reloaded the shotgun with his eyes back on Ananda. Any plans she might have hatched to use the weapon on him had died in the urgency of saving him to save herself. And Imagi, M-girl.

Leaning back, he popped the pistol's magazine and checked the barrel. Then he snapped the action and turned it over. His eyes settled on the trigger. A moment later he used a fingernail to prise a tiny twig from the firing mechanism.

"Now give me back my gun," Ananda said.

He leaned forward. "What did you say?"

"I said I want my gun. I could've shot you. I didn't."

"You are un-fucking-believable. You just gave me the most miserable fucking night of my miserable fucking life."

"Yeah, and then I saved it. Could be a little grateful."

He raised his hand. She ducked and flinched, but he was covering his mouth and beginning to shake. His eyes pooled and he exploded with laughter.

"Oh, Jesus, you are something else. 'Could be a little grateful,'" he repeated in a singsong, which made him laugh harder. He shook his head. "Here, put this on." He tossed her a smelly shirt big enough for a behemoth. "I don't want them staring at your tiny tits. I got enough problems. And throw this on Brains over there." He gave her a holey blanket for Imagi.

"She's got burns. You got anything for that?"

"Yeah." He glanced over his shoulder. "I got a burn unit in the front seat. Nurse Patty, would you come back here please." He looked at Imagi. "She'll survive. I've seen worse, especially with them. She got away before they ate her, anyway."

Imagi stared vacantly at the gouged metal floor.

Burned Fingers gave Ananda a crooked smile and loaded the magazine into the semiautomatic. "*You* are a pistol." He slid the gun under his belt. "Anyone ever tell you that?"

"Yeah." *My dad.* But she'd never tell him.

"I'll bet. What about that name of yours? You know what it means?"

"Bliss." *Like my sister's name.* He'd never hear that, either.

He lowered the shotgun, but the strange, double-eyed symbol of infinity still stared at her. Her dad once said that eternity's all those barrels ever got you.

"You know the whole thing? *Satchidananda?*"

"Existence, consciousness, bliss." She'd known it since she was old enough to talk. Hindu for pure form. Perfect love. "I also saved you from that guy with the axe." Reminding him now for whatever it was worth.

The crooked smile thinned. "That's called survival, sweet cheeks. You figured out that your friends change fast around here. But you'd better be smart enough to know something else. You know what that is?"

She shrugged.

"Speak up."

She wouldn't. All the questions made her mulish. And now a command?

"I'll tell you anyway." The last of his smile vanished. "Your friends change back even faster. So if you try to escape again . . ." He picked up his knife and wiped the blade on his pants, leaving a red streak. ". . . I'll cut you open and feed you to the snakes."

What snakes? But a more pressing question came back to her: "Did you find Bella?"

"Yeah, I found her," he yelled, grabbing Ananda by her

baggy shirt and pulling her to inches of his face. "Did you hear what I just said? You think I *won't* cut you?"

"No, I don't think that," she sputtered. The blade pressed against her gut.

"You cost me one single girl and I'll take your fucking head," he said, forcing her face down by his knife, "and I'll make you eat your fucking insides."

He sat back, sheathing the blade slowly, staring at her like he'd stared at the pistol, like he was trying to figure her out. Like if he stared long enough he might find a twig that was fucking her up.

"In two weeks we'll be there, and then you'll find out the raison d'être. Since you're so fucking smart, you know what *that* means?"

"No." Too frightened now to defy him with silence.

"It means the reason for all this."

"I know the reason." Her voice trembled. She couldn't help it: the reason terrified her, and she'd never known anger like his.

"You think you do, but you have no idea." He pulled out a bone-handled knife and scraped under his thumbnail before looking up. "The reason's old as the earth." He wiped his blade on his pants, too, smearing grime next to the blood. Then he looked her dead in the eye. "They all want a piece of Little Miss Bliss."

Chapter Ten

U.S. Frees Canada
President declares "oil and water for God and
country"
WhiteHouse.gov

India Cuts Off Vital River
Pakistan threatens nuclear attack
Millions mobilize on borders
Muslim-Hindu Peace Association Emergency Report

Jessie held out her crutch to stop Bliss and Hannah.
Hansel heeled immediately, waking dust from the
sleepy lake bed. It drifted past their feet and paws, set-
tling on the panther tracks. For three days the sun had forced
Jessie to squint and keep her eyes low. She'd spotted poisonous spiders big as her hand, and snake holes that could
swallow a foot. The shadows of vultures wheeling above had
darkened their path and warned of their demise.

Nothing to alarm her until now.

She knelt on her good leg and studied the prints. About five
inches long. At least half a dozen beasts. Solitary animals
for eons, panthers were already forming packs when she'd

first studied wildlife biology twenty-five years ago. They'd adapted to scarcity by hunting like coyotes and wolves. Like the marauders. Back then the behaviors of scores of species had started changing, from garden willows to jungle apes, from lone lizards that learned to survive in teeming clusters to dogs that sheltered in large pits seething with snarls and pup-killing. Only the minimizing spin of policy makers had remained steadfast in the aftermath of the collapse: "The warming appears to have exceeded the projections of climatological studies in the century's first decade" was the ever-careful finding of the last White House Council on Climate Change. Jessie couldn't shake its obtuseness from memory, nor the footnote she would have added to any statement about the century's first decade: oblivious.

"Scat. Over there." She spoke to herself as she had when she conducted field studies, during the painfully brief year when biology had been her profession. In the unforgiving era that followed, the knowledge had provided survival and a means for understanding it. She hobbled over to the crusty fecal links and knelt once more.

"What have they been eating?" Bliss asked.

Jessie heard the girl's fear and understood it well. She'd taught her daughters to always look for human remains in waste, including in the waste of humans themselves.

She probed the scat with the tip of her crutch. Bone matter. Masticated, but she could see the fragments.

"Snake." The bits of bone told her less than the poorly digested scales.

Hannah sat on the cart.

"Get off that," Bliss said.

"Let her rest."

Hannah thanked her. Jessie didn't respond. Her eyes had returned to the ground. She was no tracker, like Eden, but she'd picked up a lot over the years. She wished she had the round magnifying glass so she could study the prints closely. She pressed her cheek to the hot earth to see if the topmost grains looked loose enough to spill, as they will when freshly settled.

She puffed twice. The grains shifted as easily as nut flour. She swore silently. The panthers might have passed within minutes. She looked around. Didn't see them. But they were the tawny color of the earth and shrewd enough for stillness. She rose, shaded her eyes, gave the reservoir the full three sixty. Still no sighting, but Hansel snuffled one print and then another, and the hairs on his back stood straight as quills. Another ancient enmity sharpened by severity. The cats were wily, ferocious, and when six or seven circled they were almost impossible to escape. Eden always said that you had to shoot as soon as you saw them, *before* they could launch an attack. Twice they'd come for him. Twice he'd survived. Until another, more murderous pack had brought him down.

"We saw six of them on our way here," Hannah said.

"That's what I just counted."

"I was glad I was in that truck. They didn't have any fear." Hannah also eyed the environs. "It was just after we came down from the dam."

Through distant heat shimmers, Jessie glimpsed the destroyed wall spilling to the mirage of blue water that had tantalized them since leaving the camp. The illusion had never appeared crueler than it did by the gaping mouth of the dry reservoir, the shattered concrete like broken teeth.

The last time she passed over the thirsty lake bed, Bliss had been a two-year-old, towed in the very cart that her daughter had hauled from the camp. They'd pushed across the expanse for days, hobbled by babies, children, and grandparents weakened by the long journey south. They forced themselves to move on so that in a world without cars they would always be safe. And then the cars arrived and they were all but annihilated.

"That's concrete?" Bliss hurried to the base of the dam

and touched it. "The stuff they made with sand and water?"

"And gravel and ash."

"It's huge." The girl eyed the massive remains. Even blown up, the dam appeared impressive. She gripped a length of rebar and tried to bend it.

"This is what reinforces it?"

Jessie nodded, growing impatient. Twilight was swallowing the shadows.

"Why'd they ever destroy it?"

"It's complicated, the reasons. Let's go."

"What's that huge hole that's broken?"

"A spillway. There were others."

"That's a spillway?"

Jessie and Eden had taught them about dams, but their words, and the pictures they drew in dirt—even the memory of the models they'd made from sticks and mud—could not compete with the huge chunks of fallen wall, or the tall lengths that still stood on both sides of the rubble.

The girl shook her head in wonder. All around her, grit and tendon. How could she imagine millions of gallons of water exploding from the hollow, crumbling half circle— brilliant sparkling torrents crying joyfully in the sun until every last tear had dried and turned to dust?

"Where's the spring?" Jessie asked Hannah.

The old woman pointed to a huge boulder hundreds of yards away. It had been pounded by trees, dirt, and rocks that spilled from the eroding forest high above. Other than alerting them about the panthers near the dam, Hannah had spoken little during the trek. She looked ruined. At times she'd nearly fallen.

After hopping a few more steps, Hansel poked his snout into the air, as he did whenever he smelled water. Only now did Jessie stop worrying that Hannah had lied.

They moved past the jagged trail the marauders had driven up in their armored vans, SUVs, and truck. Jessie saw black streaks from tires, and couldn't imagine how they climbed the debris. Or traveled anywhere in a world that she thought had put cars to waste. Her most vivid memories of them were the riots that destroyed millions of vehicles in North and South America, Europe, and Asia. Always a target of mob violence, cars became an enraging symbol of what had gone wrong. For a two-year period people wealthy enough to buy black market gas—and unwise enough to insist on driving—had been attacked and murdered, their cars plundered and burned. Government officials, including several heads-of-state, were savagely torn from their limousines. In the most vicious incident, more than a thousand homeless veterans, many missing limbs or facial features, had stormed the play ranch of a former U.S. president closely linked to the oil industry, dragged the feeble old man from his luxury pickup, and beheaded him. They hung him by his ankles from the cross beam at the ranch entrance, leaving him to drain like a deer.

Jessie had been horrified by the brutality, but understood the outrage of the vets whom he'd sent to war. As president, the "oil brat," as he was called, had even joked that his political base was the "haves and have mores." Fated, she'd always felt, by his swagger.

As she took a final step past the dam, she spotted the bleached skull of a woodchuck. Fragile as an eggshell, it rested in the dense shade of tumbled concrete, a headstone in the quandary of a graveyard.

Then the notes of a hooded warbler stopped her as surely as the panther tracks. A songbird? But *Wilsonia citrina* had been declared extinct. Were they coming back? Here? That made no sense. Yes, this was part of their old migratory route, but when the lake brimmed with water. What were they living on? They'd have stopped migrating when the food disappeared, and then *they* would disappear.

Again the notes sounded. Not a bird, she realized, but a bird *call*. And not a very good one. Off half an octave. She slid out of her ammo pack and grabbed an extra clip for the M-16.

"Mom, what's going on? Was that a bird?"

Bliss had never heard a songbird. All she'd seen were crows and vultures. Scavengers, flesh eaters. Jessie hated to answer.

"I don't think so. I think it's a signal." She shoved the spare clip into her pocket.

"Humans?" Bliss asked, as if the species were foreign to her. She unstrapped her shotgun.

"You never know what to call them these days." Jessie turned on Hannah. "If you've led us into a trap, you're dying first."

The old woman plopped down on the cart. "I haven't led you into a trap. Don't you think I know you'd kill me?"

The sky was darkening. Jessie knew they didn't have much time. Spending the night exposed on the lake bed this close to the dam was terrifying. Three women. Supplies. Guns. Water. They'd be inviting targets to anyone armed.

"Give me something," Hannah pleaded, eyes on the unloaded weapons.

"I'll give *you* nothing."

"I didn't lead you into a trap," Hannah insisted. "Why would I want to hurt you? I'm at your complete mercy." She looked down, shaking her head. "I'm no expert on this place. I've been here once. I told you this whole trip was insane."

She sounded anguished. But Jessie had heard the same beseeching tone when Hannah pleaded that KK was too weak for an interrogation. And for all she knew, Hannah had killed him herself.

The birdcall again. Anyone but a birder—or wildlife biologist—might have been excited. Jessie heard murder.

"We need to get to that spring and see if it's occupied. If it's not . . ." Jessie turned to Hannah. "How easy would it be to defend?"

"I'm a nurse, for God sakes. I don't know anything about that."

"I'll go with you, Mom."

Jessie shook her head. "I want you to stay here. We can't take all the guns and supplies with us. I don't want to leave them with her."

Hannah looked up. "Where do you think I'm going to go? Fucking Rio?"

Though fatigued and angry, Jessie, had to stifle a laugh.

"I thought Rio was one of the dead cities," Bliss said.

"It's an expression, hon."

"Look, Mom, I'm taking Hansel. It's crazy for you to go alone. You can hardly move except in a straight line." Bliss had already hand-signaled the dog to her side. The animal's snout was still in the air.

"I can't let the only daughter I've got go in there by—"

"No, Mom, I'm going. Watch her. Guard the cart. I'll send Hansel in first."

"Wait." Jessie turned to Hannah. "Is there only the one way in?"

"I think so. That's all we used, and I didn't see any others."

"Are there places to hide in there?"

Hannah thought for a moment. "Plenty, I'd say."

Jessie looked at Bliss. "Don't go in till he comes out. And if he doesn't come out, don't go in looking for him. Take this." She handed her a flint and a small candle.

Bliss hurried toward the huge rock strewn with forest debris.

"Why would you let her do this?" Hannah asked. "Or even think about going yourself?"

"Because if that's a scout we're hearing, we may only be minutes ahead of a tribe heading to that spring. And if what you say is true—and it better be—then defending it's going to be a lot easier than trying to save ourselves out here."

Jessie searched the lake bed for tracks, a tribe of humans not her sole concern. She found nothing but the cracks left by the sun, and they radiated everywhere at once, like a maze or memory, or the broken lines of life itself.

Without the cart roped to her waist, Bliss moved swiftly, avoiding the fissures while eyeing the broken trees, wary of creatures that could be hiding behind the splintered trunks and limbs.

Hansel kept pace, even as he hobbled on his three remaining legs. "Good boy," she whispered. "Heel, heel." Patting her hip gently to keep him by her side.

She pressed her back to the boulder, shotgun ready. Combat here would be close range, and she wanted the wide spray pattern of the twelve-gauge. A pile of fallen trees stood to her left. The entrance, if Hannah could be trusted, was around the rock to her right.

No birdsong now. She wondered if her mother could be wrong.

She crouched by the dog and led him around the edge of the boulder. The opening was a black oval about five feet high. "Hansel, search."

His nose dropped to the ground and the hairs on his neck and back stood up again.

What's he smelling? She watched him disappear into the darkness. Her father had put him through dozens of cave searches over the years. The biggest creatures he'd ever flushed were bears, and they weren't nearly as big as they used to be. Mostly bones and stringy meat. Bears had grown so lean they couldn't hibernate. Not that they needed to escape frigid temperatures; even in the northern climes winters had warmed. But the heat had also interrupted their estrus, cutting down their numbers. The decline was exacerbated by the sows' eagerness to eat their cubs, infanticide as common among bears as it was among their distant canine cousins. No animal goes extinct gently, her mother had said. *Humans least of all.*

Bliss held out the shotgun, ready for anything to come flying out of the cave. If Hansel growled, she'd know.

Only silence. She pocketed a small stick. The night crawled closer.

Hansel hopped out with a snake egg in his mouth. She would have sworn he was smiling.

"Good boy. Eat it."

He gulped it down before she realized that she should have checked to see if it was poisonous. Still in its shell, it wouldn't sicken him, but it could have told her whether to be wary of the snakes.

With Hansel by her side, she entered a cave so dark it was like she'd passed from blackness to blindness in three steps. And quiet, as if it had never known the deceptions of sound.

She snapped and shredded the stick into tinder, then pulled out her flint, made a small fire, and lit the candle. It barely illuminated the high ceiling. The pool glimmered in front of her. It looked about eight feet wide. Just to the right of it she saw a dark passageway. Cautiously, candle in one hand, weapon in the other, she followed it to a widening, where she smelled salt and saw what she figured was the brine pool. She spied no other openings to the cave.

Again she commanded Hansel to search. The dog checked the shadows and returned to her side with an expression that as much as said "Told you so."

"Good boy." She turned down the passageway and hurried back to the first pool. The candle flickered. She set it on a rock and tested the water. Clean as rain, and cooler than she could have imagined. She scooped up a quick mouthful, then a second, and ran outside, waving to her mother.

Hannah grabbed the ropes and tried to pull the cart.

"Hopeless," Bliss grumbled to herself, then ran down and took over for the older woman. "It's there," she told her mother. "I think the brine pool's in the back. Hansel even found a snake egg."

As they neared the entrance, they heard the birdcall.

"It's coming from up there, Mom."

They peered at the rugged shoreline as a section broke loose, spilling a small dead tree and a cascade of rocks and dirt. But no men.

When the dust settled, they looked up again. The dusk had swept away all but the darkest shadows.

The spring was a miracle. Jessie hadn't seen one since months before they moved to the lake bed. Big enough to bathe in, but she wouldn't. Fresh water was far too precious.

"I can't believe Dad didn't know about this."

"I can't, either," Jessie said. "But if he did, he might not have said anything. Everyone would have wanted to come, and it would have been too dangerous. Can you watch the entrance?"

Bliss exchanged rifles with her mother. She'd need the M-16 to make sure nothing could draw close to the cave.

"Show me the rest of it," Jessie said to Hannah.

The nurse picked up Bliss's candle, and they made their way back to the brine pool. The walls were moist, a miracle in a land parched as a tomb. For Jessie, the smell of salt brought back the sea at her grandparents' home in Hatteras. She hadn't thought of it in years. Waves breaking near the shore. Beach grass. Dunes. Shells. All of it had vanished into the rising ocean.

She tested the brine pool. Hot, but not too hot.

"It'll be good for that wound," said Hannah.

The pool had formed in smooth rock, as if the saltwater had mined its resting spot over millennia.

Satisfied that the only way in was the entrance, Jessie made her way back to the spring.

"Bliss, have you had water?"

"Some. You go ahead."

Jessie nodded to Hannah. "Drink."

The old woman didn't stop for a couple of minutes. She sighed as she sat back on her heels. "I haven't had water like that in so long."

"I thought you said you were here with the marauders?"

"I was, but they didn't let me near it. I was *their* prisoner, too. I keep trying to tell you that. I had to watch them help themselves. One of them gave me a cup. Not like this." Her eyes settled back on the water. "Thank you."

Jessie kneeled, tempted to plunge her head into the spring, to let it soak in coolness. She contented herself with splashing it on her face, tasting it slowly before drawing handfuls to her lips.

She limped over to Bliss and took the M-16, standing at the entrance while her daughter drank again.

At the cave mouth, she stared at the descending night. The dam was barely visible. No birdcalls. But whoever they were wouldn't need them now. As easy as the cave would be to defend, it would also serve as a perfect trap.

They ate dried berries, strips of dehydrated lizard, and split a beet. Hansel rose to sniff the snake hole, which had been burrowed a few feet from the entrance. Jessie eyed it with relief. A snake would eat the rats, which had become fierce as mongooses. The dog then resumed his duty at the entrance. Nobody would get within a hundred yards of the cave without him knowing.

"You should soak in that brine pool," Hannah said.

"Would you watch the entrance?" Jessie asked Bliss.

"Sure. Go take care of your leg."

"Then you can go."

"Okay." Bliss brightened. She'd never been in a pool of water.

Hannah lit a second candle and led Jessie to the back of the cave. They stripped off their clothing without comment. Jessie peeled the bandage from her thigh, wincing at the angry, infected flesh as Hannah helped her into the salty water. The brine burned her wound, but the initial pain quickly ebbed and she began to relax.

Hannah immersed herself slowly in the other end, as if fearful of slipping.

"How old are you?" The proprieties of her own youth had no place now.

"Sixty-seven."

Very old these days. "I'm forty-four."

"I'm lucky to be alive," Hannah added.

Jessie wondered how much of her "luck" could be attributed to good fortune and how much to ruthless cunning. Her silence might have suggested as much to Hannah.

"They're killing old women," she went on.

"They're killing everyone."

"No, I mean they're going after women, especially older ones, saying we're witches and burning us at the stake."

"What?" Jessie sat forward so fast she rippled the water. "The marauders?"

"No, not them. I mean all the hysterical people out there."

"When did this start?"

"I don't know exactly." Hannah calmly splashed water on her arms and face. Jessie forced herself to lean back. "We started hearing reports about three years ago. They're blaming the heat on us. There's a lot of craziness out there. You don't know. You people had your own little paradise."

"Paradise? I wouldn't call it paradise."

"You will. It's the same thing that happened during the Little Ice Age. You know about that one, don't you?"

Jessie nodded. The Little Ice Age was the time of colder weather from the 1600s through the 1800s.

"That was the last time people went crazy about witches. It's no coincidence. If you can't blame your god for screwing things up because he's too perfect, then you go around blaming whatever devils you can find."

"What are they doing? Raiding camps?"

"No, they're not hunting us, like the girls. It's more a case of them turning on women wherever they are, and then it turns into a frenzy. They think if they sacrifice us the heat will stop. I know three women in another camp who were burned to death. One of them was about your age."

"That kind of ignorance is just—"

"Unbelievable. I know, and it's everywhere. They're even more suspicious if you have any education. When the marauders took me, I thought they were going to burn me. But it was because I was a nurse. Turned out they couldn't care less about witches." She looked at the candlelight on the water. "I didn't know what they were capable of until we got to your camp."

"They didn't kill anyone at yours?"

She shook her head. "But we were all older. We didn't have any kids there. They just took what they needed—me. Did your girl know why they wanted her?"

"She knows about the disease and what causes it, just general information. We tried to spare her the worst details, but the girls talk, the older ones."

"You didn't have any Wicca in your camp?"

"None. But we left just as it was getting really bad, and it was already becoming clear that sex was death and that absolute abstinence was the only way to survive. I was already six months along with Ananda when we got away."

"Then you were spared the worst mutations."

"We figured as much. How many have there been?"

"Several, going back at least thirty years. Do you remember when all the vector-borne diseases were starting to spread?"

Vector-bornes were the infectious diseases transmitted to humans and animals through blood-feeding arthropods, like mosquitoes, ticks, and fleas. Jessie recalled the definition from her undergrad days, when the diseases started to migrate to the northern latitudes and to higher elevations, infecting millions with no immunity at all to malaria, dengue fever, West Nile fever, and equine encephalitis. Meantime, the warming also prolonged the mosquito breeding season and shortened the maturation period for the microbes, all of which sped up the reproductive cycles of the viruses and increased their ability to adapt quickly to any human defense. The warming even increased the amount of blood mosquitoes took with every bite. It had been an extraordinary time to be a scientist. And then it turned into the worst possible time to be alive. Unless you were a pathogen.

"Sure," she said, "back when Ebola was wiping out Athens and Rome, and spreading all the way up through Europe. It was really bad."

"But it was nothing compared to what Wicca was becoming. At that point, even though men and women were both carriers, only women were getting sick. It was awful stuff, but not like HIV/AIDS, and that was always our benchmark. If it didn't approach that kind of mortality, those of us in public health didn't worry too much because we had so much else to worry about. But the whole time the vector-bornes were spreading, Wicca was incubating in bodies everywhere. It was a classic case of a virus being virulent enough to infect new hosts, but not quite so virulent that it would kill their hosts and sign their own death warrants. It was brilliant that way, like the common cold. And by infecting through sex, it was spreading to millions of people."

For the first time in many years, Jessie was listening to a fresh voice talk science. Despite the dire subject, she was undeniably engaged. And from what the nurse had said, she knew about the worst mutations. Jessie encouraged her to continue with a nod.

"Wicca was trying out lots of genetic variants, just like any virus. In its own way, it knew that the more variants it produced, the higher the odds that one of its mutations would really prosper. We always see more mutations in pathogens than in hosts, so even at this phase people could never have hoped to build a quick immunity to Wicca.

"The women who were getting sick were getting really

sick, and they had terrible blisters, but most of them survived. That's when we began to see that the immunity in
girls lasted only for the first twelve months after they started
their menses. But even then the outbreaks didn't look any
worse than influenza, except people were already complaining about visual distortions, like the kind you can get with
migraines."

"The first signs of the hallucinations." Jessie remembered
the earliest reports. Epidemiologists theorized that highly
resistant psychotropic molds had entered the food chain—
never considering that a virus could prove so pernicious to
the mind.

"That's right, and they got plenty sick and some died,
but the virus was still not AIDS. When women did start to
die by the thousands, a lot of us assumed the breakdown in
public health systems was to blame. We had no idea that
nothing was going to stop Wicca from turning into the most
lethal virus in history. But once the second phase hit, we
realized the impact. That was when the virus triggered the
full-blown hallucinations and psychotic episodes that drove
millions of women to suicide."

"When we left, they were starting to die in huge numbers.
Men were caught up in it, too."

"'Caught up in it,' that's right. But they weren't sick yet.
That happened after you left, because otherwise the men
in your camp would have infected their partners with the
most lethal mutation. It was the one that attacked the limbic
system—the reptilian brain—which made men far more ag-
gressive *and* increased their sex drive. It also affected the
hypothalamus, which controls sleep, right? So insomnia
became rampant, which caused even more irrational behav-
ior. This is going to sound ridiculous, but the truth is that
there are still millions of men out there running around like
sex-crazed zombies."

"So what else is new?"

They both burst into laughter. Jessie, against her better instincts, let a measure of comfort settle over them.

"That mutation was the key to killing men." Hannah's smile faded. "It was a cruel twist because it played right into a species' instinct to propagate madly in the face of extinction. I guess I don't have to tell you that Wicca increased geometrically."

"Because even the women trying to abstain from sex—"

"Couldn't. Rape was pandemic, and women were also having those violent hallucinations. Men were getting them, too. That's when we began to see mass suicides of both sexes. People were hurling themselves off buildings because they couldn't bear the hellish visions, or the rapes. Men were also getting raped in numbers that defied imagination. There's still no one out there to stop the violence. No police, no armies. Just bands of men roaming for whatever they can find. It's like *they* are the microbes."

"How did you survive?"

"Same way you did. We isolated ourselves before the worst mutations hit. We're all older women, so until the marauders showed up we were okay. We even have an old solar-powered shortwave radio, so occasionally we'd get Radio Tierra."

"A *radio* station?"

"It was down in the Chilean Andes. But it went dark over a year ago."

"A government station?"

"No, not hardly. Just some survivors. There are no governments anywhere. At least from what we heard."

That figured, unfortunately. She knew that most countries had fallen into chaos before she and her family had fled south with the rest of the camp. They all belonged to a commune fighting to hold onto land fed by an underground spring in Appalachia. A private army paid by a league of wealthy heirs to the survivalist industry had tried to drive them off. The mercenaries failed, but fear of Wicca eventually did the job for them.

Jessie shifted her wounded leg. "I'm a wildlife biologist by training. So was—*is*—my husband. So I know something about viruses, and that long incubation period while Wicca infected most of the planet sounds a little too ingenious."

"Not really. Measles can do it for seven or eight years inside the body, and HIV/AIDS and herpes all had long latency periods. Wicca was indolent, if you're familiar with that term."

"Not really."

"It was brewing slowly. And that ensured its survival. Strictly from a scientific viewpoint you could almost admire Wicca, if it weren't such a nightmare."

"What doesn't add up for me is why give girls a year of immunity after their first period?"

"You're right, you'd think that would be a hole in the theory, except that it leads to a lot of death as men kill one another over girls who are safe for sex. Think of your own camp. One hundred twenty-one dead, right? To get five girls? That's a ratio any virus would envy. Giving girls short-term immunity keeps the killing going on, but from the virus's point of view it also keeps itself alive by providing new hosts. Those girls will get pregnant, and a lot of them will have babies who will probably end up carrying the virus. Wicca's like any other virus—it does what it has to in order to survive."

Like us.

"What about the marauders, and the men in the Army of God?" Jessie asked. "Why aren't they raping and dying?"

"In the case of the Army of God, that's precisely what they're doing. If that's not coercive sex—"

"No, of course you're right. But that's not what you described with the epidemic of rapes."

"No, it's not. *All* women who contract the disease die, but a small percentage of men don't. I'd guess somewhere between two and three percent. Which is also great for Wicca. A high priority is placed on reproducing girls for sex, and that small percentage of men is left alive to do the impregnating. If all the men who carried it died, the disease *would* burn itself out."

"And humanity could become extinct."

"Remember, some people survived HIV and never had a symptom. But they were still highly infectious. That's the situation with the men who haven't gotten sick from Wicca. And that's what's so dangerous to those girls when they're with them. The men may not be sick, but a lot of them are carriers."

Jessie stared at the candle. "I've got to find them."

"For what it's worth, I heard the marauders saying that the girls really don't get touched until after they have a period."

"I think Ananda's close."

"At least she won't be sacrificed on some altar. There's a Pagan cult that believes Wicca is the earth's revenge on humans for causing the warming and killing millions of species. They've got a whole death ritual for any descendants of prominent climate-change deniers at the beginning of the century. I heard of a two-year-old girl getting killed by them. They think it's a way of letting Mother Earth," Hannah rolled her eyes, "know they care."

"It's a little late for that." Jessie was beginning to think that maybe they *had* been living in paradise.

"Try telling them that. Any deniers in your family?"

The question shook Jessie, and not only because of what she'd just heard. "No, none," she lied.

"Good. They call themselves 'the Plague,' in honor of the bubonic plague."

"I don't get the connection," Jessie said, still recovering from Hannah's artless probe. If that's what it was.

"Well, they point out—and this much is true—that the plague killed so many people in the Middle Ages that forests started growing back on deserted farms, and carbon dioxide diminished in the atmosphere by five to ten parts per million."

"Wicca would seem to be doing that for them."

"Their point precisely. It's enough to make you think that global warming was the planet's own survival strategy. It let things simmer along so most people wouldn't take it too seriously, and then by the time they did wake up, it was too late."

Jessie found the implications—the earth turning on its own—more frightening than Wicca's history, and she resisted them: "That's too much anthropomorphizing for me."

Hannah shrugged. "I'm only saying there's a definite parallel. You can bet those greenhouse gases are going down, and 'the Plague' sees themselves as hurrying that along. Now there are also people—and I wouldn't dismiss this out of hand—who believe Wicca is a chimera virus developed by the old U.S. Army."

In the long ago, scientists had created chimeras by combining two viruses to make them more deadly. During Jessie's undergraduate days it was widely suspected that the Americans and Russians had each developed "Veto," which was a combination of smallpox and Venezuelan encephalitis. It was also rumored that scientists had been working on making HIV infectious through the air by combining it with influenza.

"It doesn't really matter anymore where it came from," Jessie said. "Those people are all dead and the virus is still alive."

"What matters is that the men in your camp lived in isolation. If they make contact with other people now who haven't lived in isolation, they'll get sick and infect all the women, and you'll die. The same thing will happen if you get raped." She lowered her voice. "Or if your daughters are forced to—"

Jessie silenced her with a quick wave of her hand. She couldn't bear to hear it. She stood, testing her leg.

"How does it feel?" Hannah asked.

"I can bend it a little."

"Good. Try weighting it more when you move around and see how that feels."

They dried off and pulled on their clothes. Jessie heard Bliss trying to slip down the passageway. She called out and caught up to her.

"You were listening, I take it."

"Hansel's watching the way in," Bliss said quickly.

"I'm sure he is. Do you want to talk about what you just heard?"

"No, I just want to get Ananda and the others and get back."

"Me, too."

Jessie took the first shift. Hansel settled by her side. No birdcalls. No movement. Quiet as any night in the camp. When the moon arced midway across the starry sky, she nudged her daughter, who had taken a leisurely bath in the brine pool. She awoke in an instant, like the dog she adored.

Bliss rubbed his scruff and took her post, listening to her mother lie down. She smiled when she remembered her mom and Hannah laughing about men being sex zombies, even though getting infected out here really did scare her. She'd always feared the disease. From the time she first started feeling like a woman, she'd been told she would die if she gave in to her desires. The girls and boys had all been quietly instructed on how to satisfy themselves. Not that they did. Not a lot of them. There were girls who went with girls, and even a few boys with boys. The only kisses she'd ever known had come from girls. Some of them really liked it, but she preferred fantasy.

Bliss touched herself, wondering what it would be like to be with a boy. Maybe just to make out with him and feel him all hard against her. Touching *him*.

Hansel's ears twitched. She didn't notice till he growled

and rose. She jumped up with the automatic rifle and stared out at the night. She saw nothing until a shadow shifted. Then another and another. Men scurrying down the broken dam like animals.

No-no-no. Those are *animals.* She could hear the *thumps* of their paws landing on the lake bed.

Don't hesitate. Her father's words.

But before she could aim, the panthers were streaking right at her, almond eyes alive in the moonlight. Half a dozen beasts, like her mom had said, their hunger beating a fresh trail in the dust.

Chapter Eleven

Israel and Jordan War Over Water
Regional powers threaten nuke response
Bat Shalom bulletin

Russia Brings Order to Frozen, Broken Europe
Czar declares "nation's finest hour"
Moscow Times

Burned Fingers looked left then right before springing from the front seat into the nasty morning sun quick as a lizard's tongue. His scarred hand held his sawed-off shotgun, and the other wielded the pistol Ananda had briefly claimed as her own. Anvil kept the engine idling.

Edgy seconds passed before Burned Fingers lowered his weapons and pulled water canisters out of the back of the hulking vehicle. After handing out rations, he retrieved a rusty monkey wrench that had been rattling around in a side panel. He caught Ananda staring at a canister and poured her a half cup more, then cranked up the armor that served as a windshield with its eye level slit, giving them a wide-open look at the land. Not even glass to get in their way. From what Burned Fingers said over the past few days, the glass had long ago been turned into spear points, booby traps, spikes, knives. Something awful.

She leaned over the front seat, drawn by the view, repulsed by Anvil's smell. The view won. The road was cratered, the pavement plowed-up for at least a hundred yards. It might have been bombed.

"Lookin' better," Anvil said to Burned Fingers, who dropped the wrench back into the side panel.

That morning, Burned Fingers and Anvil had started the drive by staring through that narrow opening at "Injun country." They hadn't spotted any "hostiles," so they stopped to raise the armor.

Now, Anvil accelerated slowly, and air finally drifted over Ananda's face and arms. So much better than their cooped-up stink. She looked forward to seeing the outside world the way she had to playing circus with her father. When he'd get back from scouting, she would balance on his shoulders, eyes everywhere. Like she could see forever, even if it was only the reservoir. She'd pretend to be on stilts. The other kids loved it. She'd been learning to juggle on his shoulders in the days before . . .

Her thoughts trailed off like the dust raised by the wheels. She had to think. *Think.* In the days before *they* came. Burned Fingers. And Anvil with his ginger hair and beard that looked wild as tumbleweed, and the other marauders in the two vans and SUV that followed in the convoy.

The land was kind of like a desert with lots of broken junk. But it was a whole new world to her, even the junk. Only the sky seemed the same, wrung dry of every drop.

The highway looked just as burned, but it could change in a blink. Sometimes they'd find it split apart for a quarter mile or more. Anvil could usually straddle the crumbly asphalt, but when they came upon gaping holes gouged by roadside bombs or land mines, he had to slowly snake along the edges of the scalded pits. What puzzled Ananda, though, were entire sections of highway that had sheared-off and dropped a good ten feet, or risen up like walls that blocked the roadway.

"Isometric fucking rebound," Burned Fingers said the first time they'd piled out so his men could slide heavy wooden ramps off the side of the van. "The crust of the goddamn planet's moving all over the place. You get billions of tons of water burning up into the air, the land starts bouncing around like some fat lady on a fucking trampoline. Plays hell with the roads."

Which sounded like poetic justice to Ananda, but for once she'd kept her mouth shut. Only she opened it again a few moments later.

"How do you know so much?"

"Educated at Oxford, don't you know," he'd said in a flimsy accent. "Fuck it, I don't know shit. *Nobody* does." Sounding like his scary self again. "Only thing I know for sure is that driving ain't what it used to be. Forty miles a day, if we're lucky. Used to be five hundred miles, no sweat. *'Shantih, shantih, shantih,'* my fucking ass." He'd flipped off the arid landscape. "*This* is the fucking wasteland."

Ananda had no idea what he was talking about with that *shantih, shantih, shantih* stuff—and hadn't dared ask—but it didn't look like a complete wasteland. She'd spotted rare bits of green poking up near the road. They grew vegetables at the camp, but every last leaf had to be nursed. These things may not have looked like much, but they were sprouting on their own.

"Weeds," Burned Fingers said, shrugging when she'd pointed them out yesterday.

But they're growing . . . all by themselves, she wanted to shout.

More than weeds or broken roads, she'd seen rubble. Huge cloverleafs with concrete stanchions holding up nothing but air, the overpasses destroyed long ago. Blown up. Or stolen—sometimes there wasn't even rubble. Where'd it go? Who'd want it? She'd heard that all these roads and bridges and ramps once buzzed with movement. Now they'd disappeared, or were still as death.

They'd passed entire subdivisions scarred with faded graffiti, and stripped of windows and doors and decks and anything else that could have been carried off. Not even the abandoned gas stations looked like they'd drawn any interest in decades. Anvil navigated around a crater in front of another one.

"You think there's any gas left in there?" Ananda asked.

"Not out here." Burned Fingers barely glanced at the ruins. "This used to be interstate, so it got picked over plenty. I'll bet they used straws to suck the last drops out of that pissant place. Back there," he meant the town by the reservoir, "it's the middle of bumfuck nowhere. Out here you'd have better luck finding a fucking frozen pizza than gas."

"So where'd you get it?" Each of the vans had a big smelly barrel of it.

"The people who pay us have plenty. The government used to keep tons of it underground. You got the guns and men, you can still get it."

"Me?"

"No, not you. Jesus."

"Who then?"

"Rich people," he grumped. "Makes them richer. Always has."

"So they give it to you?"

"They don't give us dick, Little Miss Bliss." Boy, did he sound pissed. "It's all part of the deal."

"Like us? We're part of the deal?"

"Yeah, like you. I'm guessing you're worth two pints of crude on the futures market."

"What's the futures—"

"Aw, shut up."

Another jarring hour passed before Anvil gave up on the road and drove through a dried-up marsh. Not ten minutes later they came upon an "exurb." Burned Fingers had said there used to be tons of them. "Biggest fucking joke ever. Idiots stranded miles from anything. No gas. No food. Just guns. Bet that was fun."

This one had huge, sun-chewed houses with garages half as big as the camp. Some had been burned out, or had caved-in roofs, but most of them still stood behind a wall of heavy steel spears with sharp points aimed at the sky.

"They look like they're in a cage." M-girl was sitting against the other door. Between them rested Imagi, who'd said very little since they escaped the skells.

They'd seen lots of walls, most with razor wire still clinging to the tops, but this one had a frightening elegance, even though part of it lay on the ground. "Just enough to let the hordes in," Burned Fingers said. "We're not passing this up. Pull over."

Ananda saw where scavengers had tried to cut off the spears but failed, or were driven off by others who'd been driven off themselves. Or they'd been killed. Or eaten. Burned Fingers had joked plenty about cannibalism. "Get hungry enough, you'll eat your young'uns," he'd said last night in a twangy voice that made him laugh and sound stupid. Which he wasn't, though her mother also would have found him "completely inappropriate." But Ananda liked to hear him talk about the world. She only wished she could share it with Bliss, who would have been amazed at what her little sister was learning.

He kicked open his door again, going through the same gyrations with his eyes and guns as he leaped out.

Imagi woke up. For two days she'd run a high fever. Some kind of infection from the burns. When it got so bad that she didn't know who anyone was, Burned Fingers said she'd most likely die. After the fever broke, though, she returned to a quieter version of her former self.

"Go on, get out," Burned Fingers told M-girl and her. "Piss or whatever you've got to do."

He knew they weren't going anywhere, not with the

memory of the skells and the horrors they'd witnessed two days later at their first roadblock, a tangled mass of bed-springs on a naked truck chassis. After Anvil had flashed a pass at the "banditos," Burned Fingers looked out and said, "Go running off and what you see is what you'll get."

The highwaymen, wearing dirty bandannas and little else, had wrapped a man and woman tightly together with crinkled baling wire and were rolling them away from the road, legs mean as peaveys. Rats teemed in their wake, snuffling blood.

A boy and girl about Ananda's age sat in the dust and stared at clothes that had been torn off their backs and bottoms. Four men, bodies eager, grabbed them. They screamed for their mother. She called back in a choked voice. Their struggle ended when the men paired off and forced them belly down to the baking earth.

Ananda closed her eyes and covered her ears. M-girl didn't and cried the rest of the day.

The two of them now looked for a private spot to pee. Gilly and Bella huddled and whispered. Still sleepy, Imagi stayed in the SUV.

Burned Fingers headed directly to a two-story brick house. Not a window remained. Every last shard of glass had been taken, along with the frames. Someone had started to take apart the entryway but gave up, or decided that in a world of sweat and stone, hauling away bullet-chipped bricks made no more sense than praying for sunshine.

"It's worth a look," he said when Ananda and M-girl walked up.

He kicked aside a small boulder sitting in the middle of the doorway, then jumped back, realizing it could have been a booby trap. People set them to keep away looters, a powerfully hopeful act; but few ever returned to their homes, and none to their former lives. Burned Fingers looked at the girls.

"Rich folk figured they could hoard their way through

the hard times. Food, guns, bullets." He forced a chuckle; Ananda knew when he was truly amused. "They died for their sins." Now that was a real laugh.

In that moment, and that moment alone, he reminded her of her dad, who'd raise his eyes to the sky and say "Thank you, Lord" whenever something really stupid happened in the camp. Her father was going to find her. She was sure of it. Wherever they were going, he'd come. And they were "damn near," Burned Fingers had said just this morning, giving Ananda her first jolt of the day.

He slipped out his sawed-off shotgun as he entered the house. "You coming?"

They followed him inside. Better than hanging around Anvil and the other marauders. At least she knew exactly what Burned Fingers expected of them—"no fucking escapes"—and what he'd do if you did try to get away—"make you eat your insides."

He eyed the empty living room. Not a stitch of furniture, not even flooring. Balancing on the joists, he took a few careful steps before lowering himself to the shadows.

The last time he'd searched a house, he told them that people usually hid their supplies in cellars. "It's cooler down there." But he also said that packs of scavengers had looted everything everywhere, so your only hope was that the owners had been smart about stashing stuff. And that was hoping for way too much because most people were "dumber than dirt."

"Like Anvil," she'd chanced.

"Watch yourself," he warned.

Ananda crouched on the joists, then hung down below them and dropped. "Come on," she said to M-girl, who sat with her long legs dangling down and shook her head.

"You're bad as me." Burned Fingers turned to Ananda. "So you're going to do okay."

Not where you're taking me. Not that she actually knew where she was going, only that they were called the Army of God and wanted girls bad enough to hire Burned Fingers and his men—and didn't care how many people they killed. She also knew they wanted her for sex after she had her first period. It made her so anxious that every time she peed she checked to see if she'd grown more hair. Seemed like lots since her capture, and that couldn't be good.

The cellar was dark, and as empty as the living room. She thought they'd clear out fast, but Burned Fingers started tapping one of the concrete walls with his fist. She'd forgotten about that. Up and down. Up and down.

"The ones with half a brain," he'd explained, "actually sealed up most of their shit. 'Course, they gave it up when the hordes came."

He tapped a rough pattern near the floor. Did it again. "That big rock by the door?" He looked up at M-girl. "Go get it."

She lugged it back. Waited.

"Just drop it through, will you?"

M-girl made a face and let the rock drop.

Burned Fingers picked it up and smashed open a thin layer of concrete. He tore it away, then cleared out the lath behind it to reveal a three-foot square opening. "Well-well-well, what do we have here?"

He dragged out a wooden box about six feet long. "Fucker's heavy. Better be guns or ammo. Not some goddamn coffin. Last thing I need is another fucking stiff."

Ananda backed away. The box reminded her of the crates holding the snakes the marauders roasted every night for the "feed."

Burned Fingers pried open the top carefully with his big knife. Whatever was inside lay hidden under a long sheet of white paper. The whitest white she had ever seen. Sure didn't look like snakes. She reached for it.

"Don't!" he snapped. "Could be a goddamn nail bomb— some asshole's 'Fuck you' to the world."

"Come up here," pleaded M-girl.

Ananda shook her head, then resumed watching Burned Fingers, who shifted the paper with his blade. It lifted easily, not tucked or glued or stapled. "Foodstuffs," he said.

Gingerly, he took out glass jars. Apples and plums, peaches, cherries. He stared at the fruit, then studied the metal lids and ran his finger over a slight swelling in one of them. He shook his head, like he couldn't believe what he was seeing, and threw the jar at the wall. The glass exploded and peaches plopped on the floor. He kicked the jars he'd pulled out, shattering two more. Ananda backed up.

"What a fucking waste," he shouted. "No one's seen a fucking peach in fucking years, and all this shit was going bad down here."

Ananda didn't feel the loss. She'd never eaten tree fruit. Just berries. The kids were allowed two or three every day. Their treat.

Her eyes landed on a book with a black leather cover sitting in a corner of the box. She glanced at Burned Fingers.

"May I?" She nodded at the book.

"'May I?'" he mocked her. "Sure, what the fuck. Go ahead."

But when she reached for it, he smacked her hand away.

"Hold on, sweet cheeks."

Using the blade again, he opened the book, fanned the pages. "Okay, take it."

The cover felt dry, cracked. She thumbed through it gently, worried the pages would crumble. Only about half of them had been used.

"I'll be cutting those out." He pointed to the blank pages in the back. "You don't see paper like that anymore."

A book of letters. Ananda skimmed them quickly. Each one started with the same date, April 20, and the same greeting: "Dear Emmeline on her Birthday." And each one was signed "Love always, Dad."

She closed it and took it back to the convoy.

* * *

The roadblock appeared right over a rise in a stretch of passable highway. They were blind to the gunmen till the last second, barely glimpsing them as they scattered to the sides of the SUV.

"Here we go again." Burned Fingers drew his favored weapon.

Ananda tensed at the rustle of leather and steel. She held the book to her chest like a shield.

Anvil opened the door no more than a foot before a long black revolver pressed against his cheek. Slowly, he held out the pass. "Army of God."

Burned Fingers tried to ease open his door. Someone slammed it shut. Two other gunmen leaped in front of the vehicle, aiming their rifles at them. Asian-looking men.

The pass was snatched from Anvil's hand. Ananda heard muttering. She hugged the book harder. Her tender nipples ached, another forbidding sign of puberty; but she couldn't relax her grip.

The two front doors jerked open. More Asian eyes stared in. Burned Fingers hadn't raised his shotgun. Anvil tried to look bored, but Ananda had learned to read his moods. Angry.

A gaunt man with sunken eyes held the revolver on him. "Tell Zekiel to pay or next time we'll kill you and take them." His eyes flicked at the backseat.

"I'll tell him," Anvil said.

"This is bullshit." The Asian spoke with his eyes on Ananda. They widened when he glimpsed Imagi.

"You cooking her?"

"She got caught in a fire," Burned Fingers said.

"Like you. Maybe that's why you like her."

Burned Fingers didn't reply, but Ananda saw a vein pulse in his neck.

"What do you have for food, then?"

"Snakes."

"Give us five and you go."

Their first night out Burned Fingers had told the girls that snakes were currency. "Real as coin." Also the best kind of road food. "Even better than jerky. Those fuckers," he'd pointed to a pile of fat rattlers curled up in one of the crates, "are always fresh. You don't even need to be feeding them, long as you toss them a rat or two before you go."

The doors remained open while Burned Fingers lifted out one of the crates in the back of the SUV. Ananda hated the idea of those things getting loose.

"You take them out, you get your five," he said to the Asian with the revolver. "I have to do it, I'm holding one back."

A stumpy man poked his butt with a hunting rifle. "Five."

Just give him the fucking snakes, thought Ananda. Neither she nor the other girls had ever sworn much. Or at all. Now they did it lots. *Even in my thoughts,* she realized. The marauders were a bad influence, that was for sure.

She'd counted six of the Asian men already. All armed. They'd been eyeing M-girl and her. Talking in their strange tongue. They never smiled. None of them. Maybe boredom was too serious to take lightly. All they had was an outpost with a shade shelter. And usable road. *Don't forget that. They must plunder plenty.*

Her groin tightened at the evidence of others who had tried to pass—scraps of bloody clothes, bent belt buckle, abandoned boot, torn sack—and she hoped her parents wouldn't come up on these guys by surprise. *Don't worry, your dad wouldn't do anything like that,* she told herself. *He's a scout.*

Burned Fingers pulled out the snakes with a forked stick. They twisted and squirmed, and their rattles fried the air. He had to pin each one to the ground until the Asians claimed it. Two of their men were already firing up a stone pit a few feet from the road. Bones bleached by the sun or blackened by flames littered the ground. The men looked starved.

Burned Fingers climbed back in and told Anvil to drive

on. After cracking his door to make sure the rest of the convoy passed the roadblock, he turned back to him. "Zekiel's fucking up."

Anvil nodded, eyes on the road.

"It's getting worse."

"No shit." Anvil rubbed his hairy cheek. "That fucking gook had that thing so close I could smell the bullets."

Couldn't have smelled worse than you, Ananda thought. She loosened her grip on the book and opened it to the first birthday letter. Emmeline's dad said that she'd had colic until she was three months old.

About 5:00 or 6:00 every evening you'd begin to cry. We'd walk you back and forth, and if that didn't help we'd try driving you around. One time we were driving you up an orchard road in the upper valley. The sun was setting right in front of us. The colors were amazing, just brilliant, and right then you settled down in your car seat.

Ananda looked up. What a peaceful life, *driving up an orchard road*. Those plums and peaches and cherries must have come from there. But could "there" be here? The land was so dry.

At about nine months you started kissing us. You would take your hands and press them on each side of our face and plant a big wet kiss on our lips, though my mustache would make you crinkle your nose.

She closed the book. Longing was boring a hole in her heart. She handed it to M-girl. Her turn.

Late in the day they turned off the road and drove for about two miles, pulling into a tight circle behind a denuded hill. Beyond its thickening shadow the land stretched fea-

tureless and flat to the horizon. Burned Fingers assigned two
men to guard duty. Anvil started a fire.

Water rations had been adequate, and Ananda savored a
second cupful as she stared at the dancing flames, remembering the ballet recitals that she and the girls had put on for
the camp.

"Our last night on the road. Here's to the catch of the day."
Burned Fingers toasted the girls. The marauders laughed.
Ananda felt mocked again.

Anvil skewered four snakes. The serpents rattled and
writhed horribly over the fire, snapping their heads like they
were screaming.

Ananda sat next to Imagi, who picked at her food. She'd
lost weight since they'd been taken, and her eyes leaked constantly. The pain had to be bad, though the worst patches on
her belly and back had scabbed over.

The men quieted as the flatlands melted into the gloaming, and the hill disappeared into the night. Burned Fingers
assumed a sullen mien, and the girls appeared wary, even
when they looked at one another in the fading firelight. They
couldn't hold off tomorrow any more than they could have
crushed the days that had brought them here. The Army of
God had caused all the terror, and the girls would arrive at
their gate by late morning.

Sleep, and it'll be a matter of hours, Ananda warned herself. But as the fire snuffed itself, and the coals paled, she
did close her eyes. Taunted by time, her heart beat madly
against the bare earth.

When she awoke, the seconds and minutes swelled
quickly to miles, and they drove into a broad valley
formed by brown hills. Another half hour passed before
she spotted the fortress. Stone walls rose fifteen feet high
and spread over rolling acres. Guards in dark hoods stared
down. She couldn't make out their faces from this distance, but she could scarcely avoid a towering, glittering

cross on a tall wooden gate. It sparkled like diamonds in the sun. As they drew nearer, she saw that it was formed of broken glass; thousands of clear shards had been embedded in the dark, heavy beams. Their points and edges, sharp and scary, jutted defiantly.

Burned Fingers climbed out and walked to the gate. He spoke to guards who peered at him from the top of the wall. The gate swung open, catching sunlight so fiercely that she had to lower her eyes. When she looked up, a girl about her age stood alone in the entrance staring at them. No smile. No blink. No wave. Just the biggest roundest belly Ananda had ever seen.

A hooded man walked up to the girl, hair and beard white as his robe. He wrapped a wrinkly, liver-spotted arm around her narrow shoulders, claiming her like they were a couple. Her stare never wandered, eyes empty as the sky.

Ananda curled up on the seat, once more hugging the book of birthday letters. But she felt no comfort and certainly no protection, not with that girl before her. A sickening filled her own belly and raced to her limbs, a sensation not unlike the mortal fear of fire in a dry land.

"Don't leave us here," she begged Burned Fingers. *"Don't."*

Chapter Twelve

India's Indus River Fails
World's largest irrigation system dry
Indo-Asian News Service

Phoenix Temps Top 130
Dome attempt ends
Desert turns graveyard as thousands die
hunting water
From survivor accounts

A phosphorous flare burst high above the lake bed, showering the panthers with milky light. They raced right at Bliss, pale coats rippling like white velvet, paws a scatter beat of muffled thunder. She raised the M-16 as Hansel howled and hopped toward a deadly, futile fight.

"No, come!" she yelled, wasting a second when she should have fired. Ruing the loss the same instant, long before she'd have time to wonder about a blast of light so unearthly that it could have been the spectral gift of an exploding star.

Rapid gunfire tumbled the first panther across the dust, raising a curiously bleached cloud that swept away from the stilled creature. She stared at her hand, knowing her finger hadn't moved. Automatic weapons claimed two more cats. Fighting off confusion, she joined a fusillade that cut down the last three beasts less than twenty feet from where she crouched.

Hansel looked about wildly. Bliss stared at the destroyed dam where she'd first spotted the panthers. Her head snapped back to the dead animals, trying to reconstruct the shooting angle. Sharp echoes faded with the ghostly light.

What the hell?

A man slammed her into the cave, knocking her breathless. He ripped the rifle from her hands as two men hauled her mother outside. She heard Hansel snarl.

"Call off the dog," a grizzled face loomed inches from her eyes, "or we'll kill it."

"Hansel . . ." Starved for air, Bliss struggled to speak. ". . . down." Hansel dropped to the ground with a growl.

Another man raced in with a torch and a handgun. "Stop or I'll kill you," he yelled at Hannah, who was reaching for the shotgun. Her hand fell from their last hope.

A taller man ducked under the entrance. "Who else?" he shouted at Hannah.

"No one."

"Get out," he yelled at her. "Her, too," he shouted at the man holding Bliss.

He dragged her to the lake bed and dropped her next to her mother. The last of the white light leaked away. She heard a magazine slammed into a rifle and boiled with fright when a man aimed at them. Two others established a perimeter with their guns pointing to the darkness.

The taller man hurried over with the torch. "It's clear in there. Jaya's starting a fire. I want them back inside, and I want that meat." He waved the torch at the panthers before shoving Bliss with his boot. "Get in there, the three of you. Don't try to run."

Shaking, she helped her mother up. Her own legs jellied

as she walked to the cave, fearing the horrors it could hide.

Inside, the one named Jaya was adding branches to burning tinder, raising asphyxiating smoke. Bliss coughed and her eyes watered, but she'd glimpsed him, surprised at his youth. About her age, maybe a year or two older. Lean like her with hair the same length but much lighter. He wore no shirt, only ragged pants chopped off below the knees. Smooth-faced before the flames.

The man who'd ordered them back to the cave stepped in. Bliss saw that he had but one arm.

"Take the entrance," he barked at one of the gunmen who'd guarded them. "The dog." He turned his dark eyes on Hannah. "Is he worth a damn? Does he guard?"

"He's mine," Jessie answered. "He does. Don't hurt him."

His eyes switched to her. "What's the command, then?"

"It's 'Hansel, guard,' but he's not going to leave us now."

"Then put him in the 'down' over there." He pointed away from the pool. "And if he moves he's dead."

She hand-signaled Hansel. The dog whined but obeyed.

"Search them," he said to the men crowding the cave. "Flick, you do it with Brindle."

Flick looked ancient, but he grabbed Bliss's wrist with a grip that felt like a steel clamp. He and Brindle, younger but not like Jaya, touched every part of her body in seconds, finding the flint knife that her father had made her years ago. She rarely used the treasure, kept it sheathed insider her pants for emergencies, and now, in the midst of one, she'd forgotten it. Though its use would have been limited, given the firepower they faced.

The two men searched her mother and Hannah. In one of the nurse's greasy gray braids they found a six-inch steel spike sharp enough to scramble a brain. Hannah shrugged when Bliss stared at her in shock.

The one-armed man forced them at gunpoint to sit against a wall. Smoke drifted out the entrance, driven by pressure differentials that Bliss had never understood. She stopped coughing and her eyes cleared.

"Get water," he said to his men. He glared at his captives. "You didn't do anything to it, did you?"

"No," Jessie said.

The men kneeled by the pool, scooping water, as thirsty as Bliss had been hours ago. The one-armed man helped himself before crouching before them.

"Who are you? And what the hell are you doing out here?"

"Who are you?" Jessie demanded, worrying Bliss, who looked to the side. Two men held weapons on them.

"First, *you*." He jabbed his finger at her mother.

Jesus, just tell him.

In less than a minute her mom did, ending with the massacre but not a breath about the girls.

Jessie caught his lips narrowing at her mention of the marauders, like he was biting down on the word. She didn't know what to make of it. Or of them. So she asked him again who they were, softening her tone.

"Not so fast. First, I want you to know that I believe you."

Believe me? It hadn't occurred to her that he wouldn't. After pausing to sit, he went on.

"You're not the only camp attacked. They killed most of our people six weeks ago. We had a camp down near Lafayette, and we've been tracking them ever since. They ran their trucks over our huts, water tanks, kids, they didn't care. They crushed everything." He studied her closely. "You didn't say anything about losing girls, but I'm guessing you did and that you're going after them. We lost four. They took my twins. Eleven-year-olds." His voice splintered, and she breathed for the first time since waking to the gunshots. Even nodding before she thought better of it.

"How many?" he asked.

"Five." Nothing about Ananda.

"We're out to find ours, too." He looked at Jaya setting up a spit over the fire. "The boy there's from another camp. They took his sister. We met him here getting water. This place draws everything. Cats, bears, other animals."

"'Specially the t-two-legged kind," Brindle stammered. He was short and bony, and like the other men, he'd relaxed his guard.

"What's your name?" she asked the one-armed man.

"Coxwell."

"How'd you lose it?" Hannah eyed his arm. "I'm a nurse," she added quickly.

"A burst from a Kalashnikov. Only thing holding it on was some skin."

"Is it healing? Any infection?"

"A lot at first. It swelled to twice its size, but I got lucky. I'm just about done with these." He held out his stump. In the firelight they saw maggots crawling over his wound, gobbling up dead tissue. World's oldest medicine.

"A bullet passed through her leg." Hannah glanced at Jessie. "She could use some."

He smiled for the first time. "I can spare them."

Jessie felt acutely uncomfortable, not about the maggots, which were a blessing, but about exposing her upper thigh. When she hesitated, he ordered his men to look away and averted his eyes.

Hannah held his stump right over her leg. "Now tap your arm," she said to him. "They should fall off. I don't want to do it and hurt you."

Coxwell slapped his stump harder than Jessie would have thought bearable, and a clump of maggots fell onto her wound. He loosened two more clumps before Hannah eased his arm away.

Twenty or thirty of them squirmed on Jessie's raw flesh. After lowering her pants leg, she thanked him; her chance of beating infection had increased greatly.

She sat against the wall and tried to ignore the itchy feel of the larvae. A man lugged in a fresh cougar carcass. In minutes Jaya had it roasting on the spit.

Jessie hadn't eaten panther in more than a year. The sweetish odor made her hollow with hunger; but relief spilled into fatigue, and she didn't awaken till first light. A hairless man in shredded overalls now guarded the entrance, armed with a long blade and rifle. And a ruthless gaze.

Coxwell lay curled by the fire. The roasted panther was on a rock they'd used as a cutting board. Only about half of it had been eaten. Hannah slept. So did Bliss. Jessie wondered if they'd had any.

The itching returned to her leg, and she felt a desperate urge to claw the wound. But she dared not harm the little life givers.

As soon as she moved, Coxwell opened his eyes and propped himself on his only elbow.

"Hungry?"

She nodded.

"Help yourself."

He watched her take the knife. She didn't blame him; she would have been all eyes, too. She sliced off a narrow strip from a rib and bit off only what she thought she could chew of the tough flesh. After days of dehydrated lizard, the lean meat, with its rich taste, sparked a smile that made her feel foolish when Coxwell noticed.

"Been a while, I take it."

"Been a long while," she answered softly, wary of waking the others.

"Same here. We were hunting the whole pack when the boy spotted you down on the lake bed."

"Was he the one making the birdcall?"

"He was letting us know he'd spotted you. We figured the cats were heading to the water when they picked up your scent. Soon as they made their move and got out in the open, we had to make ours."

"Where'd you get the flares?"

"My grandfather was a captain in the marines. He secured cases of them before the collapse."

Secured? Nice way to put it. Looted more likely, but Jessie had no complaints. They'd fallen into the right hands. Seemingly.

"Were there other camps near you?" she asked.

"None. All by our lonesome till they came."

"Same for us."

"Where?"

The question surprised her. It shouldn't have—she'd asked him—but there was no telling where the information might end up. "Sorry, I can't. We—"

"That's fine." He raised his hand. "I could guess easily enough but we'll let her lay. So you've been walking on that?" He indicated her leg.

"Crutches." Her leg felt like a safer subject. "I'm starting to move around on my own. I'm hoping your little friends help." The thought of the maggots set off the itching again. "Do you know where you're going?"

"Not exactly, but all the tire tracks were heading north. Then a rainstorm wiped them out. Got us this far, though."

"She says she knows." Jessie glanced at Hannah, sleeping with her mouth agape. She also noticed Bliss listening with her eyes closed. That girl didn't miss a beat. "You can open them, hon." Bliss sat up as Jessie turned back to Coxwell. "Hannah's her name. She came with them. She says they grabbed her out of another camp and forced her to examine the girls. Then she says she played dead when they left ours. Who knows?"

"Playing possum was smart. The one who came to our camp was shot in the head as soon as she finished up. Right in front of us. It was so brutal that we knew there was no sense holding back. If that's what they were doing to someone they brought, there was no hope for us. We opened up on them and tried to kill as many as we could, but we didn't stand a chance."

"If they had a different nurse, they must have been a different gang. The leader of the ones who attacked us had two burned fingers on his right hand."

"I didn't see anyone with burned fingers."

"They'd have been hard to miss. He kept them wrapped around a sawed-off shotgun. Did you hear anything about the Army of God?"

"No. Who are they?"

She explained the little she knew. "We got that from a wounded marauder."

"He talked?"

"He didn't have any choice."

Coxwell nodded.

"He said there were other gangs working for the Army of God. His was just one of them. She says," eyes back on Hannah, "that we've got weeks of walking ahead of us. *Don't* try stopping us."

He smiled. Kind? Cruel? She couldn't tell. Her stomach clenched when he reached for a pile of weapons.

"Won't you need this?" He handed over the M-16. The hairless guard jerked his attention from the lake bed to Jessie. "You can have all your stuff," Coxwell said. "We're not marauders."

Her only response was to pop the clip. Mostly full. Taking her mother's cue, Bliss retrieved her shotgun and flint knife. She checked for shells and snapped the barrels back together, waking Hannah and the rest of Coxwell's men.

The nurse caught on and grabbed her spike, casually sliding it back into her braid as if it were a barrette.

"We were thinking," Coxwell said hesitantly.

"What?" Jessie's eyes darted around the cave, then back to Coxwell.

"We were thinking last night that maybe all of us should go together. It makes even more sense this morning after hearing what Hannah knows. You've got a pretty good idea where you're going, but you've got no idea what you're up against. We took you down in seconds. You could use our help, and we could use yours. We've all got guns, and it sounds like all of our girls are going to the same place."

Jessie saw the obvious benefits, but the unknowns were frightening to consider. She stared at Coxwell, trying to unveil the future while telling herself that if they'd wanted rape, they'd have been at it all night long. *He didn't even steal a look at your body when he gave you the maggots. And if they'd wanted murder, you wouldn't have seen the morning. He sure wouldn't be handing over our guns. They'd just grab Hannah and go.*

She caught Bliss's eye. Her girl had been stealing a look of her own—at the boy. Bliss gave her a nod.

"You can come with us," she told Coxwell, "but remember that I'm trusting her." She looked at Hannah, who said nothing. She turned back to him. *Like I'm trusting you.* Her eyes moved over the other men in the dimly lit cave. *And you and you and you . . .* Spending a final glance on the hairless guard with his unbending gaze.

"There's a lot of trust in the air," Coxwell said to her. "Maybe that's all we'll have till we get our girls back." He peered at his men, much as she had. "So let's all take a deep breath."

Jessie reached for one of her pistols. Shaking so slightly that no one could have noticed, she handed the gun to Hannah.

Only then did she remember to breathe.

At the top of the dam they spotted the charred cab that had almost crushed Eden against the camp's iron gate. The doors hung open in the sandy river bottom, metal plating smoke-seared and twisted, the driver's body no better. Jessie figured it for the vehicle that the marauders had used to abduct the girls.

She rushed from the burned cab to the severed cargo carrier. The front was scorched and mangled, as if the truck had been ripped apart by a bomb, but the rest of the carrier appeared undamaged. She gave a quick prayer that the girls had escaped unharmed.

But where? This is skell country.

Coxwell hurried to her side. They both looked at scores of large footprints. The tracks formed no particular path, extending randomly to both sides of the riverbed.

Jessie studied the dense, dead forests that crowded the banks, listening intently. Waiting. She heard nothing but a vast, unyielding silence.

Then the air shifted, prickling the hairs on her arm. A howl followed quickly, rising like a ghost in a graveyard of sand and fallen screams.

Chapter Thirteen

Chinese Drought Destroys Wheat, Rice Crops
300 million march for Siberian farms
Russia deploys troops on border
UN observer accounts

New Delhi Sacked, Taj Mahal Destroyed
Riots in cities as India starves
Indo-Asian News Service

Three burly guards pressed their shoulders to the inside of the massive wooden gate. Above their bearded faces ARMY OF GOD had been burned into the beams. The words were huge and charred, so black they could have been smoldering in the sun.

The gate creaked loudly. Ananda watched Burned Fingers back out of the fortress, edging past the thick stone wall. Bumps erupted on her bare arms, a hard chill beneath the blinding orb. Vicious rays. She clutched the book of birthday letters, now bundled in a rag. "Take it," he'd whispered at the end, melted fingers brushing her damp palm, leaving her with nothing but the aching pages. No gun. No knife. No—

"This way." One of the guards surrounding them jabbed her jutting hip bone with a rifle butt.

Wincing, wanting to scream, cry, collapse, she turned to the compound, streams of sweat dripping down her dusty neck. The gate *clunked,* shutting out a breeze so slight that she didn't realize she'd felt it until the air was gone. It was as if she'd been inhaled.

The guards lined them up side by side on a dirt footpath. Imagi stood last in line, glaring at the ground. The leader, Zekiel, eyes ever shadowed by his hood, studied his five new female captives with his arm still draped around the pregnant girl's shoulders, hand a wrinkled epaulet.

Unshaded, the path ran along the wall and down a hill, then climbed a rise and disappeared. Armed men kept watch on the world from towers on top of the barricade.

A stone-and-mortar building loomed to the left. A tall concrete crucifix rose from its front peak, Jesus a tortured figure of red glass shards glittering in the sun like the clear fragments that formed the cross on the outside of the gate. Ananda had never seen an undamaged structure so large.

As they moved past it, a man in a white robe like Zekiel's opened a metal cage and led a chained brown bear on to the church grounds. The emaciated creature trundled behind him, heavy links hanging from an iron nose ring. Ananda stared, shocked by the sight of the starved animal.

The man jabbed the bear's bony flank with a stick. It sat on its haunches, paws clawing the hot air for balance. Or food, she thought.

"Bosco's waving to you." Zekiel spoke for the first time. "He's saying 'Welcome.' Wave back."

Ananda thought the Army of God's leader was trying too hard to sound cheerful, no more his real self than the bear.

Bella and Gilly waved. Imagi never lifted her eyes from the ground. Ananda felt M-girl take her hand. A stout guard slapped them apart.

"Your Lord said wave." He glared at them.

Both girls offered a weak effort.

The bear dropped to its front paws and huffed. Its head swayed, and Ananda heard links clinking softly in the still air.

Over the rise, amid a rolling expanse of parched cheat-grass, four fields of row crops flourished at right angles to one another, tended by girls in white bonnets and long white dresses. Where the crops could have intersected to form a green cross, an iron stake higher than a man's head had been driven into the center of a dark, rocky circle.

A water faucet sprouted in each field like a steel-stemmed plant. Zekiel pointed to the bounty.

"Our fruits and vegetables reach to the heavens from the sacred ashes of consecration. They fill our fields with the life so justly denied to the defiled." He turned moist, unblinking eyes on them. His beard quivered. "The infidels among us."

Now he sounds real, Ananda said to herself. She watched him walk on. They followed without prodding.

A boy in rags hurried a dog cart past them. Wooden barrels jiggled against the sides. He glanced at the girls, catching Ananda's eye.

"He's not one of us," the stout guard warned them.

Zekiel turned so quickly that his gown swirled around his spindly legs. "What is it?"

The guard thrust his rifle toward the boy, still hurrying. "He *looked* at them."

"Stop," Zekiel demanded. The boy halted the cart, and his shoulders crept toward his ears, as if he expected a blow. Or worse. "Turn around." He appeared to Ananda no older than her. "Dare that again and you will be whipped and your trade will end."

The boy bowed like a servant and drove his dog forward. Ananda's eyes settled on the animal, big as Hansel but with a longer, lighter coat. She wondered if Hansel had survived the attack. And that started her worrying about her mother and father and sister and friends.

She tried to focus as they trudged along on the sunlit path beneath their feet. She walked on Zekiel's large footprints, imagining herself crushing him; M-girl stepped on the smaller ones next to them. The contrast of an old man with a pregnant young girl sickened Ananda, and she looked away, squinting across the expanse at habitats dug into the side of a wide hill hundreds of yards distant.

With their earthen, half oval faces and wooden doors, the homes were difficult to distinguish from the hillside. Only windows broke the monotony of more than a dozen identical residences set side-to-side.

Far to the left of them she spotted a grotto with a dark entrance. A third cross glittered above it as if to mark a sacred site. A metal cylinder, taller than the truck that had taken them from the camp and almost as wide, stood near the opening. The truck came to mind because she smelled an odor similar to its fumes, and noticed that the faint breeze cut off by the closing of the gate had returned, revealed by the murky current of scent.

Her eyes fell back to the footpath, which angled away from the wall and stopped at a corrugated steel Quonset hut. Shading her face with her hands, she spied a smaller, windowless stone building on the slope below it.

Her parents had drawn and described many kinds of buildings, but she'd never seen or heard of one shaped as queerly as the Quonset hut, like a half moon snatched from the sky.

Crimson tulips grew in beds on both sides of the entrance, a wondrous, mystifying sight until she saw that they'd been carved from wood and painted with a viscous stain.

Zekiel turned to the girls and raised his palms, as if in blessing. Guards on both sides of Ananda and M-girl stopped them by swinging out their rifles till the muzzles nearly touched. The sun burned down on her so intensely that she could feel her scalp cooking.

"You will now enter our Welcoming Center. This will be your first step to joining the Army of God. This is an honor bestowed upon few females. You are truly among the most fortunate. Mary will lead you inside. Let her be an inspiration to you. Do what you are told and do not speak unless you are spoken to."

He stepped aside and watched Mary struggle with a dented gray metal door. Ananda and M-girl trailed her into a dim anteroom. Zekiel stared at them till they passed from view.

"Take off your clothes. They are foul." Mary held her big belly as if it might drop. "Pile them there." Her eyes bowed to an ashy hollow where the building's rock foundation had been left open to the earth. "They will be burned." Her words had the practiced ring of a pronouncement.

Ananda glanced at the other girls. None had begun to disrobe. Bella looked pained.

"Why?" M-girl asked.

"Because," Mary replied, "if you refuse they will wash your eyes out with lye."

"Lye?"

"It will blind you." Mary still spoke as if rehearsed.

Ananda had heard of lye. Her parents, probably. *Soap.* That's it. The stuff for making soap.

"They wouldn't," M-girl said, not in defiance but fear.

"You will see girls with strange eyes. They are milky and can no longer see. Take off your clothes. *Please.*" The plea was so strong and sudden that Ananda knew she wasn't lying about the blinding.

Ananda put aside the bundled book and stepped out of her pants. Her sparse pubic hair and puffy nipples made her feel more naked than at any time of her life. M-girl, she noticed, also had tiny breasts. Ananda lifted her eyes to her friend's face, struck anew by her prettiness.

The girls dropped their dirty pants and shirts in the fire pit. Imagi remained stubbornly clothed.

"The cursed one must do it," Mary said. "All of you will be bathed."

Be bathed? *Someone touching me?* Ananda's stomach

tightened, but for Imagi she tried to sound happy. "You'll get to sit in water. It'll be fun!"

Imagi shook her head.

"The cursed one *must* do it." Mary looked behind her.

"Stop saying 'the cursed one.' It's not helping." Ananda took Imagi's hand. "Come on, Imagi. It's like a game."

Imagi looked up, and her stubbornness softened. She took off her clothes, exposing burns so scabbed and pink that Ananda could have cried.

Mary nodded, as if grateful. "Would you put all that stuff in there."

Ananda scooped up Imagi's clothes and added them to the growing pile.

"That, too." She looked at the rag hiding the book.

Ananda had feared that Zekiel or one of the guards would grab the worthless looking rag and find the book. Now *she* would have to reveal it. Would they blind her for hiding it? They sounded completely crazy. She never should have accepted it. But it was the most beautiful object she had ever seen, and she'd wanted to know what happened to Emmeline. In the last birthday letter that she read, her father mentioned that there were "problems" in the country.

Ananda tossed the rag into the pit. Naked, she held the book.

"Is that a . . ." Mary didn't say the word, as if it were forbidden; but she peered at the book with a cat's instant curiosity, still holding herself with both hands to try to ease the pressure of her swollen belly.

Ananda couldn't imagine being that big. The baby must be huge, she thought. When she was three she'd noticed her vaginal opening for the first time, and she asked her father what it was. He explained that when she grew up she might give birth to a baby through it. She'd looked at him and said, "I sure hope it has a tiny head." It became a family joke, though it didn't feel funny now. Not with Mary's oversized appearance. *But you've never seen a pregnant girl,* she reminded herself. *You don't know.*

"What kind is it? Please tell me." Mary sounded scared, as if the pages would burst into flames. Ananda was surprised to find that she felt sorry for her.

"It's a book of birthday letters. A dad wrote them to his daughter. See." She fanned the pages. Her thumb landed on the inside of the back cover, where she felt a circular, recessed object. Hard like a coin. She glanced down as casually as she could, but saw nothing unusual. Hidden, she realized, under the paper pasted to the cover.

Footsteps sounded from inside the hut. Mary took the book and put it to the side. Ananda didn't resist. A door that she hadn't noticed opened behind the girl, and a graying woman stepped out. Hair fell alongside her cheeks, reddened from effort or heat, and moist enough to sop up dozens of strands.

The woman was as tall as her mom, with the same lean arms. But that's all she could see of her body because a soiled white dress, like the ones worn by the girls working in the fields, covered her from the neck almost to the floor.

The woman eyed them closely, lingering where Ananda wanted herself stared at least. She shifted to the side to try to hide her sex, but the damage had been done, though she had only a hesitant sense of the violation.

"Follow me." The woman's voice carried all the force that Mary's lacked.

Ananda queued behind Imagi. As they walked out, she watched Mary open the book upside down. She flipped through it, eyes no more comprehending than pebbles.

The girls filed into a room filled with light from two windows with clear glass—broken pieces that had been leaded together. A pair of salvaged tubs squatted beneath them. A girl with a brush, bristles worn and bent, waited by each one. They looked older than her. Maybe Bliss's age. Like the woman, their faces appeared moist with sweat, dresses dulled by dust.

"She'll go last," the woman said of Imagi.

"It's better that way," Ananda said.

"What did you say?" The woman turned such a fierce glare on Ananda that her heart quailed.

"I was just saying that you're right. It's better this way. She can see it's okay."

"It's 'okay'? Get in." Each word sounded harder than a sharpening stone.

The girl by Ananda's tub pressed her shoulder until she lay back. Warmth spread over her skin. It was the first time she'd been fully immersed in water, and she had to fight a growing panic when the girl dipped her head under. Then she shampooed her with soap that stung her scalp. When Ananda lay back again, the water browned, astounding her with her own filth. Since her abduction, there had been no water for washing.

The girl had her stand so she could work the brush over her arms, back, and legs. Then she soaped a cloth and used it on her chest and feet, silently offering her shoulder for balance. Pointedly, she did not touch Ananda's pubic area or bottom.

As M-girl stepped into the tub beside them, the girl soaped the cloth again. She handed it to Ananda and with the briefest gesture indicated that she should wash her face. Ananda scrubbed and rinsed, opening her eyes not on the girl but on the woman. The woman told her to lift her foot to the edge of the tub, then flicked her thighs to spread them before rubbing a fresh, sudsy cloth against her sex. It felt warm and soft and sickening. Ananda's stomach muddied as much as the tub water.

"Turn, and put your leg up on the other side." She repeated the same nauseating motion between her buttocks. "Get out."

Ananda followed the woman into a stone cubicle, where she pulled a cord, washing her off her with cooler water from a bucket that hung from the arched ceiling.

She handed Ananda a small rag for drying, and a metal comb. "Do you know what this is?"

"Yes." They'd had one at the camp. Her father said it was an old dog comb.

The woman watched her use it before handing her over to Mary in the next room down. The two of them sat on a wooden bench, Ananda with only the damp rag on her lap, wet hair spilling onto her shoulders; Mary leaning back, hands on her tummy. Ananda wondered about a six-foot wall that cut off the other side of the room. After a brief silence, Mary spoke in a hushed, hurried voice.

"I started it." She held up the book.

"You did? You can read?"

"Shush." Mary's eyes darted to the door. "Don't *ever* let them know that. They'll think you're a witch."

"A witch? That's crazy. All of us can—"

"And don't let them hear you say that they're crazy. They'll kill you."

Ananda stared at Mary, not knowing what to make of her. "Do you really mean that?" she whispered.

"They burn girls to death at the stake. Didn't you see it at the farm? You passed right by it."

She recalled the tall iron spike at the center of the darkened stone ring. "I didn't know what it was."

"They call it the 'Sacred Heart of Evil.' They burned a girl named Sylvan two months ago. They accused her of casting spells on Zekiel so he couldn't make babies. Desana started it. She's the one who brought you in here. Stay away from her. And whatever you do, don't make her angry."

"Did you actually see the girl burned?" It sounded like a crazy rumor, like the ones that sometimes spread through the camp and made her mom and the other moms sit all the kids down and say, "Did you actually see it?"

"We *had* to watch. They wouldn't let us look away. It was horrible. They did the fire real slow. She screamed and screamed."

Mary looked so shaken that Ananda believed her. She tried not to imagine what it was like, but the memory of the stake made it horrifically real. And Desana already hated her, which made it worse. Just the way she'd looked at her when she said to get in the tub.

"So be really careful," Mary went on. "I've heard that they only kill the ones who started their periods over a year ago, but they've blinded three of the brides since I got here."

"Brides?"

"The ones who have to get married as soon as they have their period. Like I'm married to Zekiel."

"They really blinded them? How long have you been here?"

"Ten months."

Ananda couldn't comprehend the cruelty. *Blinding girls?* She took a breath and asked if any of the men could read.

"Some. Zekiel can. But they're men so they can't be witches."

"Are you going to tell them I brought the book?" The possibility had her gripping the bench.

"I have to, but that doesn't mean you can read." Mary flipped it upside down and her eyes turned to pebbles again. "See what I mean? People grab anything that looks valuable." She opened the back cover. "Don't they?"

They stared at each other.

"I found it," Mary said, voice lower than ever.

"Found what?"

"You know what."

Ananda grabbed the book and turned away, searching for the hard, hidden object. She wheeled on Mary. "What did you do with it?"

"Quiet," Mary whispered. "You're going to get us both killed." She held up a gold coin.

"You took it."

"I'm not 'taking' it." She handed it to her. "It's a Kruger-rand. It's incredibly valuable."

Ananda looked at a man's face gleaming on one side. The other held a likeness of an animal.

"It could buy our freedom." Mary leaned as close as she could. "I *have* to get out of here. I need help. I'm going to have my baby any time, and they'll take it from me. That's what they always do. And then the mothers disappear."

Ananda rubbed the coin between her thumb and index finger. "Could it get my friends out, too?"

"Maybe. Probably. You should give that back to me. You can't hide it," reminding Ananda of her nakedness.

"How could it buy our freedom?"

"The traders. Sometimes they get paid in gold dust, but they don't make that much in a year." Mary spoke quickly and kept checking the door. "They're always coming to Zekiel's house. I hear a lot. You're lucky you got that all the way here. The marauders would kill for it."

Footsteps sounded from behind the door. "Give it back," Mary said. "I'm not kidding. They'll find it and think there's more. They'll beat you, burn you, blind you, anything they have to. They'll never believe that's all—"

Desana entered the room with M-girl, who was attempting to cover herself with a tiny rag.

"Sit on the end, away from your friend."

M-girl obeyed. Desana studied the three of them before shutting the door behind her.

They sat in silence, Mary staring straight ahead. Only once did she glance at Ananda, and then only to shake her head.

The next time the door flew open, Bella and Gilly appeared. Minutes later Ananda heard Imagi crying. She slumped in with a fresh bruise on her cheek, and her burns looked raw, like they'd been scrubbed too hard. A long one on her stomach oozed blood. She sat next to Ananda and threw her arms around her. Ananda wanted to kill Desana. More so when she rushed over and separated them.

"Do not comfort her. The cursed one does not listen."

Ananda tried to hold back her temper. She did manage to speak respectfully. "Please call her Imagi."

Desana smacked Ananda so hard that her hands flew to her face. She remembered the coin only when she felt it pressing against her burning skin. Carefully, she balled it up in her fist and let her hands sink to her sides.

"Zekiel will hear of your insolence. It will not be tolerated. Stand up. It's time to examine you."

Ananda followed her behind the wall and almost bumped into a wooden table with metal stirrups. Mary was right: naked, she had nowhere to hide the Krugerrand. Her fist felt as obvious as a flag.

Desana strapped her feet into the stirrups, and with a fierce expression knotted the coarse leather. Zekiel joined them, staring over Desana's shoulder as she drew a shiny steel speculum from a shelf under the table. Ananda had never felt so exposed.

"She comforted the cursed one. And she corrected me."

Zekiel nodded, but he continued to stare openly and didn't appear to have listened.

Ananda squeezed her eyes shut at Desana's first touch. Now both hands had turned into fists and her breath came in short bursts.

"She is a virgin," Desana said, abruptly withdrawing the device.

Water leaked from Ananda's closed eyes, and her fists pressed down on the hard table. She felt the leather bindings loosen, and pulled her feet from the stirrups.

Zekiel took her hand, the one with the balled-up coin. It felt larger than ever. "You're one of God's chosen ones. You can relax now."

They'll beat you, burn you, blind you.

She could barely breathe or swallow. What if he tried to open her hand?

But now he touched her shoulder, holding it as he had

Mary's. She took halting steps as he guided her to the last room of the Quonset hut. His eyes were thieves plundering her body. He handed her one of the white dresses and a white bonnet.

"You will await your womanhood with us, here in the world's most blessed place." He studied her as he spoke. Not her face. Though Ananda held the dress close, she saw that with every passing moment he stole more of her skin.

When he stepped back through the door, she slipped on the clothes and searched in vain for a pocket. By the time Desana marched them to a dormitory, the coin dripped with the sweat of her palm.

"Pray," the woman ordered before locking the heavy wooden door and hurrying away.

The dorm had been cored out of the wide hillside, like the other residences, but the inside of the front wall was reinforced with mortared stone that Ananda noticed only now. To the right of the door a window leaded together from more broken glass faced the distant fields. Outside, thick metal shutters hung on chains. They looked like they could be dropped and locked in seconds.

Jigsaw shadows from the late afternoon sun spread across the wood floor; but after the dim and frightening hut, the dorm felt like a bright and private reprieve to Ananda.

Then her eyes adjusted to the play of light and shadow, and she started at the sight of five girls sitting on crude bunks toward the back of the long, narrow room. One of them was the young woman who'd bathed her.

"It's time for prayer circle," she said. "Come back here. It's cooler."

Ananda didn't move. Neither did the girls beside her. The sun beat on their backs.

"We don't bite. Promise." The young woman might have smiled; Ananda couldn't be sure at this remove.

"My name's Teresa." She stepped forward, lowering her

voice to a near whisper. "We're all in the same boat that you're in. We're your friends. Come on."

The air did feel a breath cooler back there. Ananda noticed the twins first. Identical. She'd heard of twins, but nothing could have prepared her for the mirror images of Mia and Kluani smiling at them. They both had long shiny brown braids and big brown eyes. Dressed identically, too, in white bonnets and soiled white dresses. All the girls were dressed alike. Only Teresa, several years older, and another girl about her age, had been spared a bonnet, which Ananda found hot and uncomfortable.

"We'd better get in our circle fast, before someone looks in," Teresa said.

They settled in the shadows, Imagi to Ananda's left, M-girl to her right. Teresa kneeled directly across from them, eyeing the windows and door every few seconds. Bella and Gilly huddled next to Kluani.

"Keep your head down, like you're praying," Teresa said.

"How do you pray?" Gilly asked.

"Just mumble along with us if *anyone* comes in. We'll teach you some prayers as we go, but right now keep your heads down. This is when we meet every day. Sometimes Desana stays and prays, but most of the time she doesn't, and we can talk."

"And try to plan an escape," Mia said firmly.

"That's the main reason we do this," Teresa said. "But first, what are your names? And are you okay? I mean, do you have any injuries, stuff like that?"

They introduced themselves. So did the other girls. The newcomers noted only Imagi's burns. Bella told them about the attack on their camp. Teresa said that she'd been taken from a cavern community in the old West Virginia, and that a different group of marauders had kidnapped the younger girls from a camp near the Gulf Coast. None of them knew if their parents or friends had survived the raids.

"Same with us," Ananda said, aching with the fear.

The smallest, frailest girl, with white blond hair and freckles on her arms and face, started to cry. Kluani took her hand.

"Cassie," Teresa said softly, "not now. We've got to tell them while we can."

Cassie quieted.

"This is *the* most important thing to know," Teresa said. "Eat as little as possible. They'll try to fatten you up so your period will start sooner. Then they'll make you marry one of the older men, and you'll have to have sex. Do you know what that means? Sex?"

The newcomers nodded.

"You'll die. Even if you feel like you're starving, eat just enough to keep going. It'll slow down your growth and delay your first period."

All the girls did look skinny, Ananda saw. Even thinner than the ones from her camp.

"Do they ever touch you before you have your period?" M-girl asked.

"Not that I've heard of. It's supposed to be a really big sin for them to do anything to a girl who hasn't had her period. But the *day* it happens, they make you get married and it starts."

"You must have had yours already," Ananda said. "How old are you?"

"Sixteen, and I have, but Desana put me on bath duty when I got here, and that makes me untouchable to them. See, the men are really scared of us. Don't ever forget that. They're scared that if we're not absolutely one hundred percent pure, then they could get Wicca from us. So they were probably worried about me because I was touching so many naked girls. It's the same for Bessie here." She nodded at the other young woman from the Quonset hut, who was kneeling to her left. "And now we really could be infected—by *them*. That's why they want you. Not that they care about us, but they're worried to death that if they have sex with Bessie or me, they really could get it."

The whole time Teresa talked, she kept glancing at the window and door.

"Are girls really blinded?" Ananda asked. All the girls looked up.

"Heads *down*," Teresa demanded. "Yes, they are blinded. It's horrible. They do it for disobedience—and that can mean *anything*. The ones who are blinded or hurt in other ways are kept in a separate dorm. You'll see them. It's really sad."

"What about you?" M-girl asked. "Talking like this."

Ananda had been thinking the same thing.

"No one's ever betrayed me," Teresa said, "but I know it could happen. I've put my faith in every girl who's ever come through that gate out there. Sometimes I had a feeling that I had to be extra careful, and I was, but I've tried to trust all the girls. This may sound weird but I think I've survived because the world needs someone—and it doesn't have to be me, just *someone*—who's memorized the names of every single girl who's ever been here. There was a girl before me who did it. She taught me before she got pregnant and disappeared. Another girl had taught her. There were dozens of girls going all the way back. We're the 'Keepers of the Names'—that's what we call ourselves. I know the names of all two hundred and ninety-seven who are gone. I practice remembering every day. Now I know yours.

"That's always the first thing we do—get the names. Memorize them. As long as we're alive and can keep passing on the names, the girls who are gone will never be forgotten. I keep hoping that someday the world's going to care and want to know who they were, and I'll be able to tell them. Or little Cassie will." She smiled at the frail girl who'd been crying. "She's memorizing them now. She wanted to. She's up to forty-seven. Mia and Kluani are doing it, too. Both of them are almost up to two hundred in only six weeks."

The twins nodded. Ananda could feel their pride, but her

thoughts returned quickly to the horror of what she'd heard: 297 girls had been dragged here, just like her, and then disappeared. It must have happened so many times to so many people in so many places, and most of them were forgotten. No names. No graves. No nothing.

It could happen to you.

When she looked back at Teresa, the young woman had teared-up and her voice was filled with feeling. "But it's not enough to remember. We've got to get out of here. We've got to stop them."

Most of them nodded, but no one said a word until Gilly, sounding clobbered by what she'd just heard, asked about the girls who were gone: "Where did they go?"

Teresa cleared her throat. "We don't know. Maybe some are still alive somewhere. They might have been sold as slaves. That's a rumor."

"What about the babies?" Ananda thought of what Mary had said.

"They keep the girl babies. Not the boys. They sell them. There are two little girls here now. We hardly ever see them. They don't want them exposed to any sickness. Four other babies have died since I've been here."

Infant mortality. Ananda recalled her dad saying it had been very high for decades. Like the Middle Ages.

"Do you know anything about Zekiel?" she asked.

"He's a mystery," Teresa said. "All we have are rumors. Lanina Scotia, who was still around when I got here, said she'd heard that Zekiel and Desana were once married and had kids. But I don't know if that's true. She said there was a painting in his bedroom that showed what it used to look like here, back when everything was green, and they had a rock pool with a waterfall and—"

"Here?" Ananda interrupted. "It's all dry and prickly out there."

"But you've seen the fields. They're green, and I guess that once everything you could see was green. But the water doesn't come out of the faucets like it used to. It trickles out now. Lanina, the girl who told me about the painting, said that she'd heard that if you look at the back of it, there's a picture of a much younger Zekiel and Desana with two kids. But we haven't been able to confirm that; any girl who's gotten near his bedroom was living with him and had his baby and disappeared."

"But Desana's a lot younger than he is," Ananda said. "She looks like she's my mother's age."

Teresa shrugged. "I haven't seen it. I don't know anyone who has. But he definitely likes young girls, so he might have been like that with her, too."

"Are his kids living here?" Ananda asked.

"Not the ones he had with Desana. At least not that I've ever heard of, and I think there would be rumors if they were."

"Why are all the men old?" M-girl asked.

"They're not all old. The guards are younger, but the older men make the younger guys leave if they don't need them. They take their weapons and push them out the gate. That really scares them. It's death out there if you're on your own, even if you're a guy. So they don't dare even hint at wanting a girl. The older men keep just enough of them around to protect the place. There's also a rumor that a lot of the guards are gay; and even though that's a huge sin here, we've heard that the older men like it that way. What they don't want is a bunch of competition for girls, especially from younger guys, because there aren't that many of us. The guards are supposed to be able to move up and become one of the 'elect.' That's what the men in robes are called. I've only seen one guard who actually did, though."

Teresa checked the door and window again. "We're going to run out of time here, so if you can hold your questions, I want to tell everyone that the boy with the dog cart whispered hello to me yesterday. That's huge," she said to the newcomers. "Even looking at us the wrong way can get them killed."

Ananda remembered the boy shrinking away from Zekiel.

"So there might be hope with him," Teresa continued. "He could bring us more weapons, but let him initiate contact."

"You have weapons?" Ananda said. "What do you—"

"Shush, 'Forgive us our trespasses . . .'"

What? Then Ananda heard the door opening. Desana entered and stared at the circle till they said "Amen."

"Follow me." She strode out the door.

Dinner, Teresa mouthed to the new girls.

They ate in a free-standing stone building. The food proved a powerful temptation—roast meat and vegetables seasoned with the most delicious herbs and spices Ananda had ever tasted. Dessert, too: dried berries in a sweet sauce. But she forced herself to eat the minimum with a hand-carved wooden spoon, while her free hand still clutched the gold coin.

Zekiel offered a blessing at the end of the meal, as he had at the beginning. Then he directed Mary to lead the "brides-to-be" to the church. The pregnant girl ushered them to the bench closest to a slate pulpit, which rose several feet above the stone floor. As they sat, Ananda brushed Mary's hand with her own. They exchanged a glance, and—*finally*—the gold coin.

"No one's to know," Mary whispered as she leaned forward to adjust her hem. "I'll hide it. I'll let you know where."

Ananda bent to pick at a spot on her dress. With her face also hidden, she thanked her.

Zekiel stepped up to the pulpit and watched the church fill. To his right sat nine girls in bonnets. Behind them, Desana and five young women, including Teresa and Bessie from the Quonset hut, knelt with their bare heads bowed. To his left, more than fifty men in hooded white gowns crowded the benches. They looked older than Ananda's father; some, like Zekiel, appeared much older. Only the guards wore dark clothing—rough-hewn pants and shirts—and they sat in the back.

When Zekiel raised his hands, everyone stood but Imagi. Ananda tried to get her to join them but she wouldn't budge.

"Let us pray to our Lord and Savior."

The church resounded with a prayer that meant nothing to the newcomers.

"In the name of our Lord, we welcome five pure girls to our church. Face your future husbands."

His eyes traveled from Ananda down to Gilly. Not one of them turned to the men. A hand gripped Ananda's shoulder.

"Face them," Desana said.

Ananda edged around and saw the men staring at them.

"We await the glory of your womanhood, which we will honor faithfully. You will be treated with great kindness. In return, you must obey. Sit."

Once they settled, Zekiel lifted his arms, as if to hold a big ball over his head, or maybe the world itself because after the briefest pause he said, "The Lord in His wisdom gave man dominion over the earth and all its creatures. You will be obedient to us as we are obedient to the word of God. We all have a place in His plan. I no less than you."

Imagi laughed, a sound so frightening in the strict reverence of the church that Ananda grabbed her arm and said, "No."

But Imagi's free hand pointed to Zekiel, and a smile filled her broad face. She shrugged off Ananda, stood, and lifted both arms like him. That's what had made her laugh, Ananda saw. Imagi looked ridiculous, and by extension so did he.

Zekiel dropped his arms at once, as if he realized this. "Remove her. She defiles the house of the Lord."

"She doesn't know any better," Ananda said.

"Silence." He thrust a finger toward her. "Or you won't be spared."

Two of the darkly clad guards seized Imagi, who grew crazed with fear and struggled to break free.

"Please don't," moaned Ananda.

"She is among the cursed," Zekiel thundered, "and they defy the Lord to serve their master."

"No, that's not true. She doesn't understand any of this."

He stepped swiftly from the pulpit. The guards were dragging Imagi out the door. The girl's cries could be heard after it closed.

Ananda looked up and saw Zekiel's beard quivering, as it had by the fields when he'd spoken of infidels. He signaled over two more guards. "Take this one to the laundry."

Ananda shot a panicked glance at Teresa, whose eyes never moved from her folded hands.

They hurried her through the darkness to a stone building. It looked like the woodsman's hut that her mother had drawn for an old tale she'd told them. Lye's sharp, oily odor clawed her nostrils as they forced her inside. One of the guards lit a candle, and she saw soiled garments piled by two large iron vats. A smaller stainless steel one glimmered in the soft light. The guards blocked the doorway. They said nothing and avoided her eyes, which felt far more frightening than the stares of the men in the church.

Zekiel stormed in fifteen minutes later. "Sit her down."

The guards pushed her onto a three-legged stool.

Zekiel handed her a small round mirror. "Have you ever seen yourself? Look now while you still can."

The reflection shocked her, and in that first moment she found it hard to accept that it was she who stared back. She'd once caught a glimpse of her face in a pan of water, but nothing so clear as this. It was like looking at her mother and sister, but as one person. Pretty like them, yet she had never thought of herself as pretty. Her eyes were such a bright blue that she might have been seeing the color for the first time. That she should possess blue in such brilliant abundance astonished her.

Her attention skipped to the light freckles on the bridge of her nose. Just like the ones Cassie had on her arms. No one had ever mentioned them, and here they were all but jumping out at her. She decided that she liked her freckles. She liked her nose. Her hair, too, the way it framed her face with dark waves. Clean and combed, it looked finer than any fabric she'd ever known.

Her hand rose to explore her features, and she saw that her fingers were lighter, scrubbed clean for the first time. She blinked and caught her own eye, looking into them the way she'd looked into the eyes of others, searching for herself as she'd searched for them. Remembering the glance that the dog cart boy had given her before Zekiel made him cower.

The Army of God's leader stared at her as she pushed her hair behind her ears and studied her forehead. It was smooth. That's what struck her most. Her mom's had lines. And Bliss frowned so much, which wrinkled her face. But Ananda saw that her own skin was like the porcelain her mother had once described.

She ran her fingers over her lips, so full and soft and surprising. She'd never thought of them as soft. She wasn't sure she'd ever thought of them at all.

"Beauty is a great gift of the Lord, but He aims for me to take it from you."

She heard Zekiel but the grievous meaning of his words could not penetrate the mirror's hypnotic hold. He pulled it away and ordered the guards to drag her to the stainless steel vat. It brimmed with a harsh-smelling liquid. The caustic fumes stung her eyes and made them water.

They forced her face within inches of the surface before he raised his hand. The fumes scorched her nose and lungs. She coughed and gagged convulsively. He bellowed "Holy Father" three times, and the hand that had risen fell to the back of her head, pressing down so hard that she had to struggle torturously to try to save her face. Her life.

"I baptize this girl with the righteous power of pain. I save her from the evil vanity of earthly beauty that would keep her heavenly gift from You. And Lord," his voice dropped till it could scarcely be heard above her hemorrhaging fear, "I bless her with the blinding vision of eternal belief. I do all this in the name of Jesus Christ, our Lord and Savior."

He jerked Ananda up by her hair. "We *can* blind you. We can burn you inside out in the name of the Lord. We can turn everything you've just seen into a nightmare." He yanked her so close that his beard mashed her cheek, and when he spoke next his hot breath coated her ear and prickled her neck. "Don't make me do that to you. Don't make me do it to the cursed one."

That evening, Zekiel had them gathered outside the church, where he proclaimed what their immediate futures would be.

Ananda would live under his roof with Mary, *not* with M-girl, Bella, Gilly, and Imagi in the dormitory with the others awaiting menarche. But they would all pray nightly for the blessed blood, and when it stained their garments, they would give of themselves immediately to the men to whom they'd been promised.

Teresa's words borne out bitterly. Zekiel spoke with one hand on Mary's shoulder, the other on Ananda's. Desana stared at them blankly. M-girl looked at Ananda, too, crying silently. Ananda tried mightily with her eyes to tell M-girl that Zekiel's plan would not hold. That if she slept in his bed he would never awaken, and that in the days, weeks, or months leading to that moment she would find a way to free them. *The other girls are already working on it, she wanted to remind her.* But she couldn't say any of this to M-girl. Not here. She could use only the intensity of her gaze to try to console her friend.

Zekiel, still touching Mary and Ananda, took them to his home. Like the others, it had been dug out of the side of the hill, but his stood closest to the grotto with the cross. He called the grotto a "shrine."

It smells, thought Ananda, shivering at the memory of the truck and the skells who'd blown it apart.

On that first night, Zekiel told her that she must nurse a rag doll. He said that praying for a baby with her breasts "unveiled" would hasten her womanhood.

When she appeared befuddled, he commanded Mary to open her dress. Mary's eyes once more turned to pebbles as she placed a doll's face against her pale nipple. Ananda tried to turn away. Zekiel reminded her of the vat and the fate of the "cursed one."

Ananda picked up the doll he'd given her and held it to her gown.

When it was time for bed, he gave her a thin mat and told her to sleep outside his bedroom next to Desana. *Like a dog.* He held the door open for Mary.

On the second night, Mary's water broke. Within an hour Ananda heard screams more piercing than the agony unleashed by the massacre. Mary's shrieks cleaved the night, never ceasing. Twice she shouted "Sacred Heart," her only audible words.

Zekiel ordered Desana to quiet her. "My baby must have a peaceful birth."

Nothing could quiet Mary's pain, though Desana tried. Ananda hated her even more. Almost as much as she despised Zekiel.

Five times Desana dispatched Ananda to the laundry for rags to soak up the blood. When she raced back at daybreak with the last armful, Mary lay torn apart by the birth. Dead.

A baby cried. Desana stepped aside, and Zekiel opened the infant's blood-streaked legs. Ananda saw him smile for the first time. He raised his arms, and his hands turned to fists that shook high above his head.

"Praise be to the Lord. A daughter is born."

Ananda searched for Mary's belongings on the night before her funeral. Zekiel and Desana had left to prepare the service. Ananda found only the girl's rag doll.

She stared at the door to Zekiel's private quarters, waiting a full minute before testing the handle. As soon as she entered, she saw the painting of the compound. It showed that all the land had been green. And that there had been a rock pool with a waterfall, just as Teresa had heard. She wanted dearly to go over and turn it around to see if there really was a portrait of Zekiel and his family, but she couldn't spare a single second: finding the book—the *coin*—was far more critical.

The book lay under his pillow, but the Krugerrand was missing. Unable to turn away, she began to read the last of the letters. As she quickly turned a second page, the door creaked. Zekiel stared at her. She denied her literacy, closing the book clumsily.

"You are a liar in the presence of the Lord."

The next morning Zekiel stood at the pulpit with Mary's body wrapped in rags below him, and said that only God's intervention had saved baby Rebecca. "By vanquishing the witch Sylvan, we saved the life of that precious child. Praise be to the Father."

The men and most of the girls echoed his last words. Imagi was missing from the church.

Ananda dropped her gaze to Mary's body. She could still recall her screams. When she looked back up, Zekiel's beard was quivering, and she wondered why.

"But we have not vanquished evil. Evil is always among us. Our vigilance must be unbending, our will as strong as Abraham's on Mount Moriah, willing to sacrifice a beloved son to the Lord." He nodded solemnly. "God's blessings do not come easily. They do not come without great cost. Surely, *we* know that. And now more than ever *we* must be pure. *We* must be vigilant because," his voice rose to a shout, "a witch has come."

The men swung their heads to the girls seated across the center aisle. Zekiel leaned over the front of the pulpit, his voice a whisper in the awed silence:

"Yes, the Lord spoke to me in the night. A witch has

come to spread defilement and profanity. A witch has come to weaken our God anointed will." His eyes narrowed to Ananda. "A witch has come but she could never defy the Lord's most sacred fire by taking little Rebecca." It was like he was speaking only to her, his breath hot on her skin again. "Instead, she stole the life of the blessed Mary." He shook his head as if the sorrow of the world were his alone forevermore. "A witch has come, and her dark soul must *burn*."

Chapter Fourteen

African Drought, Warfare, Bring Final Collapse, Un-
told Dead
Chinese murdered en masse at leased farms in Sudan
UN African conflict report

Top Pentagon Command Killed in Coup
Army divided, president hunted
Stars and Stripes

The howl didn't sound human.

Jessie ducked behind the marooned cargo carrier, peering from under the rear door, which hung open and cast a sharp, oblong shadow on the riverbed. Coxwell mirrored her movements. Both had their weapons ready, but neither aimed them; the source of the eerie wail was too hard to pinpoint. It came at them from everywhere at once, like an excitement of ghosts. Even in this heat her skin felt chilly, clammy.

Twenty feet behind her, Bliss and Hannah crouched on the sand, exposed as the scattered river rocks. When Jessie raised her hand to move them, Coxwell whispered, "Not a word."

The howl remained as unearthly as ever. Jessie waited for the creature to take a breath.

Hansel bellied toward them on three legs. She remembered when Eden trained their dog to do that. "G.I. Bowser," they used to joke. Nothing funny now. Least of all her agonizing over Eden.

The howl stopped, drawing her eyes to the nearest riverbank. It perched about eighty feet away in the fractured shade of dense, dead trees. She scanned the shadows, spotting a skell who stared into the distance, a flap of skin hanging from his incinerated chest. If her basic knowledge of medicine meant anything, he'd die soon.

"You see that?" Coxwell nudged her with his stump. She forced aside thoughts of his maggots—and the ones feasting on her own infected wound.

"You mean him?"

"The other ones. Right below him."

Her sight dipped to a dozen or more dead skells who were piled at the bottom of the bank. They looked like they'd been gunned down. Drag marks in the sand led to where they'd fallen.

The air shifted and an odor assaulted them so furiously it was impossible for Jessie to believe that only seconds ago they'd breathed easily. Coxwell covered his nose with the crook of his elbow, and Jessie's hand rose to her face. She smelled the cougar meat she'd eaten, but cooked animal couldn't compete with the rotting remains of dead humans.

"I want him alive," Coxwell muttered.

"You think he can talk?"

"I think he can tell us something about this." He indicated the bombed truck with a sweep of his stump. "Like where they get supplies for this kind of action. I want whatever they got."

He waved up Jaya, the smooth-faced boy whom Bliss had eyed, and Brindle. In the absence of the howl, their footsteps sounded loud in the sand. Bliss followed them to the truck seconds later.

Coxwell took Jaya and Brindle on a dash to the bank, which still left them a good sprint from the skell, who continued to stare vacantly into the distance. He appeared as insensate as the corpses below him until he raised a can and poured liquid on the bodies. Then he struck a flint. That'll never catch, Jessie thought, he's too far above them. But one of the sparks ignited, either from the fumes or from the methane of rotting flesh.

Flames spat high enough to shroud her view of his legs with streaks of red and yellow and blue, vivid in the blackened tableau of death. The harsh crackle of burning skin turned her away, but not before Jaya and Brindle tackled him.

Coxwell crouched near the fracas with his eyes on the woods, then signaled the rest of his men with his stump. Jessie watched a cinder shoot from the shadowy pyre into the sunlight. It grayed as she and Bliss ran forward, hoping to escape the wretched stink.

Flick, of the gullied face and iron grip, took the prisoner's arm. The man did not resist. He offered no gestures. Neither did he speak. He moved with the stony indifference of death as they hiked up a path littered with the snapped limbs of the brittle trees. Jessie wondered if he'd planned to throw himself on the flames.

The village appeared before them as a grid, made all the more apparent by the absence of houses, people, or vegetation of any kind. Only the pencil dark lines of streets remained, along with a handful of burned-out cars and the baked foundations of homes and businesses.

A sepulchral hush exposed their every step. In less than ten minutes they came upon the ruins of a blown-up gas station at the center of the town. The blast had excavated most of the corner and part of the intersection, leaving a crater as large and deep as a basement. A warren of pipes and the twisted wreckage of two metal tanks lay exposed. The bodies and limbs of skells littered the mangled ground. A headless torso had rolled to the very bottom of the pit.

Coxwell, speaking quietly, ordered his men to search the other burned-out stations at the intersection. "Then spread out and go through everything."

"What are we looking for?" one of his men asked him.

"Gas. Flints. Anything of use."

What Bliss and Jaya found a half hour later astonished Jessie, who didn't think the world could shock her anymore.

Bliss hurried after Jaya as he headed toward the foundations of the larger homes that had once overlooked the disappearing shoreline. He welcomed her with a smile. She was thrilled, toting her shotgun with a robust pride that she hadn't known before, as if it alone entitled her to the camaraderie of such a handsome, beardless boy.

Her exuberance made her reckless, and perhaps he felt the same giddiness. Two teens showing off for each other. A mating ritual with guns and knives and an unseen madness. As they scampered to the foundation of the first house, they certainly didn't see any of the signs that lay at their feet: footprints in the dust; a shank of filthy, wiry hair; crumbs of food crusted by the sun. Hints of humans where they'd want to see them least. Their eyes danced elsewhere—on an arm, neck, face—skipping away shyly when caught.

They didn't hear the chains rattle.

The stairs had been burned away, so they jumped into the concrete basement. Again they moved without pause. Jaunty. If they'd surveyed the perimeter, they would have seen that the foundation had been poured with three rooms; one encompassed half the cellar, the other two divided the remaining space evenly. Had they walked around the entire foundation, a simple glimpse would have exposed the danger hiding below. If they'd so much as spoken, they would have given themselves away. And that would have been good. Instead, muteness turned against them as they inched toward a doorway just to their left. The door itself had been burned away like the stairs, but one of the hinges still hung with a screw dangling from a hole in the plate.

For reasons they never did understand—they might have been showing off—they both darted toward the opening at the same time. They banged into each other, gasping loudly and spilling apart as a firebomb flew from the shadows and exploded between them.

Bliss rolled away instinctively, her clothing singed and smoking. She smacked at it and rose with her shotgun aimed at the entrance, spying Jaya slapping down sparks that were eating the ends of his cutoff pants. The wide space between them was ablaze, but the flames died quickly with so little to consume.

"Jesus fuck," Jaya shouted, staring at her with an intensity she'd rarely seen in anyone.

"You're not skells?" a cracked voice called out.

"Who the hell are you?" Bliss shouted.

"My name's Augustus. Don't kill me. Please. I didn't know."

"Get out of there. Slowly." Bliss was still shouting, but she heard her mother and the others hurrying toward them.

"I can't. I'm chained-up."

"Then we're coming in. Don't move or do a thing or you're dead!" she yelled.

"I won't. I promise. I won't move. I'm telling you, I didn't know." His husky voice cracked again.

Bliss dusted off a stinging ember and edged along the wall, shotgun clutched to her chest. She burst into the doorway with her weapon leveled. She did find a skell, but he wasn't the man who called himself Augustus. The skell lay at his feet and looked like he'd been burned to death. Maybe by Augustus. Then she saw that Augustus was black, too—not from burns but from birth. She'd never seen a black man. She'd heard of them. Her mother and father said they'd been among the first killed in the long ago. Blamed for the troubles. But so were many others, including her parents. The careful findings of scientists like them, built on the accumulated knowledge of hundreds of years of inquiry and experimentation, was jettisoned by raucous mobs that angrily denounced evolution, then climate change, before finally unleashing their guns and knives and clubs on the cool-headed core of reason itself.

Even though Augustus's skin was dark and the light dim, the two-inch cross burned into his chest was unmistakable. It had been placed right where a religious medal would have hung in an age when millions of chains had been made of gold. Before they'd been taken off—or savagely ripped away—for food and fuel.

He saw Bliss staring at the mark. "I'm a missionary."

Those startling words gave Jessie pause as she hung from the top of the foundation. She dropped to the hard floor, grimacing as she limped through tendrils of smoke to peer past Bliss. The black man looked about her age—early forties— with an odd puff of white hair sprouting from one ear. She could no more grasp his survival than his profession when she saw him chained to the dark, dungeonlike walls.

The dead skell, he told them, had collapsed the night before with the small bomb he'd just hurled at them.

"I'm sure he was coming to kill me." Augustus had to struggle to speak. "I thought you were, too."

"He says he's a missionary," Jessie said over her shoulder to Coxwell and his men. "He needs water."

Brindle handed him a canister.

"Thanks," he croaked.

"Let's get him out of those chains," Coxwell said to the bald-headed man with the ruthless eyes, who promptly unsheathed an axe hanging from his hip and approached Augustus. "But search him first, Maul. I don't care what he says he is."

Maul patted him down roughly. "Nothing," he announced.

"Don't move," Coxwell told Augustus. "Maul's going to chop those chains off. Might take a bit."

Augustus offered the one-armed man a toothy smile. "The Bible says patience is the fruit of the spirit."

Not for Coxwell, who bored right in: "How the hell did you end up here?"

"I was looking for a settlement, a camp of some kind that was supposed to be out in the lake."

Us? Who else? Jessie answered herself. First, marauders. Now missionaries? That's insane. And who's *he* told?

Augustus said that he'd traveled down the riverbed expecting it to end at the reservoir. "I thought I'd find the camp right nearby. That's when I saw a bunch of dead bodies and a blown-up truck, and then they grabbed me. At first I tried to tell them the good news about Jesus, but they were sniffing gas and wouldn't listen."

"You thought you were going to convert *skells*?" Coxwell's tone said it all.

"No, but once they had me I thought I'd try."

What Jessie couldn't figure was why the skells hadn't slaughtered him right away. She told him as much, and asked, "Any ideas?"

"Morbid curiosity?" Augustus ventured after gulping more water. "I've been putting up with it all my life: 'Hey, you a black man or you just well done?' Except I think these guys really did think I was ready for the roaster. I expected to see the head butcher any second."

Maul straightened and Augustus shook off the snapped chains. Both of them stepped over the dead skell and followed the others out the doorway.

"The bodies you saw, were they all skells?" Jessie asked. "Did you see any that looked different?"

"I saw two that had clothes. That was different."

"Just two?" Jessie pressed. "Men? Kids?"

"Grown men, I'd say. There might have been more, but like I say, they grabbed me right away."

"Where'd they get all the gas they were sniffing?" Coxwell asked.

"I don't know, but I could always smell it on them. Even their breath."

"How'd you hear about our camp?" Jessie jumped back in.

"One of the brothers back at the church said—"

"You have an actual church?" she interrupted.

"We're working on it."

"You ever hear of the Army of God?" she said in the same clipped voice.

He lifted his hand and three guns clicked. "No, wait." He dropped it quickly. "We have nothing to do with those people. We've heard they're doing terrible things in the name of the Lord."

"But you're not?" Jessie settled her M-16 by her side.

"You saw me. I was chained like a dog down here. Do I look like I'm out kidnapping little girls?"

"What else do you know about them?"

"Not much. I know I don't believe in them or their God or what they're doing. I know that all the brothers in our church think they're nothing but child molesters and murderers burning women alive."

"Burning them alive?" Jessie stared at him.

Augustus nodded at her slowly. "They're calling them witches. That's what we've been hearing from the traders."

Jessie looked at Hannah, who was standing behind her. Another of the nurse's grisly contentions might have been confirmed. But what horrified Jessie more was that the burning could be happening where Ananda had been taken.

"How close is your camp to the Army of God?" she asked Augustus.

"I've heard fifty miles. But it's not like we've ever been there."

"Fifty miles is pretty close, and they left you alone?" She made no attempt to hide her suspicion.

"They say we're 'repugnant.' That's the word they use."

"Who told the man in your church about our camp?" Jessie leaned forward.

"I don't know. I'm guessing a trader. They're the only ones passing through."

"Count your blessings."

"How come you're not sick?" Hannah asked warily.

"Only reason people aren't sick is they got out early and quit having relations. Or they're guys who got lucky. Black men, we've never been lucky, so you can figure that we got out while we could and never looked back. We're just waiting for it to end."

"Women? Kids?" Jessie asked.

"We've got fifteen families but they don't want our girls. Say we've got the 'curse of Cain,' so they left us alone. But folks like them, they never leave you alone for good. They're always seeing something you got."

"Can you shoot?" Jessie lifted her own weapon.

"I'm a man of the cloth. I—"

" 'To every thing there is a season, and a time to every—' "

" 'Purpose under the heaven,' " he finished for her. "Ecclesiastes, chapter three, verse one. Are you saying this is the season for murder?"

Look around you.

But she didn't reply. Not right away. She looked into his dark eyes knowing that he and his people didn't live on the Bible alone. No one did. No one *could*. You shoot. You kill. You survive. And blacks didn't go quietly in the long ago. They'd joined Latinos and whites in some of the fiercest resistance, holding Baltimore for eleven months against the flinty remnants of an army whose rapid decline had begun with the purging of all "questionable elements"—anyone who had attempted to defy the coup that overthrew a civilian government felled as much by drought, floods, famine, and a rapacious new virus called Wicca, as it was by guns, rockets, and tanks.

Within a year and a half the military split into factions,

giving rise to warlords and heavily armed gangs based on a strict racial code as old as the dying nation itself. White supremacists eventually bombed Baltimore to rubble, and the city's last defenders were either slaughtered outright or fled along the rotting shores of Chesapeake Bay, which had been swarming with jellyfish. "Cockroaches of the sea," a fellow biologist once called them.

"What about him?" Jessie pointed to the doorway. "That's quite a coincidence, him dropping dead just when he shows up with a firebomb."

"The Lord takes care of His own."

"The Lord helps those who help themselves," she countered.

"Yes, He does. He guides the living hand *and* the lost soul."

Given the grim evidence, she guessed that sometimes He also guided the living hand *to* the lost soul; but before she could respond, Augustus murmured something about the Army of God.

"What was that?" she asked.

"We've been talking about them."

She still had to strain to hear him. "What have you been saying?"

Augustus looked to the top of the foundation walls, as if he feared unseen ears. "That sooner or later they're coming. That we got to get ready for them. Maybe wait on the church and put up a higher wall or something."

"A wall won't do it," she said. "Trust me."

"A church won't, either," Coxwell said. "What about the skells? How many live ones did you see?"

"Eight or nine, but not for two days now."

"You got to think they're still around somewhere." Coxwell eyed his men. "Why's everyone down here? They could turn this into a barbecue pit in about two seconds." In the next instant three of them started climbing out, but Bliss stepped toward Augustus. "How'd you get all the way here?"

Good question, thought Jessie.

"I told you, I walked."

"You said you walked down the riverbed." Bliss moved closer. "You didn't say—"

"I walked all the way."

"No you didn't. I saw your feet when you were sitting. Show them."

Augustus hesitated.

"Do it," Coxwell ordered.

Augustus lifted his foot. They stared at his pinkish sole.

Bliss was right, Jessie saw at once. Not a scratch. You might get away unscathed on sand, but not on land.

"I had boots," he said.

"Where?" Bliss shot back.

"They took them."

"You had boots?" Jessie said. Who had boots these days? Almost as crazy as saying he'd ridden here on a horse. And they were extinct, eaten by the first wave of urban refugees.

"What the hell are you hiding?" Coxwell squared off with him. Jessie noticed his knife for the first time when his stump reached for the bone handle, phantom hand at work.

After staring at the blade for a moment, Augustus began to tell them how he'd traveled those hundreds of miles.

Without ever speaking, the skell captured on the riverbank led them to the foundation of a burned police station, where they found two half-filled gas cans stashed in a basement cell. When they refused him his reward, which Flick had panto-mimed with a sniff from a soiled rag, the skell collapsed and died. It proved such a quick and convenient demise that Coxwell grabbed his wrist and checked his pulse. But Jessie wasn't surprised by his death. With his vacant eyes and that flap of crispy skin dangling from his chest, he'd looked ter-minal at first glance. Only his deathly howl had shown any life, and that was the last sound he uttered.

Augustus led them up the river for the next three hours.

Maul trailed him closely. Jessie had strapped her crutch to her pack and walked with a noticeably less painful limp. They spotted numerous footprints crisscrossing the sand—such aimless wandering that she thought surely they'd find skells dead of thirst. They didn't.

As dusk approached, Augustus turned toward a short bank. Coxwell ordered him to stop and jammed a gun into his chest.

"I don't have to spell it out, do I? Us getting ambushed?"

Augustus stared at the barrel. "I wouldn't do that to you people."

Jessie believed him, but she also felt intensely alert as they trudged for another hour across mostly flat land to a railroad track. It would have been overgrown decades ago if anything but the sparsest weeds had managed to live here.

They followed the tracks for another two miles to a narrow, rock-walled pass. After coming round a bend, Augustus nodded to a handcar sitting on the tracks.

"You worked that all by yourself?" Coxwell asked.

He held out his thickly callused palms. "You don't grow these things by sitting around."

"How's it work?" Bliss asked.

Augustus pointed to a long iron bar with wide handles on both ends. The center rested on a brace with a pivot joint at the height of a man's belly. "You pump that thing up and down."

"All the way up hills?" Bliss peered at it quizzically.

"Railroad grades aren't steep, but yes I did." Augustus sounded pleased with himself.

"It's a b-b-big one," Brindle said.

Half the size of a freight car, if Jessie's memory proved correct. Plenty of space for all of them and then some. But fully exposed.

"How far do these tracks go?" Coxwell asked.

"Don't know. Way past Knox, I've heard. We have a place we stash it about five miles from our camp."

"You went through Knox on that thing?" Coxwell wiped his sweaty brow with the side of his stump.

"In the middle of the night and as fast as I could. The brothers have had it for twenty years, and I sure wasn't going to be the one coming back empty-handed. We never go near cities during the day, not that there's much left in them."

"How long do you think it'll take us to get there?" Jessie asked. Hannah leaned in for the answer.

"With teams of four working that thing, maybe a week."

Coxwell laughed. "If I didn't know better, I'd say 'praise Jesus.'"

"You saved my life so I'll say it for you." Augustus raised his eyes to the dimming slit of sky. The narrow pass echoed, *"Praise Jesus . . . praise Jesus . . . praise Jesus . . ."*

The fourth day out they passed an abandoned farm town, a single street meager with collapsed wooden buildings sapped by the sun. Only a lone wall stood, as if hanging on strings from the sky.

On the outskirts they rolled along a cemetery that had fared far better. No coffins dug up. No corpses plundered for jewels. No grass or vines choked the headstones. Death had been served well by the wasting of the land. Neat as the day they'd died, but for a sun-bleached skeleton huddled on the grave of a girl named Kelsey, BORN IN THE YEAR OF OUR LORD 2027. It reminded Jessie of an archeological dig that uncovered the bones of a mother embracing the bones of a child.

She turned when she heard Bliss and Jaya switching positions with Brindle and Stace, a smaller man in an animal skin hat with a broad brim. They alternated so each pair had a chance to look ahead as they worked the pivoting bar. Their shift would end when the sun burned directly overhead.

Coxwell settled beside Jessie at the front of the handcar, their feet dangling over the ever-receding rail bed. He asked if she'd had any more ideas about rescuing the girls.

"Just get there as fast as we can. There's no telling what they're doing to them."

"I've been thinking we'd be better off reconnoitering at the marauders' camp first, and then—"

"What?" Her disbelief burst above the handcar's constant creaking. "You want to take time to find *those* animals?"

"Hold on. Hear me out. Please."

She took a breath, forced a nod.

He went on: "If the Army of God's got marauders doing their dirty work, and they've got cars and guns and gas, they're going to be well-defended, just like that guy KK told you. But if we take down the marauders first, we can use their vehicles to attack the army."

"But then we'd be fighting two battles instead of one. Just look." She glanced back: not enough fighters, guns, and supplies to crowd the open platform. "We've got ten of us. That's all. I watched them kill one hundred twenty-one of my friends. I don't know if my husband's even alive. And that was just one group of them. I hate them but I'd rather die trying to save my daughter."

"But didn't KK say they're not all there at the same time? Don't they take breaks after a raid?"

She nodded again, no more easily than when he'd asked her to hear him out.

"So we'd be coming on a smaller force than we would at the Army of God. And we'd be surprising *them*."

"But even if we kill the marauders without losing all our people, that's going to take time. Those girls don't have time."

"It could be faster in the long run, and a lot better than trying to attack the army straight away. When they see armored cars driving up, they're going to think it's the marauders. They might open their gates, let down their guard. Especially if we show them more of what they want."

"Girls?"

"That's what I'm thinking."

"Are you saying you want to use my Bliss as *bait*?"

"Not just her." Coxwell gestured at Jaya. "The boy could pass. He's got no hair on his face, and what's there is so blond you can't hardly see it till you're next to him."

"Jesus, they're kids."

"They stole even younger ones."

Jessie couldn't fathom letting Bliss take the lead. Neither could she escape the distinct possibilities of his plan—or the blistering image of her daughter racing toward the man with the burned fingers when he was about to murder Eden. She'd pumped her shotgun and started shooting while all the adults sat rigid with fear. Bliss, she realized, had already taken the lead, and it brought them here, to what she hoped was the final trail to Ananda. To all the girls.

The memory of Bliss sparking their courage—and the meaning it held for what she could do now—made Jessie turn away and weep quietly. *Is this why you raised her? To fight battles? To be bait?* She wiped her tears and let her eyes settle on her firstborn, arms straining in the sun, and asked herself the harrowing question that had haunted her since the abduction. *How much are you willing to risk to save Ananda?*

The answer remained as clear and agonizing as ever: everything. She'd risk her own life, Bliss's, and the lives of all these people. It was her one and only creed:

You claim your own.

Chapter Fifteen

Pakistan, India Launch Nukes
Seven cities destroyed
From refugee accounts

unrise poured into the cell, and Levon's broad shadow fell on Ananda. She heard Imagi stir behind her, but dared not turn her back on the guard. Ananda's damp bottom had awakened her hours earlier, and in a heartsick second she knew that her first period had arrived. Now, as Levon ordered her outside, she also knew that her white gown—however soiled with dirt and sweat—would show the stain.

She rose, glancing over her shoulder at Imagi, who stared openly at her backside. Ananda slipped her hand past her hip and tried to wave off the girl's brazen interest.

Still, Imagi stared.

Ananda then spoke forcefully, "Good-bye. I'll see you later," attempting to will away the girl's astonished eyes.

No use.

Ananda hurried to Levon. He gripped her arm and led her out, reaching behind her to close the door. If he looked, he'd see. He'd stolen other glances.

Don't, don't, don't, she chanted to herself as he fastened the lock. She waited to hear him gasp with discovery or spin her around.

Her breath slowly resumed as they walked from the cell, which had been built into the side of the hill hundreds of feet from the habitats. She'd been locked-up at night—and under guard by Levon during the day—since Zekiel stared at her from the pulpit and proclaimed that a new witch had caused Mary's gruesome death from childbirth, threatening words that left Ananda feeling watched from every remove, as if each step that she took were a test.

There had been no more "prayer" circles with the girls—no communication with them at all. Just working in the laundry, going to church and Zekiel's house, and sleeping in the cell, where she and Imagi had been banished. It was lined with rock, and contained but a single reeking hole for their needs. Nothing to lie on. No covers to protect them from spiders and the unseen creatures making strange scratching sounds. Nothing but dirt and stone.

Yet they expected her to be clean when she washed the clothes. Every day she spent the first few minutes in the laundry hut scrubbing her face, hands, arms. This morning she'd have to attend to a more pressing task—provided no one noticed the stain as she made her way across the compound.

Levon led her within ten yards of the girls already working the fields that framed the Sacred Heart of Evil. Over the past few days, a circle of wood had risen around the stake. She'd seen the robed men spread tinder before adding small branches, bigger ones, and split logs until the deadly ring grew almost four feet high. More wood had been stacked to the side. Zekiel's threat becoming ever more real. It was as if she were on trial, and at any moment the Army of God's leader could pronounce her guilty and burn her to death. Levon had provided few clues to her fate. The only words he'd spoken came yesterday as they passed the stake: "Witches spark when they burn. They do. It's the evil exploding."

Mia looked up, and must have seen the stain: her eyes
squeezed shut in obvious anguish. Her twin, Kluani, noticed, too. So did Gilly and little Cassie, who always looked
about to cry. But none of them jolted or gave her away, and in
seconds their bonneted heads once more hung over the soil,
mulched to retain precious moisture.

The older men were never out this early. She imagined
them sleeping on mats as thick as Zekiel's. Each night, she
had to share his private table in the dining hall. She'd pick at
her meal, feigning fullness when she craved food most of all.

"Your stomachs have shrunk," he said when she first ate
with him. "All of you. You *must* eat as much as you can."

Even with his thunderous words from the pulpit still
stoking her fears, he groomed her to be his bride, as if
she might yet survive her trial—and condemn herself to
the filthy hazing of his marital bed. She sickened at the
thought of his touch, as she did when she "nursed" the rag
doll. Last night in his house he'd told her to uncover her
breasts so he could make sure she was "cuddling" it cor-
rectly. She inched down her gown, shattering with fright
over his restless eyes, and the terror that if she didn't obey
him he'd burn her or Imagi; he'd linked their existence
when he forced her face over the vat and said, "Don't make
me do that to the cursed one." After she bared herself and
cradled the doll, he adjusted the stitched mouth of the
floppy creature with his long, bony fingers. Never touching
her, not directly; but she'd felt the pressure of his hands and
heard his breath quicken.

Now, she neared the laundry hut. In another minute, two
at the most, she might be able to get out of this gown. The
stain brushed against her. She looked around. No one close
enough to see. Yesterday, right about here, she'd spotted
the boy with the dog cart. He snuck her a smile when her
guard wasn't looking, and she replied with a fleeting one of
her own, wondering again if he'd do anything to help them
escape. But he wasn't in sight today, and she was glad be-

cause the stain could draw his attention and alert Levon.

The stain did make her grateful for the first time that she worked in the laundry. Till now her duties mostly reminded her of Zekiel's threats to her eyes and life and skin.

The hut door flew open. The Army of God leader strode toward them. Levon stopped, stiffening like her. The stain felt as large and bright as the sun rising behind Zekiel's head.

He stared at her. She thought his beard quivered but she couldn't be sure because the backlighting blinded her to his features.

"She will sleep in my bed tonight," he said to the guard.

Does he know? He can't, she told herself, struggling to swallow her panic.

"Bring her to me an hour earlier." Zekiel swept past them.

Light-headed with apprehension, she took several unsteady steps before looking back at him. Zekiel had stopped to stare. Her stomach seized up. But he said nothing, and she hoped that the sun had also blinded him.

Levon held the door to the laundry. Still reeling, she turned toward him, edged past his intense gaze and closed him out. This was what they'd done each morning, and he did not resist their routine.

Sharp fumes stung her nose and eyes. She rushed to open the leaded glass window, and took a breath of fresh air. The hut offered a broad view of the compound , including most of the massive front gate; but the window would also make her most urgent plans far more perilous.

She hurried to a mound of dirty laundry, searching for a gown that looked like it would fit. This wasn't difficult; they weren't closely sized. With another glance at the door and the window, she pulled off hers and added it to the pile. She chanced a quick look at herself and discovered a brownish red streak on her upper thigh. It looked like she'd been wounded. For so long she'd anticipated her first period. Now it made her feel exposed, threatened.

She pulled on the gown she'd found. It smelled of sweat

but it wasn't stained. She'd try to figure out how to deal with her period later. At least she was covered. *Just don't sit.*

The door handle sounded and she knew that her silent, dreary coworker had arrived. Ananda braced herself against a worktable, and saw that her gown had landed on the dirty laundry with an inch of exposed stain. It looked moist, even from a distance. The girl, who'd never said so much as her name, was already stepping past Levon. She did not sleep in the dorm, and she hadn't been blinded. To Ananda, that made her suspect. At the only dinner she'd eaten with the other girls, Teresa warned the newcomers that she might be an informant, told them to watch their step around her.

The girl closed the door and walked by Ananda without so much as a glance or any kind of greeting. She'd done this every day. Like most of the other girls, she was lean with black hair.

The gowns were divided into men's and women's. *Go to the men's,* Ananda pleaded silently. *The men's.* But of course the girl didn't; Ananda didn't want to touch the men's filthy clothes, and apparently neither did the girl—they were always the last to be washed.

She picked up Ananda's gown and slowly unfurled the bunched-up fabric. The stain seemed to swell in her hands.

"Please don't say anything. Please." Ananda peered at the door, still closed; and at the window, still empty. She rushed to the girl. "If you say anything, I could die."

The girl looked directly at her for the first time. Her eyes appeared dark as her hair, and empty, as if they couldn't feel or reflect life in any form. Icy. She grabbed Ananda's hand and jerked her toward the vat where Zekiel had threatened to burn her "inside out."

"No, don't, don't," Ananda pleaded. "Why are you doing this?" she whispered feverishly.

The girl didn't respond. And she was terribly strong.

"Please," Ananda begged.

The girl dropped the gown into the caustic liquid, which

began to leach the stain from the fabric. The blood bloomed, strangely beautiful in the soft light.

Still holding Ananda's hand, she led her to a closed cabinet, withdrawing a clean, neatly folded cloth.

"I don't know how to do it," Ananda said, stricken by the horrors to follow: marriage, sex. Wicca. "How do they stay up?"

The girl winced, as if the question pained her more than she could ever say. She glanced at the window, then lifted her hem to reveal the first of her agonizing secrets: a cloth bound her sex. She showed Ananda the loops and knots, then flicked her wrist in a hurry-hurry motion.

Imagi was crouched in the corner when the cell door opened a second time. A guard left a cup of water and a bowl of bone broth. Pieces of hard cracker floated among shiny ovals of fat. Though thirsty, Imagi did not move till he locked the door.

As she reached for the cup, the door burst open again, Zekiel staring in at her. She cried aloud and scurried away, backing into the wall.

He stepped closer until he stood over her huddled body. Reaching down, he held her face. She pinned her chin to her chest, refusing to look up.

He backed away, as sudden as he had been slow, and rushed from the cell.

The guard locked the door. Imagi uncurled and felt her way to the cup. She dipped a finger in and licked the drops. This is how she drank her water—lick by lick—until the hours passed seamlessly into the salty taste of her own skin.

After repeated scrubbing, soaking, rinsing, and wringing, Ananda's gown still held enough of the stain to make the silent girl shake her head. She looked up and shrugged. She might have smiled. Ananda couldn't be sure because she never opened her mouth.

The girl walked by the window. With only a slight movement she eyed Levon, who stood outside the door. Then she
carried the gown to the corner of the hut and pried up a
floorboard, quickly stuffing the garment into a shallow hole
that had been dug beneath it. She lowered the board, but not
before Ananda glimpsed another gown—maybe the girl's—
lying in the dirt.

"Thank you," Ananda said. "Thank you so—"

Three gunshots interrupted her. They sounded distant,
and drew their eyes to small puffs of smoke drifting from a
guard overlooking the front gate.

"Did you hear that?" Ananda turned an alarmed eye on
the girl. She didn't expect an answer, and looked back as
other guards up on the wall rushed toward the man who'd
fired his rifle.

"Uh puh-gum." The girl spoke at last.

Ananda turned to her. "What?"

"Uh puh-gum," she said again, eyes widening.

But Ananda saw only the stubby ruin of her tongue. Severed. Scarred. Straining painfully to form words. In the gut-
twisting silence, Ananda swallowed and said, "A pilgrim?"

"Yeh, puh-gum. Ay com."

"They come? Here?"

She nodded. "Ay i."

"They die?"

"Ay i."

"See that?" Anvil eased off the gas and jabbed his finger at the
body of a man lying about a hundred feet from the entrance to
the Army of God. "They must have shot another one."

Ellison peered through the slit in the windshield armor
and pulled his sawed-off shotgun from his holster, wrap-
ping his burned fingers around the trigger. Yeah, he saw him
all right, but you never knew if they were really dead till
the dogs had their say. If they didn't mind being eaten, you
could bet they were dead.

Anvil drove closer to the compound, giving Ellison a better look at the body. He snorted, shook his head. This sorry sack of shit had carried a big cross, like those could have curried favor with Zekiel, who didn't want anything but girls coming to his gate. Didn't even want to see him, especially when he'd come to collect his final payment and the bonus for bringing him five ripe ones. He figured that Zekiel would try to pawn off Miss Down Syndrome. Anvil was already slapping himself happy and calling her "Little Freak," but the others were grumbling.

With Zekiel, though, there was no telling; his taste had confounded Ellison in the past. Except he knew better than to bring him ethnics. He'd done that once. What a mess. Nope, Zeke wanted nothing but "pure Christian blood." White girls, basically. The Christian part could always come later, after he'd baptized them with his body.

Assuming all the girls checked out okay, he and his men would get their bonus. He wasn't too concerned because Hannah had known her stuff. He'd seen that right away. He just wished she hadn't gone and got herself killed. She would have been handy to have around if another hymen debate got ugly. That had happened last year, with that crazy broad Desana shouting "Look-look, you can see for yourself. It's broken." As if that meant a goddamn thing. Girls broke their hymens to save their asses. Everybody knew that. Everybody but goddamn Desana. Fuck it. He'd conceded that argument anyway. He'd done a lot in his day but he wasn't about to look.

The brakes screeched like they'd been knifed, and they stopped outside the shadow of the closed gate. Ellison stepped out, weapon lazy by his side, but visibly in hand. Armed men glared down as he walked over.

"It's me . . ." *You crazy cocksuckers.* "Open up."

They turned away. Nah, there was one still pointing his goddamn gun right at him. He hated this shit—baking in the sun so Zekiel could make his grand entrance.

Quelling his temper, he let his eyes drift back to the dead man.

"You want me to ram it?" Anvil asked in a low voice.

Ellison knew he was just venting. The van would accordion long before that gate would budge, although it sure would tear up the bottom of that cross.

Okay, here we go. The gate was swinging open, and there was Zekiel, master of ceremonies. *And what's* that*? Another runt for the puppy mill?*

"Baby Rebecca." Zekiel spoke like he was announcing the birth to the world.

Ellison forced himself to nod, but even with the guards once again glaring down at him, he couldn't congratulate the vicious old coot. "You got our pay? The bonus? My guys are waiting."

Zekiel raised his chin till all Ellison could see were the patriarch's cold eyes perched above his bushy beard. The baby fussed. Zekiel handed her to Desana, who stepped from the background, then turned his imperious gaze back on Ellison.

"She is a blessed event."

Say *something.* "She really does look like you."

Ellison wasn't lying. Even his own kid had looked like a geezer baby. But the wrinkles had disappeared in days, and he'd never again been able to imagine him old. And he never could have, not after Baltimore.

"She is among the most fortunate of her breed."

Ellison managed another nod and fell into step behind Zekiel, as he'd been instructed from the start.

"We need fuel," Ellison said to his back.

The Army of God leader waved in the vehicle without turning.

Ananda spied the van, the one they'd escaped in after the skells had blown up the truck. Seconds later she spotted Zekiel and Burned Fingers. Her hopes lifted and she turned to the girl who'd had to write her name for her, using suds on the planked table. *Callabra.*

"That's him," Ananda said, pointing. "The guy who gave me the birthday book."

"Oo ki-nah u?"

"Yeah, well, he and a bunch of others did, but maybe he's here to help . . ." Her voice trailed off. Whatever Burned Fingers was doing, he wasn't coming to help *her.* Who was she kidding? Not Callabra, who looked away.

Ananda watched the van crawl toward the grotto. The driver with the ginger hair climbed out by the tall metal cylinder. Two guards stepped from the grotto's shadowy entrance, pointing guns at him. Waves of heat radiated off the cylinder and the van's armor, and made the cross above the grotto look like it was shaking.

Like her.

Callabra put her arm around Ananda's shoulders and drew her away from the window. "Ay i oo."

"I wish," Ananda whispered. Burned Fingers. Zekiel. All of them. *Die.*

Ellison had been in the lord of the manor's digs on every visit, so without a word he surrendered his sawed-off shotgun to a scrawny guard stationed about fifty feet from the door.

As much as he could figure, Zekiel likened himself to a pasha, what with all the big fat pillows stuffed with God knew what, and a silver samovar filled with his disgusting root tea. He choked down a sip as Zekiel spouted off a fresh round of pronouncements about the state of the world, heaven, and everything in-between.

"They're all virgins, right?" Ellison interrupted.

Zekiel offered a dismayed look that Ellison figured was as practiced as his preaching. "Yes, they're virgins, but I thought you'd welcome an intelligent discussion after your time away. It's just the two of us. You may speak your mind."

Just the two of us? Ellison was tempted to do a lot more than speak his mind. But he knew better than to think that Zekiel would leave himself unguarded.

As for an "intelligent" discussion, the Abraham of the Apocalypse was *always* overestimating himself. But at times he tossed out interesting tidbits, mostly from traders. On his last visit, Zekiel told him that the Russians had taken full control of Europe. It marked the culmination of a long, clumsy invasion of extremely limited value, in Ellison's opinion, because most of the continent had frosted over after the death of the Gulf Stream. But climate collapse had turned a mercurial smile on Russia, thawing vast tracks of Siberian tundra into arable land. They'd mustered food and what passed for an army—the one-eyed man being king in the land of the blind. Lucky bastards. Too fucking cold in Europe. Too hot here. And the Russians had it just right, like they were goddamn Goldilocks with baby bear's bowl.

Of course, if they'd bothered with the frozen remains of NATO, they might just help themselves to the sizzling homeland of what had once been the world's greatest military power. They could sail right across the Arctic Ocean—nothing but clear water these days—and march south. While Ellison had no regard for the vodka-fueled, disease-riddled descendants of Stalin, Lenin, and Putin, he didn't see how the ravaged offspring of Washington, Lincoln, and Obama could mount much resistance, either.

"Go ahead." Ellison brushed aside a ratty-looking rag doll and propped his elbow on one of the suspiciously stuffed pillows.

"Or maybe you're eager to get going with your little bonus girl?"

Ellison thought Zekiel's smile would have sickened a psychopath. Having been called one himself on numerous occasions, he used the term advisedly. "No, not at all, and my men can wait. What I need are dogs. They got wiped out."

"I have wolf mixes coming. Traders from the North are bringing them."

"They hearing anything?"

"Yes, they are," Zekiel said portentously. Ellison waited him out. "They say there's farming in the Yukon and Nunavut." Zekiel paused again, this time to sip from his cup. Beads of brown tea hung from his stringy mustache. "Above the Arctic Circle."

"Thinking of moving?" Ellison betrayed none of his surprise.

"Leave this chosen place?" Zekiel shook his head as though this were heresy. "But I would like to know more about northern Canada and Alaska. What do you think it would take to get up there?"

"A tanker truck full of fuel. You're looking at a few thousand miles of baked prairie."

"It would be a long expedition." Zekiel suddenly sounded fanciful.

Christ, he thinks he's King Ferdinand and I'm fucking Columbus. "What's in it for me?"

"Gold. Glory. Gas." Zekiel smiled at the ring of his words.

"The glory's all played out. How much gold?"

"More than you'll ever see finding blessed girls."

"What's in it for you?"

"We always have to consider the future of our community of faith."

"So the ground water's running out?" *Cut to the chase, Zeke.*

Zekiel ignored the question, instead lifting the lid from a gray ceramic box, offering dates lined up like little maroon mummies. "I understand they're growing near the Bering Sea."

Their scent made Ellison falter. He saw Katherine and Cody and the confections that she'd cooked up for the boy. Madness had been rising all around them—the siege was months old, privation everywhere—and somehow she'd still made their son smile. Ellison stared at the dates, but could see only Baltimore. Rubble. And the remains of the worst crime that a wife and son could suffer.

"Go ahead, have one," Zekiel said.

A rich, sticky sweetness filled Ellison's mouth, and the flood of Katherine and Cody threatened to overwhelm his voice. "How did you ever get these?" No longer could he hide his amazement. Grateful now to hide only his surge of feelings.

"The Alliance sent a mission north. The Arctic is blooming."

"Why send me, if you already know?" He wanted Zekiel to admit that he couldn't trust people of his own faith. The Army of God Alliance had been ruthless enough to lure others north, or south or east or west—anywhere—so they could take over farms and fortresses. Zekiel had to be wondering if they'd do the same to him.

Zekiel brushed off Ellison's question with one of his own: "Are you interested?"

Ellison used his tongue to tease out a morsel of date from his lone molar, but he couldn't dislodge the memory of Cody huddled in a basement, chewing a sweet as rockets gutted buildings only blocks away. And then the fighting came to the door. He shrugged.

"They say it's dying up there," Zekiel said.

"What's dying?"

"Wicca."

"I don't believe it." But Ellison said that only for the pleasure of watching Zekiel's smile vanish.

The gaunt leader responded by placing the lid back over the dates. Ellison breathed easily for the first time in minutes. In fact, he'd heard much the same about Wicca from traders, though he still found it hard to believe that the planet's most frigid remove had become its final refuge.

* * *

Ananda's arm throbbed. Days of Levon's tireless grip had left a bruise, and now he'd held her tightly all the way to Zekiel's house—an hour earlier than usual, as ordered.

Desana waited outside the door, which bore a cross of stones hard as her face. "Go to your station." She turned from Levon. "You stay right here," she said no less harshly to Ananda before opening the door.

The girl's eyes followed her, flaring when she saw Burned Fingers backing into the hallway. He was gesturing to someone she couldn't see. He started toward her, like he was leaving. No expression. No recognition. But she grew hopeful—she couldn't help herself—and then she felt the fool. He'd given her a book when he could have slipped her a gun or knife. A *book*.

He brushed by Desana in the hall, catching the door as a girl screamed. Ananda jumped, then looked past him, stunned to see Anvil hauling Bella up off the floor. The marauder buried her skinny body in his thick arms and barreled past Desana and Burned Fingers, Bella shrieking and struggling.

Burned Fingers hurried out behind them and closed the door. Ananda hadn't moved. *Couldn't.* Bella's narrow face was twisted like a wrung rag.

"Help me," she cried, reaching for Ananda, who looked at Burned Fingers; his eyes were not to be snared. Ananda had never liked Bella, but the girl's screams made her quake; they could have been her own.

Anvil stopped charging away, grabbed Bella's throat and shook her head till her face reddened and her eyes bulged so violently that they looked like they'd burst from her skull. He raged in a muffled, murderous voice. She couldn't make out his words, but Bella's terror sounded bare as bone. "Help," she gurgled.

"Don't do that," Ananda mustered the courage to say to him. "Don't hurt—"

A scarred hand closed over her mouth. "Shut up. Don't say

a fucking word. There's *nothing* to be done. Could be you, and it's worse than this."

Burned Fingers released her with a smile—shocking in the immediate aftermath—and said, "How's the golden girl?" as if Bella weren't still shrieking piteously as Anvil dragged her down the path. "Read any good books lately?" he added with a quick laugh. Desana cracked the door and stared. Without waiting for a reply, Burned Fingers slapped Ananda on the back and walked away. The door closed, leaving her startled and alone and with nowhere to go.

Good books? Good God, like her mother use to say. That birthday book could have gotten her blinded; he must have known that. And she wasn't a "golden girl." Her hair was dark and her skin browned by the sun. He'd never called her golden girl the whole way here in that stinky van. Other names—some terrible—but never golden girl.

It didn't matter, not one bit. He was leaving, getting his gun back from a guard. Now he was turning around. For what? To wave good-bye?

He had put out his hand, but instead of waving he made a fist and flicked his thumb up, like her father when he'd once flipped a worthless old penny into the air. Even as she made sense of the gesture and thought of the Krugerrand, and how Burned Fingers must have known about it—why else, she suddenly realized, the thumb *and* the "golden girl"?—she remembered Mary's promise to tell her where she'd hide the coin. But Mary hadn't. The baby came, and all she'd done was scream. Her only audible words were "Sacred Heart," which had never made any sense. The Sacred Heart of Evil was that horrid stake, and it had scared Mary. It scared all the girls. Ananda had watched them walk past it with their eyes on the ground or looking up at the sky. But never at the stake. *No one ever looks there,* she reminded herself.

"No one ever looks there." Ananda's lips moved almost soundlessly, repeating herself as Mary had repeated "Sacred

Heart." As quiet as Mary's words had been agonized.

Then *that's* where you've got to search, she told herself, lips now still. Where no one else dares to look.

She doubted the Krugerrand had been found. The Army of God would never be quiet about it, Mary had warned. They'd think it was part of a bigger treasure, and would do anything to find it. *They'll beat you, burn you, blind you, anything they have—*

The door opened and Desana said, "Your lord is ready for you now." When Ananda didn't step right in, the woman grabbed her bruised arm.

Zekiel rose when he saw her. The first sign that tonight would be different.

The second came when Ananda noticed that the rag doll had disappeared from the pillow she'd been using.

The third sign came when Zekiel said that Desana was a wet nurse. "Do you know what that is?"

Ananda didn't.

"Watch." He settled on a wide pillow and patted the space beside him. Ananda followed his unspoken command. His odor assaulted her.

Desana picked up baby Rebecca from a bassinet of woven twigs. She sat before them and offered the swaddled newborn her breast, which she kept covered.

Zekiel said nothing while Rebecca suckled; but Ananda felt his eyes on her, and saw when he leaned close.

"You'll nurse baby Rebecca now." Ananda's skin rioted. "Pretty girls have a special way with babies."

Desana handed Rebecca to Ananda. The baby squalled over the loss of milk.

Zekiel shooed away the woman, and seconds later Ananda heard the door shut. They were alone. Rebecca lay on her lap, shaking her tiny arms and kicking her legs, still wailing.

"Drop your gown so she can have you." Zekiel's voice softened, became scarier, and she heard his breath quickening again.

"Can I do it like Desana?" She didn't want him to see her chest. Especially not with Rebecca.

"Take it off. I have to make sure you're not hurting my baby." His tone hardened, like he'd rip off her clothes.

She hurried to wriggle her arms out of her gown. If he ripped it off, he'd see the cloth tied around her waist. He might see it anyway, if the top fell too far. She bunched it up under her tiny breasts.

Zekiel cupped the back of Rebecca's head and guided her mouth to Ananda's nipple. The baby clamped on, sucking hungrily.

Ananda's breath came in suffering starts. The infant felt like an animal trying to eat her.

"Hold her. Show her love," Zekiel whispered in her ear.

Ananda stiffened even more and stared at the wooden floor.

Zekiel rubbed her back. "You're becoming a woman. Soon you'll be a Mary. That's what we call every girl who has my baby. It's the most sacred name of all."

Rebecca tore her mouth from Ananda's breast, screaming.

That night Ananda lay next to Zekiel for the first time. A candle burned beside them, and he studied her from inches away, then began to lift lengths of her dark hair, rubbing them between his fingers before letting them fall back to her gown. He did this over and over. Each time he scooped up another handful, his fingers brushed her neck. She shivered.

"Your womanhood is coming soon," he whispered. "Soon." He twirled her hair around his finger and tugged, jerking her closer to him.

Ananda froze. The next time he did it, her scalp burned even more but his effort had been stayed.

"Hair is so beautiful." He returned to rubbing it between his fingers. "It will cover the most sacred part of your body. Do you know that? The most sacred part?"

She felt like he'd touch her skin any second. His lips so

close, his breath so fast. "What's a sin?" she asked him. The words came to her without conscious thought, and only a moment later did she remember Teresa saying that the men believed that it was a really big sin to touch a girl before her period.

He rolled onto his back and stared at the ceiling. The candle sputtered and cast a shifting, circular shadow above them. Ananda remained rigid as the earthen walls that surrounded them. When his eyes closed, she dared nothing. Not till he snored did she try to sleep, but she woke constantly, in fear of him and her body's lush betrayal.

She watched him when morning began to light the room. His mouth hung open, and she saw the purple-gray craters of his missing teeth. His tongue looked pale and withered, pointy as a turtle's beak.

I could kill him, she thought with no emotion at all.

Without warning he stirred, then rose from the bed as she looked away.

"Get up," he said to her.

She complied. His eyes fell to her gown.

"Turn around." It was like he could sense her nerves.

She did it quickly, as if embarrassed.

"You're so modest," he said.

She beamed, not at his words but that he'd seen no blood. Or his eyes were yet too blurred by sleep to notice.

Still uneasy, she stepped aside for him; the courtesy kept her back turned away. Without acknowledging her, he continued to his toilet. No females, he'd told her, were permitted to use it.

When he claimed his privacy, she checked her gown. Relieved, she let it fall. But she couldn't escape the gummy memory of Rebecca at her breast, the nauseating gnawing of the baby's mouth.

She stayed exactly where he left her. Zekiel had ordered her to remain absolutely still whenever he stepped away. The painting of the compound, when the land had been green and water plentiful, hung no more than six feet from where she stood. She wanted to see the other side of it, find out if there was a picture of Zekiel and Desana and their children hidden against the wall. Find out if there had ever been a human side to him. To her.

She eyed the door to the toilet, straining to hear. Was he sitting? Standing? Peeing? About to walk out?

Don't do this.

She looked at the painting again.

Seconds—that's all it'll take.

Her heart thumped with her frightful decision; but he opened the door and stared at her, as if he knew.

Her breath stopped. She felt suspended in space. Her feet hadn't strayed. Only just barely.

At noon Levon told Ananda and Callabra to go with him to the church. He took Ananda's arm.

"That really hurts," she told him. "Could you hold it lower? Please."

His sharp blue eyes looked at her so intently that she feared a blow, but he lowered his grip and eased the pressure. She nodded her thanks.

Everyone had gathered outside under the tall red glass crucifix, as segregated by sex as they'd been behind the church doors. The other girls stood near her, including her closest friend, M-girl; but Ananda didn't risk so much as a glance or a whispered greeting.

Zekiel climbed three stone steps and gazed at them. "I have an announcement from God, a blessed sign of our special role in His plans. A girl has become a woman."

Ananda closed her eyes. The heat was oppressive, the glare impossible, and her fear of his next words felt boundless.

"Lorinda's womanhood came last night. Ezra has righteously consented to take her in marriage. I will join them in holy matrimony at sundown."

A man with long gray hair stepped across the narrow divide and took the hand of a girl half his height, who couldn't have been a quarter of his age. She squinted, perhaps shyly, at the assembled.

A hymn followed Zekiel's announcement. It left Ananda with unmovable grief.

Zekiel ordered them back to work. Ananda's sorrow turned dense as stone when she saw the betrothed couple walking away from the church. Ezra had to guide Lorinda down the dusty path. Lorinda hadn't been squinting. Lorinda had been blinded.

The wedding unfolded at the altar much as her mother had described the nuptials of old. Lorinda vowed to "love, honor, and obey" Ezra; and at the end of the ceremony, he held the girl's smooth cheeks and smothered her small mouth with lips hiding in the damp cavern of his bearded face. But Zekiel added a steely-eyed command that Ananda's mom had never mentioned: "Go now and consecrate your vows till the seeds give rise to the mighty blood of life."

His words—and the hungry look on Ezra's deeply lined face—sparked a scorching panic in Ananda. She'd be next. Zekiel would make her marry him. He'd kiss her. Touch her. Make her do things. She'd get Wicca. Or she'd die from childbirth, like Mary. Torn apart. The girl's screams plagued her. Zekiel might not even wait to marry her. He could grab her anytime. *Tonight.*

Find the gold, she told herself. *Buy your freedom.* Maybe the smiling dog cart boy would help. Teresa said he'd been friendly to her, too. And Mary said the Krugerrand was worth more than all the gold dust a trader could make in a year. Maybe even Levon would help. The guards were treated poorly; only one had become a member of the "elect." Yes, Levon, Ananda thought in rocketing desperation. *Find a way out.* Callabra had been hiding her period for four months, but she herself had fallen under Zekiel's zealous eye—she'd be lucky to hide hers for four more days. And if he found her out, he might cut off her tongue for lying. Or blind her. Burn her at the stake. Or hurt Imagi.

Behind the church, the robed men gathered round a table, talking and helping themselves to generous portions of berry juice and nut cake. Levon and about a dozen off-duty guards waited for their elders to eat their fill.

Farther back, the girls milled about in their indistinguishable white gowns and bonnets.

Teresa brushed by her, whispering, "You okay?"

"Yes," Ananda whispered back. What else could she say? There was no time.

She shifted her gaze to the hill that overlooked the fields and the Sacred Heart of Evil. On her other visits to the church, Levon hadn't returned to her side till they left the grounds. Tonight—*right now,* with the sweet distractions of cake and juice—might be her only chance to find the coin.

M-girl approached her, but Ananda's eyes warned her away. They knew each other so well that a look of alarm filled M-girl's face.

Ananda glanced at Levon one last time. His stare was fixed on the diminishing cake. Three of the robed men had stepped away from the table, and several guards were jockeying to take their place. Levon waited in back of them.

Don't be hasty. Look again. And so she did before drifting toward a stone outhouse. She even glanced over her shoulder; no one seemed to notice her leaving, and if anyone did, the privy would be a safe and predictable destination.

After slipping behind the reeking structure, and finding it empty, she hurried to a natural depression that ran straight as a spine up the side of the hill. She stripped off her bonnet and lay it aside so only her hair, dark as the evening shadows, might show as she hunched over and made her way.

In two minutes she'd scrambled to the top, drawing the attention of the bear, Bosco. He huffed. His cage, like the crowd she'd left behind, had begun to blend into the deepening dusk. The guards on the nearest wall paid the beast no mind, facing the world they'd sworn to turn away.

No longer visible from the church, she fled down toward the fields, running across a wide stretch of dried cheatgrass. Her heart beat crazily till she slowed near the Sacred Heart of Evil. Then she edged carefully past the precisely stacked wood. This was the first time she'd come so close to the tall iron stake. It gleamed as if it were alive in the early starlight. She stared, frightened.

Start looking, she urged herself. *Don't just stand there.* But where would Mary have hidden the Krugerrand, *if* she'd hidden it here? A hundred or more large stones formed a fire circle around the stake, every space between them ample for a gold coin. The wood might even be covering it now.

Sacred Heart. Sacred Heart.

The unnerving memory of Mary's screams drew her to the stake itself. *Of course, of course.* She touched the smooth iron with only her fingertips, as if it still burned with the flames that had killed Sylvan, the girl Desana accused of being a witch two months ago. The one Mary had been forced to watch burn.

Ananda searched as high as she could reach, but the pole proved as solid as it appeared. Now she ran her hands down it, watching them disappear into the black shadows of the wood. Crouching, she felt around the base blindly, recoiling from the chains she found. She forced herself to drag them aside, tensing at their grating sound. Then she dug around the stake, aghast to realize that she'd plunged her hands into Sylvan's ashy remains.

Growing less squeamish—and more mindful of time— she clawed at the crumbly dirt beneath the ash. A sharp pain made her jerk her hand away. It felt like she'd been stung, but it was only a splinter that had lodged under the nail of her middle finger. She pulled out the sliver by feel and went back to digging, packing her nails with dirt that would show if Desana or Zekiel or any of them looked at her closely.

Would Mary have buried it this deep? Already, the hole swallowed her hands. Then where? Where would she have put it?

In the pause, she heard the parched cheatgrass crackle, like it had been stepped on.

Who's out there?

She glanced up but could see little in the darkness. Worse, her hands had not found the coin.

Fill it in. They notice so much. They'll see the digging.

She pressed the dirt against the stake, pounding it down so it wouldn't look disturbed. The knuckle of her pinkie struck the edge of something hard. She pawed at a circular object lodged against the base.

In the thickening night she couldn't see it, but her fingers made out the engraving of a head on one side and an animal on the other. She scooped ashes back around the stake, smoothing them as death itself might have left them settled.

Thank you, she mouthed, tucking the Krugerrand under the snug cloth that covered her sex; never again would she risk carrying it in her hand, as she had all through that horrible physical examination on her first day here.

The coin felt cool against her skin, like the insides of the earth where the dampness still lived. Cloaking herself in the shadows of the night, she rushed back and retrieved her bonnet, guessing that she'd been gone fifteen minutes. Maybe twenty.

Torches had been lit. Ananda sought the dark spaces between the light, sidling up to the table to pick at the cake crumbs with the other girls. She melded immediately with the wall of white gowns. M-girl reached for her hand. Ananda pulled away.

"Are you okay?" her friend whispered.

"Fine, but we can't do that." Ananda glanced around. Zekiel had decreed that girls could touch only men, and only with his permission. "The other kind of touching," he'd preached, "girls with girls and men with men, cursed this nation with blasphemy and abomination, destitution and degradation." But another reason—much more wretched—also kept Ananda's hand to herself.

"You sure you're okay?" M-girl asked.

"Yes. You?" They hadn't talked since she had been sent to the cell, but this was no time to tell M-girl all her worries. Even whispering like this felt scary.

"No, this is a nightmare," M-girl said. "Where did you go just now?"

Ananda deflected the question by asking, "Did anyone see me?"

M-girl shrugged, a gesture listless as the light that flickered across her face. Yet she also appeared tense, her fine skin and features about to crack. Not like the girl Ananda had known all her life. It was as if M-girl had lost more than her family and friends. It was as if she'd lost herself. Only her whisper remained the same: "Did you hear what happened to Bella? The marauders took her. She's theirs now. They can do anything they want to her. We don't know where she is. She's just gone."

Gilly looked at them. She stood a few feet away, eyes red and swollen. Mia and Kluani also glanced at Ananda and M-girl. *Stop it.* Ananda shook her head slightly. *Look somewhere else.* She set her own eyes back on the table, as if she might actually care for a crumb. When the others turned their attention away, she said softly to M-girl, "I was there when they took her." Teresa appeared by Ananda's side, listening in.

"But where?" M-girl whispered.

"To their camp," Teresa said. "She's their bonus girl."

"Their what?" Ananda said.

"They get a bonus—"

"I saw what you just did." Desana pulled Ananda away from Teresa and M-girl. The woman was breathing hard, like she'd been running. "And I know what you're up to." She grabbed Teresa's arm. "Guards . . ." Desana pointed to the older girl. "Take this one to a cell. You," she said to Ananda, "come with me."

She dragged her directly to Zekiel, who watched the commotion from the edge of the gathering, surrounded by aging acolytes.

"She went to the Sacred Heart of Evil," Desana told him.

"Bring her in the church."

Ananda wanted to hurl the coin into the night. She feared both the Krugerrand's brutal condemnation and the mute testimony of the cloth that hid it. But when she tried to jerk away from Desana, the woman slapped her and held her close all the way to the foot of the altar.

Zekiel rushed past them, impatient with the lighting of three fat candles. They burned with a foul odor.

"Why did you go to the Sacred Heart of Evil?" He raised his arm in fury, and his voice shook.

"I wanted to see . . ." She looked away, as if in shame. "I heard it's where witches burn. I'd seen the wood—"

"You are a liar in the presence of the Lord."

After Mary's death, he'd used those very words to accuse her.

"I saw her bending down behind the wood," Desana said. "I think she found something. She put it under her gown."

"There should be nothing under your gown but innocence." His voice still quavered, unsteady as the candle flames in the stirred-up air. "What did you think you could hide under there that a devout instrument of the Lord would not find?"

He reached for her hem. Ananda pulled away, but Desana's grip did not fail. He seized her other arm and grabbed her gown, baring her coltish legs, before he stopped to say, "Why would you risk your soul for such a sin? There can be only one answer for a witch. You—"

"I'm not a witch!" she cried.

"Silence!" Desana shouted.

"You went there to talk to the ones we burned. To plot against the Kingdom of God."

"Please," she begged. "I'm not—"

"You *will* be silent," he thundered. "The Lord has terrible punishment for the sinners of the eternal blight. They are the souls who must learn the most important lesson of the Bible. Do you know what that is?"

Ananda was scared beyond response.

"It is that forgiveness, so uniquely Christian, must never stand in the way of divine retribution. Now do you know what *that* means?"

His question hung before them like her raised hem. He lifted it higher and threw the gown over her head. It draped her like a veil and blinded her to what they could see.

But not to what they could do. She thought of Callabra; Lorinda; Mary, too.

And Sylvan, whose ashen horrors still coated her hands.

Chapter Sixteen

Oceans Dead
"No recovery for centuries"
Report, International Fisheries Governing Board

Slave Smuggling on Dead Seas
Ex-fishermen vie for trade
U.S., Russia, Brits drive demand
UN Commission on Trafficking in Humans

Coxwell's men had found shade for the handcar, a six-foot length of sheet metal that they tore from a flattened shed near the Tennessee border. They attached it to the platform and braced it with scavenged bricks and makeshift supports, ingenuity for which Jessie was particularly grateful after enduring her sweaty, mid-morning stint on the long metal bar that propelled them north. Now they headed toward a tunnel that posed different dangers entirely. In the century long past it had been bored through the looming mountain, an engineering feat that would save them days of grueling passage over broiling, barren windswept slopes. But none of them welcomed the impending darkness, not after what Augustus had told them about the band of men who called the tunnel home.

"Slow this thing down," Coxwell said. "We're getting close."

The black missionary nodded. "We *don't* want to go barging in there."

"What's that?" Bliss pointed to a barely discernible light in the pale blue sky. "Is that a shooting star?"

Coxwell shaded his face with his stump. "That's a satellite. They used to shoot them up there almost every day. Now they're just space junk. They go around and around sending out a bunch of signals that nobody hears." He turned to the team working the handcar's long arm. "Let's back all the way off. It takes a while to stop this thing."

Hannah, who'd teamed up with Maul, heaved herself down to the wooden platform. The bald man turned to face the tunnel. Flick and Stace eased up on the other end of the "misery stick," as everyone on board had taken to calling it.

"Weapons," Jessie prompted, sending them all scurrying.

In seconds they assumed their positions around the handcar, filling the air with the metallic clatter of cranking triggers and shotgun barrels snapping shut. Jessie checked her ammo and slammed the magazine back into her M-16. She took the front with Coxwell. Augustus, who said it would be a little less dangerous if he did the talking, stood unarmed between them. He claimed to know the toll tenders, and had said they would be heavily armed.

"*Please,* no one start shooting," he told Jessie and the others now.

"Get the meat," Coxwell said without looking back; they'd rolled within a hundred feet of the entrance.

"Got it." Jaya reached for the smoked panther.

Jessie caught him smiling at Bliss. They'd paired up on the misery stick, and she strongly suspected that at night they comforted themselves by stealing kisses and caresses, which she found understandable but extremely worrisome. Yesterday she'd pulled Bliss aside to warn her again, as discreetly as possible, about sex and Wicca. Her daughter had nodded, but in the absent, immune manner of a young woman bubbling in the hormonal soup of her first power-ful attraction. Those chemicals really did make you crazy, Jessie thought now. And if that girl wasn't not careful, they could kill her. What did any of them know about the beard-less boy? Only that Coxwell had found Jaya in the cave with the freshwater spring, and that he said his sister had been taken from a camp. Nothing of his life, really, and certainly nothing of his exposure to Wicca.

Bliss and Jaya lugged about a third of the smoked panther to the front of the handcar, then hurried back to where they'd been sitting. Jessie watched their fingers entwine, a nest of calluses and chewed nails. Hard work and anxiety. But both kids were smiling, and Jessie couldn't remember the last time she'd felt that good.

"These toll tenders," Augustus had said last night, "they don't cotton to people, and they don't want girls. They want food, and you don't get past them without giving them some. You don't do it, then they'll take you and turn *you* into food. That dog of yours, he'd be stewed right up." His eyes had landed on Hansel.

"How much do we have to give them?" Coxwell had asked.

"You give them more than you want, and they'll take less than they see. That's how it works."

A vague, unsettling formula, in Jessie's view; but at least they had food to give them. If the toll tenders wanted water, Coxwell said, they'd claim they had none, which, he'd added, "was kin to the truth."

"Stop this thing," he now said urgently. They were in the shade of the mountain, only feet from plowing into the dark tunnel.

Flick and Brindle threw their bodies on the misery stick, finally halting the handcar inches from the tunnel entrance. Jessie heard everyone breathe at once.

"Thank you, Jesus," Augustus said. Much more loudly, he hailed the toll tenders.

Jessie had never seen a more complete blackness; she doubted her vision penetrated more than a few feet of the pitch.

"No one shoots, unless *they* shoot," Coxwell reminded them in a soft voice.

If the shooting started, the plan—if you could call it that, thought Jessie—would send Brindle and Stace to the misery stick; they were the strongest and could power the handcar through the tunnel. She and Coxwell would remain at the front, joined by Maul and Flick, the oldest of the men, but agile. The two of them would drag dead toll tenders or other obstructions off the track. The rest of them would replace those killed or wounded up front, or handle incoming from their flanks; Augustus suspected that the tenders had carved out strategically hidden posts in both walls.

"Toll tenders, it's me, Augustus!" he shouted again.

Jessie shot a quick glance back, worried that all their eyes were looking forward. She saw only the tracks burning in the sun, while here at the entrance they had neither a spot of light nor a breath of air. If anything, the shade by the tunnel felt hotter, like a coal fire in a punch-hole mine.

One of Coxwell's men whispered. He hushed him. Deep in the darkness a torch blazed. It moved, lighting two more. As each of the torches shifted, more fires burst apart the blackness, but only in the distance; the light did not reach anywhere near the handcar. The torches moved in the air like phantom flames.

When the toll tenders came within fifty yards, Jessie heard footsteps on the gravel rail bed. Moments later she made out eerily white bodies and large eyes with huge black pupils, as if the constant darkness had drained away their color.

Easy targets, she thought. If I have to.

A lone man continued toward them.

"They never leave the tunnel," Augustus had said. "They got a good gig and they know it. Food comes to them—most times it walks right by. Everyone else, they got to go find it."

As the man moved within twenty feet of the handcar, his torch lit a section of sagging, cyclone fence hanging like a crude hammock from the tunnel ceiling. A gunner with a blackened face peered down at them from behind a Browning automatic.

A machine gun. Jessie realized that he'd had a bead on them the whole time. *They* were the easy targets.

Augustus sat, letting his legs dangle from the front of the platform. When he refused Coxwell's offer of a revolver, he'd said that after he preached, the tenders had let him pass unarmed, and that he wasn't about to change his M.O. now.

"We have meat for you," Augustus said to the man with the torch, who wore only a dark wrap over his privates. He looked sinewy and strong, like a figure cut from white marble. The only color that she could see were the blue veins that road-mapped his arms and chest, even his taut belly. He carried no weapon, but he was well protected by the gunner. Jessie glanced up again at the Browning. It could chew them up in seconds.

The man on the tracks waved his torch, and his compatriots—armed with guns, stakes, axes, clubs—marched up behind him. Like him, they were dressed in the scanty wrap, their skin so pale it seemed to glow in the torchlight like the marine phosphorescence she'd seen once in a biology slide show.

"We have panther meat for you," Augustus said so warmly that he could have been running a hot dog stand at a state fair in the long ago, instead of offering tribute to the ruler of this dark realm.

The leader moved his head, and a man with stiff dreadlocks rested a rifle against the wall to Jessie's right. Augustus pointed to the meat beside him, and Dreads sniffed it.

"It's good. Smoked real well. We've been eating it," Augustus said.

Dreads walked away with the meat. Though he appeared slight, he handled the weight with ease.

Their leader retrieved Dreads's rifle and handed it off, then his eyes roamed the weapons held casually by the men and women on the handcar. He paused over Hansel but said nothing.

"They never speak, least not to me," Augustus had also told them last night. "But they say plenty with their eyes."

The men didn't end their silence now. It felt deafening in the black heat of the tunnel. Their leader shook his head at Augustus.

"He wants more," Augustus said.

"A little more," Coxwell said, but the torchlit men weren't waiting for his approval. Two of them were hurrying down the side of the handcar. The first reached up and grabbed the last panther carcasses—bones that Jessie had planned for soup—and the other scooped up half of the remaining smoked meat.

Jessie nudged Augustus with her foot. *Say something,* she urged him silently. *We'll starve if this doesn't stop.*

"We need that." Augustus spoke as softly as before. "We've got ten of us, and we're not holding back on you."

Their leader waved his torch, and the toll tender who'd helped himself to the panther meat dropped it by Augustus's side. It sounded loud as beef smacked on a butcher's counter: one of Jessie's earliest memories, sawdust on the floor, blood specks and blond wood.

Still holding his torch, the leader reached behind him and drew a machete from the back of his waistband. He whipped the blade down in a blink. Augustus looked on calmly.

The leader's cohort took away what appeared to be precisely half the small pile of meat.

"I thank you for your consideration," Augustus said with a formality that Jessie hadn't heard since her college commencement.

It briefly brought that to mind now, how, at the eleventh hour, university officials moved the ceremony to an armory to avoid the exploding chaos that had already claimed the lives of eight faculty members—all beheaded on the campus commons. Within a year she joined rebel forces fighting throughout the South to try to stop heavily armed militias— soon to morph into the marauders—from taking land and wells from communes and small-scale farming coopera- tives, the last vestiges of civilized social order.

Now, she watched the leader of the toll tenders walk up to Hansel, lying next to her. *No you don't.* Protectively, she kneaded the fur on the back of the dog's neck. The man petted him, smiled, and walked away.

All but one of the toll tenders retreated with him. The remaining man jumped up on the handcar, holding out his torch to light their way ahead.

"Slowly," Coxwell said to Brindle and Stace. "Let's not run up on them."

After rolling through the tunnel for ten minutes, the ten- der's torch lit up two large caverns across from each other. Jessie stared into the one on the left, catching only glimpses of the near naked men, and bones hanging like beaded cur- tains from the low ceiling. *Oh, God.* She squeezed her eyes shut at the sight of half a dozen human skulls on a shelf that had been carved out of the earth. One of Coxwell's men gasped, but no one spoke—not in the presence of the torch- bearer.

The smell was almost worse than what she'd seen. But what you would expect, she guessed, from men who ate and relieved themselves in such close confines.

An hour passed before they spotted daylight in the dis- tance. Without a parting gesture, the tender turned, walked to the back of the handcar and jumped off.

For the first time in memory Jessie welcomed the sun. Clearly the others felt the same way. None of them sought the shade of the sheet metal for the first few minutes.

The track took them past the rolling hills and mountains that Augustus said would lead them to Knox. Traces of trib- utaries and the rivers they'd once fed appeared far beyond both sides of the handcar. The wiggly lines wound down through woods browned by the sun or blackened by fire. Their sandy beds looked like the avalanche paths that once scored sub-alpine forests. Sharp ridge lines, scalded by heat-fueled windstorms, rose up around them, unleavened by the lush vegetation that once crowned the southern high country. In the absence of bushes and trees, the crazed tracks of dust devils had scarred this blistered land, pocking it with craters wherever they touched down, drilling dirt to dust.

They'd been quiet since leaving the tunnel, as if the bones and skulls and the ghostly men had claimed their voices, too. Even Augustus, who spoke with the easy patter of a preacher, merely waved his arms to indicate that the tracks were about to take them onto a wooden trestle hundreds of feet above a dry river canyon.

Jessie found it dizzying to peer over the exposed sides of the handcar, and she had to force herself to stand so she could see what lay directly below them. Nothing but more of the crusty riverbed.

The trestle creaked loudly under the handcar's weight, and she doubted that the long neglected beams could support a real train. But the fact that it still stood was lasting testament to the skills and tools that had thrived in this once great land.

The handcar shuddered as they rolled off the trestle. Augustus warned that they were about to pass a ghastly sight.

"Like the skulls," Hannah said, acknowledging what had gone unspoken.

"A million times worse. It's a big pit where they put a lot of the dead. They're just bones now."

The mass grave must have been gouged from the earth by giant bulldozers. It was the size of a stadium, and filled with bodies stricken by the pandemic and the waves of suicide that it had triggered. A ladder rose to a rusty platform fifty or sixty feet above the bones, a killing field that had been carefully tended.

"What's that for?" Bliss pointed to the platform.

No one replied. Augustus looked around like he knew the answer, but not whether to offer it to the youngest person on board.

"Tell us," Jessie said. No answer could be worse than the nightmare they were seeing.

"It's for suicides," he said. "If you knew your loved ones had been taken here, you could die here, too."

"A plague pit," Hannah said so quietly that she might have been speaking to herself. She looked around, apparently surprised by the attention she'd drawn, and raised her voice. "They had them in the Middle Ages, too. Near the cities. That's where they took the victims of the plague."

"You heard about those people, then," Augustus said right away. "The ones calling themselves the 'Plague.' Bunch of crazies."

Jessie recalled Hannah mentioning the group back in the brine pool by the dam. She'd said they were Pagans "sacrificing" the descendants of prominent climate-change deniers from back at the turn of the century, all in the hope of appeasing Gaia, Mother Earth. Hannah had even asked her if there had been any deniers in her family tree, a question that chilled Jessie for reasons she'd never explained to the nurse.

Coxwell asked about the cult; Hannah's answer closely mirrored what she'd said in the brine pool.

Hushed once again, they left behind the pit, a silence born less of reverence for the dead, in Jessie's case, than an uneasiness about the "crazies." She kept glancing at Hannah's back and at the pistol she'd given her to use. After more than a week of putting aside her suspicion that the woman was a member of the cult, Jessie's worries had been born anew.

Not the least by her own guilt. It stretched back two generations to her paternal grandfather. He'd been a lovely man who played endless games of chess with her at his beach home, a staple of her childhood. He'd also been a geologist and executive with ExxonMobil—and a prominent denier. Even after the seas abruptly rose when the West Antarctica Ice Sheet plunged into the ocean, his blog—*Tain't So,* as in "Say it ain't so"—had attracted tens of millions of hits each month. Oddly enough, interest in it only increased as the most dire evidence of climate change mounted, as if in the face of the most overwhelming odds, people had clung ever more stubbornly to the junk science of self-interest. Her grandfather most of all.

She'd challenged him repeatedly, shouting in the midst of their stormiest session that he'd been bought off by Exxon-Mobil and his "two-bit fame." But she'd been young and impetuous, righteously impatient and often enraged, and failed to see that he hadn't succumbed to money, not in the most immediate sense, or to the easy blandishments of celebrity. Like most consumers, he simply revealed the power of cognitive dissonance—one of the most basic of all psychological theories—for if he had accepted what climate science and, increasingly, the earth itself demonstrated daily, he would have had to give up his big cars, big homes, jet travel with its large and toxic leavings, and nutrient-sapped convenience food that poisoned the land, air, and water that had given it life. And he would have been forced to face the brute reasons that his beloved country had warred so often and murdered so many millions abroad—to sustain a tiny percentage of the world's population by claiming so much of the world's resources. Very few of her forbears—certainly not her grandfather and his privileged fellows—were prepared to forgo prerogatives of wealth stolen from foreign lands and future generations alike.

A generous man with his personal fortune, he could not accept these forbidding facts about the consumption culture in which he'd flourished, any more than could his counterparts elsewhere in the developed world, or the burgeoning billions who craved what humankind had wrested from the earth and could ill afford to keep. To the very end, her grandfather reflected the unbending tension between irrefutable science and the cosseted life that he enjoyed every day, by denying the starkest signs of the coming collapse.

And then he died quietly and alone, with the ocean surging ever closer to his magnificent beach house until, a mere month later, the surrounding sea grass, playful dunes, and even the stately stone foundation were ripped from the sand and pulverized in a single afternoon by a category seven hurricane.

Mourned to this moment by his fiery and finally forgiving granddaughter, who still bore the silent wounds of the shrill arguments that had riven so many families and friendships, as if words alone, brazenly unadorned by artifice or material desire, could ever have overcome the allure of such a seductive and sparking sense of entitlement.

"I doubt there are any deniers here," Hannah said.

To Jessie's uneasy ear, it sounded like a challenge. No one responded, and Hannah—almost pointedly, Jessie thought—did not look at her.

The tracks climbed a grade that was steep by rail standards. At the top they could see Knox about fifteen miles away. Jessie fixed on the haunting void where downtown buildings once crested high above the streets, an eerie emptiness that brought back memories of old crumpled photographs of New York after a terrorist attack in 2001. Knox had been a battleground city like Baltimore, and the skyline had fallen, along with innumerable lives.

"We'll be there in about three hours," Augustus said.

And then we've got to get to the marauders' camp. Surveil it. Attack. Get the cars. That's assuming Hannah really knows the location.

Jessie looked at their dwindling food stocks, and for the first time wondered if the risks were worth the possi-

ble reward. The reality of a humbling death from starva-
tion shocked her; she'd thought of dying only in a fight to
free Ananda and the other girls. But it could come down to
simply not having enough calories to soldier on.

They rolled toward the razed city in numbed silence until
Coxwell called out a warning.

"Look at that. A vehicle." He jabbed his stump toward a
dust cloud moving along a strip that had been a busy highway ages ago. His maggots had turned to flies, leaving his
severed arm with a hard, healthy crust—the same result
Jessie was seeing with her bullet wound.

"If those are marauders," she said, "they've got guns. Lots
of them. And armor." *And they might have Ananda.*

"If those are marauders, we could really use that car,"
Coxwell said. "Grabbing it out here could be a helluva a lot
easier than in their camp."

"I don't know if we can make it in time," Augustus said,
"but see right there." He was pointing now, too. "That road
passes by this track about five miles from here. You can see
it if you look real hard."

Jessie could just pick it out, but shook her head. "That
car's moving a lot faster than we are."

"Only thing is," Augustus said, "the road gets real bad,
and then they have to stop and set up ramps to get down a
nasty, sheared-off section right where we'll be close to it."

Even as he spoke, the men on the misery stick started
pumping like mad, reminding her that they all had girls
who'd been abducted.

Jessie's hopes surged: they could start the battle here,
while they were still strong, instead of taking on a camp
while starving. *If* those were marauders. Only one question
gave her pause. "Couldn't our girls be in there with them?"

Augustus shook his head. "They're driving away from the
Army of God."

Jessie rushed to take the next shift on the misery stick.

Every few minutes a new team took over, pumping frantically as the old one stepped away drenched with sweat. The
canisters of water drained quickly.

"We just need one car," Coxwell exhorted them. "Just one."

If it's them, Jesse thought again.

As the first mile receded and the second swept them past a
cluster of ramshackle warehouses, she stared intensely at the
vehicle. A sudden sun reflection off a side panel forced her
eyes shut. "Armor!" she shouted. "Marauders!"

Them.

The men cheered, filled with bravado. The handcar
gained speed. It was as if every second of the journey had
come down to these frenzied moments. She took another
shift, pumped the misery stick till her heart felt like it would
explode, and collapsed to the platform, chest heaving, no
longer able to imagine them winning a battle at the marauders' camp. They *had* to get that car. Then they could pack
themselves into it and try to drive their Trojan Horse right
through the gates of the Army of God.

She dragged herself to her feet and sipped water sparingly.
The dust still moved on the old highway, though slower.

"How far?" she asked once she caught her breath.

"Two more miles, I'm guessing," Augustus said.

"Can they see us?"

"Not if they're using the armor on their windshield," Coxwell said.

The slits, Jessie remembered. That's right.

Ellison had refused the wheel, taking the passenger seat.
Anvil shook with frustration.

"You're not going to do a fucking thing with her," he said.
"I can sit back there and party all the way to camp."

Bella, bound and gagged in the seat right behind them,
watched wild-eyed as Ellison pretended to weigh the crazy-
looking guy's argument.

"Nope," he said after lowering the armor over the windshield. "I can't do that. You drive. I ride shotgun. That's the way it works. It's hard enough seeing out this thing, and I want both of us keeping our fucking eyes on the road. We get back, you can draw lots with the rest of them for who goes first."

They were still about an hour from the camp, and then he'd have to leave for a week or two—the grimmest time in a bonus girl's life. He'd caused more pain than he could ever remember, but couldn't abide the feeble cries of children. It had driven him mad with Cody. After the boy and his mother were raped and murdered, he'd been forced to accept that he had only one talent in a world born of smoke and rage, drought and ruin. It was the ability to block the softest call of the past so he could bear the worst of the present.

He'd block it once more, grab his bedroll and hike high into the Smokies, where a crystal spring spilled from a granite outcropping, the virgin earth that didn't know any better, still making its dumb offering to the thankless land.

He knew what his men would say after he left; a couple of them had gotten drunk enough on their hooch to say it to his face. But nobody defied his rules. He'd killed three of them in the past two years for crossing him, Grinder on this trip for putting his stinking hands all over the tall one they'd taken. But he couldn't keep his men from a bonus girl. That was a rule, too. They'd murder for it.

Coxwell had them hide the handcar behind an embankment a couple hundred yards from where the road sank ten feet. Jessie found shade for Hansel and commanded her dog to stay.

From the angle they now had of the road, she couldn't tell what kind of vehicle was heading toward them; but it had windshield armor in place. Good. Nobody looking out was likely to see more than a horizontal strip of land. But also bad because from a distance it would make shooting anyone inside the vehicle, once again, all but impossible.

Irrigation ditches surrounded them, the last efforts to farm this once verdant soil, now scrubby as the badlands of old Mexico. The ditches looked no less ancient than the ones dug by the Hohokam tribe in what used to be Phoenix, where decades ago frightened citizens made a desperate attempt to erect a massive, reflective dome over their city as summertime temperatures soared over 130 degrees, and then hit the 140s. Untold thousands died with the dome barely begun and quickly abandoned. Many others perished just as miserably as they tried to flee across the desert that once lured their ancestors with its promise of winter warmth and open wonder.

Augustus led them to a ditch that would skirt the end of the sheared-off road. Coxwell took the lead position, with Maul crawling right behind him. Jessie claimed the third spot. Bliss was fourth in line with Jaya—no surprise—inches from her heels. The others trailed out to Hannah and Augustus, who was still unarmed.

Bellying down, they dragged themselves on their elbows, trying to get beside the road before the vehicle arrived. Jessie stole a look over the edge of the ditch and glimpsed the car.

"I know that one," she announced between breaths. "It's a van." The one she'd been hiding behind when she was shot.

"Faster," Coxwell responded.

They covered the last hundred feet at a furious pace, arriving deadly close to where the van would have to stop. "We want to hear at least one door open," Coxwell had said. "Then we'll wait to hear if any others open up. If not, we'll come up shooting. No matter what, we *can't* let them get away with that car. If they do, they'll alert everyone and all bets are off."

The brakes screeched. They readied their weapons.

Setting up the ramps always made Ellison edgy. He gripped his sawed-off shotgun and reached for the crank to lift the windshield armor. But his arm just hung there.

"Open the goddamn thing," Anvil said. "I got to be able to see those boards."

"Something's not right," Ellison whispered.

"Yeah, it's me driving when I could be back there with her." But now Anvil was whispering, too.

Ellison looked through the slit for anything that moved. *Anything.* The land was dead. The dead don't move. But even in the van the still air suddenly felt unsettled.

Jessie heard a door open. But only partway. Icy tension shot through her system so powerfully, she thought it must have ripped through all of them, fast as the cold water that once flooded these ditches.

The door didn't close. It's just hanging there, she thought.

Bliss gently squeezed her ankle, mouthed, *I love you, Mom.*

Ellison raised his sawed-off and peeked past the edge of the cracked door; no window in that thing, just metal plating. His eyes roved left to right. If he'd been planning to ambush a car, he'd be down in that ditch waiting for someone to break cover. He was that someone. He fixed his sight on the dip in the dirt and signaled Anvil to keep the engine running. The bushy-haired driver had stopped complaining. He looked serious as a steel trap.

Ellison heard Bella curl up into a tight fetal position.

Yeah, even she feels it. But what?

The door creaked sharply as it opened all the way. Jessie buried her breath, trying to take air quietly—to keep her frantic nerves from betraying them. With the greatest care, she tested the clip on the M-16. Snug. The rifle felt warm as the earth. She'd set the weapon on full auto. The barrel would burn.

Waiting had become torture. Above the sound of the idling engine, she thought she heard a footstep.

* * *

Ellison halted. There was no quiet that was quiet enough at a time like this. And he'd violated it when he put down his foot. To him, it sounded like the earth had cracked wide open. If there were ears out there, they'd heard him. And if there were eyes, he'd see them any second. The air was rife with the worst of certainty.

He thought of climbing back in the car, signaling Anvil to back up. But that could be treacherous, too. There could be a dozen gunmen ready to spring up in the next breath. They could have gas bombs, like the skells. He'd be better out in the open, where he could react before they turned the van into an incinerator. And even if he and Anvil retreated, they'd still have to traverse this stretch of road to reach their camp. *Don't close the door.*

Keeping his options open, in every sense of the word; but he also hoped that if there were hidden gunmen, letting the door hang open would leave the daunting impression that others were piling out—murderous men more light-footed than he.

Something's not right. Those words kept coming back to him. *A man makes his own echoes, and he does it all his life.* His last thought before the shooting began.

Coxwell rose and fired without warning. A blast took him down before Jessie and the others could climb to their feet. A man by the front of the van was already rolling toward the edge of the sheared-off road. She aimed the M-16, opening a screaming zipper of dirt right at him. But he dropped below and she had no idea if she'd hit him.

The van was backing up. Bliss stumbled past her, heading toward the open door, shotgun in both hands. Stace, racing out from under his animal-skin hat, streaked past Bliss and drew close enough to shoot out the right front tire. The car limped like a wounded beast.

Jessie saw that all of them but Hannah were chasing the van, gaining on it; with a flat tire, it fishtailed wildly before backing into a large boulder. The crash sent a side door flying open. Now the vehicle headed straight at them before veering sharply for a U-turn, hurling a bound girl onto the cracked asphalt. With her gagged face turned away, Jessie didn't recognize her; but she was too small to be Ananda. The child tried to squirm off the road, moving only inches. Jessie glanced at the drop-off. No sign of the man, but she couldn't go after him—she had to grab the girl.

The van couldn't complete the U-turn without running into the ditch, so the driver backed up once more, forcing Jessie and the others to dart out of his way. While still in reverse, he turned quickly so he could drive up the road that had taken him here. Then he braked sharply and gunned his engine. His rear tires spun, raising clouds of noxious black smoke as he tried to race away. But he was still hobbled by the flat front tire, which peeled off the rim as Jessie watched.

"Grab her!" she screamed. The van was heading right at the bound girl, riding on the bare steel that could cut her in two.

Stace jumped on the vehicle, clung tightly to the top of the windshield armor and jammed the barrel of his pistol through the slit, firing five times. But the van didn't stop. Flick, the oldest of Coxwell's men, threw himself toward the girl, pushing her out of the way. The steel rim sliced through his spine.

The van churned ahead. Stace climbed along the windshield armor, reaching for the driver's door. The car finally slowed. He leaped off, jerked it open, and dragged out a screaming man with reddish hair and a face streaming with blood. Stace tried to shoot him again but he'd run out of ammo. Bliss stepped up with her shotgun, but Maul pushed her aside and completed the killing. Silently, Jessie thanked the bald-headed man for his brutal act of kindness.

"Bliss," she called. Her daughter looked over. "Get the girl."

Wasting no time, Jessie advanced toward the edge of the road where the first man had vanished.

* * *

Ellison had limped to a large pothole about fifty feet from where he'd rolled off the ledge. It was just deep enough to cover his hide. He figured Anvil for dead; he'd heard two different caliber bullets, but neither sounded like the driver's .32. Wouldn't be long and he'd be dead, too. There was no escape, not this time. They'd lost the van. He couldn't even run—he'd wrenched his ankle with the fall—and seen enough of them climbing out of that ditch to know that they would soon have him surrounded.

He raised up a fraction and spotted a woman aiming right at him from up above. He tucked himself back down, surprised that she hadn't shot him on sight. She had the goods—the automatic that came within a hair of tearing him in two as he flung himself over the edge—but worse, she had a powerful set of motives: he'd chained her husband to the front of the truck and forced her to show him around the camp. And if she'd chased him this far, then he would bet his last bullets that he'd taken her daughter as well.

Vengeance was a filthy beast. No one knew this better than he did. Right now, it was all hers.

Jessie would never forget that face, or his sawed-off shotgun and burned fingers. "Slide all your weapons onto the road," she shouted, "and climb out with your hands up."

When he didn't respond, she said she'd give him to a count of ten and then drop a gas bomb on him without hesitation.

A bluff. They sure as hell hadn't crawled down that ditch with gas bombs on their backs. But more than anything, she wanted him alive.

Maybe they did have a bomb—that had been Ellison's fear when he thought about retreating in the van only minutes ago. But most surely they had the numbers; he heard footfalls all around him and knew without question that he'd been run to ground. He also heard the bonus girl crying, a reminder that life spits out the strangest outcomes.

He reached up and slid his pistol onto the road. Flipped his knives up there, too. He had other plans for his shotgun.

She's a lucky girl, thought Jessie. Bella was sitting on the road, sobbing and shaking. Bliss was crouched down, peppering her with questions about Ananda and the others.

"Bliss." Jessie shook her head. "She's in no condition."

But this one—she looked down at the hole—had better have plenty to say. And soon.

"C-C-Coxwell's h-hurt pr-pr-pretty bad. Fl-Flick's dead." Brindle stammered worse than usual, maybe because he sounded homicidal.

"Do not shoot this man if he comes out with his hands up," Jessie said. "I don't care who's hurt or how bad, we need him to talk."

Like KK, she added to herself. The marauder wounded in the attack on their camp had told them plenty before he got to die. "Your shotgun!" she yelled to the man in the hole. "I want to see that, too!"

Ellison pushed the double barrel into his mouth. When you have no illusions about yourself, the end is always near. He'd known this since Baltimore, when he left Katherine and Cody in a grimy, brick-walled basement near the harbor. The three of them had found their latest refuge only the night before, hunted like other rebels by mutinous, starving soldiers of a failed army who were pressing ever closer, killing at will, and committing horrific acts of personal vengeance. They were reputed to be driving down the eastern seaboard to unite with the militias tearing apart much of the South. Baltimore was not yet lost, though holding the city appeared as doubtful as it was critical: thousands of unarmed refugees had fled the frenzied troops and huddled in the cratered neighborhood of Federal Hill.

Ellison had slipped in and out of rubble-strewn streets and shelled buildings whose walls had crumbled, leaving them open as dead, ungazing eyes. He'd spotted three squads—gaunt, hollow-cheeked men—and noted their weaponry and vulnerabilities. Then he returned to the basement before nightfall, smelling smoke seconds before he saw that other soldiers had found his family. Katherine's shooting hand and left leg had been chopped off, roasted in a fire, and left mostly uneaten. He convulsed and dropped to his knees at the gruesome retribution suffered by a woman who'd tried to defend her child and herself, and had killed a man in filthy camo whose body sprawled facedown by the door.

His wife's clothes had been torn from her and burned; a sleeve lay a few feet from her corpse like a disembodied arm. Cody's shirt had been stuffed into his mouth. That's when he saw that both of them had been raped; their bodies bore the marks.

Ellison had studied the smoldering fire, then placed his palm on Katherine's cheek. He touched his boy, too, and felt the child's fading warmth, his tautening skin.

Now he tasted the metal barrel and the bitter residue of battle, and glanced at the burning sky, wondering why he hadn't offered the same kindness to his son and wife. He'd planned to spare them the most painful terror, but when the time came—when ravening men crept close enough to claim them—he'd left his family alone and alive, succumbing to the final savagery of hope.

His fingers, scarred by the fire that had destroyed that city, slipped from the trigger. He could never take more than he'd given his family.

The curious penance of a man with no more faith in God than in his lost self.

The shotgun appeared last. From above, Jessie watched him climb out favoring one leg. She had the honest urge to shoot him, but she could scarcely imagine a sweeter revenge than taking him alive.

Coxwell's men scooped up his weapons and pressed close. He was the first marauder at their mercy since the murder of their wives, children, friends.

"Don't touch him," she ordered again. "Keep your distance."

Though Maul shot her a defiant look, most of them backed away, perhaps remembering that crowding a captured man did not constitute smart tactics; prisoners had been known to set off suicide bombs.

She had him searched and his hands tied, then dragged up a slope to the road. Maul and Stace pushed him to the ground in front of her. Sweat ran down the man's dusty face.

"Do you remember me?" Jessie pressed the muzzle of her weapon against his brow.

"I sure do."

"What's your name?"

"It doesn't matter. I'll tell you what you want to know and then you can shoot me."

"It's not going to be that easy."

Ellison told her everything that he thought would matter to them: the girls' health; their life in the compound; number of men guarding it; types of weapons; fortifications; food and water supplies; the location of the fuel depot, dormitory, and the residences of the men.

Jessie pressed him for names. He said he didn't know them, and in her view that figured: why humanize girls you're selling for sex? Treating them like cheap commodities was easier on the conscience, if he had one. But after describing the others, he remembered Ananda's name.

"How come you know hers?"

"Because we talked about how it meant bliss."

"She's mine." Jessie watched him closely. If he laughed or smiled, or made even the slightest excuse, she wasn't sure that she could control herself. But his expression never changed, and when he spoke again it was with a deliberateness that she hadn't heard from him:

"Your plan's never going to get you past the front gate."

"Yes, it will," she replied, "because you're going to get them to open it."

"They'll never do it. You'll see bodies rotting outside. There's only two reasons they open it, for known traders and girls. And I've already given them the girls."

"As of now, you've got two more."

Without shifting his head from the end of the barrel, he eyed everyone in sight, spotting a thin-boned teen with a shotgun by the bonus girl. Something about the way the older one held her weapon looked familiar. Almost as quickly he remembered her running toward him in their camp and firing, setting off the whole goddamn battle. She'd almost killed him.

He gave away none of his surprise when he spoke. "If you mean those two, you'll never get away trying to pass off the smaller one. They know her."

"We'd never send her back to them. There's another one." She jabbed the M-16 against his skull. "You going to do it?"

Jessie watched him nod. Not a wasted word in all that he'd said. Another man with a gun to his head might have floundered and begged for his life. He'd become focused.

"You'll die," she said to him, "if you don't do exactly what we say."

"I'm going to die any—"

"He's getting away!" Stace yelled.

"Who?" Jessie asked, looking around.

"Augustus!" Stace shouted as he raced after the black man, now scrambling past the embankment that hid the handcar.

"Take him," Jessie said to Maul, who jammed his pistol to the back of their prisoner's head, execution style.

Jaya also took off after Augustus. Jessie started to, but in the midst of all this Hannah yelled her name and said, "Coxwell wants you. You'd better hurry."

Jessie forced her eyes from the handcar, which Augustus had just rolled into view. *They're either going to get him or they won't.* Turning back, she rushed to Hannah and Coxwell. Blood seeped from the corners of his mouth, streaking his chin. Lead shot had opened his gut all the way from his waist to his groin. Hannah caught Jessie's eye and gave a slight shake of her head.

Coxwell tried to talk. "My girls . . ." It was all he managed.

"Yes, your girls. I can hear you." Jessie kneeled beside him.

"Mia . . ." he struggled harder to speak. ". . . Kluani. Tell them I love them. Tell them I tried—" He stopped to cough up blood.

"I promise I will. I'll tell them you love them. I'll tell them everything you've done to save them. You're a hero to them. They don't know that yet but they will."

"The girls . . ." He gripped her hand firmly. ". . . they don't have a mom anymore. No one." Even with his life seeping out of him, he turned to hide the tears washing down his bloody chin.

"They'll have me," Jessie vowed. "I'll take care of them and love them like my own."

He looked at her, his wet eyes red with pain and death and longing.

"You'll be proud of them," Jessie said. "I promise."

Coxwell's hand turned limp and his stump fell heavily to his side.

Hannah closed his eyes. Jessie stood weeping, empty and worn, thinking of Eden—left in a coma and probably dead by now, too.

She looked at Brindle, who was staring at Coxwell from a few feet away. Then she saw Maul with his gun still pressed to the head of the man who'd killed their commander, like he really was about to execute him.

"Don't shoot him," Jessie said once more, acutely aware that Coxwell might have been the only reason that his men had ever heeded her.

Maul stared at her with his cold eyes. He'd always worried her most, right from the time she first met his gaze in the cave. He rarely offered any expression, as if his blankness were a mask for the explosion that could come with any excuse. Now a powerful one lay dead before him.

She stared right back at him, unabashedly wiping away her tears. She understood the desire to murder this bastard, but she also knew that if Maul took revenge on their prisoner, she'd have to kill him. A plan to rescue the girls had been set in motion, and their most critical resource now knelt before them. As long as the man with the burned fingers did not resist her orders, he could not be harmed. And if Maul killed him—if he bowed to the fury that they all struggled to contain—then Maul would have to die.

Her trigger finger rose to the M-16's selector switch to make sure it remained on full auto; killing Maul would almost certainly mean battling at least some of the others. They had history with him, loyalties. But she could brook no challenge to her command. Once it broke down, you had the failed army and its ruthless, raging forces. But far more wrenching to Jessie was the blunt understanding that if she lost the prisoner, she'd also lose any real hope of saving those girls.

Maybe Maul sensed the impending chaos. Or maybe the words he spoke next would have followed anyway. "Mind if I put Brindle on him? They could use some help." He looked from Coxwell's killer to Stace and Jaya, who were struggling with Augustus.

Jessed nodded back, a little less empty, a little less worn.

They buried Coxwell and Flick within the hour. Simple cairns marked their graves. Jessie had taken a twine necklace from Coxwell, wondering if one of his twins wove it for him. She put it aside for them. Flick had even less to leave his granddaughter, whose parents were murdered in the raid on their camp. But he'd saved Bella's life, and the story of his courage would be his bequest.

Augustus, hands tied like the prisoner's, kept his head bowed during the burial. He might have been praying. No one cared. He'd caused them trouble when they needed it least. And now as they trudged to the van, refitted with a spare tire, the missionary bristled with anger.

"I don't want any part of your battle. That's all black people ever get stuck with—fighting some white man's war."

"The Army of God says you're repugnant," Jessie reminded him.

"Good. Keeps them away."

"And you said that folks like them never leave you alone for good, that they're always seeing something you got."

"Don't throw my words back at me. I know what I said."

"Maybe you're t-too sc-scared to f-fight," Brindle said.

"The man's not scared," the prisoner with the burned hand said. "Augustus Blackwell doesn't scare."

Augustus stopped feet from the van and stared at him. "Do I know you?"

"Bay Street? Baltimore? You were leading the League of Black Resis—"

"Holy blazes. Ellison?"

"I've been called worse." The marauder offered a tight, flickery smile. His first.

"You *know* who this man is?" Augustus asked them.

"A marauder," Jessie answered. "A murderer who led the massacre of our camp."

Augustus looked back at him. "That true?"

Ellison didn't respond.

"What in the name of sweet Jesus ever happened to you? Last time I saw Ellison here," Augustus turned to them again, "he took over a tank and turned it on a block full of crazies killing everyone they could." He eyed Ellison. "I saw them hit you with white phosphorous. *Twice*. I thought you were dead."

"No such luck," Jessie said to Augustus. "Now get in the car. You and your buddy here can trade war stories later. I want *you* all the way in the back." She planned to hold the missionary until they freed the girls. If she let him go and he betrayed them—for food or supplies or whatever the information might buy—they'd be gunned down as soon as they drove up to the gate. They were running that risk already without adding to it.

But Augustus's words did make her wonder about Ellison. About Augustus, too. From all reports, Baltimore had been a grinding, murderous siege. For the last five days, a massive force of renegade soldiers shelled the resistance until every last battlement was reduced to rubble. Then they tried to overrun the rebels, who mounted a furious final stand behind piles of broken concrete and burned cars on Bay Street. Fighters of all colors—the "Rainbow Resistance," as they came to be known—held the last few yards of pavement for another twelve hours—buying time for thousands of refugees to flee their camp and join the "unarmed road of flight," in the song of a long-dead balladeer.

Captured fighters were force-marched to the harbor and executed. The dank, mustering water choked on bloated corpses for weeks. Jessie had heard that the rebels who escaped fled with deep and lasting scars. Not just the kind you can see, she thought as their two prisoners climbed into the van: one had turned to God, the other to murder. Even now she couldn't say which of those pestilences had wreaked a greater carnage. Or where one began and the other left off.

Brindle drove and Stace rode shotgun. Jessie sat behind the passenger seat with Ellison on her left. She held a pistol to his ribs; but a bullet, which could pierce him and hit an unintended target, would be a last resort. Maul sat on his other side with a six-inch blade to the man's belly; the knife was the preferred option. Jaya squeezed between Maul and the side door at the back of the driver.

No one held a gun or knife to Augustus. They'd simply wedged him in the third row between Bliss and Hannah. Bella rested her head on the nurse's shoulder and slept. Hansel curled at their feet.

Bliss, in contrast, looked tense, jumpy. The handcar had been the fastest vehicle she'd ever ridden; and after Brindle picked up speed, Jessie saw her daughter's face tighten even more.

"Cars are pretty safe," Jessie said to her.

"No traffic jams anyway," Stace joked. Only Brindle at the wheel laughed.

"It's weird moving when you can't see anything," Bliss said. Light entered only through the slit in the windshield armor, leaving the interior mostly dark.

"When I was your age, cars still had windows," Jessie said. "And seat belts. We'd have to buckle up before we could go anywhere."

"Why?" Bliss asked.

"In case another car hit us or we went flying off the road."

"Nobody wants seat belts now." Stace turned to face them. "You want to get out of these things fast as you can, if you have to."

"You won't be able to get out of this thing fast enough," Ellison said, "if you go ahead with your plan and drive right up there."

"Shut up." Maul threatened him with the knife.

"Hold on," Jesse said. "What's wrong with driving up? They know this van. They must."

"But there's a protocol. You can't just drive up and expect the gate to open. If you do that and don't do anything else, they'll *kill* us."

Silence followed Ellison's warning. It rankled Jessie that he might take this for consideration—much less respect—so she told him to explain himself.

"We always stop about thirty to forty feet from the gate. No closer. Then I always get out right away and everyone else stays in the van. I go over and talk to the guards; they're up on a walkway. I've got my shotgun pointing down, but I make sure they can see it. There's no trust with them. Not on either side. You hear me? And seeing me again so soon will make them nervous. They're sure not expecting me to show up with two girls, because there's no way I could have been on another raid since I left there today."

"You got lucky," Jessie said. "You tell them that you ran across some refugees and murdered the girls' families. That'll sound about right."

"Pilgrims," he said, ignoring her scorn. "They never see refugees around here anymore."

"What do you mean, 'pilgrims'?"

"There's a rumor that the Army of God is a holy site. People show up sick or crippled, starving, and want to get in. The guards shoot them. There's a dead guy out there right now who showed up with a big cross. They weren't impressed."

"Fine, then you walk up and say you killed some pilgrims. But you're not taking your shotgun."

"I'll need it *and* my pistol and knives. They notice everything."

"Not in your wildest dreams."

"Then empty my weapons and give them to me. But I'm going to need them, and I'm going to have to take one of the girls with me. It's going to be really unusual for me to go back there so soon, so it makes sense that I'd recognize that fact and show off a girl this time."

Bliss as bait. The imminence of it tore at Jessie. So did the ruinous vision of her girl arriving at the gate in the hands of this killer. *Just like Ananda.* But what he said possessed a murderous logic. "You'll have your unloaded guns. But no knives."

"I'm not going to take her hostage, if that's what you're thinking. The minute I drive up, I'm casting my lot with you people. I've got no choice but to go through with it."

"You're not taking a knife," Jessie said firmly. No matter his words, he could try to take Bliss hostage and tell the guards that the van had been hijacked.

"All right," he said. "As long as I've got my guns, they might not notice the knives, or they might not think anything of it. I'll have one of the girls in the front seat, and when I get out I'll take her with me. I'll leave the door open, but at an angle so they can't see in. That's protocol, too: we never leave ourselves exposed, in case they get trigger happy. They never have with us, but you never know."

"Are they going to wonder if the girls have been examined?" Hannah asked from the back of the van.

"Probably. I'll have to tell them no. They'll never believe that I had them checked all the way out here. But I can say that their parents begged us not to take them because they're virgins . . ."

He said it so matter-of-factly that Jessie knew he'd said it before.

". . . and I can also tell them that if the girls turn out to be used, they can sell them on the slave market."

"The slave market?" She didn't know how much more of Ellison she could take.

"I've never had anything to do with slaves. The point is that it's not credible that I had two girls examined out here."

"What about the girls in the compound? What are they going to be doing when we get there?" Jessie asked.

"They'll be locked up in their dormitory for the night. We'd be a lot better off showing up around mid-morning tomorrow when most of them will be out in the fields. That way they'll see you and come running. If we hit the compound tonight, the guards will be very skittish; we never go there at night. No one ever goes anywhere at night. But even if we got inside the gate, we'd end up having to fight our way to the dormitory in the dark. And they really lock them up tight. It's like a fortress within a fortress."

"How far away are we?" Jessie asked.

"Two hours."

She turned to the others. "I hate the idea of waiting one more minute than we have to, but tomorrow makes sense."

"T-Tomorrow," Brindle agreed as he drove. The others nodded. "And if f-for s-some r-r-reason w-we c-c-can't p-pull it off, at l-least the g-g-girls are g-going to s-see that we tr-tr-tried to s-save th-th-th-th—" His last word failed him.

"Them," Maul said decisively. "That we didn't just let some scum like him drag them away so they could be fucked to death." He looked ready to gut Ellison.

"We *need* him," Jessie said to Maul. She turned to Ellison. "But you're a dead man if you give us away."

"I'm dead either way." Ellison spoke calmly, as he had when she'd pressed the muzzle of her M-16 to his head. His eyes flicked at Maul. "It's a fait accompli."

"No, it's not. You help us get our girls out, and you get to live."

"He *killed* Coxwell," Maul said.

"You have a daughter in there, right?" she said to Maul.

"No," he said, surprising her. "My girl was killed by the likes of him." Madness wracked his voice, left it creaky as a rusty hinge; and Jessie understood that grief had left him steeped in vengeance.

"I'm so sorry," she said. "But you have to ask yourself, what do you want more? Those girls back or his death?"

"I want both."

"We're making a deal here." Jessie turned to the rest of them. "And we *will* keep it. You think I don't want to kill him? He and his men wiped out my camp. I *saw* what they did. He put my husband in chains and shoved a shotgun to his head. Eden was in a coma when I left, and he's probably dead because of him. Then he took my youngest daughter, and now I have to use my only other child to try to get her back. But we have to give him a reason to help us, and there's no better reason than the lives of our children. Look, if he gets us inside and does nothing to betray us, then we've *got* to guarantee his life."

She wasn't sure that she believed her own words, but she had to make Coxwell's men *and* Ellison believe them. Everyone agreed but Maul. He stared at his blade as if it were the only answer he could ever give. Jessie thought better of pressing him.

Miles passed. With Maul's knife still pricking his side, Ellison broke a long silence. "Who's the second girl, anyway. I only see the one in the back."

Jaya sat forward. "Me."

The prisoner studied the boy's beardless face. "Let's hope we don't have to use him. He'll only work from a distance. This one," he glanced at Bliss again, "has to be screaming like her heart's getting ripped out, right from the time we pull up." He spoke to her directly: "Your family's just been murdered by me and the men in this van, and we're dragging you to a place that's a nightmare. You've got to scream like you mean it. You fight me hard as you can. If you don't make it real, everyone dies."

Bliss nodded. She looked numb.

"I smell gas. Do you have any for making bombs?" Ellison asked.

"In the back, two half empty cans," Jessie said.

"You know how to do it?"

"Of course," Jessie said.

"Then make two of them. When we show up, the guards up on that walkway always gather just to the right of the gate. It's stupid, but they're bored and that's what they do. When we get inside, someone's got to hit them with a gas bomb. Whoever's got a strong arm. It's a risky move, but we've got to take them out right away. Even if they don't die, a bomb will slow them down. The second bomb's for the gas depot. It has a cross in front of it. They treat it like it's the Holy Land. We should drive straight for it and blow it up. That'll set off a huge fire. The grass is dry as tinder. We want a fire that'll burn down the sky, spread everywhere. If we get that going, it'll start getting crazy in there, and we can grab the girls and go. If for some reason I'm not with you—"

"You'll be with us," Maul said. "You won't be going *anywhere*."

"I mean if I'm dead, then you get to the depot by following a wagon road that cuts to the left of the entrance. It goes up over a hill and takes you right to it. Just look for that cross."

"Why are you telling us this?" Jessie asked.

"If any of it's true," Maul said.

"It's true," Ellison responded, but he kept his eyes on Jessie. "What else am I going to do? My life depends on getting those girls out. Look, I don't care about the Army of God. It's not like I buy their bullshit. And they're finished. They had groundwater, and they wasted it. Everything's dry as bone, ready to burn, and now they're thinking of heading north."

"So the gravy train's pulling away."

"That's the way it looks, but it's not just that. They're bad as the assholes who brought down the planet in the first place. They sucked the life out of their own little squat, and if they get half a chance, they'll do it again. People like that never learn. It's all 'God's bounty' and a thousand hosannas and the End Times are coming so let's use it up fast as we can." He shifted to face her. "I don't expect you to believe this, not now, but if we get those girls, you'll find out that I tried to help them. I gave yours a book that we found—"

"A book? What was she supposed to do with *that*?"

"Nothing, but it had a Krugerrand pasted inside the back cover. Open the thing and you couldn't miss it. Your kid is sharp. I figured if she had few minutes alone with the book, she'd find it."

"And do what with it?"

"Buy her way out of there. Bribe the guards. It's bleak for those younger guys. They have to wait for the older men to die before they get to move up the food chain. That much gold will buy a new life for someone like them. Some of them want it. I see it in their eyes every time I go in that place."

"You're a coward," she said. "You're scum. You could have saved her, but you flipped her a goddamn coin." *I could kill you.*

Ellison said nothing.

If he'd had no conscience at all—if he'd been another KK—she could have disregarded him; but he bought off whatever feelings he had for her child with a Krugerrand, delivered a death sentence to her and the other girls, and then taken his thirty pieces of silver—with kisses of betrayal to come later.

"Why didn't you give her a gun or knife?" Jessie demanded. Using her own weapons had never felt so inviting. "Something she could have protected herself with?"

"Because she would have been totally outgunned, and if they found anything on her, they'd have blinded her or burned her at the stake."

Jessie looked away, once more forcing on herself the reasons that his life mattered: Ananda, Imagi, M-girl, Bella, Gilly.

"I should tell you that Zekiel took a liking to her. He runs the show."

"What's he like?"

"Old Testament with Uzis. I'd have no trouble killing him. He's a child molester who thinks he's Abraham."

"And you procure for the prophet."

Again Ellison offered no response.

"So this Zekiel's having his way with my daughter?" Jessie had never felt sicker, or more willing to kill. Primed for the worst.

"I don't think he's touched her. He believes that it's a sin to do that before their first period. Then he parades them around on his arm. He's not doing that yet. But if he comes to the gate with her, then you'll know."

As the last of the sun settled, they pulled behind the same hill where Ananda and the girls had been forced to camp on the final night of their journey. Jessie had Ellison tied to the front of the van and put under guard. They did not light a fire. In the blanketing darkness, it could have been a beacon to anyone in the back country. Neither did they eat. With their provisions almost spent, they saved their last meal for the morning, when they'd need their strength.

Jessie stirred before the cracking dawn, feeling like she'd awakened to another world. She wondered if it was the one you entered right before your death. Every movement of air lit up her skin, and she smelled the lingering demise of the land more fiercely than ever before. Her senses felt stropped by fear and desperation. By nightfall she'd be dead, or have her daughter back.

They dawdled over their morning meal, killing time. Each moment unfurled slowly, yet once in the van the minutes moved at a furious, unflinching pace. It was like the battle had already begun.

Ellison rode shotgun with his empty weapons. Behind him, Bliss sat next to Jessie. Her daughter would move up front when they neared the compound. The girl's hands were bound, but not so tightly that she couldn't break free, and she had a knife strapped to her thigh.

Brindle gave a stuttered cry when he spied the walls. Bliss climbed up next to Ellison. She turned to share a long look with her mother. Jessie squeezed the girl's hands. No one spoke. The air in the van felt heavy and warm, strangely listless on the way to war.

When Bliss turned forward, Jessie stared at the land glimmering through the narrow slit. The brakes sounded, and she saw a giant cross of shattered glass embedded in the gate, burning in the sun.

Bliss's screams strangled the fading brake noise. Ellison dragged her out the metal-plated door, giving no hint of his ankle injury. She fought like a trapped animal. Guards gathered above and stared as she kicked Ellison and tried to punch him with her tied hands. Screaming always, so hard that Jessie thought she was already hearing the horror of her daughter's death.

Ellison holstered his weapon and slapped her to the dirt. The crack of his foul hand scarred the air. Then he kicked her in the belly. Jessie heard the *thump.* Her own gut ached.

Bliss had no breath to scream. She lay curled in the dust, gasping in pain. But when Ellison looked up at the guards, she lunged for his crotch, doubling him over. He grabbed her hair, twisting it, forcing her face to the ground.

Enough's enough.

But Jessie could do nothing to help her girl, and her frustration turned to rage for all the brutal reasons that had brought her here. She gripped the M-16, aching to kill him.

"Tell Zekiel I've got two more for him!" Ellison shouted.

Bliss wept loudly, defeated. She uncurled, and Jessie saw blood and dirt caked on the girl's face. This was not an act. She was hurt. But in the next few minutes Bliss regained strength and fury, kicking at Ellison as Brindle spoke up from the driver's seat.

"G-G-Gate's op-opening."

Jessie kept her eyes on the slit, moist hands on her weapon. A man in a white robe stared at Ellison. Ananda was not by the man's side. That's what Jessie saw most clearly—that this molester in priestly garb wasn't parading around her daughter like a prize.

Bliss climbed to her knees. Ellison, hand still in her hair, yanked the girl to her feet. She yelped, screamed. He muzzled her mouth with his good hand.

"I've got two more for you, Zekiel. Pilgrims. Found them on my way back." Ellison forced Bliss to face the Army of God leader. "She looks better without the blood."

"I was going to summon you today," Zekiel said, curiously ignoring the marauder's prize. He held up a gold coin.

When guards rushed up and seized Ellison and Bliss, Jessie knew that their prisoner had told the truth. She also knew that now nothing could go according to plan.

She shoved Brindle, "Go, *go*," her heart hammering her chest.

The van lurched forward. Almost stalled. Guards up on the wall started shooting. Bullets crackled against the roof, front, sides.

Jessie threw open the sliding door and hurled herself out. Gunfire kicked up dirt inches away. She darted left, right, left-left—a crazy pattern—and saw her shadow killed several times as she raced for the gate.

But it was already closing, and Bliss had disappeared.

Chapter Seventeen

World Population Drops 3 Billion
Higher mortality "unstoppable"
Final UN Report on Climate Crisis

Glaciers Gone, Millions Doomed in South America
Patagonia outpost overrun by refugees
Radio Tierra

With her gown draped over her head, Ananda could see only the glow of the three church candles. But she could feel Zekiel's fingernails. Each of them—sharp and untrimmed—raked her skin when he yanked down the cloth that covered her sex.

The Krugerrand fell out and clattered loudly on the floor. Then she heard metal scrape stone as he picked up the gold piece from the slate.

"Fix that," he said to Desana, who quickly snugged the cloth back into place.

Zekiel pulled the gown off Ananda's head and thrust the Krugerrand in her face. "Where did you steal this from?"

After all her fear, not a word of her menses. Ananda stared at the coin, then glanced at Desana. The woman's eyes were wide; but she, too, gazed only at the gold.

Zekiel grabbed the back of Ananda's head and jerked her forward until she could smell the dirt and ash that clung to the Krugerrand.

She said nothing. His grip tightened, wrenching her hair so violently that her scalp ripped and her eyes watered.

"Mary gave it to me." *He can't hurt her.*

"Mary?" Zekiel pressed the finely corrugated edge of the Krugerrand against the lower rim of her eye socket. "That's a lie. Where would Mary have found *this*?"

He twisted the coin and tore her skin, then thrust the edge into the soft belly of the socket, a sudden lever under her eye. His thumbnail pressed against her squeezed lids, and his other hand tightened mercilessly on the back of her head. "The cursed one," he said to Desana. "Bring her here. I want this one to watch."

The woman ran down the aisle, her robe flapping as nosily as her bare feet.

"I told you not to make me hurt the cursed one." Zekiel forced Ananda to her knees in front of him. "You failed her."

He towered above Ananda, his eyes shifting between her tear-streaked face and the gold glinting in the soft light.

Ananda turned from the sour smell of him. He seized her head with both hands and made her face him again. She fought sickness.

"Do you want to tell me now where you got this, or do you want to face the consequences?"

Beat you, burn you, blind you.

Before she could speak, Imagi cried out. Desana was hauling the child into the church. The girl broke away and ran toward Ananda, who didn't dare turn from Zekiel's soiled gown.

But he moved, grabbing Imagi and pushing her to the altar. He stood behind her, gripping her shoulders. The girl quieted, but Ananda saw her eyes and sensed her terror.

"The cursed ones bring darkness," Zekiel proclaimed.

"But they have blessedly brief lives. Hers will end when I burn her to death at the Sacred Heart of Evil. Unless you tell me where you got it. Now."

"Burned Fingers."

"Do you mean El—"

"The man with the burned fingers. The guy who brought us here."

Zekiel stared at her: "He wouldn't give you a gold coin, not for anything. The man gives away nothing."

"He didn't give it to me exactly. He gave me that book of birthday letters, and it was in the back, hidden. You can feel the spot where it was."

Zekiel shoved Imagi toward Desana. "Take her to the cell. Leave her there." Then he dragged Ananda to her feet. "You are deceitful. You hid the gift of life from me. You have lied from the start. You have defied an instrument of the Lord." He lowered his face to hers. "You cursed Mary twice, first with her death, and then her sacred memory with a lie. Tomorrow, at sundown, you will burn."

Desana, leaving with Imagi, wrestled the girl back to them. "Teresa cursed the church by speaking of the 'bonus girl' to the others. I heard her spread this lie myself."

What Ananda heard in the woman's excited voice was the plea for another girl to burn.

"Have the guards bring her to the dorm window," Zekiel said. "This one, too. Wait for me there. The others must see everything. Every step."

"Yes, yes." Desana pulled Imagi back down the aisle and shouted for guards.

Five of them rushed in and hurried Ananda out the door.

The older men were assembling. Torches burned, flames a foot high. The men glared. None spoke. But Ananda could feel their keen attention to her every breath, as if they were already watching her burn.

She had two guards on each arm, holding them straight

out, forcing her up the hill from the church, a procession of white robes and red flames in a sea of stillborn blackness.

Ananda heard the brush of gowns against aged skin, and dozens of bare feet crushing the dry cheatgrass; but her own body felt numb, as if touch had perished, while sight and smell and sound came sorely to life.

Even time—the most fleeting sense of all—did not escape her now, when she wanted nothing so much as the refuge of stillness. She could have numbered the seconds that swept her to the dorm, where four more guards held Teresa under the torches of another crowd of old men.

"They're going to burn us." Teresa's eyes spilled.

Ananda said nothing. Saw only the shutter rising and the glare of flames on glass, the swiftly lit faces of the girls inside. M-girl stared at her.

The old men parted for Zekiel. He strode to the window and pointed to Ananda and Teresa. "They will know the Sacrament of Fire at sundown tomorrow," his voice louder than ever. "We will light the eternal darkness with their sins."

Guards marched Ananda and Teresa past the stacked wood at the Sacred Heart of Evil and shackled them upright. The girls' spines were mashed against the steel stake, their backs pressed into each other. Rusty links cut their ankles, hips, chests, and—worst of all—throats. Like they'd been garroted but left to live.

Levon stayed to guard them through the night. And this gave Ananda hope; when she complained of her sore arm hours ago, he'd eased his grip. But Levon would not answer her entreaties now, and he turned from Teresa's tears.

They heard him sleeping, and struggled against the chains, but the links cut deeper. Silence settled over them. Teresa no longer wept, and Ananda tried to lose herself in glimmering memories of childhood. Only to be startled by her friend's fierce whisper:

"Number two twenty-four, Gabrielle Kinsey."

It took Ananda a moment to remember that Teresa was a Keeper of the Names. But why here? she asked her. Now?

"Because if you survive and I don't, more girls will be remembered."

"But they're burning us both."

"It's what we do, Ananda. We promise to remember until we can't anymore."

"Number two twenty-four, Gabrielle Kinsey," Ananda repeated, an allegiance to the unknown.

They continued reciting names as night gave way to day, delivering more than fifty girls from the darkness of forgetting.

"Number two seventy-eight, Heather Cookenboo," Teresa said.

Ananda's throat was so dry she could barely speak. *Heather Cookenboo, Heather Cookenboo,* she repeated to herself.

They paused to watch their friends enter the fields, eyes meeting eyes under the gaze of guards. All of them turned when they heard a long tanker truck lumbering toward the grotto. Ananda was thinking she could walk faster than it was moving when gunshots rang out from the front of the compound.

Jessie slipped sideways between the wall and the massive gate, narrowly avoiding being crushed, then plunged into the dense shadows of a wooden catwalk. The broad planks shielded her for no more than a second from guards patrolling the upper wall. She used the moment to turn her M-16 on two men who were closing the gate. They toppled into each other, dead before they could finish their job.

A creak in the catwalk alerted her to a guard reaching down with a Ruger. Jessie opened the automatic, shooting right through the rough boards that held him and the others. Wood chips rained on her. The guard with the handgun died instantly; so did another who fell hard enough to rattle the walkway. Three men squirmed on the planks and moaned, gripped senseless by bone-cracking wounds.

"Mom!" Bliss screamed.

Wheeling around, Jessie saw a guard trying to aim a revolver at her, thwarted only by Bliss's failing grip on his arm.

"Now!" her daughter yelled, rolling away. Jessie gunned him down.

A wounded man spilled off the catwalk and hit the ground by the gate. He writhed in the dust, arms wrapped around the blood, bone, and sinew of his ruined knee.

One of two guards hauling off Ellison turned and fired a pistol wildly at Jessie. The shot nearly tore off her daughter's head, leaving a red streak across the side of Bliss's skull as she fell in a belated attempt to protect herself.

Two guards from farther down the catwalk ran toward the battle. They crouched to avoid cover fire from the van. Jessie threw her back against the wall and tried to gauge their position from the pounding of their feet.

The guard who'd almost killed Bliss now dragged her away. Ellison turned on the lone man now holding him, kneed him savagely, then beat and stomped him unconscious in seconds. He dived at the guard who'd grabbed Bliss.

Jessie heard the reinforcements stop right above her, saw their shadows aiming at Ellison, and blasted through the planks again. She wounded them both.

Maul and Stace forced the gate open wide enough for the armored van, while Ellison grappled with the guard who'd shot Bliss, freeing her. The man's gun landed on the ground. Bliss, bleeding, crawled toward it. Ellison head-butted the guard's face. Blood gushed from his nose and mouth; his front teeth dribbled out on strands of red saliva, dropping like bruised fruit. Ellison grabbed his crotch and shirt and drove him backward, skewering him on the six-inch shards of the gate's huge cross. The guard died with his eyes opened wide, mouth agape.

Ellison spun around, looking everywhere.

A pause: momentary, murderous.

Bliss staggered to her feet with the weapon that had wounded her. She reeled, had to catch her breath and balance. Jessie ran to her, pulled her close, stared at the bloody gash in her scalp. She couldn't imagine that a mother had ever been more grateful: millimeters more and the bullet that grazed her daughter would have taken her life.

The van rolled up, doors open.

"Get in!" Ellison shouted. Guards were running toward them from distant points of the compound. Zekiel had vanished.

Maul, Stace, Bliss, and Jessie piled through the side door. Ellison scavenged for weapons and executed the wounded, each pop of gunfire singular and stark. Jessie looked away.

The van turned toward the wagon trail that appeared to the left of the gate. Ellison raced up with two rifles, a slide action shotgun, and three pistols, tossing the spoils on the floor by the front passenger seat.

He jumped in and pulled out his sawed-off shotgun. "I need my ammo!" he shouted with a breathlessness that might have been nerves. Hard for Jessie to say. He'd killed like it was a career. Murdered the maimed. Saved Bliss. Now he turned to Brindle: "Floor it. They're coming." To everyone else: "Close the fucking doors." He slammed his own.

Jessie shut the side door, closing off a view of guards massing about a 150 feet away. She rummaged under the seat for a leather sack packed with shotgun shells and bullets. She handed Ellison his knives, too.

"I don't know about this," Maul said to her.

Ellison threw him a look that Jessie knew she would never want to catch herself. Her doubts about the man with the burned fingers had died at the gate. He knew war. He *looked* like war. He was brutal, fast, feral—what they needed now.

She watched him crack his door. Peer out. The church was coming up on their right. "Get your gun ready and take a look," he said to her. "Timing's good."

Jessie opened the side door a few inches and saw the towering concrete cross—and the guards rushing toward the van.

"Twilight time," Ellison singsonged strangely.

Jessie slid aside the door and opened up on full auto, cutting down three of the guards before the others dropped of their own accord.

The church cut off return fire. She kept watch. In another minute or two she might see Ananda. They just had to get over a hill that rose before them like an ocean swell. The climb worried her; the van already strained under the weight of ten passengers. She heard Bella crying all the way in the back next to Hannah. Hansel made odd growling sounds at their feet.

"Any automatics in that haul?" Maul asked Ellison.

Ellison shook his head. "Take this." He handed him the slide action. "Nothing better for tight combat." He sounded like he relished the prospect. "It'll work well with that." He eyed Maul's pistol.

Maul took the slide action without comment or thanks.

"Anyone else?" Ellison looked back. "It's a real grab bag up here."

Jesus, he sounds almost cheery, thought Jessie.

"I'll take a rifle," Hannah said. Jaya reached for a pistol. The weapons disappeared like food after a fast.

"I just want my shotgun," Bliss said from behind Jaya. Her hand rested on his shoulder.

Jessie picked it up off the floor and handed it back. Bliss pumped a shell into the chamber, then wrapped her arm around Jaya's chest. He settled into her embrace.

For several more seconds Jessie's view of the guards was

cut off by the church. Stone and mortar, crudely configured, it looked medieval to her. Another crime against the age.

The van labored harder as the hill steepened. She saw forty or fifty men in white robes racing away in the distance. That made no sense. Back in their camp, the wounded KK had said that the older men were armed, too. Not these guys. Not yet anyway.

Automatic weapon fire riddled the rear of the van. Jessie flinched, ducked, closed the side door. Ellison scratched his head.

"Once we reach the top and start down, you're going to see that grotto with a cross and a big storage tank," he said to Brindle. "Head right to it. We've still got those gas bombs?"

"They're back here," said Hannah, sitting between Bella, still crying and gnawing her fists, and Augustus, whose lips moved in prayer.

"Get ready to hand them up."

"What about the girls?" Jessie said. "We should be seeing them, right?"

"I have my doubts." Ellison spoke without glancing back.

"But you said—"

"That they'd come running, but that little tête-à-tête back there gave them time to round them up. I can't imagine Zekiel leaving them out in the fields at this point."

He's right, Jessie realized. Nothing could go according to plan, just as she'd told herself after he and Bliss had been seized at the gate.

Still chained to the stake, Ananda and Teresa watched the guards run up to their friends and order them back to the dorm. The girls didn't move. Not at first. The darkly clad men had to strike and shove them. M-girl cried out, yet had to be pushed again. Mia and Kluani waved to the two of them, boldly defying the guards before they forced the twins to turn away.

Ananda squirreled her hand back until she found Teresa's fingers. In an instant they were entwined as tightly as the chains that bound them.

When the van reached the top of the hill—chased by guards only a hundred feet away—Jessie inched open the side door, hoping against all reason that the girls *would* be running to them. But the fields were empty.

As she closed it, Ellison said, "We need that."

"What?" She sat forward. So did Maul, next to her.

"This tanker truck." Ellison pressed his eyes to the slit in the armor.

She leaned over the front seat and spied a long vehicle trundling toward the grotto.

"Why?" Jessie demanded. "It'll blow sky high."

The tanker truck stopped suddenly, as if the driver had heard the shooting and now spied the van.

"Because it changes everything."

"*You'll* need it, maybe!" Maul yelled at him.

"*We'll* need it. To get away from here, far as we can. We don't want to be anywhere near this place once the word gets out."

"We have no intention of *staying!*" Jessie shouted, not just in anger: they had to make themselves heard over the screeching brakes. The wagon road was deeply rutted on the downhill side, forcing them to creep along. The shooting had stopped, at least; Jessie figured that the van had dipped below the guards' line of sight.

Ellison turned to her. "Where are you going? Back to that camp of yours?"

"That's where we live."

"Not anymore you don't. As soon as word gets out, you'll have the Alliance, marauders, my own goddamn men all descending on this place for the plunder. There's food stocks, water, weapons. Anything we take, they're going to want."

"And you'll give it to them. All of it," Maul said.

"No, I won't be doing that. My men are going to want my head after this, and they'll take it straight to Zekiel, or whoever's left, so they can keep trading girls for gold." He eyed the others. "We have to take everything we can out of this place or we'll die out there. Separate or alone, we'll die. So we'll set off the gas in the grotto. Without fuel, no one's going to be able to chase us down. It buys us time. We take that truck, we've got a rolling gas station and can outrun them all."

"*We're* going back," Jessie said.

"Not without fuel. Not without food. Not without water."

"No," Maul yelled. "We fight for the girls, not for some goddamn tanker—"

Ellison grabbed Maul's throat and jerked him forward. "Stop fucking with me and start *thinking* or you'll never see your kid. They won't blow that thing up. They blow it up, the whole fucking place turns to ash. That's *our* job. Right now it's a fucking barrier. Our *only* goddamn barrier. We've got rocket launchers behind us, guards in the grotto, and a driver with an armed crew on that truck. We take it. We fucking *die* for it. Till then, anything else is up for grabs."

Ellison shoved him away. Maul choked and coughed, his throat red and bruised. The van stopped. Brindle pointed a gun at Ellison. He swatted it away like it was a wasp. "Drive," he ordered. "Or do you want to kill *all* of us?"

A vein fat as a bloodworm pulsed in Maul's brow. Jessie thought that he'd murder Ellison, spatter him right there in the front seat. Without realizing it, she rested her hand on Maul's arm, trying to calm him.

"Ellison's right." She spoke to all of them, resenting the concession; but she knew it was necessary. "That truck opens up a whole new world. It doesn't mean we can't go back. It just makes it easier. Till now, all we could hope for was getting the girls and surviving somehow."

The growing problem—and she had seen it coming—was Ellison. He'd taken over. She watched him peer out the slit in the windshield armor—wound up and ready to spring. Yes, he did know war; and when this was over, she'd make sure that he knew its final price.

"Rocket launchers?" Jaya said in the strained silence.

"One," Ellison answered. "Short guy in the back's got it. But they're hard to handle, and if they miss and hit that truck or the grotto, they're doing our work for us. That's why that goddamned truck stopped. If it gets blown up, they don't want to set off the gas in the cave, too. So they're going to be real careful with rockets. We get close enough to that truck, they won't dare use them." He picked up Brindle's gun and handed it to him. "Don't threaten me again. And drive faster. My driver would have had us there by now."

"Y-Y-Your dr-dr-dr-driver w-was an ass-asshole."

"Yeah, he sure was, wasn't he?" Ellison laughed.

Scary, Jessie thought. In two minutes he'd gone from calm strategist to brutal enforcer to genuine . . . *laughter*?

They'd moved halfway down the slope. Only the back of the van was exposed, and the shooting hadn't resumed. Jessie opened the side door and saw the guards deploying on the crest of the hill. Then she looked at the open acreage to their right, hoping she'd missed the girls with her first glance.

The letdown came quick as sun glare, but the green fields astonished her.

They formed a lush cross in a huge expanse of dry cheat-grass—the latter a scourge *and* an apt symbol of the warming, in her studied opinion. Escalating carbon dioxide levels in the atmosphere had pumped up its biomass—its fuel load—by more than seventy percent. "The national flower of the collapse," she'd once said to Eden, except cheatgrass was a weed, rooty and predatory enough to have colonized most of the country as temperatures rose and wildfires raged. But it had been driven back from this vegetation, the thickest she'd seen in decades.

A large circle lay at the intersection of the fields. At its center stood a metal pole crowded by a wall of wood. The pole appeared cloaked with bulky white fabric. Maul stared over Jessie's shoulder, still rubbing his throat.

"What's *that*?" He pointed to the strange sight. "There's something going on there."

Ellison opened his door and looked closely. "Sure is. They're getting ready to burn a couple of girls."

Ananda and Teresa spotted the armored van driving toward the tanker truck, which had stopped well short of the grotto. Guards on top of the hill were aiming down at it but holding their fire.

"The people in that van must be okay," Teresa said, "if Zekiel wants them dead." The taller girl faced away from the vehicles, and had to strain against the chain throttling her neck to look over her shoulder.

"What's that big gun?" Ananda's dry mouth made speaking a struggle, but she'd never seen a rocket launcher, and it looked scary. Neither had Teresa.

A man tried to steady the RPG on his shoulder. Another guard jumped up to help him. They looked like they were aiming at the van.

Ananda could just make out an open door on the side of it. She thought someone might have waved. "Mom? Dad?" she said urgently, with no real hope of being heard. Or maybe Bliss. *Burned Fingers?* It looked like his van. She strained against the chains, wishing she could point to the big gun. *They probably can't see it.*

But the van turned behind the tanker truck and was no longer visible to them or to the guard, who dropped the rocket launcher to his hip.

In seconds four armed men crawled out from under the truck trailer, where they might have been hiding. One of them looked around and crept back into the shadows. The other three climbed the metal ladders and braces that framed the long cylindrical tank. They must be with Zekiel, Ananda thought, because they didn't look worried about the guards shooting them in the back.

All the guns were quiet. A tense reprieve. Ananda worried about the guy who'd slipped back under the trailer. She wished she could have screamed out a warning, but even under the best of circumstances her voice wouldn't have carried.

"Should we go on with the list?" Teresa coughed. Her throat sounded raspy. "We don't have much time."

"I guess." Ananda couldn't peel her eyes from the gunmen on the tanker trailer. It was like watching a spark about to explode.

"Number two seventy-nine, Billie Compton," Teresa said with effort.

"Number two seventy-nine, Billie Compton," Ananda repeated, trying to find a lick of moisture in her mouth. Then gasping, "Who's that?"

"I don't know." Teresa sounded exhausted. "A girl who was here a long time—"

"No, *him*." Ananda twisted her head to see better. A man in a white robe was running toward them with a burning torch. "Is that Zekiel?" Teresa had a clearer angle from her side of the stake.

"Oh no. *No*."

Zekiel held the torch high above his head, like a lance or a cross or some other weapon of war. The red and orange tongues roasted the air. Black smoke billowed, sucked to the sky—more heat for the heavens—but Zekiel never once looked up. He stared only at the fire to come, not at the flames he carried.

"If a b-b-bullet h-hits th-that t-t-tank, is it g-g-going to bl-blow?" Brindle still gripped the steering wheel after braking alongside the truck.

"Bullets can't set it off." Ellison looked to his right, where the back end of the tanker trailer sat, even though his windowless door remained closed. "Only rockets. That truck," speaking faster, glancing out the slit, "has four guys on it, plus two in the cab. That's the standard setup. They're freelancers; all they do is run trucks. Army of God will have two of their own in the grotto. They'll shoot us if they can, but they're not supposed to leave it."

Ellison peered out the slit again, put up his hand for quiet, and kicked open his door, gunning down a man stealing up on the side of the van. Before his target hit the ground, Ellison leaped all the way out, waving the others to come.

Jessie stepped into the truck's broad shadow, checking above, weapon ready. A man behind a one-foot wide walkway on top of the tank rose to shoot, but ducked when she fired off a quick burst. Immediately, she checked for legs and feet exposed on the other side, thinking he might have jumped down. Nothing. All of them must be on the trailer, she figured. Just to be sure, she scanned the undercarriage, and saw Ellison dip in front of the big wheels of the rear axle. Then she glanced toward that distant circle where the girls were bound to the stake. The rolling land blocked her view.

Jaya, Stace, Maul, Brindle, and Hannah fanned out quickly. Bliss ordered her dog to stay and slipped out of the van last. Augustus and Bella remained in it. A shot rang out from the grotto.

From under the trailer Ellison yelled, "Jaya, pin them down. Hannah, keep your eyes on the hill."

Bliss teamed with the boy by the back of the van. They fired at the cave, hitting no one; but when they stopped, the grotto was quiet.

Jessie kept her eyes on the tanker trailer, worried about the freelance killers on the other side. Twelve, fifteen feet away. She heard a ladder creak—and their breaths, no more hidden than a hard wind.

An ammo belt shifted. Metal grazed metal. Violence immutable as ever. Close as blood, and deadly surreal.

She stepped toward the front of the truck lightly, as if treading on a minefield.

Maul might have spotted the man she'd seen ducking because he started climbing the metalwork. He'd strapped his shotgun across his back and led with his pistol.

Right then, the truck engine started. Stace raced toward the armored cab. With great caution, Jessie moved forward, too. They couldn't let the truck pull away; it would expose the van to rocket attack. Their lives, she knew, had become hostage to the dull gray hulk of a fuel tank.

Just like in the long ago.

The truck lurched and accelerated slowly. Stace, gun in hand, yanked on the metal-plated driver's door. It wouldn't give, and then it flew open, the brute weight bashing him to the ground. The wiry man jumped up, but before he could raise his revolver a shotgun blast ripped off the top half of his face and launched his animal skin hat into a brief, fluttering flight. His body crumpled, spasmed, stilled.

Jessie watched a battered, prosthetic arm reach from the cab. A steel claw hooked the door and slammed it shut.

In the dark locked-down dorm, the latest gunfire gave M-girl hope. She'd been weeding a row of mustard greens when she heard the first shots, and figured that more pilgrims had been murdered near the gate. But the flurry that just made her look up came from deep inside the compound.

The shutters rose with an unnerving clatter. The girls took one another's hands and drifted like a web in the wind toward the front of the room.

M-girl wanted to see the exuberant faces of her mom and dad and everyone who'd fought to free them. But before she neared the window, her stomach turned with the memory of last night, when the shutters opened for the chaining of Ananda and Teresa, surrounded by Zekiel and dozens of his torch-bearing disciples. M-girl had sickened at the sight, sure that they'd burn the girls right then. But Bessie, Teresa's red-haired workmate at the Quonset hut, had said Zekiel would never do that. "Not without us being down there to watch," she explained. "Zekiel says that if a sin is big enough for a burning, it's because it's big enough for God to destroy this place. So burning girls is like a sacrifice for him, a way to buy off his God; and he makes us watch from close up so we never forget what happens if we disobey him."

Now, the window didn't reveal the jubilant faces of rescuers. M-girl felt such meager disappointment that she knew her hope had never been great. A guard still stood outside the door, but the truck that had stopped shy of the grotto started to move. Men might have been clinging to the metalwork—hard to tell at her remove—but she could definitely make out the dark shadow of another, smaller vehicle jutting beyond the far side of the long tank trailer.

Little Cassie pointed to the Sacred Heart of Evil. It was hard to see in the bright sunlight. "What's that?"

"What's what?" Mia bent next to the girl, still holding her hand. "Show me."

Cassie pointed again. "Is that Zekiel with a—"

"He's lighting the fire!" Mia sounded stunned. She straightened, pounded the window. "He's burning them!" she shouted.

"What?" M-girl pressed closer to the glass. All the girls did.

"Zekiel's *burning* them." Mia's voice shook. "You can't hardly see it but he's doing it *now*."

There's no one to stop him, was all M-girl could think.

The door banged open. Desana and the guard rushed in. "You must follow me to the Sacred Heart of Evil," she yelled, "for the Sacrament of Fire."

She walked out the door and waited for them. M-girl kept her head down as she lined up, trying to look solemn, though her mind felt fevered, insane with impulse. This wasn't planned, she thought in a fleeting moment of clarity. It's not what Bessie had said or what she'd heard from the others. Before Sylvan was burned, the girls were grouped right there in a prayer circle with Desana, then marched by a phalanx of guards down to where the terrified child had been chained. It's not even what Zekiel had said last night. He must be worried that if he waits, she thought, he won't get to burn them, which filled her with both hope and horror.

M-girl restrained herself until all the girls had stepped out the door. Then she bolted. Desana snagged her arm for only a second before Mia smashed her fist down on the woman's wrist and jerked her free. The two of them raced off. So did Kluani and Bessie. But the guard grabbed Gilly, and Desana started after Cassie, shouting, "Stop or you'll burn, too," which only made the towhead run harder.

Desana gave up and yelled at the guard, "Get her." She pointed to Cassie. He dragged Gilly over to Desana, but in the handoff, Gilly broke away. And she was fast.

M-girl, Mia and Kluani, Bessie, and now Gilly were sprinting toward the Sacred Heart of Evil. They saw flames. Smoke. Heard Ananda and Teresa screaming, and Desana yelling, "All of you, stop! *Stop!*" But that's all the older woman could do—shout and hurry after them by herself— because when M-girl looked back, she saw that Cassie had led the guard away from them. Intentionally or not, she'd done them a favor.

Maybe herself, too, M-girl thought. Running toward the fire felt like the end to her. It could have been written on the blank slate of the sky, for all the certainty that flooded her in those stricken moments. The gunfire had surely been aimed at whoever had fought their way close to the grotto. The gas.

Battle lines above. Battle lines below.

A wild rush of adrenaline nauseated M-girl and made her legs feel like stumps numb on the land. Yet she'd never moved faster. Ananda had always been the courageous one who ran all the risks, like stealing away last night after that disgusting "wedding." *Not me,* M-girl said to herself, eyes soaked with self-recrimination. *I've always been scared.*

Scared senseless now, but not slowing. She ran with the

great weight of her guilt, knowing in the bleakest yet boldest terms that she couldn't let her best friend burn. She'd rather die than live with that, and the reason was so simple: she loved Ananda. Not Zekiel's twisted love, but her own kind. She knew he'd burn her, too, if he knew her heart. And in moments he would because, sick with fear and never braver, she raced screaming into the flames.

Chapter Eighteen

Wealthy Build Lake Superior Enclave
100 mile walled, armed "Christian community"
From word-of-mouth accounts

Ananda and Teresa's shrieks deafened them to M-girl's screams, and their crippling agony sealed their eyes to her sudden presence. Zekiel scrambled around the circle in a frenzy, sweeping his torch over the last few feet of kindling, daubing spots he'd missed, a painter turning his canvas red.

A nightmarish crackle heralded the horrors of this parched and brittle world, but Ananda's most grinding fear—rising above raw pulses of raging pain—was the gunpowder that could sear her skin at any second. Zekiel had mixed it in a mud paste and rubbed it on their thighs, bellies, and under the necks of their gowns. Hidden places. He'd never said a word, but she knew the odor. And she'd understood Levon's odd remark when he first marched her past this abominable stake: "Witches spark when they burn . . . It's the evil exploding." A grisly ruse to dupe gullible guards and ignorant old men.

The brutal heat eased from Ananda's feet; blessed, she

thought, with the first numbing effects of death. Then she opened her eyes on M-girl kicking and tossing away logs—and saw Zekiel wielding his torch like a club above her friend.

Ananda yelled a warning. It came too late. He smashed the flaming length on M-girl's back. She crashed face first into the burning wood. Crying, she heaved herself aside as the first stone struck Zekiel.

Kluani followed Mia's attack with a rock of her own. All the girls threw them. The Army of God's leader whipped his torch around, trying to bash them, burn them; but they scattered like ravens and regrouped to throw more rocks. They bloodied him quickly, which made them bolder.

Mia fired a stone directly into his face. The impact sounded a distinct *crack*. Bone or teeth. The girls turned into a ruthless, vengeful pack, picking up rocks bigger than their fists, hurling them with the fury of innocence burning.

M-girl never saw their attack. She had eyes only for the flames that she smothered with her bare feet, and the tinder and smoldering logs that she strewed with her singed hands. She never stopped moving, defying pain, driven by outrage and galvanized by qualities of life and love that she was only beginning to grasp.

She cleared her way to Ananda and Teresa, yanking futilely on the chains before turning to Zekiel, as if he might have a key. His mouth bled through his beard as he raised a hand to protect his face from the girls who swarmed him.

"The chain's knotted down there," Ananda cried, casting her eyes to her feet. "The metal's hot." A voice shaken by final fears. Blisters rose on her toes and insteps and bubbled along the links that gripped her ankles. Teresa might have been suffering worse; Ananda heard her weeping.

M-girl's palms sizzled when she tore at the links, and she cried out twice; but she jerked the chains apart and pulled both girls from the fire that she'd defeated.

Desana rushed up and tried to grab Teresa, burned bloody

on her lower legs. The girl's shins smoked, and blisters big as snake eggs had ballooned on her feet.

Bessie spun Desana around and punched her in the mouth, clawed her face. The woman tried to cover her eyes, releasing Teresa. Bessie picked up a sharp rock and pounded Desana flush on the ear. Blood spilled down her neck. She tripped, fell, fled—driven away in less than a minute.

Bessie turned her wrath back on Zekiel. Ananda looked for a stone. Mia advanced close enough to batter his shoulder with a log. He lashed at her with the torch, but she retreated deftly, having distracted him long enough for Gilly to smash his sandaled foot with a rock so large that she'd had to lift it with both hands.

Ananda saw him falter and knew they could bring him down. Her pulse quickened. She threw a rock as hard as she could, bellowing when she missed.

Kluani, a few feet away, drew back her arm and pitched a big stone that smacked the back of Zekiel's skull with such force that he spun around looking dazed, dropped his torch and pitched sideways.

The girls circled him, closed in, beat him. Kicked him viciously. Bessie grabbed his robe. "His feet," she yelled. "Get his feet."

He tripped, fell to one knee. Ananda clapped his face with a flat rock. Did it again harder. Felt something give and wanted him dead. Mia seized his arm, twisted it.

"Break it, break it!" Bessie shouted. Spittle flew from her mouth.

Gilly returned to his foot, pounding it like a hammer with a rock. Bessie buried her hand in Zekiel's hair, wrapped it around her fist and tried to wrench him over backward.

"The guard!" M-girl screamed. "He's coming!"

Bessie, Mia, Ananda—all of them—looked up as if snapped from a trance. The guard who'd chased little Cassie was barreling right at them, truncheon raised.

* * *

Maul clung to a steel ladder on the tanker trailer that rolled him slowly past his dead friend, Stace. He stared at the body bleeding in the dirt, face ripped away by the shotgun blast fired by the man with the steel claw. Maul's head shook. He looked like he'd scream, but he lunged up the last few rungs, surprising and shooting the freelancer whom Jessie had targeted when she stepped from the van. His body smacked the ground on the other side of the tank. She crouched, saw the cloud of unsettled dust, and edged closer to the cab.

She heard movement below the tank and spun toward it with her M-16.

"Don't shoot me," Ellison said. As the truck wheeled left, he swung himself up onto the back of the cab, which was reinforced with a thick slab of armor. Then he studied hoses that fed into the vehicle through a portal, jammed his pistol in the opening and fired five or six times. Jessie lost count.

She scurried around the front of the lumbering truck to try to open the passenger door. Before she could move close, however, it exploded open and a screaming gunman jumped out, blood spilling from his buttocks. She killed him with a quick burst.

Ellison pulled himself on top of the cab and reached down with his pistol, shooting once at the driver through the slit in the windshield armor. The truck still rolled into what looked like a U-turn.

Jessie scaled the running board on the passenger side, now out of range of the guards on the hill. She heard Hannah gasp, "God Almighty," but couldn't risk a look back. She pulled out her handgun and threw the flapping passenger door all the way open. A thick black snake slithered past her face and over her shoulder. She pivoted wildly to the side but held on. The serpent spilled off her and fell to the earth in a squirming clump.

She anticipated a larder of them—broken loose in battle—and fired blindly before she dared look in. She found the driver with the artificial arm slumped over the wheel with a neat wound in his forehead, and three more in his hip and leg. No snakes, and surprisingly little blood.

"Go!" she yelled to Ellison, who'd started taking fire from the guards up on the hill.

He jumped off the roof, shadowing her briefly. She hoisted herself into the cab, spied wires hanging from the ignition socket and pulled them apart. The truck shuddered noisily and stopped only halfway through its U-turn, but it had rolled far enough to open the van to rocket attack. *Christ.* Now she had to back up this beast or move their vehicle beside it. And fast. She shoved the dead driver out his door, closed it, and held the wires back together to try to start the truck. They sparked but she couldn't get the engine to turn over.

Get out. *Now.*

She didn't move fast enough. The driver's door opened; strangely, she saw no one. As if a phantom had visited. Tense, she reached to shut it, shocked breathless by a bearded face swinging down from atop the cab—the perch Ellison had abandoned only a minute ago. A toothless man stuck a snub-nosed pistol in the cab; but before he could aim in the tight space, she stabbed his eye with her bone-handle knife.

Wailing, he pulled the trigger, missing her by a wide margin. She gripped the haft with both hands, weighting it so heavily that she lifted herself off the seat. The blade scraped down the gritty cone of his orbital cavity as she dragged the screaming man head first off the roof. He crashed to the dust and staggered to his feet, clawing insanely at the blade still buried in his head.

She grabbed her guns and jumped out, acutely aware that the van was too far away to protect her from the guards in the grotto. Jaya, she saw at once, had moved to cover them, perhaps foolishly: he'd bellied down on the exposed ground with his rifle trained on the dark opening. Nothing shielded the boy but his own temerity. Jessie didn't see her daughter.

The stabbed man spun around, arms flailing. She gunned

him down with her pistol, and retrieved her knife with a hard jerk that snapped his lifeless head off the ground.

Two more shots issued from the rear of the long tank. Now Jessie chanced a look, spotting a truck guard backing up, dropping his gun and raising his hands. The same instant, a shotgun blast blew him back several feet. She hoped it was Maul with his new slide action, but Bliss poked her head out from behind a wheel to survey the damage and pumped another shell into the chamber of her smoking weapon.

Jessie spied a thicker, blacker plume over her shoulder. She couldn't see the fire from where she was, but the monstrous meaning of Hannah's "God Almighty" clobbered her: *the girls are burning.*

Even as she quelled a tumultuous impulse to risk their lives by driving the van to the stake, Ellison yelled, "Back that goddamned—"

A rocket obliterated his last word, exploding about thirty feet in back of their vehicle, spitting shrapnel loudly against the metal plating.

The van shielded Jessie, but Bliss took a hit that bloodied her leg, and a freelancer stealing around the rear of the trailer was hit so hard that he buckled to the ground. Hannah, keeping watch on the hill, shot and killed him when he tried to crawl back to safety.

Jessie sprinted for the van's open side door, certain that she was racing against the next rocket attack.

Her dash set off gunshots from the grotto and from guards up on the hill. Just before she launched herself into the vehicle, a hot pain flashed up her leg.

Blood spilled to her foot. She didn't look. Didn't care. Roaring with adrenaline, she wanted the wheel. But Augustus was climbing into the driver's seat and—with the front doors open—into the cross fire. With his hands still tied, he slammed the door next to him, then lunged for the other, praying aloud all the while. Jessie spotted the rocket launcher aiming at them and heaved the side door closed.

Augustus cranked the ignition—"Forgive us our tres-passes . . ."—and struggled to throw the transmission into reverse. ". . . as we forgive those who—"

"Move, *move*," Jessie shouted, gripping the back of his seat.

Bella wept softly behind them.

The rocket explosion by the van stopped the girls' flight from the Sacred Heart of Evil. Ananda had never seen anything like it. Clumps of earth bigger than their bodies erupted into the air, and shrapnel kicked up tiny clouds of dust within yards of where they huddled. Riotous flames scalded the crater, and suffocating smoke drifted over them. But through the pall, she could see that the van remained unscathed several hundred feet away, and that the truck had been stopped only partway through a turn. But the van was still very much a target: she spotted two men on top of the hill reloading the rocket launcher.

The girls had outrun the guard, and when they neared shooting range of the intruders—seconds before the blast tore a hole in the earth—he'd raced back to Zekiel. The guard had never fired on them. Neither did the men on the hill. The girls themselves had fled with no thought of the rifles and pistols that could slay them, but they were the only ones who would not be shot. Burned to death, yes. Murdered by sex and marriage, absolutely. But never gunned down without Zekiel's express consent. The guards and old men wouldn't dare: the girls were the Holy Grail of the gulag. Ananda looked at all the weapons—none aimed at them—and understood this.

"Go!" she shouted at the others. "They won't shoot you. But don't stop till you get to the big truck."

"Aren't you coming?" Teresa exclaimed.

"Not now," Ananda said, quickly assessing her own burns—painful, increasingly so, but not crippling. "*You* need help. Go."

Bessie grabbed Ananda's arm. "You're coming with us."

"No." Ananda sounded fierce. "I've got something I *have* to do."

"What about you?" Bessie asked M-girl, who'd sidled over to Ananda.

"In a second."

The two older girls raced off with the twins and Gilly.

"Thanks for staying," Ananda said to M-girl. "I really need your help."

"What's wrong with you? This is—"

Footfalls silenced M-girl. Ananda spun around. Little Cassie ran up breathing hard as a bellows.

Where had she been? Hiding? Ananda had no time to ask. "Follow them." She pointed to the girls. *"Now."* Cassie took off.

"That's what *we* should be doing," M-girl pleaded. "Let's get out of here." She tried to drag Ananda away.

Ananda jerked her arm free, wincing with pain. "They're not guarding Imagi. Don't you see? They're all up there." She looked to the hill where the robed men were armed and gathering behind the guards. "They only had the one guy for all of us. Imagi's going to be locked up but we can try to get her out."

"*I* want to get out," M-girl yelled. "They're here for *us.*"

The steel in Ananda's spine would not bend: "Whoever they are, they're here for all of us."

"I don't want to go back for Imagi. I want them to save me." M-girl wept from fear and longing, burns and slow-settling shock. "We're always having to help her. She's going to get us killed, goddamn it."

"I really need your help."

"I can't." M-girl pawed her wet eyes. "I'm sorry, I just can't."

"We've got to move fast," Ananda said, as if she'd never heard her friend. And M-girl followed, as if she'd never spoken.

* * *

Augustus floored the accelerator. Jessie felt them speeding
wildly forward, no visibility but the slit in the windshield
armor. She feared crashing into the tanker trailer and blow-
ing all of them up as much as she feared the rocket, which
exploded at that moment—close enough to lift the rear of
the van off the ground like a horse bucking.

Bella screamed. Jessie thought they'd flip over. But Augustus had the presence of mind to keep his foot off the
brake, and the front wheels pulled the heavy vehicle out
from under a crushing tumble.

The van crashed down with enough force to blow open
the front doors. Before Augustus could slam the one next
to him, two shots from the grotto tore into the seat inches
below his bottom. He jumped up but kept his foot on the
gas, never slowing till he pulled even with the tanker trailer.
The van screeched and stopped just inches from a group of
girls gathered by the side of it. Blood splotched the back of
one of their gowns.

We almost killed them. The wrenching irony didn't escape
Jessie, who'd missed their desperate arrival in the blur of
prayer and panic in the van. "Ananda," she called softly.

None of them responded. They might have been too
stunned to speak. Before she could hurry to them, Ellison
waved and caught her eye. "One more," he mouthed as he
edged along a horizontal brace on the bottom half of the
tank. Brindle trailed him.

Jessie crouched and forced her eyes from the girls. Another shot rang out from the grotto, hitting the tank inches
from Brindle's head. He swore without a stutter. Frustrated,
Jessie screamed, "Jaya!" and turned her automatic on the
dark opening. The boy, rushing to his post by the rear of the
van, opened fire. No one returned their volley.

Ellison climbed off the trailer and took the full cover of
the van. Brindle shadowed him, and Jessie saw that their

driver had been covering Ellison's back—a surprising tribute and another gritty irony: minutes ago, on the way down
the hill, Brindle had stopped the van and pointed his weapon
as if to murder the marauder.

A girl reached for Maul as he hurried past. He squeezed
her hand and spoke softly, swiftly, before ordering all the
girls down on the ground.

He scanned the trailer's elaborate, shadowy undercarriage. Like a hornet's nest, thought Jessie, but they had to
search it: they'd accounted for only three of the four truck
guards.

Bliss called Hansel from the van and ordered him to join
the hunt under the tank. The three-legged dog sniffed like
he was starved for work. He made his way quickly from the
back of the trailer to the front, growling by the forward axle.
A semiautomatic pistol pointed flush at the animal's face.
Ellison fired his sawed-off shotgun from close range, ripping the gun loose—along with most of the man's hand; the
bloody remains dangled from splintered bone and exposed
cartilage.

A guttural scream split the air. Hansel sunk his teeth into
the injured arm and yanked the freelancer from his roost.
Bliss called off her dog, and Maul shoved his gun to the
man's head.

"No," Ellison said, surprising Jessie. "Make him go to the
grotto." He pointed his weapon at the man. "You, show them
what we'll do. Tell them that all your men are dead. Tell
them that we have gas bombs and we'll burn them alive if
they don't come out."

Jessie couldn't tell if the man heard. He was doubled over,
hyperventilating, and gripping his nearly severed arm.

Maul searched him roughly, finding a stiletto in his belt.
He gripped the back of the man's neck and shoved him in
front of the van. "Do like he says."

The wounded freelancer weaved his way toward the

grotto. The guards shot him from the dark opening before he could speak.

"If he'd come back, would you have spared him?" Maul asked Ellison.

"Only a miserable life."

The two men made a final, perfunctory pass down the side of the tank. Bliss crawled under it after Hansel's nose twitched in the air. As the girl and her dog neared the cab, Hansel growled again. She swore loudly and rolled out from under the trailer like she'd been stung. Ellison raced over, reached past the agitated dog and came back with a long black snake twisting around his arm. He allowed a smile for the creature that had startled Jessie.

"All clear. Truck's ours. So's this. We'll eat it." Ellison tossed the snake in the van, alarming Augustus, though his impassioned cry—"Oh, sweet Jesus"—could have been confused with prayer until he and Bella tumbled out the side door.

Jessie and Bliss rushed to the girls still cowering by the rear axle. They saw at once that Ananda was not among them. Neither was M-girl or Imagi.

"Where are they?" Bliss asked Gilly.

"They were just with us, but then Ananda stopped. And M-girl said she was going to be coming but she didn't."

"What about Imagi?" Jessie asked. The girl never strayed far from Ananda.

"We haven't seen Imagi since we got here," Gilly said. "She's been locked up."

"So they didn't burn them?" Jessie asked, wary eyes on the smoky sky.

"No," the girl named Teresa said. "Zekiel *tried* to burn Ananda and me. M-girl saved us. All these girls helped." Her legs were badly burned, Jessie saw as Teresa took Bessie's hand. "We fought him with rocks. Rocks," she repeated sobbing.

"Ananda wouldn't come," Gilly told Jessie. "I think she went back for Imagi. She was really worried about her."

Ellison stepped forward. Gilly screamed and backed into Jessie.

"He's the one!" Gilly shouted. "He threw me in the truck at the camp!"

Jessie hugged her. "I know. But he's helping us now."

"What?"

"Do you want to see Bella?" Ellison's presence was much too complicated to explain to an upset child—Jessie was still puzzling it out herself—so she redirected Gilly. A battle didn't alter the basics of child-rearing.

"Gilly?" Bella raced over. The girls hugged and jumped up and down. Jessie made sure their exuberance didn't drive them from the van's limited shelter.

"Guards are coming!" Hannah shouted. She'd never taken her eyes from the hill.

Before Jessie could react, Ellison grabbed the M-16 from her hands and rolled under the trailer. She pulled out her pistol and joined him. Seven guards had launched what looked like a suicidal attack.

"Shoot them," she said to Ellison.

"Hold your fire," he ordered loudly.

"Kill them." She waved her pistol at Ellison. The men had drawn perilously close—less than a hundred feet from the truck. She aimed at them.

"Dinna fire till ye can see the whites of their eyes," he said in a Scottish accent and chuckled. Then he shot the legs out from under them, the burst like a scythe cutting wheat in a forgotten world. Howls filled the air. Ellison hadn't killed any of them.

Why would they try something so stupid? Jessie wondered. The answer appeared immediately: the robed men who fled earlier had reappeared on top of the hill. They were heavily armed and had taken command of the guards.

"Put them out of their misery," she said to Ellison.

"Never. It's a warning to the rest of them that if they listen to those old fools, they'll pay a huge price."

As if to underscore his words, one of the wounded, already hoarse from screaming, rose to his knees and shot himself in the head. His body crumpled like a sheet.

"Oh, Jesus," Jessie said. *But he's right.*

"Sorry to grab your weapon like that," Ellison kept his eyes on the hill, "but if you don't mind, I'd like to hold onto it. Just for now. In case more of them try the same thing."

Jessie backed out from under the trailer, hearing, "Dad? Dad?"

A heart-faced towhead looked around. Jessie also saw twins who looked as lost, and knew they must be Coxwell's. The first child took her hand. "My dad's Stace. Stace," she repeated, as if to defeat the grief on Jessie's face. Grief for this girl and the twins. Grief for Ananda. Grief that never seemed to cease. The girl's eyes were already racing to the dead bodies, her faceless father among them.

Maul appeared by Jessie's side. She saw tears on his cheeks. "Come here, Cassie." A big man whose words trembled. He took Stace's child in his arms and whispered to her. A wail rose from the girl. And rose and rose and rose, and she beat Maul's back with a ferocity that defied her innocence—or what passed for the last of her youth. No mother. Now no father. Maul held her long after he sank to his knees, weeping with her.

Jessie removed herself from their agonizing moment. *What can he say to her?* she asked herself. *What can any of us say to that girl? Or Coxwell's twins? Flick's granddaughter? Orphans all. Or your own girls, if Eden's dead? If they even survive. And I do, too.*

Tending to Teresa's burns, Hannah raised the back of her bloodstained gown. "See that," she told Jessie. "He spread mud with gunpowder on her and your daughter so his 'witches' would put on a show when they burned up. I thought I'd seen everything."

Jessie stared at the dark streaks, stunned. *Ananda's still out there.*

"And this is shrapnel." Hannah's hand circled a brutish looking wound on Teresa's lower back. "It just missed her spine, but it's buried in deep tissue. I can't take it out till we can boil water. But we should do it soon."

"How's your leg?" Jessie asked Bliss, who'd hurried over.

"It's nothing. Ananda must have—"

"Let me see it," Hannah said.

"Later. I want to—"

"Please let her," Jessie said.

Bliss relented. Jessie became aware of her own wound for the first time since the hot pain had flashed up her leg. Left calf. Blood streaks to her ankle. But surface only.

A peculiar hush had descended. No shots. No attacks. The howls of the wounded had subsided. Maybe they've bled to death, she thought. Maybe the rest of them are counting their casualties. Like us.

Hannah spread apart the tear in Bliss's pants, exposing an oddly circular cut about two inches above her right knee.

"We'll have to clean that out, too," Hannah said to Jessie.

"Not now. Mom . . ." Bliss pointedly turned away from the nurse. "Ananda must have gone after Imagi. It's the only thing that makes any sense. She *always* does. And M-girl would have gone with her."

Because she always does, thought Jessie.

She managed no more than a nod to Bliss before slipping under the trailer.

"I want to take that van and go find my daughter and her friend," she said to Ellison.

"There's another way. We take the grotto. Then we've got control of all their gas." He tapped the tank without lifting his eyes from the guards and old men aiming down on them. "It's full. They hadn't delivered yet. We hold the gas as ransom for the girls. All of them. There's more than just your kid and her friend at stake."

She hadn't slowed enough to consider that other girls were

imprisoned in the compound. Surprised that he had. "Why do you care? You put them—"

"Zekiel's no fool. He survives on trade. If we don't bargain like demons, he'll sense weakness."

His answer was too quick, too pat. She didn't believe him, which felt different from not trusting him. More important in a way that she couldn't say exactly. He was talking again. "What was that?" she asked.

"We might end up having to leave the married ones. They're going to die anyway. And the ones he's blinded."

"We're not leaving a single girl to him, if we can help it. In any condition."

"That'll be a handful."

"We should be so lucky."

He laughed. She hadn't intended humor.

He went on: "The thing to remember is that no girl's as important to him as gas. It's his seed corn. He rations it like food in a famine. It'll be months before he gets more of it—maybe a year—there's no telling anymore. That's a long time before he can even think about getting new girls. It's not just him—he's got a lot of men who expect them. But we've got to get that thing first." He pointed Jessie's M-16 up the hill at the RPG. "Fuck, I wish we had ours."

"Why don't you?" They'd had it at her camp. Almost got to use it, too.

"We keep that thing locked up unless we're on a mission. Some asshole gets hold of it, the whole balance of power changes.

Does he hear himself? she wondered. *Some* asshole?

"Soon as we get it and the girls," Ellison's eyes were back on the bulky weapon, "we convoy out of here."

"Convoy?" She looked down the length of the tanker trailer. "You want to take this whole thing?" *Like moving an island.*

"Just like I said the second I saw it."

"But that could risk a deal for the girls. I don't want to risk them."

"The deal's with the devil, and the devil take the hind-most."

"What's to stop them from killing us then? Using gas bombs, IEDs, whatever they've got?"

"Fire. Same as it's always been. That'll keep them busy. It's going to get wild." He didn't sound disappointed. "They'll kill us anyway, if they can. And they'll burn every one of those girls for trying to escape. There's no going back for any of us."

"They could be killing my daughter right now. I can take that van and get them. Christ, they've missed the damn thing twice."

"You're underestimating them. They'd have blown it up if they weren't worried about hitting this tanker. We can't risk that van. Or you." He looked at her for the first time since she'd crawled back under the trailer. Then he rested his hand on her arm.

Jessie recoiled, but his touch shot through her so fast that she felt pierced. Crooked fingers that would have fired a shotgun into Eden's face had violated the tormented sanctity of her own skin.

His hand returned to the weapon, his attention to the hill.

She turned away and saw smoke thickening the sky. They'd tried to burn Ananda to death. And still her girl went back. She might have felt pride, if grief hadn't engulfed her, along with the fear that her daughter's ashes would yet rise on unseen currents and inescapable hate.

Chapter Nineteen

My name is Maria Thomason. I'm thirteen years old.
Thousands of men attacked us four days ago. They
used dynamite and battering rams to break through
the west gate this morning. All day long it's been horrible bloody fighting door to door. My friends tried to
escape and were cut down and hacked to death. The
men are downstairs now. My mother is screaming.
They're killing her. Please, God, help us.
Painted on bedroom wall, Christian Community, Lake Superior

Ananda knelt by a faucet in the last of the fields that surrounded the stake. She scooped up water, splashing her
face and soaking the bib of her gown. She didn't notice.
Wouldn't have cared. The trickle felt like a torrent rushing
over her parched lips and gums. Fire and thick smoke rose
from the cheatgrass near the Sacred Heart of Evil, already
spreading from the torch that Zekiel had dropped. But she
paid the flames no mind: she had water—*water*—for the first
time since last night. She drank shamelessly while M-girl
watched.

"It's *so* good," Ananda said, breathless from gulping.

M-girl drank only briefly before glancing at the fire, creeping closer, crackling softly.

Ananda took another turn, then looked at the men on the hilltop. Smoke and distance blunted their features, but she still asked M-girl to stand in front of her while she peeled off her gown.

"What are you doing?" M-girl demanded. "Let's get Imagi and get out of here."

"Just a sec." Ananda wet her thighs, belly, and neck, scrubbing away the gunpowder paste that Zekiel had spread on her body.

"What is that stuff?" M-girl asked.

Ananda explained. "He did it to Teresa, too."

"That's insane." M-girl washed off smears from her friend's back.

"It almost worked." Ananda drenched her gown and put it on, feeling cool for the first time in memory.

"Who's that?" M-girl pointed to a figure darting behind a rise.

Ananda caught only a glimpse of him before staring at empty space. *He saw me naked.* Chilly water dripped from her gown and stung her blistered feet.

The cheatgrass burned behind them, red and ravenous as army ants.

"This is Ellison!" the marauder shouted to the grotto. "Remember me? Throw out your guns and get the hell out or I'm going to bomb you." From behind the van, he dangled a gas can with a rag spilling from the spout.

The guards didn't respond.

"Let's go!" Ellison yelled at Brindle.

The driver started the motor. Ellison sparked the gas-soaked rag, and a *whoosh* rose above the engine idle. He waved the can in the air. "Here we come. Get ready to *burn*."

Two rifles and a handgun flew from the grotto's dark

opening, raising crowns of dust. The pair of guards stepped out, hands up. Ellison snuffed the burning rag.

Jessie flooded with relief. There was no telling what Ellison would do, and throwing a gas bomb into the grotto could have killed them all.

"Keep coming!" the marauder yelled. "I've got a job for you!"

Ananda didn't think the guy behind the rise was a guard—someone hiding was someone scared. "But we've got to keep watching out for him," she also told M-girl, "just in case."

"We should go back. *Now.*"

"No." Ananda tugged her friend to a row of greens, where Teresa said that the girls had buried their weapons. She kneeled in the mulch, but before searching, she stuffed chard into her mouth and held up a bunch of leaves to M-girl, who still kept watch on the rise.

"I'm not hungry."

"I'm starving." Ananda ate her offering and clawed the dirt, almost impaling her palm when she unearthed a flint knife. She used the blade to dig up more ground, efforts that yielded nothing.

That's it? She wanted guns, rifles. She hacked the earth and came up with a single-bladed axe. *Guns,* she pleaded to the smoky sky.

Five more minutes of feverish effort produced no more weapons. *This* was their arsenal?

Ananda worked her way down the row, eating fistfuls of chard with one hand and turning over clumps of dirt with the other, wide-eyed when she unearthed a . . . spear? Hard to tell till she dug out the long flint point.

She hefted the weapon. The balance felt good.

"I want this," she said.

M-girl shook her head. "This is Stone Age crap. They've got guns."

"But what's *he* got?" Ananda eyed the rise.

* * *

The grotto guards stood in the shade of the tanker truck, drinking water that Augustus hurried to give them; Jessie had untied his wrists after he saved the van. One of the guards had been wounded in the shoulder, and winced as he lowered a dented canister.

Ellison pointed his weapon at them. "You're going up that hill with a message for your buddies."

"We surrendered. They'll kill us," the wounded man said.

"They might. I definitely will, if you don't do exactly what I say. You walk straight up that hill. You try to run off, I'll kill you. You try to grab a gun from the guards I shot up there, I'll kill you. You tell those crusty old fucks that we want all the girls—deaf, dumb, blind, married, pregnant, virgins—I don't give a shit who they are—or I'll turn this place into a living hell. I'll set off the gas in the grotto, I'll blow up this goddamn truck, I'll burn down everything and everyone. I'll make that grass fire out there look like a fucking matchstick. You got that?"

The men stared at him.

"And the babies," Jessie said.

"The babies?" Ellison turned to her. "We're not taking any—" He checked himself and looked back at the men. "How many babies are there? Little kids?"

"Three," the wounded man said.

"How old?" Jessie asked.

"One's a week old, maybe two. The others can crawl." The wounded man still spoke for them.

Ellison raked his hair with his hand. "Fine, the babies, too. And make sure you tell those old assholes that it's me—the burned-up crazy fuck."

He dragged the wounded man to the rear of the tanker. The other hurried to follow. Augustus handed Ellison a scrap of white cloth torn from a girl's gown.

"Wave this," the marauder told the men. "Maybe they won't shoot you. And if you see Zeke, give him my regards."

* * *

His name was Erik Ambers. The dog cart boy. He remained crouched behind the rise, waving Ananda and M-girl over.

"What are you doing?" Ananda saw his big dog lying behind him, tongue out and panting.

"I can't let them see me talking to you. They'll kill me. What are *you* doing?" He stared at her spear.

"Going to get my friend." She told him about Imagi. "Do you know if all the guards are up on the hill?"

"I think so. Except for the one with Zekiel. He helped him back to his place. Desana went with him, too."

"Zekiel's still alive?" Ananda did not want to believe this.

"Yeah, he was limping, but he was getting back there okay."

"What about all the other old men?"

"They're all up there now." He tilted his head toward the hill.

"I saw them running toward that weird-looking building with the bathtubs, and now they've got guns. Where'd they get them?"

"The armory. It's right below it."

"Do you think they've got any more down there?" Ananda asked.

"I don't know. They never let me near there."

"Let's go look."

"I'm dead if they see me doing that."

"You want to be with them, go be with them." Ananda jabbed her spear at the guards and robes. "But they're killing girls, burning them, blinding them, cutting out their tongues. And you've been trading with them. What are you bringing in here, anyway?"

Erik looked down. Wouldn't say. Ananda realized that he was younger than she'd thought. Her age.

"What do you bring them? I swear, you'd better tell me." She pounded the base of her spear on the ground.

"Gunpowder." His voice barely a whisper.

"You're bringing *them* gunpowder?"

M-girl hushed her. "You're too loud."

"You should be helping us, not them," Ananda said. "You have any now?"

"No, I brought some yesterday, and then all the shooting started."

"They keep it in the armory?"

He shrugged. "I don't know. They could be hiding it anywhere."

Ananda looked at his panting dog. "He needs water bad."

"I know, but they might shoot me if I go down to the fields."

"I'll take him," Ananda said. "They're not shooting girls."

"Yet," M-girl said.

"But you better help us. What's his name?"

"Razzo."

"Come on, Razzo." Ananda snapped her fingers at his dog. "Let's get you some water."

"He's scared of fire." Erik watched his dog walk up to her.

"Any creature with half a brain's scared of fire," Ananda said. "But it's lots worse being scared of being scared."

The grotto guards trudged up the hill, passing within yards of the men Ellison had wounded. Hoarse cries greeted them and bloody hands reached out. Gaunt faces rose from the cheatgrass, only to fall back.

Gunshots rained down from the hilltop, hitting the unscathed guard in the chest. His legs buckled and he sank to his knees, face to the murky sky. Before he pitched back and rolled several feet, the man beside him was running toward the charred pan of cheatgrass, zigzagging, sprinting faster than Jessie would have thought possible for a guy who'd already taken a bullet to his shoulder. A spray of gunfire— *pop, pop, pop,* sounding tragically innocuous—chewed up the earth near him, and he tumbled to the bottom of the hill.

She thought he'd been hit, but he heaved himself to his

feet and staggered on, erratic movements that might have
helped him dodge the shots. But she gave him little chance,
and was surprised that Ellison didn't want to finish him off
with the M-16. The marauder caught her glance.

"Good stuff," he mused. "They're killing one another. The
crazier it gets, the better for us. I'm just sorry it's the half
dead one. Full of piss and vinegar, though. Look at him go."

"What about them talking to the old men?"

"I'd say that's a bust. Maybe you should get up there, see
if they're more amenable to your presence."

He sounded serious. She watched him turn back to the
wounded guard, who was still trying to outrun bullets.

"He might want to consider switching sides," Ellison said.

Like you, Jessie almost replied. But nothing about the marauder felt settled.

"When it's good and dark," he stretched his arms high
above his head, like an athlete of old, "I'll mosey on up and
let them know what the deal is. But from what I'm seeing,
they're going to force our hand."

An unarmed guard in a bloody shirt staggered toward the
rise. Ananda stepped out, wielding her spear like a pike. He
saw her but didn't stop till he stumbled and fell on his back.
The girl, little more than half his size, raised her spear.

"Don't, don't," he pleaded.

"What's going on?" she shouted.

"A marauder . . ." He swallowed air with difficulty.
". . . made us go up the hill. Our people, they shot us."

"Why'd he make you go up there?"

"They want girls, babies, or they'll burn everything."

"Who's with him? A woman? A girl who looks like me,
but older?"

"A woman," he gasped. "Older. Dark hair. Automatic."

Mom. It's got to be. "A man with long hair? Shotgun?"

"I don't know. Black man. Others I couldn't see." Still his
chest heaved, and he gripped his side.

"Which marauder?"

"Ellison."

Burned Fingers? "What's he doing with my mom?"

"I don't know, I don't know." Fresh blood seeped into his shirt where he held himself.

"You know where they keep the gunpowder?"

The guard's neck cords stuck out. He rocked slightly, hip to hip.

"You better tell me," she said. "The gunpowder?"

"So you can kill me?"

She raised the spear above his chest, gripping it with both hands, a girl about to sink a stake. "I'll kill you if you don't." Her words came as naturally as her desire for food and water, and felt no more shocking to her.

"Armory. Down from the Quonset hut."

"Is it locked?"

"Always. The robes"—she was surprised to hear him use the same shorthand as the girls—"were rushing around to get their guns. Maybe it's open."

"Is there a key?" Ananda hadn't relaxed her spear.

"Zekiel keeps it."

She never considered killing him after he talked, or that he might alert others. She simply ran. And M-girl followed. But what stunned them both was that Erik and his dog came with them, too.

"Remember the bear?" Ellison walked up beside Jessie, who was wiping down her dusty weapon.

"What bear?" She had no interest in a bear. They might be under siege at any second, and she had yet to find her youngest daughter. She leaned her rifle against the van.

"Zekiel's pet, Bosco. The one in the cage near the church. We could use him. Didn't you see him?"

"I was a little preoccupied with the guards at that point." Consumed now with the speed of the falling night, smoke soaking up the last of the light. She saw the gloaming lit like a stage, flames for footlights. The fire had crept across acres of land, left it dead. Crawled on. A blaze like this could skulk along forever and leave vast black blankets of char. Deserts without sand. But Jessie was also glad for the flames. They'd started up the hill. Not far. Not fast. Steady as the hand of death. A strong ally. They didn't need a bear, and she'd had enough of Ellison's craziness. The guard who'd run off could be out there killing Ananda and M-girl. "Let's leave his pet out of this."

"Think about it," Ellison said. "That beast running amok would scare the hell out of them. They never feed him much. I doubt he's had anything since we showed up. He's going to be nice and hungry."

"You want that bear loose? He could turn on us."

"He could, but they're opportunity eaters. Scavengers. They like easy prey, food that can't run away. Roots and berries and stuff like that." He smiled. "You'll see."

The stone armory had a thick wooden door with a metal grate over it. A heavy hasp lock sealed it shut, and looked inviolable in the twilight. M-girl ran her finger over the mortar, then bore down on it with the axe. Her second swing broke off a sizable chunk. It was cob, not concrete, like the stuff they'd been using on the wall at the camp. Ananda and Erik took turns. Ten minutes later the three of them used the spear shaft to pry a stone loose. Five minutes after that two more popped out. When another tumbled away, Ananda squeezed through the opening.

She saw nothing but darkness in the windowless room, but the smell of gunpowder was strong enough to irritate her nose. Moving slowly, she swept her hands over bare shelves that might have stored pistols and knives, clubs and pipes and other bludgeoning tools. The walls held rifle racks, but they were empty, too.

She lowered herself to the cool slate floor and scoured the corners, finding two compact wooden barrels like the ones that Erik had been hauling when she first saw him. She rolled one of the kegs to the opening. He reached in and moved his hand over the round top.

"That's it," he said.

"There's another one."

"Won't be needing it." He helped her wrestle it out. "This could blow up a whole building. You're talking a door, right?"

Flames edged up the bottom of the hill, moving toward the wounded men. How long till they start to cook? Jessie wondered. An hour? Some of them were trying to drag themselves away from the smoke. But the rustling of the cheatgrass never lasted, and their cries grew frantic.

Ellison called over Brindle, Maul, Jaya, Bliss, and Augustus. He asked Hannah to stand guard, and told the escaped girls to stay in the van.

"Everybody seen Bosco the bear?" Ellison asked in his most cheerful, unnerving voice. No one had seen the beast. "Maybe I should go, then."

"No," Brindle said, revealing a burst of anxiety.

"What do you need?" Augustus asked Ellison.

"We've got to get Bosco out of his cage, let him stir things up."

"I'll do it," Augustus said without hesitation.

His snap response reminded Jessie that he was a veteran of the Battle of Baltimore, part of the shattered rebel force that had cobbled together every scrap they could find to slow down a mutinous, anarchic army.

"Me, too," Bliss offered. Jessie dearly wished she hadn't. "Is he locked up?" Bliss asked.

"No." Ellison shook his head. "There's a bar on the side that faces the church, and it slides right out. But be careful. He looks like some big plaything, but he ripped off his trainer's ear when he got pissed off. So when you open it, get the hell out of there. And if he charges you . . ."

Oh, Christ, thought Jessie.

". . . don't kill him."

"What?" she said.

"Try to scare him with a shot." Ellison still addressed Bliss and Augustus. "If you have to, shoot him in the leg. Make him irritable. Just don't go killing him. We want him ornery as hell. He probably already is. Check your bullets. That goes for everyone. What about you?" He pointed to Augustus. "You're not going to do this without a gun, are you?"

"I see no glory to God in getting eaten alive by a bear." He took Ellison's pistol. "Praise the Lord and pass the ammunition."

"'Nanda!" Imagi screamed, beating the inside of her cell door.

"Shush," Ananda said.

"'Nanda!" Imagi screamed again.

"Shut her up." M-girl looked in every direction at once. Erik's dog growled.

"Imagi, the game," Ananda said gently.

"The game," Imagi repeated in a softer voice.

"What's that mean, anyway?" M-girl asked.

"To be real quiet and secret, like hide-and-go-seek in hell," Ananda said. "Imagi, I need you to go far away from the door. We're going to open it."

"Open door," Imagi insisted.

"Yes, we will, but you have to go all the way back and stay there. Back where you sleep."

The girl retreated. Ananda turned to Erik. "Let's do it as fast as we can."

He pulled out a hefty ball of gunpowder wrapped in a rag.

"You ever done this before?" Ananda asked him.

"I watched my father do it plenty."

"Where's he?"

"Dead."

* * *

The cage creaked. Bliss could just make out Bosco pressing his huge side against the steel bars.

"Door must be over here," Augustus said. "I'll get it."

"Give me a warning."

Bosco's head followed Augustus. His flank bristled inches from Bliss's hand. She'd always wanted to see a bear. Her father had seen lots of them. But till now, bears had been no more real to her than mythical creatures like unicorns or centaurs.

She reached in and touched his fur. The beast whipped around and smashed his face against the cage so fast that she stumbled and fell, finding herself staring up into his open mouth, teeth gleaming in the pitch. Eyes, too.

"Holy shit."

"You all right?" Augustus paused by the door.

"Yeah, I'm okay." Her voice shook. So did her legs when she backed away. "If he comes at me, I'm not keen on just making him more ornery."

"Can't be blaming him. This thing's so small he can hardly turn around."

"I'm not blaming him," Bliss said. "I'm just not letting him take it out on me."

"You ready?" Augustus took hold of the sliding bar.

"Go."

He shoved it aside, and the bear pulled open the door with his big head, knocking Augustus to the ground. The beast barreled out making a gurgling noise. Then he climbed to his hind legs and tottered toward Bliss. She scurried backward and raised her shotgun; but before she could blast the creature in the chest, Augustus shot him in the hind end.

The beast bellowed and dropped to his front paws, turning quickly. Augustus jumped in the cage and slammed the door.

Bosco batted the bars, then huffed past Bliss, pounding the earth as if he could outrun his maddening pain.

* * *

Ellison heard the gunshot just as he started up the hill. He tore his eyes from a thin column of flames climbing the slope to his left and listened. In seconds he heard the bear and readied his weapon, waiting for the darkness to explode with teeth and fur. But as the animal's efforts grew louder, he placed the beast farther uphill. Then, as if to confirm his blind estimate, a ghastly scream rose from one of the men Ellison had wounded. The bear had lifted him with his teeth and slammed him down. A bone cracked, loud as a tree limb. But even that noise paled when the beast crushed the man's skull like a nut. His scream could have shattered rock.

Ellison edged to his right, away from drifting smoke, but mostly to give Bosco a wide berth. *Don't get him going,* he warned himself. *Not now. Not when everything's setting up touchier than a hair trigger.* He figured the bear would feed on his victim till that fire inched close enough to scare him, and then he'd drag off his meal, though Ellison had no intention of letting him finish it, a strategy based both on the looming needs of battle and a basic understanding of *Ursus americanus.*

Erik used a steel roofing nail that he'd inherited from his father, and the flint on Ananda's spear tip, to set off a narrow stream of gunpowder. It ripped across the dirt with an angry sizzle. Both of them raced toward M-girl, crouching behind a boulder with Erik's dog.

A three-foot flame lanced the darkness, but the explosion sounded muffled. Nothing like Imagi's scream, which came from deep inside the cell.

Ananda ran back and saw that only the bottom of the door was splintered. Erik started kicking the smoldering boards with his bare heel. In moments he forced an opening. Ananda found Imagi balled-up in the back of the cell and hugged her. "I missed you so much, Imagi."

The girl's screams subsided, but she shook terribly, saying only "'Nanda, 'Nanda, 'Nanda."

Both girls started coughing from the dust and smoke.

"We can go home now," Ananda took the girl's hand, "but we have to be very quiet, like the game."

Burned Fingers had circled around Bosco and climbed within a hundred yards of the hilltop. He could still hear the bear, loud as a dinner bell, and thought the guards and old men must be listening, too. And nobody could have missed the man's agony. But even that hadn't spurred them to hunt down Zekiel's hungry—and prized—pet in the dark. *The stars are aligning,* he told himself. *Now let's keep the bolides at bay.*

"This is Ellison." His voice a shadow over darkness. "I've got a proposition for Zekiel. Take it to him, unless you're up there, Zeke."

No response.

"We've got all the gas. We've got the grotto and the truck. You can have it all back, but we want the girls—blind ones, married ones, all of them. No exceptions. And the babies."

Still no response. The only sound was the bear's chewing.

"You hear me? I know you can hear Bosco. We opened the cage. He's eating one of the men you sent on that stupid suicide mission. Think about that, guys."

The bear sounded louder than ever.

"Tell Zeke that if we don't get the girls and babies, we'll burn down everything—all the gas in the grotto, the truck, and everyone in this place. All of you. They'll be nothing left when we're through. We'll be gone and you'll be burning. So this is how you'll do it. When it's light out, you get all the girls and those babies on top of the hill. Then the girls carry the babies down to the van on their own. No guards. We'll clear out Bosco, if he's still stuffing himself." He wouldn't be, but Ellison wasn't about to tell them that. "Zeke's got till sunup to give me his answer."

Ellison didn't find their silence surprising. Most of them wouldn't have dared speak for Zekiel, and they probably thought their rocket launcher could trump any escape attempt in the van, a calculation that did have merit. But the threats he'd used to try to disarm them were also real, and far more potent than they might imagine. Hours ago he'd put his plans into play, and under the right circumstances he reckoned he could fire up even more fear than an exploding rocket. He'd been turning the horrors of men to his own gain since Baltimore, when he first glimpsed the real value of his nightmare's naked core.

He retreated to the truck and van and ate a few bites of jerky. Drank water. He suggested the others do likewise. The very last of the provisions were cleared out. No point in saving them. In a matter of hours they'd either plunder and leave or they'd be dead.

Ananda and Imagi didn't stop coughing till they crawled outside the cell, which overlooked the distant fire. A red islet had burned almost to the top of the hill, lighting the ghostly figure of the guards. "We don't have to go near them," she told Imagi. "But we've got to get you moving." Ananda looked to her right, where Zekiel's house was burrowed into the same hillside as the cell, no more than a fast walk from where they were.

M-girl took Ananda's hand. "Okay, so let's get out of here. We've got her."

"I'm staying." Ananda turned to Erik. "You go back and get somebody with guns. Tell them that we know where Zekiel is, and that he's only got one guard with him."

"What are you talking about?" M-girl tried to drag her away. Once more Ananda pulled back.

"You always cut off the head of the snake," she said. One of the basics of battle, according to her father. "Our people are going to want to know where Zekiel is."

"Then go tell them," M-girl said.

"Then we won't know if he leaves."

"You should come," Erik said to Ananda. "You don't want to be out here all alone."

"I'm not going to be alone. We'll be together, right?" Ananda stared at M-girl, who grimaced but didn't disagree. Ananda went on: "It's dark, we can go back any time, if we have to. When you get near the truck, make sure you shout out that we sent you. And say that you have Imagi." She turned to the girl. "You go with Erik and his dog. His name's Razzo, and he's really nice. See, you can pet him and walk with him. We'll be there soon."

"We hope." M-girl made no attempt to hide her fear.

Ananda worried that despite Imagi's love of dogs, she'd balk. But the girl stroked Razzo's head and gently patted his back. Then she took Erik's hand and led him away, as if he were the one who needed help.

Ellison headed back up the hill, directly toward the bear. In the past few minutes a wedge-shaped offshoot of the fire had started burning across the slope; but none of the flames had moved close enough to bother Bosco. The beast still feasted on his victims, crunching bones with unsettling enthusiasm.

The marauder didn't trouble with stealth, and the bear let him tromp within fifty feet before he charged. Ellison waited till the creature sounded like he was going to bowl him over before he fired just above the thunder. The powder flash lit up the animal's wild eyes, and buckshot nicked his shoulder The beast roared, a bellow that tore open the night, then turned and raced uphill, much as Ellison had figured.

He reloaded and hurried after him, not at all disappointed to have hundreds of pounds of wounded, raging bear running interference. He heard men shouting and panicking up above, and veered left, using the fear and confusion to close in on the area where he'd seen the two guards with the rocket launcher. He'd watched them till the last of the light, and if they hadn't moved, they'd made a critical, tactical error that he never would have tolerated.

He shot at the sound of men scrambling, a blast that lit the blackness and took down one of the RPG guards. A tick of movement in the corner of Ellison's eye revealed the other guard lunging for the prized weapon.

Ellison fired again, and heard him topple amid the sharp clatter of weaponry. The marauder moved toward the fallen, reloading without pause. Wild shots and groans and staggered, abrupt screams arose from his right. He braced himself as the bear's efforts grew clamorous and closer. When Bosco sounded near enough to break out of the darkness, Ellison banked on the beast's innate intelligence by firing his shotgun into the air, wanting no part of killing the chaos that he'd so carefully set into motion.

Bosco raced away before Ellison ever saw him, trampling back over maimed and crippled men. More guards fired their weapons—the bear howled, might have been hit—but the marauder never heard the animal falter.

Searching blindly, he found the RPG in the limp hands of one of the men he'd killed. Others raced by but never saw Ellison grubbing in the dark for rockets. His hand landed on a canvas bag with three of them, and he lugged his bounty off the hill.

Jessie saw him hurry around the rear bumper of the tanker trailer, hauling the RPG. Everyone gathered and gaped at the weapon. Maul kneeled and ran his hand over the blue steel like it was a sacred relic. For the first time, Jessie thought they might actually bargain their way out of the Army of God with all the girls.

None of them noticed the two approaching figures. "Ananda sent me," a boy yelled. "I've got Imagi."

"Home? Home?" the girl called.

Jessie ran to Imagi and cupped her cheeks, astounded at

her survival. But Jessie's attention moved swiftly to the boy: "Where's Ananda?"

"She's up near Zekiel's place, keeping an eye on it."

"What the *hell*?" Jessie's frustration could have crushed stone.

"She's making sure he doesn't get away," he explained, "and she wants me to bring back somebody with a gun."

"I should go," Ellison said.

"I'm going. She's my daughter. And one of us better stay here." An unstated acknowledgment of their co-command, but mostly she didn't want to give him a chance to make private deals with the leader of this hellhole.

"Are you sure Zeke's in his place?" Ellison asked the boy.

"I saw him go in with Desana. I guess he—"

"Who's Desana?" Jessie interrupted.

"His aide-de-camp. Go on, Erik," Ellison said.

"He could have come out before I got back there with Ananda. I don't know."

"What kind of shape was he in?" Ellison leaned closer to him.

"Well, he had blood on his face, and he wasn't walking real good."

"What kind of shape is Ananda in?" asked Jessie.

"She's got some burns on her feet," Erik answered, "but she's getting around okay. M-girl's with her."

"I'll give you odds that Zekiel's holed up nursing his wounds," Ellison said to Jessie.

She kept looking at the boy. He'd been with Ananda only minutes ago. Her girl was *so* close. "Are you part of this place?" she asked him.

The kid shook his head, but after offering so much about Zekiel and Ananda, he remained suspiciously quiet about himself.

"He's a trader," Ellison said. "Brings them gunpowder. He's—"

"Gunpowder?" Jessie said. "Why are you—"

"To survive," Ellison answered for Erik again. "This place is the only game around. People do what they have to. His father was a trader, too. Erik took over when the old man got killed two years ago." Ellison tapped the boy's shoulder with his burned fingers. "You got any powder now?"

"We broke a keg out of the armory. Another one's still inside."

"Where's the one you got?"

"Up near Zekiel's. Ananda knows. I left my dog back there a ways. Is it okay if I call him?"

Ellison nodded. Erik issued a short whistle, and Razzo trotted up. Hansel hopped over on three legs. The dogs sniffed, wagged tails.

The marauder held up his stumpy shotgun. "If you're going after him," he said to Jessie, "you'd better take this."

"I'm not going after him. I'm going after my daughter and her friend, and I'm bringing them back."

"I'm going, too, Mom."

"No." Jessie shook her head. "I can't let you do that. If anything happens, I don't want you to die, and I don't want your dad left all alone. Come here," she said, and opened her arms.

"Mom, I *want* to see Ananda."

Jessie held her tightly. "You will soon, but you're not going."

"Then you have to come back, Mom," Bliss whispered. "That's the deal: no dying."

"No dying," Jessie said, repeating the meaningless vow.

Her girl felt fragile and strong, and weak and hard, and smelled of salt and cordite and love, and every hot, dusty step they'd taken here. She buried her face in Bliss's hair and told herself to remember. *That's all we take from this life. And that's all we give.*

They stood wrapped in each other's arms for another full minute. Jessie's daughter wept softly. Her shoulders shook.

No one spoke, not even Imagi, who stared in round-faced wonder. Then Jessie kissed Bliss's brow and let her go.

She took Ellison's weapon. It was deep night, hard to see, harder to aim. She would have to hunt by sound. She gave him the M-16. "Better for holding off the hordes."

The trade felt final in a way that didn't lend itself to the comfort of words.

"It needs loading." Ellison handed her his sack of shells.

She tied it around her waist and cracked the barrels.

They felt warm, like blood and skin and touch. Like everything she'd lost, and everything she wanted back.

Chapter Twenty

Jessie charged through the smoky blackness, eyes and throat burning. Erik struggled to keep up. They raced past the Sacred Heart of Evil, bare feet oblivious to the charred cheatgrass, still warm in the slow aftermath of flame. The boy whispered fevered directions on the long hill to Zekiel's house, but their breathing grew so loud that it smothered the footfalls rushing toward them.

In seconds the steps loomed near enough to seize Jessie's attention. She grabbed Erik's arm, stopping him, then tracked the sounds with Ellison's short-barreled shotgun, already hunting blindly. She heard a girl's plaintive cry only feet away and reached out, pulling her close. The child gasped and stiffened. Before she could scream, Jessie said, "It's me. Mom."

"Jessie?"

Not Ananda. That's all Jessie could think. She choked down her disappointment.

"M-girl?"

Ananda's friend fell into her arms. Jessie held her, stroked her hair, and when the delay became unbearable, asked, "Where is she?"

"Zekiel's got her," the girl cried. "We were—"

"Whisper," Jessie said.

"Sorry. We were listening really hard for anyone coming out of his place, and then the door opened and we heard someone and we thought he was escaping. But it was a guard, and he walked right up to us. I swear we were hardly making any noise at all."

"It's okay," Jessie said. "What happened?" *Just tell me.*

"He got really close, like a few feet away, and Ananda stood up with her spear. I could hear her, and I was sure he could, so I shouted, 'Don't shoot, don't shoot.' Ananda got really angry at me, but she was going to get us killed with that stupid spear."

"Stop crying." Jessie held M-girl by the shoulders. "I need you to think clearly. Where *is* she?"

"At Zekiel's. The guard dragged us over there, and Zekiel tied her up right away. He said there weren't going to be any deals, and that I had to go and tell you guys that he'd kill Ananda and all the girls if you didn't surrender. He was really scary."

"So she's in his house?"

M-girl nodded, still crying. "And he wanted to know who else was out. He had a gun, too, and I thought he was going to shoot me, so I told him, and as soon as I said that we got Imagi, he started shaking me and wanted to know if the other girls got out. I told him no, but he yelled at the guard to go check, and that's when he told me to go back and tell you what he'd do if you didn't surrender."

"How long ago did the guard go check on the girls?"

"A few minutes."

"Five minutes? Ten?" *Think, M-girl.*

"More like five."

Jessie turned to Erik. "Could he get to the girls and be back by now?"

"Maybe, if he ran real hard. But it's dark, and we'd see him if he had a torch."

"Take me to Zekiel's," she said to him. "Then you two go back."

After hurrying up the last of the hill, Erik drew her close, speaking so low that she could hardly hear him: "His place is right there. If you go straight, you'll walk right into—" He stopped at the sound of faint footsteps.

"That's him," M-girl whispered. "The guard."

"Go back as fast as you can," Jessie told them. "If he tries to catch you, I'll get his attention. *Go!*"

They ran off, and the guard paused. But he didn't chase them, confirming Jessie's belief that he was there to protect Zekiel.

She crept forward, inching close enough to the house to make out the guard's deliberate approach. She raised Ellison's weapon, careful not to brush her pants or breathe deeply. *He'll have to open the door,* she said to herself. *Probably unlock it. There will be noise.*

Her fingers closed around the trigger. It felt warm, rested, welcoming.

He stopped. Sounded close. Maybe ten feet away. Did he sense her? All she'd done was hold her ground. And breathe, barely. But she knew that even hidden eyes can raise the hair on your neck, when the reptiles we were become the reptiles we are.

After you shoot, move. *He'll try to kill you if—*

A single metallic noise, like a *click,* stilled her thought. Alive now only to the stark beckoning of sound. She heard it again. *He's right . . . there.* She squeezed the trigger, ravaging the silence and lighting the darkness with a yellow flash that showed the guard smashing face first into the door.

She didn't move. She stood numbly and fired again. Saw a flicker of him falling, holes bored in blood.

Now she forced herself left and drew her pistol, listening intently. She heard only a shrill ringing in her ears.

Dropping slowly to her hands and knees, Jessie inched through the dust and gun smoke, nose sharp with the smell of urine. But she took no risks, firing her pistol into his inert body before reloading the shotgun. With the fat muzzle to his chest, she searched his hands and found a heavy revolver. She stuffed it in her pants, pointed the shotgun at the door, and tried the handle. Locked. He must have had a key—it sounded like he'd been using one—but she wanted no part of searching him or the ground.

Standing to the side, she placed the sawed-off near the handle and fired, cringing when she needed the second barrel to blow the door open. It banged against an inside wall, and she waited, invisible as a dust mote in the dark.

"Zekiel," she called. "I'm Ananda's mother. I've come for her. I don't care about anything but getting her back. Give her to me and you can have your gas."

Her words fell into blank, black uncertainties. She slipped two shells from Ellison's sack and cracked the barrels, seconds without her pistol in hand. Stealing time from eternity. But she would not edge past that entrance without a loaded shotgun.

Before she could snap the barrels together, a handgun pressed against the back of her head.

"Put it down."

She lowered the shotgun to the ground and stood back up. He'd been watching, skulking. Whoever he was. She didn't dare turn. The hard pressure on her skull never eased. He pulled her pistol and the guard's revolver from her pants, leaving her without a gun.

"Walk inside. Don't try to run."

Jessie stepped into the swarming darkness of a house burrowed into a hill. No exits. After counting five steps—the only bread crumbs she could leave in the pitch—she spied a soft glow at the end of the hallway.

A room with a candle opened to her right. Ananda lay bound and gagged on the floor.

"Don't go near them." He hadn't spoken since the door.

Beside Ananda an older woman with a bloody face slumped against the wall. Her eyes were closed and her limp hands rested next to a photograph on her lap.

"Sit against the wall." Still guiding her with the gun.

She adjusted to the candlelight, and saw Ananda's terrified eyes on her. Weeks of the most grinding fears, and then to find her child still a world away.

Jessie forced herself to turn to him. Slowly. His face was bruised, smeared with blood. Bearded like so many others. Gowned like them. But he had to be Zekiel. He had the air of ownership: of them, the room. The moment.

"Are you the leader?" Offering the honorific, believing that he, of all people, would demand it. She was wrong.

"I'm Zekiel." He spoke as if from a pulpit, accenting all three syllables of his name, letting them linger in the etched silence. "And you have violated my world. You have brought sin, and there is no forgiveness for what you have done. Not on earth, and not in the heavenly kingdom of God."

He kneeled next to her and pressed the gun to her temple. "Your daughter is a demon. That's what the godless do, they raise *demons*. We try to save them. We anoint them with the blood of the lamb. But her soul is stained, and she must be burned back into the land."

"May I speak to her?" Jessie heard a tremor in her voice and willed it away. *Don't let her see you die scared, not from the likes of him.*

"You *will* speak to her, but not as you mean. You'll speak to her now when she sees you perish. You'll speak to her of the demon times when witches and heathens defiled the sacred Word."

I should have died at the door. Spared her this horror.

The candle flickered. He controlled her, Ananda; and with the endless, passing minutes, he controlled time.

Jessie spied a bullet hole in the woman's chest. "Did you kill her?" *In front of my daughter?*

"She worshipped a false image from a fallen world. She hid that picture from me for many years. I found her *praying* to it"—he jabbed Jessie's head with the barrel, as if she were to blame for the blasphemy—"after you came and started your killing."

Jessie stared at the streaks of blood that had dried on the woman's cheeks and brow, and the moist red circle on her chest, and she knew—because she'd seen it before—that he'd chained her with his beliefs, and then murdered her with his hands.

"The old females are cursed with the eternal weight of the past. Even she"—Jessie felt his eyes drift to the dead woman—"could not resist the lure of the fallen world. Only girls may live now, and only with those who are building sacred lives."

"You're killing them." Jessie looked at Ananda, offering her a final act of defiance. "You take their virginity and you give them Wicca. You murder them."

"You," he bellowed, "know *nothing* of the righteous healing power of the Lord."

He grabbed her hair and jammed the muzzle in her face, and Jessie knew that he'd kill her now. She shouted, "I love you, Ananda."

The gunshot roared. Her daughter deafened, and squeezed her eyes shut on the grim vision of shattered skull.

It took a full second for her mother to note the body fallen beside her, and another convulsive moment to lift her eyes to Bliss. Her eldest had executed Zekiel with a pistol, saving her life as she'd saved Eden's only weeks before.

Bliss stared at the blood. "Is that—"

"Yes." Jessie reached for his gun, unwilling to trust him so readily to the dead. "That's Zekiel."

She held the weapon away from his body and checked his pulse. Then she rushed to Ananda, tore off the ropes and pulled out the filthy rag that had been stuffed into her mouth. She rocked her daughter, the moans of mother and child primal as light.

Bliss wrapped her arms around them, and Jessie thanked her over and over. The three embraced with an almost violent fervor.

"We'd better go," Jessie said after no more than thirty seconds.

"Mom, wait." Ananda slipped the photograph from the dead woman's lap and studied it. Jessie and Bliss looked over her shoulder. The photo showed an easily identifiable Desana with a man and two girls, all of them sitting in front of a Christmas tree. The colors had paled but Jessie and her daughters could still make out the reds and greens, and the gold cross worn by each member of the family. "That's him, isn't it?"

Jessie nodded. Zekiel's dark eyes appeared as daunting as they had been at death. She wondered about the girls in the photo. They'd be young women now. If they'd survived.

"See if there's anything on the back," she said.

Ananda turned it over and they read a faded inscription:

*Rachel (6), Simone (7), Desana and Zekiel, The Year
of Our Lord . . .*

The date had disappeared completely, as if even the neat, linear past had lost its hold on history.

"Women and children always suffer the worst in bad times." Jessie wanted to remind Ananda and Bliss of compassion. Even here. Even now. Even though she knew that her own heart might never heal. "I think that she probably lost everything that ever mattered to her. Grief can make you a better person"—she thought of losing Eden and wondered about her words—"or it can make you worse. It always leaves you empty, so people fill their hearts with love or hate, or sometimes"—and now she thought of Ellison, without knowing why—"they fill it with both."

They heard far-off shouts and gunshots. First light brought alive sound as well as sight. Jessie reclaimed her pistol and gathered up Zekiel and the guard's handguns. Then she tried to herd her girls away, but Ananda begged for one more minute.

She laid the photo back on Desana's lap and hurried into Zekiel's bedroom, returning with a book.

"What's that?" Bliss asked.

"Birthday letters. Burned Fingers found it."

Burned Fingers? Jessie led them to the door before she remembered the first time she'd seen Ellison. He'd climbed down from the top of a steel-plated truck, his scarred index and middle fingers curled around the trigger of a sawed-off shotgun. Her eyes fell to it now, lying inches from the guard she'd gunned down. She reached for the warm barrels, unable to fathom their fiery path. Logic, ever so sure of itself, could never untangle the skein that had delivered Ellison's weapon to her hands.

A hellish spectacle greeted them outside. The grass fire had blackened more than half the compound, and burned to death the wounded guards on the hill. Thick, oily smoke rose from their distant corpses. And the flames that had consumed them were still marching up the rise. Another arm of the fire had reached within a hundred feet of the tanker truck and van.

Small groups of guards were spreading out, slinking like pack dogs behind ribbons of smoke. Jessie heard automatic weapon fire and saw Ellison holding off a contingent that had tried to circle behind him. He waved at the truck cab, and it completed the U-turn it had started hours ago and began rolling away. With a quick step up, he was on the side of the trailer and pointing to the van, which drove off in the opposite direction toward the Sacred Heart of Evil.

Jessie took hold of her girls. "I want to see what they're doing."

The three of them huddled in front of Zekiel's house and watched a guard hiding near the metal stake jump up and rush the van. A flash of firepower from the side door cut him down immediately, detonating what must have been a gas bomb in his hand. His lifeless body burned only feet from where girls had been chained and set afire.

While the tanker truck moved farther from the flames and stopped, the van raced up the long slope, its destination no longer in doubt.

The brakes screeched as loudly as ever, and Jaya threw open the side door, rushing to Bliss, holding her tight. Jessie herded them and Ananda into the vehicle, then jumped in the front seat.

"C-C-Close—"

Jessie slammed the door. Erik leaned over Brindle's shoulder, speaking hurriedly: "Go left just before the Quonset hut."

"What?" Jessie stared at the boy, then Brindle. "Turn around and get out of here."

"Ellison said to get all the food and water."

"Ellison's insane!" Jessie shouted over the engine noise. Erik grabbed the back of their seats to steady himself. "We've got to get out—"

"W-W-We d-do l-like he s-says. L-L-Long w-way to g-go."

Not *that* long, Jessie thought, impatience almost boiling over. She had both of her daughters. *Let's go.*

But he knows war, she said to herself once again. *And what are we going to eat? Food's all gone. Water, too.*

The Quonset hut appeared. Erik directed Brindle down an easy two-track trail to the storehouse. The two of them kicked in the door, and they all carted off crates of dried fruit, nuts, vegetables, smoked and salted game, and jugs of water. The provisions filled most of the van.

"We're going to be hanging on that tanker truck to get out of here," Jessie said.

"That's the plan." Erik squeezed behind the front seat again.

Jessie had never seen this much food, not even in childhood. The Army of God must have been trading with hunters and gatherers from all over the continent.

"W-W-We g-got to g-g-get the b-b-babies, g-girls, n-now."

Jessie winced visibly. In her struggle to get Ananda, she'd forgotten about them. The risks never stop rising, she thought.

They drove past the dead guard lying by Zekiel's door. She looked back at Ananda and saw her perched on a crate, helping herself to a fig. Her daughter looked famished, and her feet were filthy scabs. "Burns," the girl said when she saw her staring.

Erik grabbed Brindle's shoulder. "Stop, I almost forgot." The boy jumped out and rolled a keg of gunpowder from behind a fat boulder. He stored it by Jessie's feet. She eyed the explosive warily. So did Brindle.

"Ellison said to make sure we got it," Erik said. "Just keep going this way. The girls are right up here."

Jessie shifted her feet away from the keg, and Brindle turned his grimace back to the slit in the armor. He followed Erik's directions to what looked like a jail that had been built into the hillside. A metal shutter covered a window, and the thick door was chained shut.

Jessie got out and pounded on the wood, yelling that they'd come to free them. Someone pounded back. A weak voice cried for help.

"Stand back," she shouted, blasting the rusty metal links with a shotgun shell. Then she rushed inside, finding four girls and the three babies.

Ananda ran in yelling, "Callabra, we're getting out."

The tall girl smiled, and Jessie could have wept for the misery revealed by Callabra's tortured tongue.

Jaya took Callabra's hands. The young man had been a portrait in self-control since Jessie had met him at the destroyed dam; but when he heard his sister try to speak, he bawled. So did the girl. Callabra pulled him close and they clutched each other, shaking horribly, the sole survivors of their family.

Ananda watched them, her own lips trembling, then joined the others in helping the girls find places to sit on the crates. The babies started crying, and didn't stop until they were back in the arms of their blind caregivers.

The van was too packed to close the side door, so Bliss and Jaya dangled out the opening. Bliss held the roof with one hand; the other braced her shotgun against her hip, ready to fire.

Brindle started down the slope, braking constantly from the heavy load. The screech was nonstop. Five guards ran toward them, firing wildly. Against all reasonable odds, a bullet passed through the slit and ricocheted off the paint-chipped interior, just missing one of the blind girls holding a baby.

Brindle backed off the brake, spewing profanities without a single stutter. Then he swerved right to shield the open side of the van, before cutting back sharply to run over two guards. Jessie felt the quick thumps and heard bullets smacking against the back of the vehicle till they made it past the Sacred Heart of Evil.

Brindle swerved one more time—to skirt the grass fire—and pulled alongside the truck.

Jessie sprang out then. Ellison tossed her the M-16 and took back his sawed-off shotgun. "We need you up there." He pointed to the top of the tank. "Hold them off. I'll be right up." He hoisted the rocket launcher to his shoulder.

She pulled herself up on the trailer, and heard Hannah trying to calm the first group of girls. They clung to the met-alwork or were berthed beneath the tank where the truck guards had hidden. Augustus checked each girl's handhold. "Hang on," he told them. "No matter what."

Jessie paused by Bliss's side. "I love you," she whispered. "Don't ever forget that."

"I love you, too." Bliss tapped her chest right above her

heart, then propped her shotgun against her hip as she had on the ride down there.

Jessie crawled up on the walkway on top of the tank, eyes never more alive. No quick targets, so she popped the clip, relieved that Ellison had saved most of the ammo. He joined her moments later with the RPG. "Go!" he yelled.

Maul jumped in the cab, and the long, ungainly tanker truck shuddered and began to roll. Jessie saw Hansel and Razzo alongside the trailer; both dogs appeared as eager to leave as their masters.

Brindle, driving the van with Jaya riding shotgun, took the lead. Ananda, Callabra, and the blind girls with the babies were wedged, once more, among the crates of food.

Guards, trailed by the older men in robes, sprinted across the cindery cheatgrass toward the rear of the tanker truck, which could only lumber up the wagon trail. Jessie watched Erik hurl a lumpy rag almost a hundred feet. It landed in the midst of three guards and broke apart, spilling gunpowder that flared and engulfed their legs in flames. Jessie fired her gun, slowing more of the attackers, but was acutely aware that every round cost them.

"Cover my ass." Ellison rose with the rocket launcher. More than a dozen guards had spread out and now surged past the fallen men. Erik threw another gunpowder grenade, but they'd seen the damage and dodged it easily.

Jessie hoped Ellison would kill them all with the RPG, but he pivoted left and fired.

The rocket ripped through the smoky dawn in a second so scant that she wasn't sure she'd actually seen it. The dark opening of the grotto exploded in brilliant red and yellow flames that ignited the tall cylindrical storage tank. A deep concussion shook the earth so hard that she felt the truck quake.

A mushroom cloud erupted from where the tank had stood, climbing to the sky on a thick stem. A fatter, deadlier tube of fire shot from the grotto with a scream so piercing it was as if the earth itself had come to life. The flames streaked across hundreds of feet of ground, broadening into a wide V, fueled by deep, twisting underground caverns brimming with gas. The fire roared like a monstrous acetylene torch up the hillside to where the guards had bivouacked, immolating men so swiftly that Jessie saw skeletons burned to the bone before they fell.

Waves of brutal heat washed over the tanker, and she feared that it would also explode. Her hair crisped. She had to shield her eyes. When she could look up again, the men chasing them had vanished so completely they might have been vaporized; but up ahead she spotted other guards and robes running madly along the hilltop to try to intercept the truck, which now held the only fuel in the compound. She took a deep breath, steadied her weapon, and cut them down.

Maul drove hard, and she felt the heat fade, amazed that none of the girls had cried out. Even now, flames hissed from the grotto.

And then they felt the hot wind. It whipped around the open field, and vast stretches of cheatgrass—spared the slow, relentless fire of the long night—blazed in seconds, as if suddenly teeming with millions of red rodents.

"Firestorm," Ellison shouted. His hand rose to cover his face. "Like New York, Madrid, Copenhagen, Paris."

He knew his history. So did Jessie. Before the Gulf Stream died, massive bombings by ferocious political and religious rivals had set off firestorms in the parched heart of each of those cities, and left them deader and darker than the leaves that had once rotted every autumn on their broad, beautiful walkways.

Cheatgrass ignited within twenty feet of the tanker trailer before the winds swirled in a new direction.

Ellison turned to the front of the truck. Maul was driving up the last of the hill that led to the front gate. The church stood to their left. So did Bosco's cage. Jessie wanted them both to burn: for the church to turn to ash, like the girls whose lives it had claimed; and for the metal cage to melt, so the beast could be held no more.

At the first sight of the closed gate, Brindle pulled to the side.

"I like that driver," Ellison said to Jessie. "He figures it out all on his own."

Ellison loaded the rocket launcher and obliterated the cross and heavy beams that had barred the world. Brindle navigated the smoke and ruin. Maul followed closely behind. As the tanker drew even with the wall, Ellison pointed to guards racing toward them on the catwalk. Jessie emptied her weapon, and they rolled into the open.

The sun had risen above the hilly horizon but couldn't be seen in the smoke-choked sky over the Army of God.

Jessie spotted the bear bounding out of the compound. Men, too. Neither bothered with the other, or chased the truck or van. The guards and old men had their eyes behind them, stumbling and falling and shouting, filled with fear of fire and death.

Epilogue

One hundred twenty-two dead.

Mounds of powdery ash stood at the reservoir's edge where the pyres had once darkened the sky, remains as still as stolen breath. The camp gate hung open, derelict in the heat. Solana, long black hair pulled back, limped from behind the wall, hesitation in her eyes, a gun in her hand.

Without a word, Bliss and Ananda ran toward her. Jessie shouted to her oldest friend and raced after the girls, cautioning them to be gentle: Solana's machete wounds had been savage and deep.

But her daughters wanted word of their father. "Where is he?" Bliss yelled as they drew near.

"He's fallen."

Jessie would never know why those words came to her before Solana shook her head. She'd never used them for the many dead she'd known. *He's fallen.* As if to the ancient hollows of the earth, as believers say "He's risen" to speak of their savior and his reckless, beguiling sky.

Her girls stared at Solana, numbed by the news. Jessie pulled them close.

"He's not dead," Bliss shouted. "He's not." She jerked away from her mother, screaming, "No, no!"

Ananda sank to the ground, weeping so quietly that only

her shoulders hinted at her grief. The unspeakable vow of emptiness.

Bliss stormed into the camp, fierce to redress the madness that had murdered her father and stripped her naked there. That left her mortally exposed even now.

Jessie kissed Solana in silence and left her with Ananda. Her friend lowered herself gingerly, lending a frail hand to a fragile girl.

Just inside the gate, Bliss beat her belly mercilessly with her fists, shrieking, "Dad, no. *No*," over and over. Jessie rushed up and grabbed her hands.

"Mommy." The girl could scarcely speak and her eyes were wild: "I miss him. I miss him." She collapsed to her knees, hugging herself, gasping still.

Jessie rubbed her back and began to rock her. Eden's death could destroy her daughters. She felt this in her hands— Bliss's constant trembling—and knew this from their history. Eden was a man who'd loved to be needed, and his girls always needed him so much. She would have to help them survive his death like she'd helped them survive the Army of God. *When they start to heal,* she promised herself, *you can start to feel.* Sorrow could swallow her for months, and she had no time for mourning: delays could prove lethal.

"He loved you." Jessie hugged Bliss tightly. "He loved you and Ananda more than life itself. People say that but he lived it every day."

"He died gently." Solana stood over them with her arm around Ananda. "He didn't suffer."

"Did he ever wake up?" Ananda asked.

"Once," Solana said. "On the morning you left, he took my hand and squeezed it. He could hardly talk but he said your names, and then he shut his eyes."

"If one of us had stayed . . ." Bliss couldn't finish.

"It wouldn't have made any difference," Solana said. "You saved him once, but no one could have saved him again."

Jessie looked at her daughters. The love that gave rise to

their pain made her more grateful than ever for the years she'd shared with Eden. Brilliance burning through heartache.

"I have his ashes," Solana said.

Jessie would not spread them here. Eden would rest where trees were growing and the land had begun to green.

Maureen and Keffer Gibbs waited deeper inside the camp, not far from where they and their three children had survived the slaughter by burying themselves under bodies. Maureen had gathered the other survivors by their tent, one of the few that had been raised back up.

Four children stared at Jessie. She knew them all, and smiled. They didn't respond. They looked stunned. So did the lone man who'd overcome a gunshot wound. He sat holding a crutch made of branch, like the one she had used when she left to find Ananda. All of them looked exhausted, worried, hungry.

Jessie hurried to the gate and waved to the van. They'd left it far from the camp, knowing that its steel-plated appearance would have been terrifying.

Brindle and Jaya joined in feeding the survivors their first ample meal in weeks. When they were done, Jessie spoke.

"People know we're here, it's not safe anymore. And the water's running out. We knew that even before they came." Her eyes swept the crippled, empty camp. "But up in the Arctic, the Inuit are doing well. Trees are growing. The ice has melted, and the land is coming alive. That's what the traders are saying."

"There must be thousands going north," Keffer said.

"That's not what we've heard," Jessie told him. "It's very hard to make it across the dead zone. The deserts go all the way into Canada now. I don't want to mislead any of you. We've got gas, a lot of it, but it's going to be tough to get there. There's an alliance of groups like the ones that grabbed our girls, and men dying from Wicca and committing insane acts of violence. And there's a cult murdering anyone who ever had a grandparent or great-grandparent who denied climate change. There's trouble out there. A lot of danger. It's not going to be like it was here, but this is never going to be what it was. We had our own little paradise, we really did." Strange to be the one saying that now. Not long ago she couldn't have imagined those words; less so the wanton plundering of their lives. But what Hannah said was true: They'd had paradise here. They'd had food and water and family. "But we have to leave. If we stay, we're not going to survive."

Two hours later they rode out with Jessie, who now worried about having to tell them about Burned Fingers; he'd taken a liking not only to Ananda, but to the nickname she'd let slip the day after they escaped the Army of God.

Jessie broached the explosive subject of the marauder with them when they took their first break. After watching them stretch their legs, she gathered them together for the news. They reacted with predictable horror at the prospect of teaming up with the leader of the massacre.

She listened patiently, then explained what he'd done to save the girls and why their survival might hinge on the man who'd chained her husband to the front of an armored truck. She'd tried to prepare for this moment, and pointed to Bliss and Ananda. "Their father is dead because of him. *My* husband. If there's one man in this whole goddamn world I wanted to kill, it was him. But—"

"You've forgiven him," Maureen interrupted. "Well, I'm not ready—"

"No," Jessie said. "I haven't *forgiven* him. I will never forgive him. But I will not sacrifice their lives . . ." She eyed the children. ". . . or yours, or mine, or Keffer's, or any of us for a self-defeating act of vengeance." Then she said aloud what she'd only thought till then: "He knows war." She let those most telling words settle like dust, like death itself. "And he fought for the rebels in Baltimore."

"So he changes sides whenever it's convenient." Maureen shook her head. "Great."

"He did change sides, Mo. That's true. But there was nothing convenient about the Army of God. He could have turned on us. He could have killed us. But he fought like a demon to get those girls out of there."

Ananda stood slowly. "I know it's weird, but like with me, he took me to the Army of God, but then he saved my life."

"How do we even know that he's going to be there when we show up?" Keffer asked.

"We don't," admitted Jessie.

But when they arrived, Burned Fingers greeted the survivors briskly, then stepped aside so they could be with the children they would all be raising.

Ananda hurried over to Teresa, lying in the shade of the tanker truck. The girl's burns had become infected, and she was glassy-eyed with fever. Her dry lips moved slightly. M-girl, by her side with the birthday book, leaned closer and spoke softly. "Can you tell me again, please?"

Teresa whispered, and M-girl wrote down the name of another girl who'd been killed in the compound.

Ananda took Teresa's hand. She didn't appear to notice.

"How many do we have now?" Ananda asked M-girl.

"Two hundred and ninety-four. The last time she could really talk, she said we only had a few more to go."

Ananda sat with Teresa through the night, stricken by the fear that her name would become the final one on the list. But the girl slept deeply for the first time in days, and when she awoke at dawn her fever broke. Sweat beaded her forehead, and her eyes brightened. She smiled at Ananda and recited the last three names. Ananda recorded them, then dabbed Teresa's brow with a damp rag and gave her water. They spoke softly of trees and wild green grass and other wonders that might await them.

An hour later Ananda eased Teresa into the van. The two of them shared it with M-girl, Callabra, Imagi, and the three blind girls who sat in the back with the babies. Jaya rode shotgun, separating Bliss—a sentry on the truck—from her boyfriend. Her mother wished she could work the same magic at night.

Jessie performed a head count of both vehicles: fifteen adults, including the older teens; twelve children; and the three infants. The two dogs would have to walk. A long haul for Hansel on three legs.

Before they pulled away, Hannah checked on Teresa once more. Then the nurse took Ananda's hand and said, "If her fever starts back up, you tell me right away."

Ananda promised that she would. Teresa thanked Hannah.

"You're strong girls," the nurse told them.

And you're a strong woman, Jessie thought as the sixty-seven-year-old climbed to her perch on the tanker trailer. She wanted to go north with them, not back to her own compound, and Jessie had agreed, extending her trust to another invader. Maybe Hannah really hadn't known the marauders' plans for the camp. Maybe even that didn't matter anymore. She was a healer. Burned Fingers was a warrior. They needed both.

On the third morning out, Burned Fingers told them over breakfast that they'd now traveled beyond the easy reach of anyone from the Army of God.

"And the Alliance?"

"They won't know what's happened for a while," he said. "It could be months before they find out."

"Or days?" Jessie said.

"Possibly. We don't know, so we go." He rose, and Jessie gathered up the girls. Some of them moaned about taking their places on the tanker truck or cramming themselves into the van. The complaints—so simple after so much madness—made Jessie smile.

In seconds they were rolling north again, leaving fresh tracks in the dust.